Praise for Ross Leckie and *Scipio*

'Leckie's Rome is certainly alive and kicking . . . a fine achievement, a thoughtful and stylish piece of historical fiction.' *Daily Telegraph*

'The character of Scipio is central, admirably done, full of interest. Yet this is also a novel of action, and very exciting action . . . All the battle scenes are terrific. So, indeed, is the novel, even better than *Hannibal*.' Allan Massie

'This novel teaches an interesting passage of ancient history and is replete with the facts and figures of Rome's civic and military life.' *Scotland on Sunday*

'Many readers will be fascinated, even involved, by this meticulous recreation of ancient Roman life.' *Sunday Telegraph*

'The descriptions of Trasimene, and of the subsequent carnage at Cannae, are breathtaking. Leckie brings the battle-tactics and manoeuvres almost cinematically alive and the sense of blood and sweat, chaos and horror linger powerfully on . . . utterly gripping.' *Scotsman*

'In Leckie's descriptions it's possible to smell the stench of sweat and fear, hear the roars of warhorses and elephants, see the blood-stained armour. Informative and utterly compelling.' *The Times*

'Visually rich and satisfyingly credible in detail . . . *Hannibal*'s triumph is to bring the world of Carthage to life again.' *Spectator*

'Enthralling . . . The politics of Hannibal's makeshift alliances, the corrosion of his humanity and the ghastly mechanics of war, are brilliantly described.' *Independent*

'Full of wonderful scenes: cosmopolitan, chaotic Carthage – an ancient incarnation of New York – heaving with people from all corners of Africa . . . What was once cold history with echoes of adventure becomes full-bodied adventure with echoes of history.' *The Times*

D1017664

Also by Ross Leckie

Hannibal
Carthage

Μηδὲν ἄγαν: *nothing in excess.*

ἄγαν:

SCIPIO

ROSS LECKIE

CANONGATE
Edinburgh · London · New York · Melbourne

First published in Great Britain in 1998 by
Canongate Books Ltd, 14 High Street,
Edinburgh EH1 1TE

This paperback edition first published by Canongate in 2008

1

British Library Cataloguing-in-Publication Data
A catalogue request for this book is available on
request from the British Library

ISBN 978 1 84767 100 4

Typeset by Palimpsest Book Production Ltd
Grangemouth, Stirlingshire
Printed and bound in Great Britain by
Clays Ltd, St Ives plc

www.canongate.net

τίς γὰρ οὕτως ὑπάρχει φαῦλος ἢ ῥᾴθυμος ἀνθρώπων ὃς οὐκ ἂν
βούλοιτο γνῶναι πῶς καὶ τίνι γένει πολιτείας ἐπικρατηθέν-
τα σχεδὸν ἅπαντα τὰ κατὰ τὴν οἰκουμένην ἐν οὐχ ὅλοις πεν-
τήκοντα καὶ τρισὶν ἔτεσιν ὑπὸ μίαν ἀρχὴν ἔπεσε την
Ῥωμαίων, ὃ πρότερον οὐχ εὑρίσκεται γεγονός;

Surely no one can be so worthless or apathetic as not to want to
know by what means and under what system of government the
Romans, in less than fifty-three years [220–167 BC], succeeded in
bringing under their rule almost the entire inhabited world, an
achievement without parallel in human history?

POLYBIUS, *Histories* 1.5

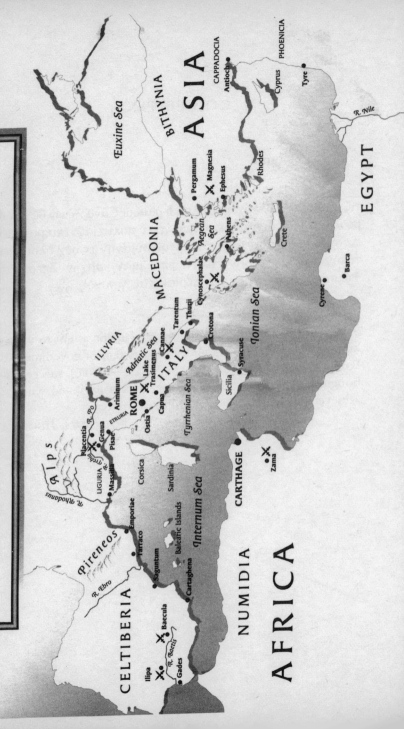

THE WORLD OF SCIPIO

PHOENICIA

CAPPADOCIA

ASIA

BITHYNIA

Euxine Sea

Antioch

Cyprus

Tyre

R. Nile

EGYPT

Pergamum

× Magnesia

× Ephesus

Rhodes

MACEDONIA

Aegean Sea

Athens

× Cynoscephalae

Crete

Barca

Cyrene

Ionian Sea

ILLYRIA

Tarentum

Thuqi

Adriatic Sea

Ariminum

Lake Trasimenus ×

ITALY × Cannae

Crotona

ROME

ETRURIA

Capua

Syracuse

Ostia

Tyrrhenian Sea

Sicilia

Placentia

Genua

R. Po

Pisae

Trebia

LIGURIA

Alps

Massilia

× Zama

CARTHAGE

R. Rhodanus

Corsica

Sardinia

Internum Sea

Emporiae

Pireneos

Tarraco

Balearic Islands

NUMIDIA

AFRICA

Saguntum

Cartaghena

R. Ebro

CELTIBERIA

Ilipa ×

× Baecula

R. Baetis

Gades

CONTENTS

PROLOGUE

The deep drums throbbed as the senators, their togas white, their faces grave, filed past us to their seats. My brother and I stood straight, still, on the platform in the centre of the chamber, looking forward, arms by our sides, in the way we had agreed. I could feel Cato, I could smell him as, last as usual, he approached. I had promised myself not to look at him. But as he passed, I had to meet his eyes. I saw hate in their deadly blue, pure aquamarine – who could doubt his bastard Celtic blood? – under those beetling brows, the low, bald, peasant head.

Our eyes met, and he sneered. Walking past, he raised the index finger of his right hand. The sign for victory. He thought that he had won.

The drums stopped. The senators sat down. The voice of Fabius Pulcher, father of the house, rang out. '*Patres et conscripti*, senators of Rome, the trial of the brothers Scipio is resumed.'

One hundred senators sat in silent rows around us. Behind them, their armour shining, at attention, the soldiers of the senatorial guard ringed the room. Many of them had served me, or my brother. They had fought for me, as I had fought for Rome, in the mountains of Celtiberia and Asia, under far and foreign skies, in the valleys and plains of Gaul and Italy, in the marshes of Macedonia, across Africa's desert sands.

I was never beaten. I saved Rome from the vengeance of Hannibal, and Carthage from the vengeance of Rome. I defeated Philip of Macedon, and Antiochus whom they called the Great. I brought honour to my stock. I gave Rome her army. I sought, as had my forefathers beyond men's memory, to serve the Republic of Rome. Under my hand, Rome has mastered the world. From being a city state, nearly destroyed

1

by Hannibal, Rome has become the city and the world, and all this I gave to her because Rome has been my life, my love, my song.

Now, those who owe me their very power of speech have used it to impeach me. The people say I am a god, my peers but a man. I know that is what I am. And as a man I feel utterly alone. The injustices of life, the absurdities, buzz in my brain like flies, fetid, black. I have lived life to the full, and now I know the tears of things.

Fabius stood up. The silence was chilling. The light from the high cupola was strong. I saw, on this last day of our trial, a new adornment of the court. On a low table beside the prosecutor's lectern sat the voting urn, and before it in neat rows a hundred small tablets of boxwood, covered in wax. On these, in time, my peers would write one letter with styluses: *L* for *libero*, acquittal, *C* for *condemno*, condemnation – two lives to be determined by two letters.

'Senators,' Fabius called out. 'What is the charge today, and who brings it?'

Cato moved with his crab-like limp from the benches to a lectern on our right. He claims to have been wounded in some war. I did not see him there, and there have been no wars in our lifetime without me. I believe the story that he was, in fact, kicked by a mule. That is how he broke his hip.

What a runt, I thought. You can hardly see him above the lectern from which he will prosecute his case. That vulgar voice. After all these years in Rome, his accent is still strong.

'The last of the charges, Fathers, is extortion, and I, Marcus Porcius Cato, bring it, on behalf of the Senate and people of Rome.'

'Whom,' asked Fabius, 'do you accuse?'

'These two men before you, Lucius Cornelius and Publius Cornelius Scipio – whom,' he said with contempt, looking straight at me, 'they call' – he spat out the word – 'Africanus.'

'And what penalty do you ask for?'

'From the evidence I have already brought you, Fathers, and from what I will tell you today, there can be only one penalty. That, as the law demands, is death, by strangulation.'

'Very well, begin.'

That was almost a month ago. We are waiting for judgment, on our bond not to flee from Italy, I here at my villa on the coast at Liternum, my brother at his house in Rome. The bond was the final insult. 'I have never fled from anything,' I said. 'Shall I now flee from Rome?'

I might hear the verdict tomorrow. It might take months. The Senate must heed the voice of the people. But through almost thirty years as a soldier, I have learnt to live life without fear. By sickness or sword – or strangulation – no one can tell when it will end.

My brother seeks in wine a black oblivion. My solace is in my farm here, and this account that I am dictating to Bostar, my secretary and my friend. The Senate, or the gods, will take my life from me. But this account they cannot kill. Bostar will copy it when I have finished, and see the copies safe.

Even without it, I shall not wholly perish. Neither time nor man, not famine, tempest or disease can destroy what I have done. The deeds of Scipio are his marred, magnificent memorial. What you now read is their account. A building up, a breaking down: the life of Scipio before, soon, it is time for him to die.

Forming

*Nostra autem res publica non unius esset ingenio, sed
multorum, nec una hominis vita, sed aliquot constituta
saeculis et aetatibus.*

But our state was founded on the genius not of
one man, but of many; not in one generation,
but through long years and many lives.
CICERO, *De republica*, 11, 1.2

The leaves are turning now. I see from where I sit how the season, cold, is blighting their veins sere and yellow, passing soon to brown. And so it is with me. I feel age upon me; the ache of damp, of wounds, of long days and short nights, of too much turning in my mind. I feel the weight of memories, calling me from far away. And as I wait for the judgment of the Senate and the people, I feel old and cold and weary.

The moon grows and dies and comes again, the sun, the grass. Does man grow and die and never come again? I wonder what I have made. Or Hannibal. He forced me to perfect what he meant to destroy. It is said that he's alive still, in Bithynia. They will send for him; Cato will see to that. But Hannibal will not come. I think only of how much love he must have lost to hate so much.

Hannibal hated. I have loved. Loved Rome, loved life, loved the beauty to be found in proportion. These thoughts and things console me. Consider, for example, this chair in which I sit. Consider from this the manner of man I Scipio, I Publius Cornelius Scipio Africanus, am.

This is no ordinary chair. It is not a simple, unadorned frame of beech from Andalucia. It came from the city of Syracuse on the island of Sicilia, one of the fruits of the sack of that city by my cousin Claudius Marcellus twenty-eight years ago. I was in Celtiberia then. That I missed the siege is one of the few things I regret. They killed Archimedes then, you know. Some damn fool legionary just chopped his head off. He was drawing, apparently, in the sand, and wouldn't be arrested until he had finished the theorem he was working on.

What we could have made of that man! For two years he

7

defied Marcellus with his ingenious machines. 'Give me a firm place to stand on and I will move the earth,' he said. Well, at Syracuse he invented a huge crane. From behind the city walls, it plucked Marcellus' galleys from the water. His catapults sank many others. Each time Marcellus moved his ships back, Archimedes adjusted his catapults to throw further.

Although a mathematician – I have several of his works in my library here – he perfected the science of mechanics. We Romans may take pride in ourselves as mechanics and engineers, but the truth is that this too we learnt from the Greeks.

My accusers, especially Cato, say that such observations prove me to be a Hellenist, and not a true Roman. That's nonsense. It should be no insult to be philhellene. At the same time as I acknowledge our debts, I observe that only a people such as ours could have formed of them that which we have made. Yes, our craftsmen could not have made a chair such as this on which I sit, its feet of lions' heads, its back carved with winged sphinxes, its seat of inlaid ivory and lapis lazuli. But only we have the power, through war, to make a peace. And it is in peace, not war, that painters paint and weavers weave, that poets polish.

To get this chair to its perfect position I had to move it perhaps two inches forwards before I sat down. I used to remonstrate with Aurio, my body-slave, as I still think of him, though I gave him his freedom many years ago. Each time he cleans this room – I let only him and Bostar come in here – he moves this chair and never puts it back on the right spot.

'Aurio, Aurio, no, no!' I always used to say to him. 'Come and sit here yourself.' And he would come shuffling forward, his eyes fixed on the ground.

'Sit down.' As usual, he hesitated. 'Go on! Now, sit the way I do. Yes, back straight. That's it. Now, look out of the window.' I always had to move aside for that. Aurio would not look up if, in doing so, he could see me. 'Aurio, what do you see?'

'I see your garden, master.'

'Yes, yes, but what else? Can you see the quince trees?'

'Yes, I can.'

And each time, so many times, I asked him, 'And how many can you see?'

'Three, master, three.'

'No, Aurio, no!'

And Aurio would stand up and move away, sandals shuffling, shuffling across the face of Minerva, the mosaic on the floor. And I would move the chair forwards and sit in it and see. Five quince trees forming a quincunx, where Aurio, the chair too far back, his view blocked by the window-sill, saw only three.

I gave up this game perhaps a year ago. There are some things that cannot be changed. Now I move my chair myself.

The quince has always been my favourite tree. Stock from Cydon in Crete, I planted these before me now to mark my fiftieth year. They first flowered three years ago, and soon each day I will see their bursting flowers, creamy white and richly red, through the greyness of the winter's cold. And then as well there is their fruit, astringent, aromatic, strong. I love a little added to the apple pies that Mulca, my cook here, makes so well. All this from a tree so small. Few men give forth both flower and fruit, and some neither.

So here it is I sit and look upon my quincunx. I think and dream and I remember. And I dictate to Bostar.

I love this man. I loved him in his prime and now I love him in his twilight, in his pain and anger, in his shame. Of course I have never told him, never will. Saying something gives it life and death. Besides, love is polymorphic, and language not. Not Latin, anyway. Would 'amo, I love' be a description or a definition? Greek has six words for 'love'. Perhaps I could use the right one, and tell him in Greek. But he would understand.

SCIPIO

I have served Scipio for almost twenty years. I will serve no one else now. I am as old boots, formed to his feet, and I will fit no more. We have lived here at Liternum for two years. In that time, we have been to Rome only for the trial, since which we have resumed our ordered life. Mulca serves breakfast early, warm milk and pastries, fresh bread, cheese and, in season, fruit. She must get up very early, even if she leaves the dough rising as we sleep. I like that thought, of dough rising in the house of Scipio each night as we sleep.

Until mid-morning, Scipio is with his bailiff, Macro, seeing to the land and often working on it too. I know what he's going to do when I see what he's got on. To ride round the estate, he wears a blue cotton shirt, white Gaulish trousers and knee-length doeskin boots. 'The herms are fine, Bostar,' he says to me when he gets back from such an outing. Yes, herms, Greek herms. He had them placed, crude statues of strange country gods, at regular intervals round the boundary of the estate.

We often discuss boundaries. 'I mark them when and where I can,' he told me once. 'That is why I mark my boundaries here. So much cannot be bound.'

'But why place boundaries, Scipio? Everyone knows what's your land. And your life has hardly known boundaries.'

'Ah, but it has. You must understand, Bostar, that I have only been able to break boundaries when I have known where they were.'

But he does not only check his herms. He rides round his land to ensure he knows what is going on: which stream is dry, which pastures are green, which orchards need manure. He is keen on manure, Scipio, especially at this time of year. He likes to see the land lying through the winter covered in manure. He threatens to write a treatise on dung. I can think of other subjects more worthy of his pen. Anyway, will he have time? We may hear the judgment any day.

But if only others were like him, there would be less trouble ahead. Too many patrician Romans exploit their land. They increase rents; they terrorise their tenants and neither know nor care whether their farms are growing millet or maize — so long as it pays.

Scipio is different. He is very interested in agriculture and, when he returns, always tells me what's going on. 'Stone-clearing in the Quintucia fields today, Bostar,' or 'The wheat's lodged in the night. There must have been heavy rain, but I didn't hear it,' or 'The cowherd Stultus is down with a fever. I'll send Aurio to him.' And then, with these mundanities around us and behind us, knowing that the rhythm of the land goes on, unchanging, Scipio sits down in the chair where he is now and, in time, begins.

I sit at this table behind him. I always have at least ten tablets ready, and spare styluses. I have perfected a system of shorthand of which I am proud. I call it tachygraphy, but Scipio thinks I should re-name it brachygraphy from the Greek brachus for short, as opposed to tachus for swift: that's the sort of word-game we enjoy. Anyway, whatever it's called it allows me to record Scipio at the same speed as he speaks. I must write an account of my system. Soon, soon.

For a while, we each sit alone with our thoughts. Aurio brings marjoram tea, sweetened with a little honey from the beehives on the hills where the wild thyme grows. Then for two hours or more, without interruption until the midday meal, Scipio dictates and I record, record the life of Scipio.

In the afternoons, I transcribe my notes. Later, not from notes but from my memory, I add what I have known and, at times, I record the present, not just the past. The two are one and form, of course, our future. This is an account, then, of two lives in one, two pasts, two presents. I shall let the two merge and mingle, like the shifting sea.

I can see the sea here in Liternum. I have always loved to look at the sea. Perhaps it was my childhood, the winter storms breaking on our door and walls. And I would get up, shivering in my blanket, and slip out and stand and watch and feel and hear the crashing of the waves' undying beating on the beach. In the sea are all the colours, green and blue and black and red and grey. I have seen in it vermilion, ochre, jade. In it are all emotions, the rising and the settled and the spent. I have heard the sea whisper like lovers and roar like lions, caress the land, attack. In the sea all these things are one as they have been at times, I thought, in Hannibal. I can see the sea again now. As boy, so old man, one who has served two men who tried to change the world and found the world to have a balance of its own.

And so I move now to my memories. I shall begin with those of things that happened long before I first met Scipio, or served him. When I can, I shall continue them. In recording Scipio's life, I shall perhaps account also for mine.

I stood until I saw his ship slip out of sight, until my arm, raised, palm held out in valediction, benefaction, ached and shook and I could hold it up no more. And then I sat where I had stood upon a beach in Italy and looked out to the sea bearing Hannibal home. Still, he will go on searching until he learns, I thought. Then he will make the final journey and he will ask of the gods a judgment. Who knows what they will say?

I had joined Hannibal as a mapmaker in Celtiberia, before he crossed the Alps and invaded Italy, almost twenty years ago. Until the hatred in his heart consumed him, I was by his side. Now he had sailed back to Carthage because, unable ever to defeat him in Italy, the Romans had invaded Africa. At last, Hannibal heard from Carthage. They called him home. But where he was going, I knew I could not help him. Only the dead ever see the end of a war. Hannibal had left Italy. I stayed, alone.

Darkness gathered about me where I sat like a hen with folded wings. There is nothing more gentle than the slow coming of the dark. Man rests. The earth rests. Much renews. Wrapped in my cloak, I lay back and waited for sleep, my thoughts filling with the swelling of the sea. My dreams were of him, as they so often are. That night I dreamed that Hannibal was a meteor, brilliant, coruscating, flaming, not a dull and distant star.

On the dew of golden morning I walked away, inland, north. I had only my satchel with my maps and some few things inside, and the clothes I wore.

*　*　*

FORMING

Can you imagine what it is to be born a Roman and a Scipio? It is to assume greatness, to learn with your wet-nurse's milk that, though you have rights, you have responsibilities. Take our name. It means 'staff'. My great-great-great-great-grandfather was blind. His son Cornelius acted as his staff – *patrem pro baculo regebat*, as our history records – and we have borne the name Scipio with pride since then. We have been Rome's staff. Our family tomb, at the Capena gate in Rome, contains the bones of many, many Scipios who have died in her service.

But yes. I see already that this might seem didactic. I am already giving form to things that are assumed. That is the case with great people. They are the stuff of great events, ones that reverberate through time. And yet, for the most part, they were responding. How many saw, and made? How many created history, before it overtook them? I have, I know in my bones, been one who did. Rome is something I made. I own her, I owe her. She has been and may yet be what I meant her to be. Rome is mine. And so I allow myself the luxury of being didactic. I shall set down what I think it is to be a Roman. This pride is a fault. There are worse. Bostar, you may edit it accordingly. But something has been made that before me was unmade. So it is mine, and I shall try to account for it.

I was born in my father's house, which is now mine, though I no longer go there. Its shutters are barred. Its hearths are cold. Only the old porter, Rurio, is there, as he has been for sixty years. He is meant to deter burglars, but is now almost completely deaf. The city Watch keep an eye on the place, though. I arranged that they should. I still have some friends in Rome. When Rurio dies, I shall sell the house. Not for the money, which I do not need, but for the peace.

I have learnt to let go of things. I care for all the beauty I have gathered about me here, my rugs, my sculpture, my vases. I have carvings from Nineveh, silver jewellery from Cappadocia, alabaster, myrrh, amber, ebony and ivory, emeralds and diamonds,

13

glossopetri fallen from the moon, and I have gold. Yes, I have many precious things. I touch this silver brooch, for example, griffin-faced, the one holding the folds of my tunic. It is Etruscan, from Praeneste, three or four hundred years old, priceless. Its back bears the inscription *Manios med fhefhaked Numasioi*, proto-Latin for *Manius me fecit Numerio*, Manius made me for Numerius.

I look at this many times each week, for as many reasons. Even our language has Greek origins. Bostar thinks this inscription is Chalcedonian, a Greek alphabet adopted by the early Latins, perhaps by way of the Etruscans of – where, Bostar?

Cumae.

Yes, Cumae. I knew, but I had forgotten. An interesting thought, that. Isn't it strange that we can say, 'I do know, but I have forgotten'? How can knowledge be knowledge if it can be forgotten? Plato deals with this question in one of his dialogues, the *Meno*, I think. I must look at it after supper. Remind me, please, Bostar.

This brooch is compelling for other reasons. Who was Manius, and who Numerius? How did they live, how die? I feel this brooch is alive with the life of the man who made it. It is always warm in the hand. And yet now the Etruscans are only a name. We eradicated them. We should spare a defeated people, not destroy them. I fear for Carthage. I fear that I have failed. Yes, we have achieved much. Have we destroyed even more?

I am turning my signet ring round and round on the little finger of my left hand, twisting it with the thumb and first two fingers of my right. I always do this when I am troubled. I am always troubled when I think of Carthage. Its fate is not far removed from that of this ring.

I heard that, Bostar. You always give that low cough when you think I digress. But what you don't know is how hard I had to fight in the Senate for the simple right to wear a ring, let alone for Carthage to continue to exist. Cato went on and on about how the Spartans forbade anything but iron rings.

'If we must be *Greek*,' he said contemptuously in the debate, looking of course at me, 'let us be Spartan!'

My grandfather went to Sparta once, on an embassy. He dined in their famous public mess. He was asked about that when he came back. 'It's no wonder,' he said, 'that Spartan soldiers don't fear death.' Sparta produced no art, no literature, no philosophy. It was a state built on slaves. And Cato wants us to be like that.

Well, Cato wanted us to pass one of his innumerable sumptuary laws banning rings made of anything but iron. I beat him on that, at least. I'm quite proud of my *ius annuli aurei*, under which I and many others may wear our signet rings of gold. But I would gladly give up that right to know that Carthage is safe.

I was talking of possessions. Theogenes, my art dealer, comes here from Rome each month with more. But these things do not own me. The house where I was born, though, is too big for me to let go of while it is still mine – though they may take it from me when they reach a verdict. That house is my last tie to Rome, and Rome has been my life.

I smelled the woodsmoke first, and then I heard the yapping of the dogs. I can still remember that first village I came to, and its name, Secunium. It sat in a defile. A stream ran through it. Its midden stank and steamed as I looked down from the hill above. Its huts were mean, their thatch unkempt, their gardens overgrown. I almost turned away, but hunger drove me on. When had I eaten last?

Only dogs, mangy, curl-tailed curs, met me at the bottom of the hill. Italian peasants eat dog. I never have: I think the meat unclean. I hoped for bread, perhaps, or cheese, or a melon would have done.

I shooed the dogs away, walked on. A young boy, filthy, his hair greasy, his face blotchy, stared at me from the doorway of the first hut. As I drew near, I stopped. 'Salve,' I said. He darted in. A curtain of cowhide swung after him. I walked on. The curtain of each hut swung shut as I approached, and then I was at the end.

My stomach growled. Where there were people, there must be food — though not for the dogs, if the limping, grey bitch, a yard to my left, one eye oozing pus, her ribs protruding, teats hanging, right flank festering with sores, was anything to judge by. I turned, walked back to the middle of the village where the dogs, uninterested now, lay and scratched and sniffed.

'Viator sum,' I shouted. 'I am a traveller. I come only in peace. Give me some food, and I'll go.' Silence. Only the buzzing of flies, and the sun, hot on my head. I thought how still Italy is, now Hannibal has gone. I tried again. 'I only want some food.' I waited. Nothing. I saw a hawk high overhead. Perhaps I, too, would have to hunt. 'Then I'll go, and spit on your shrine as I leave.'

Each Italian village, however mean, has its own shrine, usually to parochial gods or spirits known only to those who live there. Hannibal destroyed each one he found. He meant to break the Roman mind. He failed. In fact, I think he hardened their resolve. To insult a people's gods and superstitions is to push too far. The Romans always let a conquered people keep their gods — so long as Rome's collector of taxes is paid.

I had passed this village's shrine as I came in — a half-dome of clay and wattles, hip-high. In it stood a wooden statuette, a priapus, rough-carved. I had seen many like it before. Most had a small bowl of water and a barley cake before the image of the god. This had neither. All around it, though, dry or drying on the grass and ground, was blood.

This, as I saw from the bones, was the blood of an ass. The Italians seem to think the ass the embodiment of lust. I cannot understand that. To all the other peoples I know, the ass is the symbol of stupidity. Stubborn, but stupid. Perhaps that is appropriate for Rome.

I adjusted the straps of my satchel and started walking towards the shrine. 'Hic!' came a voice from behind me, an old man's voice, weary, worn, 'Stranger, over here!'

* * *

Light. What I remember most of that house in Rome is light.
My great-grandfather, Lucius Scipio Barbatus, built the house
on the Palatine Hill. His death-mask stands there still, in one of
the recesses, the left, I think, off the central court, the atrium. Or
is he in the right-hand recess? There are so many masks and busts
– my family has borne the *ius imaginum*, the right to have oneself
represented in painting or statuary, for hundreds of years. But I
haven't seen the busts properly since I was a child. There was
never time. Now I have the time, I do not have the will.

Scipio Barbatus was, like four of my ancestors before him,
consul. Only a Roman can understand what that means. Or
can you, Bostar? Can you? No, I did not think you would be
distracted from your brachygraphy. Anyway, you probably do
understand.

Our two consuls are the supreme military and civil magistrates
of Rome. Their office is fundamental to the Republic, which
replaced monarchy as the government of Rome three hundred
years ago. Tarquin the Proud, an Etruscan, was king then, but
the people rose up against him, expelled him, and the Roman
Republic was born.

The consuls' authority is complete. My grandfather, a war
hero who had himself been a consul, once came to talk to his
son, my father, who was then consul. My father was watching
a military parade on horseback, surrounded by his lictors, or
officers. My grandfather didn't dismount when he rode up. My
father was furious, and told one of his lictors to command my
grandfather to do so, even though he knew my grandfather was
rheumatic and found mounting and dismounting very difficult.
As he climbed down, my grandfather called out, 'I congratulate
you, Publius Scipio. It is good to see the respect due a consul
upheld.'

Rome's consuls are elected, not appointed, and their calling
is to serve the state, subject to the rule of law. I say 'the state'
advisedly. The state, not the people. It is greater than the Senate

or the people. It is the sum of all its parts. The people have their representatives, the tribunes, who are also elected. They and the consuls and the aediles and the censors and the praetors, these together run the state. It is a matter of balance – or was.

What, you may say, has this to do with the house where I was born and its light? Well, there was always a sense of lightness, a calm serenity in the house of a family that had for so long served Rome. There was order, peace. Each morning, in clean togas, my father's clients came to greet him, each awaiting in the atrium his turn. All of them, like the servants and the members of the household, knew their proper place.

I can see it now. When I turned eight I was allowed for the first time to stand behind my father in the main reception room, the *tablinum*, as, one by one, his clients came forward to greet him in his chair. Only the buildings further up the hill prevented the whole room from being bathed in morning light. As the last of the clients turned to leave, I moved forwards to my father's side. 'Father,' I asked, 'why is our house here?'

'Why here, Publius? I don't understand. Where else should it be?'

'Further up the hill, Father. Then the houses above us would not block the light.'

My father smiled. He had a very gentle smile, spreading softly from the corners of his mouth. And when he smiled the wrinkles round his eyes showed. They were small and fine and tender. Strange, I always wanted to touch them. I never did. 'What a boy, what a boy,' he chuckled.

His smile faded. 'Come and stand in front of me, Publius.' I did of course, back straight, arms at my sides, as I had been taught since I could stand, heels together. 'You are right. The houses above do block some of our light. But you are wrong. Why might that be, Publius?'

'I don't know, Father.' I held his gaze. His eyes were brown, like mine, but the whites of his eyes were very, very white.

'My grandfather built this house only halfway up the hill for a reason: so that the people should never think the Scipios too far above them. Others are free to build as high as they want to. But no Scipio will ever rise above his station.'

He coughed, got up, paced across the room. Then he turned sharply and looked across at me. 'This is important, Publius. Are you listening?'

'Of course, Father.'

'We may live on the Palatine, and the plebs opposite us on the Aventine, but we are the same people, equal before the gods and the law. Remember that, Publius.' With a nod, he dismissed me.

I have never forgotten. I have only ever sought to serve the people.

As a child, I learnt to enjoy such light as we did have, the light pouring in at midday through the unroofed atrium, diffusing into the rooms ranged round it, the bedrooms, storerooms, my father's offices. But it was the light beyond that. Past the atrium, on through the *tablinum*, beyond its cedar doors and out into the peristyle, our colonnaded garden, once again unroofed – there was the light I loved.

The floor of the cloister round the garden was of porphyry, quarried in Egypt, and green marble. I have always got up early. One spring morning – was I eight, nine? – the household sleeping, I walked, shivering in the cold, through to the garden. Beyond the peristyle, slanting light flowed. The porphyry glowed, deep reds and incandescent ambers. The world was alive with light.

I stopped, turned. I saw him. He was small, stooped, standing in the doorway of the last hut I had passed. His hair was lank and matted, grey. His shirt was patched and filthy, his trousers torn, his feet bare. He gestured to me to come. I took the ten steps or so towards him.

19

'Salve, senex. *Greetings, old man.*' *He didn't reply, but nodded in acknowledgement. He stared. He screwed up his nose.* 'Armatus?' *he muttered.* '*Are you armed?*'

I held out my arms. 'No. I come in peace. I want only a little food, and then I'll go.'

'I know, I know. I heard you, I heard.' *With surprising speed, he darted into the hut. I heard him speak, a woman's muttered reply. He came back out with a small stool in each hand. Kicking a sleeping cur so that, whimpering, it moved away, he put the stools down by the door.* 'Sit, stranger, sit.'

He put his hands on his knees. Both, I saw, were missing their thumbs. I had heard of Italians chopping off their thumbs to avoid conscription as, in the desperate days after Cannae, the Roman press-gangs scoured the land for anyone who could hold a pilum *and a shield.* 'Why?' *I asked him, pointing at his hands.* 'Surely you were too old to be conscripted?'

He hawked and spat and grinned a toothless, sour grin. 'Older than me were taken! Anyone who could stand was marched away to fight against that Hannibal!' *and he made the sign against the evil eye. I simply nodded, feeling my way.* 'But I am no coward!' *he went on.* 'I fought in Sicilia for Rome, in the last war against Carthage. I was a decurion, in the legion of the Vettulanti—'

'Then why did you avoid service this time?'

'Don't judge me, stranger!' *he said sharply, and he looked at me fully for the first time. I saw strength, purpose, in his haggard eyes.* 'Because there is more to life than war. This is my village. I am its headman. I have a wife here. I had children. My two boys fought at Cannae. We waited for months'* – his voice tailed away –* 'before we realised they'* – *he screwed his eyes shut, swallowed –* 'before we realised they would not be coming home.'* Cannae. Hannibal's great victory over Rome when the dead, it was said, were too many to count and the River Aufidus ran red to the sea. That, by the way, is true. I know. I was there.*

Silence settled. Flies buzzed, and I heard the sounds of goat-bells on the hill and, from inside the hut, of someone stirring.

'Yes, I have paid my debt to Rome,' he said softly. 'But you, stranger, what brings you here? Are you a pedlar? By your looks you come from the east.'

'Yes, I was not born in Italy, though I have been here for a long time. Sixt—' I almost told him. Had Hannibal been sixteen years in Italy? Had he really gone? 'Yes, for a long time,' I said instead. 'But no, I'm not a pedlar. I am' − I had prepared for this − 'a teacher. My name is Bostar. What's yours?'

'Sosius,' he said. 'A teacher? What do you teach?'

'What I can: languages, astronomy, geography—'

'Pah!' spat Sosius. 'We have no need of learning here!' He scratched his groin. 'Can you work a hoe?'

'Yes.'

'Good. Then, Teacher, you can stay. Food, you said. Woman!'

'Ready!' came a muffled reply. I followed Sosius inside.

Light and shade, deep shadow and dazzling light. These I remember from the house where I was born. My bedroom, the *tablinum* and my schoolroom were always dark. The panes of selenite over the small windows let in little light. But then the atrium and peristyle would be ablaze with light. I thought both light and shadow private, just for me.

That seems risible now. But our house was private, inward-looking, its walls closed to the world, its windows small, all its doors opening inwards, its rooms giving on to each other. The one door was guarded night and day by a porter and salivating bull mastiffs. As a Roman home, so a Roman family. That is how I was reared.

We Romans are bound together by many things: our laws, our sense of destiny. We are a people hardened by the many wars which gave us painful birth. But we are a people formed within our families.

Consider, for example, our names. Barbarians mock these.

They should instead consider the strength that they impart. 'Publius' is my personal name. 'Cornelius' is my cognomen, which defines a branch within my *gens* or clan, and that of course is 'Scipio'. 'Africanus' you can discount. It is an honorific name, for the conqueror of Africa. Some still call me by that name. I don't object to that, but I have had my fill of honours. Perhaps the Senate, if they do nothing else, will take them away.

Roman clans are tied by more than blood. The clans Pinarii and Potitii, for example, looked after the rites of Hercules at the ancient altar in Rome's cattle-market. When, a hundred years ago, the Potitii betrayed the secrets of that ritual, all died within a month, twelve whole families of them, so it is said. I have seen enough to know such things are possible.

I value being a Scipio more than I value my life. Almost as soon as I could read at all – was I four, five? – my father took me out. I remember the heat, the crowds. He kept stopping, his toga white in a sea of brown, to greet or to be greeted. He seemed to remember every name. 'And how is your aunt? I hear she's been unwell.' Or, to someone else, 'And the new warehouse? Is it finished?' It was a long walk. I was tired, and did not understand.

The iron gate into the mausoleum creaked on its hinges. The silence was sudden, after the noise of the Forum, the markets and streets. The tomb was huge, I thought. All round it figures were carved. They frightened me. Below the figures were inscriptions. My father knelt. I did the same. He was silent for a long time. Ants crawled up my shins. I wanted to scratch. I didn't think I should.

Still kneeling, 'These are your ancestors, Scipio. Revere and learn from them,' my father said. 'Now stand up and read me the inscription nearest you.'

I didn't stumble much. When I did, my father helped me. 'I increased the merit of my race by my upright standards,' the inscription ran. 'I begat children. I followed the exploits of my ancestors so that they rejoiced I had been born to them. Honour ennobled my stock.'

'Good, Publius, good. That was written for your grandfather. You should be content if, when you die, it could be written for you – as I would be. Don't forget it.'

I never have.

His memory is prodigious. One day I must ask him when or where he learnt that skill. Nature gives some men better memories than others, but memories like Scipio's are formed by use and art. Someone has written a treatise on The Art of Memory. *A Greek, of course. Aristotle? I must look in the library tonight.*

'No, no, no!' Sosius screamed, shaking his stick at me. 'Not so deep, not so deep!' *Well, it was a long time since I'd held a hoe. After sixteen years travelling with an army, the man I had served being now in Africa, here I was on a smallholding in Bruttium, hoeing beans.*

Sosius came up. 'If you hoe so deep, you'll let the sun too far into the ground. The roots will dry out, and then, and then . . .' *He tailed off, looked down, looked back up at me.* 'Then, Bostar, we'll have no beans!'

We both laughed. We had eaten beans, I gratefully, Sosius with a grumble. 'Beans again, woman?' *But I had four helpings, and as many barley cakes. At least it isn't dog, I thought.*

An interesting vegetable, the bean. Pythagoras banned it. Perhaps he believed that if his adherents ate it they'd fart when they were about to metempsychose into a priest or a holy man and end up instead as a dog. But then I've always been suspicious of that story. The Greeks used beans for casting votes. I wonder if, in prohibiting the humble bean, Pythagoras wasn't telling his followers to stay out of politics. If he was, he was a wise man indeed. But the first interpretation is certainly more interesting.

I learnt from Sosius of ravaged Italy. It was astounding that Rome had fought on. Sosius said his village was typical. There were no men left there over fourteen or under sixty – well, no whole men, anyway. There was one in his twenties, called Ostio, I think, but he had lost both legs to the surgeon's saw after Trasimenus.

That was one of Hannibal's most effective ploys. The Romans were used to the straight sword-thrust, trying to push past the shield and through the breastplate. Either that, or the hacking swing down to the neck and the space between breastplate and helmet. In Celtiberia, for hour after hour Hannibal had his men practise both those cuts on dummies filled with straw. But then he introduced a third.

I remember the evening. We were sitting round the fire, eating. Castello, one of Hannibal's lieutenants, had been saying we must move camp, because where we were seemed to be the centre of the world's flea population. We all had them. 'Yes, yes, Castello,' Hannibal said, distracted, pushing the stew round and round in his bowl.

Then he leapt up, and we watched him as he strode across to the exercise ground and the dummies. In the weakening light, we saw him take off his greaves and strap them to a dummy's legs. He stepped back, concentrated, still.

'What's he doing?' Castello said. 'His supper's going—' I remember how quickly Hannibal drew his sword. I've never known anyone who could do it faster. The blade shone in the last of the light as it swung, back and down and then sweeping up to cut off the dummy's leg at the thigh.

Hannibal was smiling when he ran back. 'There. I've got it,' he said as he sat down. 'Castello, tomorrow a new drill. Everyone. It's an awkward stroke, but we'll learn. If Achilles had been a Roman, I'd have found his heel! Now, where's that stew?'

Hannibal taught his men well. The stroke needed more room than most, but there are many one-legged Romans living who can show how well it worked.

Ostio sat all day in his hut, morose and alone. I saw him only once or twice, swinging himself along on his hands to the latrine.

'What does he live on?' I asked Sosius.

'His grief, Bostar, his grief.'

The only other younger man had his legs, but no hands. He was the village's goatherd, rarely seen. The first time I saw him was when he came to the spring and Sosius' wife filled his water-gourd, held between his stumps. I was turning hay nearby with Sosius. 'And him?' I asked.

Sosius didn't even look up. 'Deserter.'

'But I thought the Romans crucified deserters.'

'They do, when they have time. It would have been better for him if they had.'

Sosius was an intelligent man. I learnt from him something I had not understood before. Because only Capua had joined Hannibal, I had assumed that the whole of Italy was loyal to Rome. 'Never,' said Sosius as we talked one night. 'I am a Bruttian, not a Roman.'

'Then why did you serve Rome?'

'Because until the Carthaginian came, curse him, Rome brought us peace. There was that pirate Pyrrhus, but they soon saw him off. Our roads were safe from brigands, our seas from pirates. We could trade. The year I returned from Sicilia, this village sold twelve wagon-loads of barley. Twelve, even after we had paid to Rome the decuma, *the tithe of a tenth of our grain! Come and see, Teacher.'*

Putting down his hoe, Sosius walked off. I followed, across the ford, up the rise, north. We walked in silence to the top. 'Now look.'

On the plain below, stretching into the distance, were fields. Or, rather, what had been fields. Their walls were crumbling, their irrigation channels blocked. I saw the odd stalk of barley, but the crop of these fields was weeds. 'Now we can barely feed ourselves,' Sosius said.

'But this can be put right,' I replied.

'It could be, but won't be in my lifetime. Our whole country is laid waste, teacher. Our young men are dead or maimed. Our—' Sosius' voice cracked. 'Let's go back to our beans.'

How had Rome fought on?

A Roman's *gens*, his clan, is not all. Consider how our families are bound together even by our language. *Familia* means not just immediate family but the entire extended household, including slaves: the word comes from *famulus*, slave. A paternal uncle, *patruus*, is only *pater*, father, with a different suffix. Our words 'grandfather' and 'grandchild' are almost the same as those for maternal uncle and niece. I knew my paternal uncle's wife, Julia, as 'amita', the same kind of word as 'mummy' or 'nanny'. My mother's sister, Antonia, I knew as 'matertera', in effect 'mother'. All my maternal cousins were – and some still are – *sobrini* or *consobrini*, obviously connected with *soror*, sister—

All right, Bostar, I heard that. The cough again. You think I should be dictating my memoir, not a treatise on linguistics. What is my point? That Hannibal was fighting not individuals but members of a *gens* and then, too, members of a *familia*. In killing one member, he drew on himself the vengeance of the rest. Hannibal would not have won so long as one Roman remained alive. It was through ties of blood that Rome fought on. This point may be over-didactic. But it is true.

Not only that. There is an extraordinary stubbornness about these people – but that is not the word. It is more than that, the quality I mean. It is a capacity to endure, always to go on. Any other people would have surrendered after Cannae. But when news of the disaster reached the Roman Senate, the praetor mounted the rostra *in the Forum to tell the people and 'Pugna magna victi sumus' was all he said. 'We have been defeated in a great battle' – that and nothing more.*

There cannot have been in all of Italy someone who had not lost a father, husband, cousin, friend. Yet the Senate declared a prohibition on mourning – which was, of course, obeyed – and raised new legions. When we heard they were made up of slaves, Hannibal laughed. What we didn't understand was that, as Scipio has just observed (actually, my cough this time was genuine), these were not slaves as Carthaginians know them. These were all members of a familia. *They may not*

26

have been free, but they belonged. They didn't fight for their freedom, granted. That didn't matter. They fought for Rome. Those who were not slaves were men like Sosius.

He and I were hoeing, again. He worked hard, despite his lack of thumbs. He had been telling me, matter-of-fact, of all that he and his village had suffered in the war. 'But why did you put up with all this?' I asked him. 'Why didn't you just give up and go away?'

Sosius straightened, squinted in the sun. With the back of his hand, he wiped the sweat off his forehead. 'Teacher, we are born to this, born to fight for Rome. My father fought in the first war against Carthage. My uncle was killed in the battle of Ausculum, trampled by one of Pyrrhus' elephants. His people almost starved.' Sosius kicked a clod of earth. Disturbed, the ants underneath it scurried away.

'My father's favourite story, Teacher, was about a Bruttian peasant, much like him or me. His wife died in childbirth. His sons were killed in Gaul. His crops were ruined by a freak hail storm. Then, to crown it all, his hut caught fire and burned to the ground. When he saw the smouldering remains, he fell to his knees and raised his eyes to heaven. "Jupiter, Jupiter, why me?" he called out. "Why me?"

'Well, there was a flash of lightning and Jupiter appeared from a cloud. He looked down on the terrified man and said, "Because I've never really liked you."

'I suppose, Teacher, that's why we've kept on.' He looked up at the sun. 'Come on, another hour to go.'

Underpinning all, we Romans have the law, under which even I have just been tried. Plebeian or patrician, we are all equal before the law and for us the law lies in the Twelve Tables. Inscribed on sheets of bronze, they stand in the Forum, where everyone can see them. When Rome was burnt by the Gauls two hundred years ago, the first thing the Senate did was replace the Twelve Tables. They are Rome's soul.

Like every Roman child, I had when I was eight to learn them by heart. 'I am your *fabrus*, your blacksmith,' my father told me, 'and the first thing I want you to understand is the law.'

I found the learning easy. '*Si in ius vocat ito, ni it antestamino, igitur em capito*: if a man calls another to court, he must go; if he does not, call him as witness, and thus seize him. If a patron commits fraud on a client, let him be *sacer* – sacred, accused, outside the law . . .' The laws, after all, seemed to me to be common sense. But then I suppose one of my grandmother's favourite sayings is right: 'There's one thing about common sense, it just isn't common.'

I heard the drumming of the horses' hooves, pulsing through the earth. I was awake and up and out. In the half-light, I saw them come, nine horsemen, bearded, wrapped in furs and armed. Mine was the nearest hut. I stood outside.

A pilum thudded into the ground at my feet. 'Stay where you are!' came a voice, and the first of them was upon me, his bay stallion rearing, phlegm from its snorting landing on my chest. The rider was tall. He wore a Gaulish helmet and, under his furs, a leather jerkin. He carried a sword and a battle-axe. His cheekbones were pocked. I can still remember his rank, sweat-soaked smell.

The nine formed round me in a semi-circle. 'Move and you're dead,' the tall one growled. 'How many of you are there here?' I couldn't place his accent. Ligurian?

'Perhaps thirty,' I said clearly.

'Any women?'

'Some, but . . .' The tall one gestured with his head. Three of them turned their horses. I heard them canter down the street.

'But, bastard? But what?' and suddenly his horse was forward, his sword-point at my neck.

'But they're old,' I said very slowly.

He guffawed. 'We'll see if they're too old for us!' The other five joined in their leader's laugh.

A jab with the sword. 'Any gold, silver?'

'No. This is a poor place. See for yourselves.'

The sword was dropped. The leader turned. In the growing light, he surveyed Secunium, its shabby huts, its dozy, skulking dogs.

'It may or may not be poor, but it sure stinks.' Another gesture of the head. Three more rode off. I stood still. The man to the leader's left, swarthy, dark-skinned, took out a flagon, drank, belched and passed it on.

It wasn't long before the first three came back. Stumbling up the street in front of them were Sosius' wife, Sulcipia, and five other old crones. 'Is that the lot?' the leader asked.

''Fraid so,' one of the three replied.

'Not even any girls?'

'No.'

'Damn. I like 'em young. And we haven't had a virgin for bloody ages. Oh well, we'll see what we've got, eh, lads!' Again, that barking guffaw. 'Right, you lot,' he said to the women, 'Strip!' Sulcipia wailed. 'Shut up, bitch!' the leader shouted. 'Strip!'

The sun had just come over the hill above Secunium. In that clear, soft light, the six old women took off their clothes before us, crying and snivelling in shame.

So, our families, our laws. Then, third, we Romans are bound by our gods. It's hard for me to know what to say on this subject, because I no longer know what I believe. Bostar and I were discussing the founder of the Eleatic school of philosophy, Xenophanes of Colophon, a night or two ago after dinner.

'If donkeys had gods, they would conceive of them as donkeys,' Bostar said.

How right he is. Jupiter is merely a manifestation of anthropocentrism. Perhaps I am with Xenophanes a monist. I probably think that there are no gods. Is there, instead, a single, self-sufficient and eternal consciousness? And, if so, does that consciousness not govern through thought the universe, with which it is itself identical?

But I wouldn't try this on Cato. It is for such beliefs, and others, that I have been tried. Cato and others of the reactionary brigade – I wish I could say old, but they are mostly young – really do, I think, believe in the Pantheon, in Mars and Mercury and Juno and Diana and all that lot. I remember the last opening of the Saturnalia I attended. Cato was doing the invocations on the Senate's behalf. He went droning on, '*per Iovem, per divos, per astra, agimus vobis gratias, quantas possumus maximas . . .*' as if his life depended on it. Perhaps it does. I remember thinking how hot it was, and wishing he'd get it over with.

Well, our Pantheon is simply the Greek one, however hard we try to pretend we've made it ours. It's the one aspect of Greece that leaves me cold. I can't accept those stories in Homer of the gods coming down to earth every ten minutes and meddling. A battle's going on, and suddenly Athena or Ares or even Poseidon or someone's right in the thick of it. Preposterous. At times, Homer even has the gods fighting each other. Greek gods are simply men with bells on.

No, by our gods I suppose I mean our religion. Our word *religio* means, after all, a non-material bond or restraint. I have no quarrel with such things. They are one of the glues that hold Romans together. The patricians like Cato may think themselves close to Olympus. But the gods and the religion of the people are much closer to home. Their gods lie in their hearths and hearts. Their gods are the Penates and the Lares, Vesta and the Manes. Such I understand.

I squeezed my eyes shut, pressed my chin down on my chest. I had seen the rape of Similce, Hannibal's wife. I could bear to see no more. That memory engulfed me. I felt sick.

I heard the man dismount, smelt him come: sweat, garlic, wine.

FORMING

The pain when he jerked my head back by the hair was sharp. The dagger at my throat was cold. 'Open your eyes, dickhead, or die.' The leader's voice was soft. I had seen and done enough with death. I wanted life. Or did I? Was a part of me willing to see more of the madness that can be man?

I opened my eyes slowly to the light. Of the six naked women standing in a huddle, some had crossed their arms to cover their breasts. The two at the front had their hands across their privates. Their breasts were shrivelled, flabby, old. All the women but Sulcipia were sobbing quietly with lowered heads.

'Bring the rest of the village here too,' the leader shouted.

Prodded by pila *and swords, Sosius and the others, old men and young boys, soon formed another huddle near the women.*

'Right, lads, who's first? Not exactly virgins, but a hole's a hole, boys, a hole's a hole!'

The six men who had dismounted shifted uneasily on their feet. The two on horseback looked at each other. Flies buzzed. No one moved. A small, blond-haired man with an enormous nose and a long, red scar across his forehead spoke. 'After you, Tertio.'

Tertio took his dagger from my throat. 'All right, matey. Come and hold this one. Make him watch.' Scarface's dagger was at my back.

Tertio moved forward, dropping his fur, then unbuckling his belt as he went.

Every Roman household, plebeian or patrician, has its shrines to the Penates and the Lares. The first are the guardian spirits of the family larder. Their name comes from *penus* for store-cupboard. In our house in Rome, their shrine was in an alcove down the passage leading to the kitchens. Its lamp never went out. The votive barley cakes were renewed each day.

That eternal light has never left me. In later life it stayed with me, burning on. Often as a child when I could not sleep I slipped out of bed, through the sleeping house and sat down in the passage before the shrine. The flickering lamplight cast shadows and gleams on the figures of the gods, two men crudely carved in ebony. I used to wonder why their wood was black. I came to see a balance in it, in the light and dark—

Yes, Aurio? What is it?

Lunch, master.

Goodness! Can it be that time already? Tell Mulca we're on our way.

Shuffle, shuffle, then the softly closing door. I am fortunate in my servants, although I suppose by comparison with some masters they are fortunate in me. Cato, for example, prides himself on treating his slaves like dirt. As soon as they can no longer work, he kicks them out. So do many others. I don't. I support my old slaves until they die.

I have been praised for this, and criticised. I am indifferent to both. Such kindness comes from my nature, and my upbringing. I was ten, perhaps eleven. School had been hard. I was tired, hungry. I was to dine with my father, who had important guests. He had sent his own body-slave, Festo, to help me dress. I was fidgety. When he slipped the pin of the brooch I was to wear through the fabric on my chest, he went too deep and pierced my skin. I howled and, without thinking, slapped Festo in the face. He ran from my room.

The dinner guests arrived. I was called. I remember long and heated conversations about things I didn't understand. After the last course, before the wine was brought, my father looked across the room, caught my eye and nodded. I went to bed.

He woke me early in the morning. He held a strap in his hand. 'I am going to beat you, Publius,' he said quietly. 'You must never, ever, strike a slave or servant. It demeans not only you, but also them. But before you learn your lesson, I want you to understand. Sit up and listen.'

I sat up, drew a blanket over my shoulders. My father sat on the end of my bed. Its leather thongs creaked. 'You know,

Publius, about the building of the Athenian Parthenon, and how every citizen of Athens contributed as best he could?'

'Yes, Father,' I said rather weakly, unsure where this was leading. But of course I remembered the stories of the building of the Parthenon. Only last year Rome had sent an embassy to Athens to see how it had been done.

'Well,' he went on, 'when the building was finished, do you know what the Athenians did? They turned loose the mules that had worked the hardest. They declared them exempt from further service, and put them out to grass for the rest of their lives at public expense.'

'Remember that, Publius, when next you're angry with any living creature. Now, get up, and bend over the end of the bed.'

I did as I was told, and I have always remembered.

I never knew the name of the woman Tertio grabbed and threw down on the ground. He knelt on top of her, forcing her legs apart with his knees and hands. She moaned and mewled. The only other noise was Tertio's grunts.

Suddenly he pushed himself up. 'Shit!' he shouted. 'Even with my eyes shut, I can't keep it up.' He kicked the woman sharply in the side. 'Get up, you filthy slag. The rest of you, get dressed.'

His legs were pale and hairy. He buckled his belt, looking at his men. 'No silver, gold, lads? Nothing?'

'Nothing, boss,' Scarface said. 'We looked in all the usual places. But hang on.'

The pain was so unexpected, so sudden and so intense I can recall it now and wince. Scarface wrenched the silver earring from my left ear, the earring I'd been given when— That does not matter now. But my left ear lacks its lobe.

I felt the sting, the blood trickling down my neck. Scarface held up the earring. 'At least there's this!' he chortled.

'Keep that bauble if you like,' Tertio said. *'Let's get out of this dump. It stinks.'*

And they were gone as suddenly as they had come.

I was working in the fields this morning, clearing irrigation channels. Macro, my bailiff, many years ago gave up trying to stop me working with the men. He knows by my dress what I intend, and simply accepts it. Yesterday it was my patched brown woollen tunic, my old straw hat and boots. That meant work, manual work.

First we had to mend the water wheel. I loved wading out to it in the middle of the dam, cool water in the softness of the morning when the larks and finches sing.

The water wheel was my idea. We use it to move water uphill to a feeder tank. From there, the water has enough head to flow right through the fields – if the channels are clear. Before we built the wheel, the lower fields were dry and yielded much less.

But it is, I accept, a fiddly thing, constantly going wrong. This time, it had slewed on its axle, so its buckets were picking up hardly any water. I unhitched the mule that turned the wheel and gave its bridle to Macro.

'We need to grease it more often, Macro, at least once a week. Have you enough tallow?'

'Yes, Scipio.'

'Well, give me some.' Holding a jug of tallow I waded to the wheel. 'The wedges have split,' I shouted to Macro. 'They got too dry. Bring me some more, will you?'

'How many?'

'Four should do – oh, and a mallet, please.'

I fixed the wheel, and waded back as the dragonflies darted on the water. I stood on the bank, watching the wheel turn and the drops of water dance. I thought of my trial, of the judgment.

When will it come? Dragonflies, I thought, will dance. Water will be wet, regardless.

For days afterwards, Secunium was silent. I saw people when I went to the well, the latrines, but no one spoke. I worked, hoeing and irrigating beans. There is a peace that comes from the life of the body, not the mind. When a man can think no more and feel no more, all he can do is be silent, and let his well of life refill.

As it must be all over the world, the life of peasants is governed by the rhythm of the earth. Awake at first light, eat, work, eat, sleep a little during the hottest hours, work, eat, sleep when the sun goes — where does it go? — down.

I had never lived like this before. I have not since. I felt the sun beat on my back as the hawks wheeled overhead and the flies buzzed round my bloody ear.

I worked alone. Even Sosius kept to his hut; until I saw him walking towards me in the field on the fourth day, or was it the fifth?

I stopped, put down my hoe, looked up and wiped the sweat from my forehead. Sosius came nearer, stooped, I saw, his step not neat but shambling. I have seen men walk like that when drunk. As he came closer, I saw his shirt was torn across the chest. It and his face were covered in soot. I did not understand.

'Come with me, Teacher' was all he said, in a weak and faltering voice.

'But what—'

'Just come.'

I followed him back across the field where the soil I had just watered was beginning to steam in the strengthening sun. Back on to the path that wandered through the acacia bushes, the brambles and the thorns and opened out back at the well. From there we walked in silence up the street that was Secunium, shabby, dirty, poor. From such as these, I thought again, Rome's greatness comes. She is the sum of many parts, lives lost, hearts broken, pains borne.

There were, I saw, no fires burning. Even the dogs were still. Sosius passed his hut, then went on past mine up to the end of the village where the abandoned huts were, roofless and forlorn.

He stopped outside one of them. He didn't look at me, just said, 'In there, Teacher, in there.'

I went in. Sulcipia's body was still swinging, very slightly, on the rope across the beam from which she had hanged herself. Her head lolled forward, her limbs were slack. She seemed a puppet, or a doll.

I have seen many, many dead. None has moved me like Sulcipia, whom I hardly knew. Aristotle says of Oedipus that his tragedy is so powerful because first you fear for Oedipus, and then you fear for yourself. This old woman, who had nothing, had, it seemed, her pride. To any passing soldier, pedlar, merchant, Sulcipia's would seem a life not worth living. But she had her heart, I thought. Simple, no doubt, ignorant, uncomplicated, but still hers, still free somewhere beyond the drudgery of her days. Those men who came had broken it. Since it was all she had, that she could not bear.

She was a small woman. Her belly swung almost level with my shoulders. I took the knife from my belt. I put my left arm round her thighs and, reaching up, I cut her down.

I blinked as I came from the darkness of the hut to the blinding light, dead Sulcipia in my arms. Sosius was standing where I had left him. He still did not look up.

'Will you . . .' He cleared his throat. 'Will you bury her for me?'

'Of course, but . . .'

'We cannot bury a' — *he could not manage the word 'suicide'* — *'those who have taken their own life.'*

'I understand.'

Sosius looked up. 'Now I am truly alone.' He was crying, I saw, silently. 'It was the shame, the shame. She could not bear the shame.' He turned, and walked away.

I was the rest of the day burying her. I chose a place high above Secunium, a shelf on the hillside. The ground was hard and stony, yet I had to dig deep to keep her from the dogs.

As I dug, I thought what I might do to mark her passing, what I might want for mine. When I stood up to rest my aching back, I saw the vultures, already wheeling high overhead. How do they do it? I wondered. Does death so soon have such a smell, or is death a sense? Perhaps it is just sight. They say that vultures can see clearly over many miles. Could one chance-passing seeker after carrion have seen Sulcipia's body lying beside me on the ground? There are many things man does not understand.

When I had finished, I climbed further up the hill. There was a glade there of birches, and the little spring that fed them made the grass green all around. I saw a sapling that was straight and healthy. I dug it up with care, carried it down and planted it in the stony earth above Sulcipia. Then I went up and back several times to refill my water-gourd and soaked the birch's roots. They would have good feeding in time.

I left Secunium the next morning, at first light. I remember well what I had with me: those things with which I had come. The clothes I stood in, boots, black cotton trousers under my leather leggings, a simple cotton shirt and over that my light summer cloak. In my satchel were my winter cloak, a pair of sandals, four maps of Italy, two unused wax tablets and three styluses. Hanging from my belt were my knife and water-gourd. The only things I left with that I had not brought were calluses and an even heavier heart.

I walked north, up and through the ruined fields where Sosius had first taken me. Did I know where I was going? Not entirely. Away. Secunium's life was not mine. I have seen so many men in trouble for living a life that was not theirs, for never living their own – though it seems much easier so. When people realise their mistake, it is usually too late to change. Sometimes, as when I left Secunium, let alone left Hannibal, I did so because I had to find my own way.

'The wettest thing is water,' says Xenophanes, 'the brightest thing is light, the hottest thing is fire, the softest is air. But the hardest is to know yourself.' As I think does Scipio, I grow old learning something of that every day.

I was about to pass an olive tree, old and big but wizened, burnt. I stopped to look at it. Olives are strong. This one was already sprouting new shoots and leaves from its blackened bark. It seemed to me a symbol of hope for Secunium, a symbol, too, of the strength of Rome. You can burn an olive, and destroy a year's crop, even three, but it will fruit again. The vine is the same, with the vigour of a weed. Olive and vine must be uprooted to be killed. Hannibal thought that by burning he would do enough. As this tree and many showed, he was wrong.

Sosius stepped into my path from behind the tree. I stopped again. He looked at me openly this time. 'Go well, Teacher. Perhaps you don't know it, but you have taught while you've been here.'

'Taught, Sosius? I don't know about that. But I do know I have learnt.'

'Here, take this,' he said, pressing a bag against my chest. 'I don't need it now. Vale. Farewell.'

I watched him until he disappeared over the brow of the hill back into his village of, or so it seemed, the damned. Perhaps they would know peace again, and thrive and farm.

When he had gone, I thought it would be easier to carry one bag, not two. So I opened Sosius'. There were four barley cakes in it, two cheeses, and a little leather pouch, shut with a thong.

I squatted down, tugged the thong of the pouch and tipped it up. Gold fell to the ground, gold pieces. I picked one up. It had clay on it. So Sosius had had gold buried underground. Where? The shrine, probably. No one would think or want to look there. I scraped off the clay. 'Senatus populusque Romanus,' I made out. Roman gold. I laughed out loud as I remembered. Hannibal had paid me each month, as he paid everyone who served him – when he could – although most served for love, not gold. But I had never taken the money, just asked him to keep it for me. It never occurred to me to ask for it when I stayed behind. Hannibal had paid me in a different kind.

*   ＊   ＊   ＊*

My childhood. That is what made me, and I have made Rome, so I must give a true account. And be consistent. Chronology, then, Bostar. I shall use the order of time, and not totter about like a new-born colt. Though I am hardly that. An old warhorse, perhaps, now put out to grass. But I shall chew my grazing carefully, and dream.

He seemed immensely tall, a fair giant, my first teacher, Rufustinus. He was also very thin. My nanny, Quinta, was the opposite, dark and small and round. We were all astonished to learn, years later in Celtiberia, that they were to marry – no, Bostar, I shall not forget that I am to be Thucydidean, or try to.

Rufustinus was my *litterator*, employed to teach me to read and write when I was four. We Romans have a clear and tested system of education. A *litterator* teaches letters to an *abecedarius*, someone learning a-b-c, and that then was me. In lesser families, the father acts as *litterator*, but my father did not have the time and did, presumably, have the money to pay someone else to do it. I had a class with Rufustinus each morning for two hours in a room at the far end of the courtyard.

He came from near Verona in the north. His mother was a Celt, and that explained his fair hair and blue eyes. Of course, Rufustinus didn't tell me this. I would never have dared ask him. He kept strictly to work. I learnt what little I knew from Festo, who used to help me dress. Yes, I know, Bostar. I've already mentioned him. Anyway, Festo told me that Rufustinus had been a clerk to one of the state priests, or pontiffs, and that's why he was so clever. That meant little to me. Other things did.

'And why, Festo, is he so tall?' I once asked.

'Also because, young master, he is a Celt. Theirs is a land of many rivers and mountains. The people there need to be big to cross and to climb. Why, some of them are taller than the Aventine. They march at great speed round their country, catching animals to eat.'

'What kind of animals?'

'Huge shaggy ones called aurochs, and others called bison, ten times bigger than the biggest cow. They kill them with clubs bigger than I am, and then' — and Festo whispered in my ear — 'then they eat them raw.'

I remember this conversation because it made me curious. A little scared too, I suppose, but above all curious. Perhaps that was when I developed a love of travel I have never lost. For weeks I dreamed of giant Celts with clubs in wild and wasted lands. But it did me good. I certainly worked harder after that, and never did anything that might annoy Rufustinus.

I thought about what Festo had told me. When Rufustinus wasn't watching, I looked at him hard. Yes, he was tall, but not all that tall, I decided. So the next time Festo was sent to help me dress, I challenged him. 'Festo, you said the Celts are very, very tall, and Rufustinus is, certainly. But he's not all that tall, only two or three hands more than you.'

'Granted, young master. He was obviously the runt of his litter. Now, your sandals . . .' Well, I have known many Celts since then and travelled through their lands. I have never seen a giant. Perhaps I will one day, in my dreams.

Runt or not, I found Rufustinus' Latin strange at first, guttural and harsh. But he had an excellent reputation — otherwise, of course, my father would not have employed him — and he taught me well. Or, rather, I think he must have done, because I learnt to read and write sooner than was expected of me.

But the truth is that I cannot remember how he taught me. I remember words written down on tablets and placed on or beside the objects they described. *Mensa* on a table, *cathedra* on a chair, *lucerna* by a lamp and so on. In time, I think, Rufustinus began to place the letters in order for me in the alphabet. They came to make a pattern in my head, like a song, and I can sing it still.

FORMING

I wonder, before battle, before the killing-frenzy comes, when men know they may be about to die, or lose an arm, a leg, an eye, a hand, how many sing under their breath a rhyme they learnt at their mother's knee or, perhaps, if they are educated, the alphabet. It is not the words that ease their fear, but being safe deep down with sounds, back in themselves at a time when the world was as simple as a–b–c. But no road leads back to that place.

One morning – I must have been five – I opened the door to the schoolroom. Rufustinus was standing by the window. Beside him was my father. I can still see his white toga next to Rufustinus' brown.

'Good morning, Publius.'

'Good morning, Father.' I didn't know what to do. This hadn't happened before.

'Well, don't stand there gawking! Sit down!' my father said.

When I had, he began to walk across the room between my desk and Rufustinus' table. 'You are doing well, Rufustinus tells me. Good, good. So well, in fact, that we think you are now ready.' He smiled at me.

I was puzzled. 'Ready, Father, for what?'

'For a new language, Publius. Today you will begin to learn Greek. You will need Greek for the life you will lead.'

'What life is that, Father?'

He laughed, said, 'You will find out soon enough,' patted me on the shoulder and left the room.

I remember feeling scared. Greek? I remember the sweat on my hands. We had a few Greek slaves in the house, but they spoke Latin to us. I overheard them sometimes speaking Greek, and thought it was some kind of music that they played, running like a stream. Yet that day began the best journey I have ever made. Like all such, like true marriage or friendship, it is one that has no end.

★　　★　　★

I walked steadily on, north and east. At least there was no shortage of places to sleep, or shelter from the midday sun. There was always a hut or shepherd's cottage. Bruttium was a green desert, its fields untended, its villages burnt or deserted, testaments of war. I saw no one, only goats roaming wild without a goatherd. This was how Rome had fought on after Cannae, by stripping her larder bare.

Yet I was never hungry. I found enough fruit trees, corn. Early on, when I left the path I was following and went into the bushes to relieve myself, I came upon a rabbit snare. It had caught a rabbit, long ago, and now held only bones, stripped by ants and bleached by sun. I added it to my satchel's contents, and was to eat much rabbit in the weeks ahead. Bread I missed. I have a weakness for it. But when, I thought, I had it again, I would enjoy it all the more.

Strange eyes in the dark, an amber gleaming. I was half awake. Or was I dreaming? Then I heard the sound, a rapid panting, and the knowledge came. Dogs. Wild dogs. I had gone to sleep in a half-ruined bothy, once a woodman's, judging by the shavings on which I had made my bed.

I had roasted a rabbit that evening. That must have brought them. I sat up. I heard a menacing growl, saw teeth white in the half-light. I cleared my throat. 'Go,' I said quietly. 'Go on your way. Leave me to mine.'

I lay back, turned on my side and went back to sleep. But in the morning, they were still there, across the clearing, just in the shelter of the trees. I threw the rabbit carcass to them, shouldered my satchel and walked on. There were many wanderers in Italy then.

From the start, Greek was fascinating. First, Rufustinus taught me the alphabet. I loved the look of the letters, the strange shapes of ξ and θ, ι and μ. I practised them alone. He began to teach me Latin and Greek simultaneously. I would translate simple sentences from one into the other. I found the differences between the two languages helped me to learn both. It was all the easier to learn the Greek optative, for example, because Latin did not have one. It seemed less hard to learn the principal parts of Greek irregular verbs when I had mastered some Latin ones – although τίθημι still tricks me, even after fifty years. Words are the most fickle – and fascinating – of things. Like clouds, they change. Like earth, they endure. When a word is said or written, there is nothing you can do to take it back again.

Well, perhaps it was all harder, took much longer. These memories are far away. Some stand out, tall trees in a forest, but most have merged and muddled in my mind.

It was winter, cold and raining. We were going over the imperfects of *amo* and λύω. I recited them well enough.

'Now, write them down,' Rufustinus instructed from high above, handing me a tablet and stylus. He was like a stork, leaning down. His cheeks always seemed puffy and full. I had a chilblain on my index finger. The wax was stiff. I made a mess of λύω. I knew it.

Rufustinus glanced at the tablet, and wiped it clean with his ruler. 'Again.'

From his third rejection came the only time I crossed him. 'But that's the best I can do,' I whined, looking at my feet, wishing the lesson was over.

'Publius Cornelius Scipio, I am not interested in your best. Can you build a house without bricks, or a road without stones? No, of course not. That, by the way, was a rhetorical question.' And Rufustinus then said something I have never forgotten. 'Never forget, young Publius, *potest quia posse videtur* – you can because you think you can. Now, try and try again.'

I did not know it, but I was building the foundations of what I am. They have proved deep and strong.

Scipio has been in bed now for two days. He has a mild fever and, while he had anything in his stomach, kept being sick. Aurio and I take turns to sit with him. He dozes. We talk, though not about the trial. We read him the historian Herodotus, although this morning he asked for the comedian Aristophanes – he must be getting better. Mulca brings him her special teas. When you are ill, it is good to be among friends.

I am better, though weak. I always think when I am ill how much more, because of it, I enjoy being well. I see my quince flowers, for example, with a new eye. Several have opened since I took to my bed. I will send for Macro. I want to know what else is going on. I hope the water wheel is still working. And I can go to the latrine. I do hate chamberpots. They are so demeaning, but a necessary evil for the ill, I suppose – and the old.

The dogs followed me for days. I never thought they would attack. I did not send them any sense of fear – not because I was controlling it, but simply because I had none. I was brought up with animals. I was put when I was very small into a den of wolves. Or have I imagined that? A wet licking, a nuzzling in the night. We are not only what we are, but what we wish we might have been and hope, perhaps, yet to be – and I must practise what I preach.

From following well behind, the dogs suddenly rushed yelping towards me as a pack. The hairs on my neck stood up and my penis stiffened in fear and I held my muscles hard. 'Calm, Bostar, calm!' I said to myself, taking the deep breath of peace.

The dogs veered off to my right, bursting through the undergrowth and shrubs. Probably a pig, I thought. They need to eat. Let them.

I was in high and lonely hills, cut with sharp defiles, difficult to cross. The rich red earth crumbled as I scrambled up, often sending me slipping down. My arms and face were badly scratched from pushing

through thorns. Many of the cuts were septic, and I could not find the
herbs I needed as unguents. My progress was slowing. It was time to
turn east, to an easier way.

Preparations had been long and patient, hushed. My life was
unchanged, but I smelt and sensed the bustle in the kitchens,
saw the greenery put up to beautify our house. I was put to
bed early the night before. Quinta tucked me in, and said,
'Now remember, don't wait up for him. He only comes to
children who are asleep.'

'Who, Quinta? Who comes?'

'You'll find out in the morning – if you go to sleep.' She
kissed me on the forehead, said, 'Good night,' crossed the room
and softly closed the door. Her smell, of lavender and laundry,
stayed behind.

I fought to stay awake. From far below us in the Forum, I
heard the drums that marked the passing of the hours. I forced
my eyes wide open. I clenched my teeth, held my arms rigid. I
pinched myself, sat upright, pushed off my blankets to be cold
– but I fell asleep.

I woke with a start. What had I done wrong? Yes, fallen
asleep. I jumped up, rushed to the window and tugged the
curtain open. I could hear people stirring in the house. It
was not fully light, but enough for me to see, as I turned,
an unfamiliar little table by the end of my bed. On it were
boxes. I was running to the table when the door opened and
my father and mother came in. I checked myself.

'Good morning, Father. Good morning, M—'

'Oh, go on!' my mother laughed. 'Happy Saturnalia. Open
them!' She was fat about the middle, fatter than when I had
last seen her.

How long had it been since Quinta had told me? Six months,
five? I still didn't understand.

She had been putting me to bed. I was spitting into the bowl she held, having cleaned my teeth with the usual stem of arrowroot and my *dentiscalpium*, my toothpick, when she said, 'And by the by, young master, you soon won't be alone.'

'What do you mean, Quinta? I'm not alone. I have you, and Festo, and my father, and—'

'I mean a brother or a sister. You're going to have a brother or a sister or maybe, who knows, two of each.' Her kind face smiled, and the crows' feet round her eyes became like a spider's web and as she nodded enthusiastically her double chins wobbled.

'Two of each?'

'Or even one of each,' she said, sounding hopeful.

I looked hard at her. Slowly, I put my right thumb in my mouth. For once, she didn't pull it out. I still remember sucking hard. I don't think I did it again until I saw the carnage at Cannae and then, yes, I sucked my thumb.

Sorry, Bostar. Cannae is some way off, I admit. But the extent to which past, present and future are the same baffles me. What is an action? By asking that very question, I am presuming my past – from which I acquired the capacity to ask it – my present – in which I ask it – and my future, without which it would lose its force.

An action, any action, is surely the result of someone doing something intentionally. That intention is formed, in large part at least, by that person's past and presupposes the consequences of the future. But say I moved this chair to the door to have a different view. Say Aurio then came in to clean when we had gone to bed and, in the dark, tripped over the chair because it wasn't where he expected it to be. My action would have had consequences, yet no one could say they were intentional. Perhaps, then, we need a new word for that kind of action.

But back to Quinta.

'I don't understand. I'm going to have a brother, or a sister, or two of them, or one of each?' I asked.

Quinta tutted. I have not known since a sound so sure, unless it be the thud of a *pilum* lodged in flesh. 'It's past your bed-time,' she marched on in her brusquest manner. 'What I mean is that your mother is going to have a baby,' she said, tucking in my sheets.

'What, tomorrow?'

'No, Publius, not tomorrow.' She was suddenly gentle. She sat down on the edge of my bed.

'Well, when?'

'When, when . . . when the baby is ready. When the baby is ready, Publius, you will have a brother or a sister. Or both.' She chuckled. I saw the creases in her rosy cheeks. 'Now, you must sleep.' She leant forward across me, about to blow out the candle, and her soft bosom against my chest made me feel safe.

'Quinta?' I said softly, slipping round on my side to face her.

'Yes?'

'Have you got babies?'

Suddenly, she crossed and clenched her hands beside me. 'No, young master, no, I haven't. Except . . .' And the thing I still remember is the cheeks of my nanny, Quinta, in soft candlelight, wet with tears. I hope I have not failed her.

When they came back, three were limping. Two others had great gashes in their sides. 'So, not a pig, a boar,' I said out loud. I had begun talking to myself, as men do when they are long alone. But they all had full bellies. They had killed.

The land was opening out. Early some mornings, if the breeze was right, I could smell the sea from the Mare Adriaticum, over to the east. The dogs fell further and further behind, although I always left out for them any hare or rabbit I could spare. But those were just scraps.

They must have been hungry, as by then was I. It had been eight weeks, nine, since I left Secunium. As I left Bruttium, forage became increasingly rare. I saw villages, inhabited, but I stayed away. I did once come upon an olive store. I ate as many as I could and took as many as I could carry. I left behind a gold piece in the almost empty jar. I chuckled as I thought how I must, thereby, have added to the local lore of sprites and fairies.

The world needs more of those. I once asked my father how it was that trees grew upside down. I meant, of course, how they went up so high. You couldn't, for example, throw a javelin that high.

He scoffed, and told me not to be so silly. But I still don't know the answer.

I had reached the brow of a small but steep hill, rich in brambles and wild rose. I paused to catch my breath and look around. Below me, on the little plain, was the pack of dogs, tongues lolling in the heat. The lead dog, a big, grizzled grey mastiff, moved forward and stretched out his neck, it seemed, towards me. He gave out a long ululating howl, then barked, once, twice, turned and trotted back the way he had come. The others followed. I don't know why, but I thought this was an omen, and I thought the omen good.

They both came and sat on my bed. They were holding hands. I had rarely seen them together before, let alone like this. 'What are they?' I asked, pointing to the boxes.

'Presents, Publius, presents,' my father said with a smile.

'What kind of presents?'

'How should we know?'

'Aren't they from you?'

'No,' my mother replied. 'They come from Saturnus, a god. Today is his birthday. He brought you, and all other good children, these presents in the night.'

'But if it's his birthday, shouldn't *we* be giving *him* presents?'

My father slapped his knee at this. 'Maybe, Pomponia, we have bred a son for the courts and not the field!' Then, turning to me, 'We shall give him presents, Publius, you'll see. But come on, open what Saturnus has given you.'

I opened the biggest box first. In it were dolls, two of cloth and two of clay. I put them carefully on the table, in a row.

'These are symbols from Saturnus of your childhood, Publius,' my father said.

'Oh, I see' – not that I did, well, not really. In the next box were little jars, one containing water, the other earth, and a dagger. I looked at them, perplexed.

'These symbolise what Saturnus gives us, Italy and Rome. These are our right, Publius, but they are also our responsibility. That is why he gives you this as well.'

I unwrapped it slowly from its calfskin, bound with a thong. It glinted in the light. A dagger, steel shining, its heft of some blackwood inlaid with precious stones. I looked up at my father enquiringly.

'Saturnus gives you this for a purpose,' he said. 'Never use it in anger, but never sheathe it when what you have been given is under threat.'

I was as puzzled by the earnestness of my father's voice as I was by the strange gifts. Well, strange then. Not now. When I was a soldier, the dagger of my first Saturnalia was unsheathed for many years.

'Don't look so serious, Publius,' my father said in a lighter voice, getting up. 'Ouch, your bed is hard,' he went on, rubbing his bottom. 'We must get him a softer one, Pomponia.'

'All right, I'll tell Festo,' she replied with a smile.

'Now, we must be quick or we'll keep the servants waiting. Open the last two boxes,' my father told me, kneeling down beside me, his arm round me. His soft beard brushed my face.

I gasped when I opened the first of the two left. It was full of gold coins. 'Goodness, I am rich!'

'No, not quite, Publius. These are for you to give away, as Saturnus gives to us.'

'To g–give away?' I stammered.

'Yes. You'll see. And now the last.'

The first layers were of the softest wool. Under them, I found a ring. I held it out on my palm to the light. The red stone glanced and glowed. 'It is, it is . . . alive. Alive with light,' I whispered.

My father held out his right hand. He slipped a ring from his little finger and, as he put it in my hand beside the other one, he said, 'This was my grandfather's. That one is yours. Wear it, in time, with pride and with the blessing of Saturnus.'

'And in the meantime,' my mother said, coming over to us, 'wear it with this.'

She held out a simple leather thong. My father took it, looped it through the ring. I knew. I bent my head. He passed it over my neck. Still kneeling, he hugged me, then stood up. 'Now, quickly, Publius, get dressed.' I was in my nightshirt. 'We'll wait for you in the atrium.'

Blisters. Well, one, to be exact. A tiny stone must have slipped into my left boot. By the time I noticed, it was too late. I felt the swelling only when I stopped to eat my lunch. I remember the grove of oaks where I did that, softly whispering in the breeze. I relieved myself under one of them, adding my steaming urine to the must. But I remember those oaks not because they were fine oaks, which they were, but because of my left foot.

Of course I felt relief when I saw the road. It would take me where I wanted to go. But more than that, I felt a sense of awe. I had crossed the Via Appia with Hannibal. Then there had been much else on my mind. But from where I stood this time, in the rolling hills above a town I took to be Venusia, I stood and looked and saw and was amazed. Straight as a ruler, a vast Roman highway stretched on, far out of my sight.

I have seen nothing like these Roman roads. They are the product of refined, meticulous engineering, of course. But more than that, they are the product of the Roman mind. Ten Hannibals with twenty armies might, in time, destroy the Via Appia. But, as Hannibal found out, you cannot destroy the Roman mind.

The sheer thoroughness of it. The short stretch I could see crossed some marshes, then a river. Most people would have avoided the first and used ferries for the second. Not the Romans. They had built a causeway, then a bridge. Even on the bridge, I saw, the road kept its drainage channels, its kerbstones. This road, I thought, is the product of a people devoid of self-doubt. How did they come to be so? The Via Appia makes you feel that it, and those who made it, will never end.

And for a blistered foot it meant easier going. Men have died for want of less.

It is the noise, the colours and the smells that I remember: overwhelming. Cymbals and drums, tympana and flutes, lutes and whistles in a cacophony of sound. All the buildings were decked in bunting, garlands of flowers round doors and windows. Bright flags rippled in the breeze. Dancers in fantastic costumes of vermilion and ochre, brightest blue and crimson, indigo and violet, performed their cartwheels and undulations, oblivious of all around. And then the singing, the talk of many voices, the calls of stall-holders selling hot chestnuts, figs, sweetcakes and cordials, wine. Jesters and buffoons cavorted. Laughter was loud; I still love it, though I hear it less often now. I think we should all laugh, even when we have considered all the facts. Laughter is immense. It is immeasurable.

The Forum was packed. I did not know there could be so many people, Celts and Celtiberians, Ligurians, Lusitanians, Aecians, Hernicians, Cantabrians, Samnites, Bruttians, Volscians, Baliarideans, Dorians, people come from many miles around.

Women with masks of flowers wandered at their will, offering kisses for a penny and singing soaring songs that mixed and mingled in the noise.

There were black people, brown, yellow, olive, some as tall and thin as eucalyptus trees, others short and round as melons, babbling in as many dialects and tongues. Preceded by their walkers, as were we to clear a way, rich merchants strolled along in gold and purple, dark-eyed women by their sides, their bosoms bare and heaving and their perfumes languid in the air. Dressed in black and beating heavy drums, priests' officers pushed their way through the throng, and behind them came the augurs, mincing, nosegays pressed to their nostrils, as beggars pressed their stumps at passing burghers. The world was mad and wonderful, alive.

'Look, Mother, look!' I shouted. 'Father, look at this!'

My parents were talking to some friends. A tumbler was about to cross in front of us. In pants of crimson and a shirt of gold, he was walking on his hands, and on each of his feet there was a red ball. They rolled a little as he moved, but did not slip off his feet. I watched, fascinated, as he passed beyond us into the crowd. Did the balls, I wondered for days afterwards, ever fall, or did they stay on his feet for ever?

It was my first Saturnalia. It gave me a love of festivals I have never lost. And I gave away my gold, but not to the priests of the temples, whose collectors pressed on us at every turn. From my hot and clammy hand I gave my box to a beggar boy sitting alone and quiet under a column of the law courts. He had no nose, I remember, and his clothes were rank and torn. When I knelt down quickly and gave him the gift of Saturnus, he looked astonished. Then he smiled, before I was borne away like flotsam in the sea.

*   *   *

FORMING

When I stepped up on to the Via Appia, I felt I had left Hannibal at last. I was on a new road, and this one, unlike Hannibal's, led to Rome.

Why did he not take Rome? He hardly even tried. So many have asked me. I give the usual answers: lack of siege equipment, of support from Carthage. The truth is that after Cannae he was spent. What he had made in his mind was broken. He had drunk his loss — his father, his son, his wife — to the lees. When that was done, he found that beneath the brilliance and the fury and the anger there was nothing. He found he was only a man.

The road was deserted, reaching on as far as I could see, its far distance shimmering in the sun. Strong and sure, this road's self-confidence was almost frightening. I sat down on the kerb and drank deep from my water-gourd. I ate some dried figs. I wanted to defecate, but felt exposed, alone. The bowel, unlike the bladder, is a patient friend. I stood up again and walked on.

The first people I met ignored me. They were on a wagon, coming south towards me. Two oxen pulled it, plodding on. A haze of flies buzzed round the beasts. I started to greet them, but their driver stared straight ahead as they passed me. The others, two men and a woman, did the same. The creaking of the wheels was raucous, then again I was alone.

I limped on. I slept that night and others in a culvert, like a fox in his den. Now both my feet were sore from walking on the stones.

Even from my room I heard the banging at the door. Then the noise of voices, people stirring. It was dark and cold. I slipped out of bed and shivered, fumbled for my woollen gown. Still half asleep, I walked into a chair and stumbled as I crossed the room, but I found the door. Torches were blazing in the corridor. I blinked, and rubbed my eyes.

Festo rushed past me, a torch in each hand. I followed, past the Manes and Penates, down the corridor as so often before. There were six men in the atrium, no, seven. Crossing the room in front of them, his hair dishevelled, in a gown, his back to me, his slippers scuffing on the floor, I saw my father. I squeezed against the wall to see round him and gasped – I had never seen blood before.

'They what!' my father shouted.

'I know, it's outrageous,' said one of the three men I could see. He and another, younger man were supporting a third, who was slumped but standing, his whole face covered in blood, shining in the torchlight. I could see it ooze, glowing, from a gash across his head. His thick brown hair, there, was black. Who says blood is red? It is, but not for long.

'Festo, quick. Bandages, hot water. Pomponia, where are the chairs?' There was a new note to my father's voice, an urgency I had not heard before.

'Coming,' I heard my mother answer, though I couldn't see her.

'It doesn't matter,' my father replied, crossing the *tablinum* and pulling over a couch.

'Lay him down there.'

'But the blood . . .' said the younger man.

'Bugger the blood,' my father replied. I'm sure he did. It was the first time I had heard anyone swear.

They laid the man down gently. My father knelt down beside him. Festo approached, and reached out with a dripping cloth.

The man waved him away. 'Later.' I could barely hear him. He cleared his throat, spoke more strongly. 'We'll do this later. The cut's not deep. They tended to it on board the ship, but we've ridden hard to get here. That's opened the wound up again. Anyway,' and he looked up at the elder of the men who had carried him in, 'it's not outrageous, Ligurius.'

I saw him turn his head towards my father, reach out a hand and take him by the arm. 'No, it's not outrageous. Scipio, it is war.'

What I remember of that night is the dirt. There had been none in my childhood until that night. Everything in our house was always clean and ordered. Everyone's clothes were always the same, not in colour – on the contrary – but in cleanliness, and that crisp, clean laundry smell is one that I still bear with me from my childhood as if I was still there.

We had a laundry room at the back of the courtyard, its copper vessels gleaming, and a laundry maid – what was her name? Caria? Coria? – always with her hair tied back, her apron white and crisp. I used to hide behind a bench and through the open door watch her working and smell that slightly acid smell.

I have a fine laundry here. Mulca supervises it. Even our bed-linen, of fine Egyptian cotton, is white and crisp and clean. Mulca does not know, but often I stand in a recess in the passage outside the laundry and shut my eyes and smell and dream.

I am finding this a trifle dull. But I must let him have his memories. So I have been doing other things, and will allow myself a brief digression. I can always take it out later, when I edit Scipio's account.

What I have been doing is renewing my love affair these past few days. My love affair with numbers. In the late afternoons, when Scipio is out on the estate again or reading, I have been checking Macro's accounts. That would be tedious, even to a practised clerk, but not to me. Payments for fencing and lamp oil, receipts for lambs and corn . . . I haven't found a mistake yet, and Macro is fastidious. But he asked me as a friend to check. 'The older I get, Bostar,' he said, 'the more the numbers seem to swim before my eyes in the ledger.'

Not so with me, and I do not use an abacus. I have loved numbers since I was very small. They were and are utterly reliable, true, something I can depend on. Two plus two, everywhere and to everybody, is always four. People, by contrast, as Scipio has just demonstrated by breaking off to talk about his laundry here, of all

*things, do not behave at all like numbers. They are, on the whole,
neither dependable nor independent. I am fortunate indeed to have
known both numbers and people. The ideal state, I think, would be
one that balanced people and numbers. But most embody the virtues
of neither and the vices of both.*

Two slaves brought the chairs at last. My father sat down beside
the wounded man. 'So, Flavius, tell me. What happened? Where
is Julius?' I had never heard him so intense.

The man called Flavius sat up a little on one elbow. He
coughed, long and hacking. 'W–water . . .'

'Of course. Festo! Get some water. Or wine?'

Flavius shook his head vigorously. 'We need Mars, not
Bacchus tonight, Publius. Let me begin.'

I stood transfixed, just outside the *tablinum*, surrounded by
the images of my ancestors. A great part of what being a Scipio
meant had been brought home to me, I realised, as I watched
the stain of Flavius' blood spread across the white linen of the
couch where he lay.

'Our journey at least went well,' Flavius said, 'no storms, or
pirates.'

'Though we were faster back than going,' added the older
man, Ligurius.

'You sailed from Ravenna?' my father asked.

'No, from Ancona. We were on our way to Ravenna when
we heard that one of Paullus' ships – you remember him, Scipio?'
– my father nodded – 'that one of his fast merchant ships was
bound for Illyria anyway, out of Ancona.'

Flavius paused, and coughed again, and shivered. So did I.

'Festo, quickly, bring a brazier!' my father called. 'And some
blankets!' to Festo's footsteps. 'Flavius, we must get you a
surgeon. Ligurius, arrange it, will you?'

'Who?'

'Um, a head wound. Anything else, Flavius?'

'No. At least I don't think so.'

'Then Arimastis – you know, the Chian. No, on second thoughts get Archagathos of Kos. His surgery's over by the—'

'Yes, the Acilius crossroads. I know it. I'll be right back.'

'Good.'

Ligurius walked out into the night, just as Festo came back with a burning brazier and some white blankets. I thought how dirty they would get, and asked myself if it mattered.

My father resumed. 'Then, Flavius, you'd better tell me quickly. What happened?'

Geometry is dependable, too. Make a circle. Place one point of your compasses on the circumference. Describe an arc. It will always divide perfectly into six. Or take a piece of string and tie twelve, equidistant knots along it. You can always make a perfect right-angled triangle.

Of all the books here, the one I enjoy most is Scipio's precious copy of Euclid's Stoixeia, *his* Elements. *Here is clarity, safety. 'A point is that which has no parts, or which has no magnitude. A line is length without breadth. A solid is that which has length, breadth and thickness . . .'*

Of course, there are problems. Take Euclid's statement that 'the extremities of a line are points'. This is merely a proposition. It has, it seems to me, either to be proved – in which case it is a theorem – or to be taken for granted – in which case it is an axiom.

But this is a matter of thought. Numbers are, as I said, dependable. They reward the purest thought. But they are also mysterious. Consider the number seven. All the even numbers, of course, are divisible. Of the odd numbers, one is indivisible, three is the first stable number – a tripod will not easily fall over – and five a fistful. But seven is free. Nine is just an inflated three, but seven is so stubborn, so impractical, that it must have been made with mystery in mind, for a purpose beyond our understanding. Why, for example, are there only seven – or should I say as many as seven? – sacred substances, frankincense, galbanum, stacte, *nard, myrrh, spice and* costum? *Why seven? I don't know.*

There is a deeper mystery to numbers. How do we know that they are? Because, I think Euclid would say, they are self-evident. The earliest men must have seen, say, the fingers on their hand and made words for one to five. One stylus plus another stylus, patently, makes two. So arithmetical truths become truths about objects. But objects of what kind?

I could count for the rest of my life and not run out of numbers. I shan't, of course, but the thought comforts me. The problem is that there cannot be enough physical or mental objects for me to count. Well, there might be, but no brain could grasp them. And, even if it could, objects must be finite, but numbers are infinite. Even if that were not so, I cannot imagine or bring into my mind, for example, 3,476,212 objects. But I could easily count to that number, given enough time.

So are numbers abstract entities, that just are? *If so, I cannot understand how we can know them.*

Well, there are many things I do not understand. Life would be dull without them. I am lucky to be able to move from farm accounts to such questions – and, fortunately for Macro and Scipio, back again. I must return to my past; and Scipio's.

Flavius and three others, I learnt as I stood and listened, had been sent by the Senate on an embassy to Illyria. They were to arrange peace, to stop the Illyrian pirate ships preying on our trade with Greece and slaughtering our merchants.

They were met amicably enough, and taken on horseback straight to the tented city from which ruled Teuta, the Illyrian queen. Her tent was cavernous and dark, hung with rich tapestries and cloths, thick with the smoke of incense.

'We could barely see her,' Flavius said, his voice stronger now.

'"So, Romans. I presume you have come with a message," she said. "What is it?"'

'We had agreed that Julius was to be our spokesman. "Peace, Queen Teuta, between Illyria and Rome."'

'"Ah, peace." She drawled out the word. "So simple?" She sat back in her chair. We couldn't see her face at all. "Well, a simple proposition deserves a simple answer, does it not?"'

'She clapped her hands. A huge Moor stepped forwards from the shadows to stand in front of us. He bowed, out of respect, I thought, for our rank and station as ambassadors of Rome—'

'And as was only proper, indeed,' my father interrupted.

Flavius raised a hand in irritation. 'But as he straightened, it all happened so quickly, I saw too late a dagger flash in his right hand. We hadn't seen it in the folds of his cloak. He stabbed Julius in the heart. As Julius fell, men seized the other three of us from behind. I broke free, to go to him – of course we weren't armed – and took this sword-cut for my pains.'

I could just see my mother all this time. I'm surprised my father hadn't sent her away. She listened impassively. Perhaps she was used to hearing such things. I always meant to ask her. I never did.

My father stood up. He walked out of my sight, but I heard him. 'So, it is war.'

'And the command, Scipio, is yours,' Flavius said.

'It is, Flavius, it is. But don't worry. Julius will be avenged. I'll go straight to the Senate in the morning. Now, where is Archagathos?'

I heard the beating, drumming, on the road long before I saw them. I knew before they came what they would be. Cavalry. A turma, a squadron at least, coming from behind me at the gallop. I wondered whether to leave the road and hide. Where? The countryside was flat plain, grass. A culvert? I could see none. Well, I would walk on. My fate, it seemed, would overtake me.

I did walk, or rather hobble, on for a bit. But I needed something. I had one comfort left, so I stopped and sat on the kerb by the side of the road as I heard the cavalry come closer. I opened my satchel, and felt in a little side pocket. One last small piece of bdellium, of gum. Until the pedlar came to Hannibal's last camp at Crotona, I hadn't had any for months. It is an indulgence of mine, still; there are many worse. I had bought all he had, and now it was all but gone. It seemed appropriate to mark what was about to happen by chewing my last piece of gum.

Of course, they might not have stopped. But then, I tried to think like a Roman cavalry commander. A single man on the Via Appia without horse, carriage or wares agricultural or otherwise would have to be (a) a deserter, (b) a vagrant or (c) a discharged veteran. If (a) or (b), arrest. If (c), stop to show respect. Of course (a) or (b) would hardly sit around in broad daylight when all but the very deaf or insane could tell that a squadron of cavalry was coming. But that thought would not occur to a Roman cavalry commander. Or so I reasoned.

They rode three abreast, their colour streaming, their armour glinting. How many ranks, I couldn't see. Ten, or eleven. But anyway, far from full strength. As soon as he saw me, the commander raised his hand for Halt.

They stopped perhaps forty paces from me. 'They probably have a drill for this sort of thing,' I thought, 'a manual.' It was good to be chewing gum. The decurion in command — at least that's what I assumed he was, since each turma is supposed to have one — waved on the two on either side of him. They walked up, the left-hand horse, a young bay gelding, snorting and confused.

'Quis estis? Who are you?' the taller of the two demanded. Under his cap I could see black hair. He was barely a man, almost beardless. What would he be? Fourteen, fifteen? Yes, Rome had dug deep in fighting Hannibal.

They were restless, nervous. Both had their hands on their sword-hilts.

I stood up, and the bay reared. 'Non armatus sum,' I said, raising my arms. 'I'm not armed. I am from the east, a teacher, bound for Rome.'

'A teacher? Pah.' The boy spat. I followed the spit's trajectory and watched the little bubbles fizzle at my feet. He kicked his horse forward to within inches of my face. 'Marcus,' he said to the other horseman without looking round, 'search that,' and he pointed with his left hand to my satchel on the ground. He drew his sword. The point was at my throat. 'Teacher, or spy?'

I didn't see my father again for many months. To be honest, I didn't even know when he went. My life went on, unchanging, although each time I crossed the *tablinum* I still saw the faint stain of blood on the floor, a darkening of the white wooden tiles in the mosaic of Zeus and Hera.

Two things happened in that time. One is important, one not. The first is that my mother had her baby. She was called – she is still called – Cornelia. I used to hear her cry or mewl occasionally. That is all. Well, not quite. She did become important to me, but much later, and in ways I still don't understand. But let me keep to Bostar's chronology. I will come to Cornelia in time.

The other is quite different. When my father was away fighting what has become known as the first Illyrian war – there has been one more since and will, I prophesy, be more unless we change. But for Bostar's sake I won't go into that. When my father was away, I first met the friend who has shared my life.

It was a grey day, cold and wet. The wind whistled through the selenite. Even the fire's smoke seemed to judder, rising, in that blast. Even Rufustinus seemed cold. I noticed that he kept returning to the brazier, once he'd written on the board. The chalk, I remember, slowly spread on his dark kidskin gloves until it was like a white blaze on a brown filly. Normally, he stayed by the blackboard to elucidate and question. Not that day.

I wasn't doing well. I remember wishing I'd put on my woollen socks, not my cotton. It doesn't seem to matter at the time, when you get up fast because you're late and just put on what's easiest and nearest. '*Celerius agens, lentius dolens*. Act in haste and repent at leisure,' goes the proverb. I have found often that is true, and tried to change accordingly. Perhaps the soldier and general in me was formed in a small child wearing the wrong socks. It's possible. Why else should I remember?

We were covering the Greek genitive of comparison. 'In Latin, Publius, as you know, we use the ablative for comparison or *quam* plus the ablative,' Rufustinus said. I nodded. 'Greek uses the genitive instead, or ἤν plus the genitive. So, put into Greek for me,' and he wrote on the board:

Socrates sapientior quam ceteris.

'That's easy,' I said. It was.

ὁ Σωκράτης σοφώτερος ἦν τῶν ἄλλων. Socrates was wiser than the others.

'Good, Publius, good. Now, soon we will have a visitor, so just one more exercise.'

'A visitor? Who?'

'You'll find out soon enough. Back to the perfect and aorist tenses. What is the difference between these two sentences?' And he wrote out in that neat hand of his: ἡ θάλασσα λέλυκε τήν γέφυραν: 'The sea has broken the bridge.' ἡ θάλασσα ἔλυσε τὴν γέφυραν: 'The sea broke the bridge.'

'So, explain,' and in the cold his breath steamed.

'The perfect, λέλυκε, describes a past action whose effect is still continuing. But the aorist, ἔλυσε, means that on a certain date the sea did break the bridge. It means that was a historical fact.'

'Very good, Publius.'

It wasn't, really. I loved the Greek aorist from the start. I still do. The ability to distinguish between the perfect and the aorist seems to me one of Greek's many superiorities over Latin.

That was as much progress as we made that day.

'Come in!' Rufustinus responded quickly to the knock. I turned my head to the door. A boy walked in. About my age and size, he looked uneasy and scared. He had a mop of red, tousled hair, freckles and a turned-up nose. And his ears, I thought, were too big for the rest of him. He stood just inside the door.

'Well, come in, Gaius Laelius, come in!' Rufustinus chided. 'Don't just stand there. Sit down, over here.' Rufustinus pointed to a desk on the other side of the room. Laelius took a step forward. 'Close the door first, boy.'

Laelius sat down. His nose, I saw, was running. Perhaps he had a cold. Or perhaps it was just the cold. Rufustinus picked up his stick and tapped it against the blackboard. 'Publius, this is Gaius Laelius. He is the son of Priscus Laelius, a client of your father's. Your father left instructions that I am to teach him with you. He is said to be bright, and well advanced.'

Laelius looked shyly at me. When our eyes met, he quickly turned his away.

'But let's see what we've got,' Rufustinus went on, 'a scholar or a sow. Laelius, what are the principal parts of *sperno*?' he barked.

I saw Laelius stiffen. A tough one, *sperno*. I'd felt Rufustinus' stick for getting it wrong. '*Sperno, spernere, sprevi, spretum,*' Laelius gave back, without hesitation. His voice was high, but soft.

'And *tango*?'

'*Tango, tangere, te . . .*' He stumbled. '*Tetigi, tactum.*'

'Ah hah,' from Rufustinus. That was high praise. I was rather enjoying this. 'What's the supine of *lavo*?'

'There are two, sir, *lautum* and *lotum*.'

'Adverbs divide into which classes?'

'Manner, degree, cause, place, time and . . . and . . .' I didn't know either. Laelius screwed up his nose, concentrated, went on, 'And order.'

'Well, well. Your father has taught you properly, I see. Publius, I do believe that this young man will test you.'

He did. And he still does.

I had expected this, or something similar. 'I am a teacher, on my way to Rome.'

'Why Rome?'

'To find work.'

The boy looked at me, hard. I held his gaze. At last, 'Wait there,' he said. He turned his horse, walked back to the squadron. I saw him, though I couldn't hear, talk to the commander.

He slipped off his horse, a gelding, chestnut brown. I had seen so many horses dead. It was good to see living ones, even on a sullen grey morning, in the cold.

He walked back to me. 'Anything in the bag, Marcus?'

'Nope. Just some old scrolls. Maybe he is a teacher. But I did find this.' He handed over my little pouch of gold.

My interrogator opened it, whistled under his breath. 'Where did you get this? Did you steal it?'

'No, it was a gift,' I said.

'A gift? Some gift! Who from?'

'From, from' — I faltered — 'from a friend.'

'Teacher, you've got a lot of explaining to do. For a start, don't you know that no one travels without a pass? Don't you know there's a war on? For all we know, you might be a spy for that bastard Hannibal. Now, hold out your arms.'

So it was that, tied up and on a Roman horse, I continued my journey.

No one spoke to me. I was relieved, because I've never been much of a horseman. I concentrated on staying on my mount as we cantered, with me in the middle of the squadron, up the Via Appia. If I fell off, I knew, with my hands tied I had no way of breaking my fall. And I didn't want to break my head on stone or on the hooves behind. I needed my head. I had plans for it.

It was Quinta who explained that night, at bed-time. 'Laelius' father is a *novus homo*. A new man, of new money. He made it, they say, supplying corn to the army. His people are farmers in Bruttium. Anyway, your father's fairly taken to him. Agreed to become his patron, and appointed him one of his tribunes.'

'Tribunes?' I asked. 'What's a tribune?'

'You'll find out soon enough, in the life you'll lead, young master. But a tribune is a senior staff officer. Anyway, this Priscus Laelius, that's his full name,' she sniffed, 'he hasn't even got a cognomen, anyway, he and your father are off together in Illyria, and so we have young Laelius with us.'

'But Quinta, if Laelius' father is so rich, why doesn't Laelius have his own *litterator*?'

'Because, young master, that wouldn't go down well. Too showy, when you're still a mere *publicanus*. Why, Laelius' father isn't even an *eques*, a knight, yet. Though I dare say he might be if he does what's expected of him in Illyria.'

'And what's that, Quinta?'

'Well, win for a start. But that's more your father's problem than Laelius', who's acting as quartermaster.'

'Quartermaster? What's that?'

'Oh there never was such a boy for questions. Last one, then lights out. The quartermaster sees to supplies and—'

'You mean swords and shields?'

'Yes, those, but war's as much about a hot meal and a dry tent . . .'

A hot meal and a dry tent. I never forgot that. In big ways and small, many contributed to what I was to become.

So Laelius became part of my life. He was neither sullen nor sycophantic. We never fought, but we played; and for that I owe him my childhood. Before school and after school – as time went on he came earlier and left later – we played in the courtyard, hopscotch, marbles, hide and seek. In class, the pace quickened. He started with no Greek, and soon had more than I. He admitted to working each evening.

'Why do you work so hard, Laelius?' I asked him one day. We were sitting in the garden, after school, drinking lemon cordial.

'Why? Because, because my father told me to.'

So simple. Simplicity in life is, I think, the key. Knowing who and why and what you are. Good men admit the complex. Great men absorb it, and make of that something simple.

The next day, Laelius was to be tested on some irregular verbs; I already knew them. Rufustinus had only given Laelius two days to prepare.

He got them right, perfectly, and the lesson went on. I asked him afterwards how he'd done it. 'It took me two weeks to learn those verbs,' I said. 'How can you memorise them so fast?'

'How? I make them into pictures.'

'What do you mean?'

'Well, take a verb like τίθημι. What does it look like to you?'

'What does it *look* like? I don't know. It doesn't look like anything.'

'It does to me. It looks like a sneeze.'

'A sneeze? Are you serious?'

'Yes! The sound my father makes when he sneezes is like τιθημι. So when I had to learn the principal parts, I just pictured my father sneezing! Like this.'

He stood up and sneezed. 'A-τίθημι,' he went, 'τιθέναι,

ἔθηκα, θείς . . . and,' he said, tears of laughter running down his cheeks, 'I just think of my father sneezing like that. I see him, hear him making a racket like a winter storm.'

We laughed until our sides ached. But I had learnt a lesson. If you want to remember something, picture it. The more absurd the picture, the better you'll remember. I've been complimented, for example, for remembering people's names, even if I've met them only once or briefly. That's easy. You merely think of an image when you meet them and associate that with the name.

The Pannonian merchant Timpulus, for example, was amazed that I remembered his name when we met for the second time, after many years, shortly before I left Rome. When I first met him, he was just another merchant on the make, trying to win an army contract; there were hundreds like him. But his mouth. It was almost a perfect circle, small and full. I thought of a goldfish feeding and the sound I imagined, not that I've ever heard it, was something like 'Timp' as it sucked the morsel in. So I remembered goldfish-face Timpulus. Not that it did me any good.

We were in class. The door opened. No knock. My mother walked in. No, she didn't walk, she glided. 'Good morning, Rufustinus.' I hadn't seen much of her since my father left. She kept to her rooms most of the time. I knew my sister had been difficult, weak and often sick.

I was amazed how beautiful my mother was. First, the way she held herself. Composure. Grace. Her hair was still raven black, tied up as was proper in a bun. She wore a simple, white woollen shift with a belt of beaten gold on calfskin round her waist. No make-up. No perfume, or none of that horrible stuff whose smell overwhelms the air. I have thought since I was a very small child that strong perfumes, scents and body-oils should be banned. No, I am more temperate now. Not banned, discouraged.

Her figure was perfect, but it was her ugliness that made her beautiful. Her nose was, there is no denying it, crooked. Her eyes were too far apart and her mouth too big. But she unified it all, imbued the imperfect with her peace. How does the perfect come from imperfection?

'I must borrow the boys, Rufustinus. But they will be back.' That was typical of her. Absolutely in command, but polite, regal. She turned to us; our desks were now side by side. 'Publius, Laelius. The war is over. Your fathers are home. Go to the Campus Martius to greet them. Festo will take you. But first go and change. I want you both in the *toga praetexta*.' That was formal dress for boys of Laelius' station and above, a light-coloured toga whose purple border meant we were freeborn. My mother smiled, warmly yet almost imperceptibly, and left the room.

'But mine's at home,' Laelius whispered in my ear.

'Don't worry. I'll lend you one of mine.'

I felt many things, all at once. A child does not yet know how to marshal them; nor do many men. My father's return was exciting. But the Campus Martius was, I have to admit, a stronger draw, and abandoning Aeschylus a third. I have grown to love his plays. But does anyone understand them?

Yes, Aristotle, that unparalleled, polymath Greek. Alexander the Great was fortunate to have him as a tutor. He understood everything. Aeschylus and, from what I read last night, memory. I found his treatise on the subject, De memoria et reminiscentia. *Scipio's is a fine library.*

I shall let myself digress again from my past to the present. I have, after all, as good an excuse as a man can have – Aristotle. 'It is impossible even to think,' he writes, 'without a mental picture.' Memory, he goes on to say, belongs to the same part of the soul as imagination. It is a collection of pictures in the mind that comes to us from the impressions of our senses.

These mental pictures Aristotle likens to a painted portrait, 'the lasting state of which we describe as memory'. He thinks of the forming of a mental image as a movement, like a signet ring making a seal on wax. 'Some men have no memory owing to disease or age, just as if a seal were impressed on flowing water. The imprint makes no impression because it is worn down like old walls in buildings, or because of the hardness of that which is to receive the impression.'

This is exciting. I am almost seventy years old and yet have never before thought of these things. Here I am remembering with Scipio, without until now asking how it is that we can or do remember.

'Follow me closely, please,' Festo said. 'The crowds will be thick, and we mustn't get separated.' He was always earnest, Festo. And he looked so odd, thin and stringy like a bean, with dull, lank hair that lay across his forehead like a tent flap, a pinched head and pock-marked skin. But if a worrier, he was a kind and faithful servant.

'Now, if we do lose each other, let's meet at your Uncle Cratinus' house, young master Publius. Ask anyone, but listen, both of you. You go through the Forum, past the temple of Castor and Pollux, turn left, go straight up the street, past the temple of Diana, then turn right, then second left. Before you come to the city gate just by the pond there's a small flour mill. The drive up to your uncle's house is just beside it . . .'

'Do you honestly think he expected us to remember all that?' Laelius asked me as soon as we'd set off, Festo well in front.

'I thought you would. You could make a picture,' I replied. In the end, far from being separated, the crowds pushed us so close together we couldn't part. It wasn't bad at the beginning, as we walked down the Palatine and along the path through the waste ground at its foot.

As we followed it, Laelius asked me, 'Why does no one build

on this ground? In other parts of Rome, you'd find a thousand people living on a space like this.'

'You don't know?'

'Know what?'

'Why this ground is empty?'

'No, I don't. Tell me.'

'About a hundred years ago, a general called Vitruvius Vaccus had a huge house here, and a big garden. But he committed treason. He was fighting some northern tribe and was surrounded. He surrendered, on condition that his life be spared.'

'Which it was?'

'Which it was. But his men were massacred. When he got back to Rome, the senate had his house here demolished, and decreed that the site should stand empty for ever in memory of his shame. But—'

'Come on, you two!' Festo chided from ahead. 'Keep up, or we'll be late.'

What I read in Aristotle itself triggered a memory. I hunted for perhaps an hour, until I found it, a passage in Plato's dialogue the Theaetetus *in which Socrates assumes that there is a block of wax in our souls – the quality varies – and this is the 'gift of Memory, the mother of the Muses'. Whenever we hear or see or think of anything, we hold this wax under the perceptions and thoughts and imprint them on it, 'just as we make impressions with rings'.*

I have been thinking how best to do this. It seems to me that using this villa – or any largish house – is one good way. Say I want to remember the names of the planets. Yes, I could memorise a written list – Mercury, Venus, Mars, Jupiter and Saturn. But how much easier simply to place the five planets in five different rooms of this villa. So I stand, in my mind, at the front door. I walk in. I place Mercury in the portico. On the table in the tablinum *I place Venus, and so on. When I want to remember the names, I simply walk round the house in my head.*

I wonder if this would work with a much longer list? The towns of Italy, for example? I suppose I could use up the outhouses, and the stables. I would just have to formulate a very obvious route for my mental walk. I must try.

From there, we crossed the Forum and started to walk around the Capitoline Hill. The crowd was getting thicker now. We passed between the temples of Jupiter Capitolinus and of Juno Moneta. The buildings became denser, the smells stronger. I grimaced at Laelius, held my nose.

'It's the fullers' quarter,' he said. 'What a stink!'

Suddenly, the buildings stopped. Rolling away towards a bend in the Tiber was the Campus Martius, sacred to the war-god, Mars, a huge open space rapidly filling up. The dust was so thick I could hardly breathe, let alone see what was happening. Someone tugged me sharply to the right. I looked round. It was Festo. 'This way, young master. Come!' I in turn tugged at Laelius' sleeve, and followed Festo.

We came to some kind of enclosure, fencing off a slight rise. Two soldiers stood guard, impervious to the racket, their two *pila*, javelins, held to form a triangle, barring the way in. We stood behind Festo. 'Publius Cornelius Scipio,' he announced to the taller of the two.

The man snapped to attention. 'And him?' he said, pointing to Laelius.

'That is Gaius Laelius.'

'Gaius who?' the soldier asked. 'He is no patrician. This enclosure is only for the sons of the nobility. Publius Cornelius Scipio, you may pass. You two, stay where you are.'

I didn't even think. I pushed past Festo, looked up at the man and his brooding helmet, its chin-piece casting a shadow across his jaw. 'He may not be noble, but he is my friend. He comes with me.'

71

I saw the soldier hesitate. His eyes darted to his left, to the other soldier. I looked at him too. He stared impassively ahead. I returned my gaze to the first soldier. I did not flinch.

'Well, sir, if you say so.'

'I do, soldier, I do.' I was only a boy, but that was the time I first knew I was born to command. Both Laelius and I passed in.

I didn't know until now that it had started so early. Laelius owes all he has to Scipio. I think he knew all along what he was doing, and made the most of his chance. That's what I dislike. I don't mind Laelius benefiting from a greater man's rise. I, after all, have more than I ever dreamed of thanks to Scipio. But if he suddenly had nothing I would still be there. Laelius, though, is, I believe, an opportunist. He has made a science and an art of opportunity. I think that when it no longer suits him, he will at best drop the man who made him. At worst, he will hasten his fall.

Or am I simply jealous? If I am, it is only to defend the man I love. I am too old for petty jealousies. I have known the absurdities of love. Any fool can be jealous, and many are. But to be jealous at the right time, in the right way, for the right reason and of the right person, that is a good thing, even if no easy matter. It is one of life's many paradoxes that emotion is useful only if it is intelligently controlled.

From the top of the mound, we could see. I gasped. I saw row upon row of soldiers, facing a man on a black charger. I knew it was my father. And then, a row at a time, to a steady drumbeat from behind, the soldiers marched forward, across the hundred paces between them and my father. Just in front of him, they stopped. As one man, they laid down their shields in the dust, then their *pila*, then their swords.

And, back standing to attention, in one voice they called out, 'Publius Cornelius Scipio, we greet you.' Then they turned about, and filed away, walking proudly past my father, then running. Women called out to them, waving in the crush. 'Curius, I'm over here! Antonius, this way!' Then they were swallowed up in the shifting and the restless crowd.

For two hours or more we watched, as the sun blazed down and the pile of weapons grew and spread like a stain. Sweat trickled down my back. I remember feeling very thirsty, then feeling that it didn't matter. Rome had gone to war. Rome had returned, a Scipio her staff.

I was beginning to think I had answers. Now I feel I have only questions. I'm sure Plato and Aristotle are right – to some extent. Yes, we remember something when we form an image of it. But are we remembering the image, or imagining it? Perhaps the image we remember has some intrinsic property that belongs only to memories. Yet that won't do, because such a property can't tell us whether the image we have of the event in question was real, or imaginary. Surely we have to know what has happened before we create an image of it? So, I think, images can't constitute, can't be, memory. They can only correspond to it. The image helps me to remember, no doubt. But, at the same time, my brain is analysing. I know the image might be inaccurate and incomplete. I might qualify it, or enhance it. But if memory is more than just image, what is it?

Well, as Scipio would say, these are deep and difficult waters. I have never been a good sailor. Perhaps it's time I learnt. Anyway, it's time I returned to the past before I confuse those who may read this account – which is not mine, anyway, but Scipio's.

The crowd was drifting away. My father was still on his horse, but now surrounded by other men, his officers, I presumed.

Laelius nudged me. 'Can you see my father?' he asked.

'I don't know what he looks like.'

'He's tall, and has grey hair.'

'Impossible to see. But I'm sure he's there. Laelius, are you thirsty?'

'Not really. But I'm bursting for a pee.'

We turned to go. The other boys there – I didn't know any of them then – parted to let us through. Again, it was good to be a Scipio. We found Festo where we'd left him, outside the enclosure, and went back the way we'd come.

Capua has a very distinctive high wall, with turrets evenly spaced, towering above the fertile plain around it, the Ager Campanus.

I had hoped to go to Rome. When the squadron halted outside the gates of Capua, I sensed that this, for the time being at least, was as far as I would get.

I was marched, without explanation, straight to the city's jail and handed over to a balding, pot-bellied, bow-legged Capuan. His eyes were bleary and red-rimmed, the skin on his face mottled, blotchy, wrinkled. He had only a few black stumps for teeth. 'What's he in for, by the way?' he asked one of the cavalrymen who had brought me.

'Vagrant, or worse.'

'When's he to go before the magistrate?'

'When you're told, Capuan, when you're told.'

No love lost there, I thought. Hardly surprising, since Capua had revolted and joined Hannibal – not that it did him much good. But it did take Rome years of siege to get Capua back. Perhaps that helped Hannibal: not even Romans can be in two places at once.

Grunting and farting, the jailer prodded me with his dagger to my cell, and slammed the door. I wondered what had become of my satchel. The cell was dark and dank. The straw on the floor stank of mould and worse. It was almost evening. I lay down in a corner and tried to sleep. But then they came. People can behave as they want to. Rats do as they must.

Rats are certainly reliable. They made my first night in Capua a misery. It is their tails that are the worst. There can be few sensations as repugnant as rat tails across the face. Those dry scales. Ugh! And then, strangely, there was the horrible coldness of their feet in that fetid, humid cell. I still shudder at the memory. That is one image I do not need to qualify or enhance. All that long night they crawled over me. I could bear them on my clothed body, just; but whenever I dozed off they were back on my face. I tried sitting up, but still they ran up my back and sides. In the end I stood and sweated, and kicked out every so often to keep them at bay.

The rats were one torture. Hunger was a second. I could have put up with that, but my cell had a small, barred window. Too high for me to see out, but I could smell and hear.

The sounds were of a market, beginning soft and shuffling, then getting louder, raucous, as the sun climbed. The smell was of a bakery, and the smell of fresh-baked bread assailed me. I mastered my mind, but my body failed me. I could not stop my mouth salivating, which was strange, since it was very dry.

He came to see me early the next morning, just as I was waking up. As I sat up in bed, he hugged me. How long had he been gone? Eight months? Nine?

'I hear you came to the assembly yesterday, Publius.'

'Yes, and I was very proud.'

'Proud?'

'Yes, Father,' I answered, puzzled.

'Of whom?'

'Why, of you, of course.'

He smiled, and shook his head. 'Proud of me? That, Publius, is a mistake. Be proud, by all means, but of the army as a whole, and of Rome. Be proud, because we won.'

'What happened, Father?'

'Well, we went fishing.'

'Fishing?'

'Yes, we put out our nets, and pulled them tight.' He laughed, and tousled my hair. 'But I have to be at the Senate for daybreak. The aftermath of a war can be as long as the war itself – or longer.' Yes, longer. That I've learnt. 'So you won't see me much for a while. But I gather we have quite a scholar on our hands. Good, Publius. Keep it up.' He squeezed my shoulders, and left the room.

The routine of my life went on. How strange I find that. As a child, you take routine and rhythm for granted. You are puzzled when they are missing. As an adult, you have to work hard to find them again. Our routine here at Liternum is productive, but has been bought dear. It is the fruit of success, but also of retraction and regret.

One thing had changed. From my walk to the assembly, I had developed my love for Rome. I was born to love her as idea, as I do; but I learnt of my own will to love Rome as form.

It must have been four or five nights after the assembly. I couldn't sleep. When I felt sure the household was sleeping, I got up and dressed. There was a small wicket-gate at the end of the garden. I should have known: locked. No way past the porter at the front. Well, there probably would have been past him, but not past his dogs.

The wall was high. I managed it. I actually enjoyed the jump down, falling weightless into the night. I landed, like a cat, on all fours. Then a momentary fear. What was I doing? I could have asked permission, but I wanted to see Rome alone.

I went straight to the Forum. I stopped on the edge of it, just beside the temple of Castor and Pollux, the legendary twins who, I knew from Rufustinus, had appeared miraculously when we were losing the battle against the Latins at Lake Regillus. As horsemen, the twins fought with the Romans and we won. Is that fable or fact? I don't know. It doesn't matter: Rome was built on both.

The Romans are reared on such legends. Castor and Pollux, Romulus and Remus, the twin founders of Rome suckled by a she-wolf. I have never known or read of a people in whom the rational and irrational so combine. Their present is full of their past, myths and foundation legends, tales of bravery and self-sacrifice. Rome's, paradoxically, is a state of reason secured by superstition. But that is, I think, its greatest strength.

The moon was half full. In its light, away to my left, the temple of Saturn glowed. Beyond it, the peristyle of the temple of Concord disappeared into the dark. The breeze was gentle, almost wistful, and stirred some leaves at my feet. I heard the sacred trees rustle, and saw them bend down and back as trees, I thought, must have done since time began. Just as old, it seemed, was Rome. From far away, across the square, I heard the call of the nightwatchmen. This was the heart of Rome.

The merchants' booths around the square were closed and shrouded, still. I left the shadows and walked out, absorbed in what I saw. To my right was Rome's life political, the *rostra*, the speaker's platform, the *comitium* where the people met, the Curia for the senators. But I was drawn south, to the sanctuaries that marked the Forum's end. To walk here was to travel through Rome's memories, where lived on what had been, what was then and now; and to imagine what is still to come. *'Memoria est thesaurus omnium rerum et custos.* Memory is the treasury and guardian of all things,' Euphantus used to say. Sorry, Bostar, I haven't got to Euphantus yet. But I shall — unless the verdict cuts me off, as it were, in my prime.

I came to the place marked by a fig tree, an olive tree and a vine. I heard the trickling of the water. This was Curtius' lake. I knew the story well. What Roman child didn't? One day, hundreds of years ago, a gaping chasm suddenly appeared in the Forum. At a loss as to what to do about it, my ancestors consulted the sacred Sibylline books, bought from the Sibyl herself by Rome's fifth king, Tarquinius Priscus.

They learnt that the earth would close up once it had received whatever the Roman people valued most highly. And from then on, it would produce an abundance of what it had received.

People threw in sacred cakes, treasures, silver, gold, but the chasm failed to close. At last Marcus Curtius, a young cavalryman, begged leave to address the Senate. He said that in his view it was the courage of its soldiers that Rome held most dear, and that if one were willing to sacrifice oneself the earth would yield men of courage in plenty.

He put on his armour, mounted his warhorse, and then hurled himself into the chasm. It closed over him, leaving only a spring where, each year, on the spot where I stood, Curtius still receives Rome's offerings and prayers.

I stood there for a long time, thought and dreamed. It was then that I began to realise what Rome is. It is a city, of course, and a people. But these alone did not defeat Hannibal. Rome is a state of mind.

So, rats by night and hunger by day. Many have borne much worse. What I found hard to bear was not knowing how long both would go on. I thought of Sisyphus, in Greek myth once a king of Corinth, but condemned by the gods to Hades for his sins. There he had to roll a large stone up a hill. As soon as it got to the top, it rolled down again. What was so hard about this punishment was not the labour itself but not knowing when, if ever, it would end.

My trial, if not Sisyphus', ended around midday, insofar as a grille in my door suddenly opened. A tray was pushed in, with a bowl of some gruel and a small gourd of stale and brackish water. I ate and drank gratefully. And the rats were gone; they do not like the day. I thought of them somewhere underneath me, in their tunnels and sewers, a city within a city, copulating and squeaking, their red eyes bright in the dark.

I lay down, dozed off. The heat was stifling. I licked cracked lips, got up, and passed a little water in the bucket in the corner. I recited poems to myself from my childhood, chants from the sacred texts, walking up and down – three steps, turn, two steps, turn.

na jâyete mriyate vâ kadâcin
nâyam bhûtvâ bhavitâ vâ na bhûyah
ajo nityah sâsvato 'yam purâno
na hanyete hanyamâne saríre . . .

For the soul there is never birth nor death.
Nor, having been, does he cease to be.
He is unborn, eternal, ever-existing, undying and primeval.
He is not slain when the body is slain . . .

And I thought of my father and my childhood and was glad. I remembered the time – I was four, or five – when my brother let his mongoose out from its cage at the back of the house and it caused mayhem. Shrieking, my mother chased it through the house. Silently, I sat and laughed and laughed.

So that day passed, and the next. I disliked the rats. But I went into myself. I did not feel alone.

From then on, I used often to go into Rome at night, to walk and look and wander. Those months were settled. My mother was pregnant again. My father was at home. My time with Rufustinus was nearly over. Laelius and I had learnt from him everything we could. Our next stage was due, and my father had let it be known that he was looking for a *grammaticus*, someone who would teach us not language but the arts: rhetoric, astronomy, science.

I was closer to Laelius then, I think, than I have ever been. I felt awkward about my body, its spots, my breaking voice and facial hair. For months, each night I would peer at my face in my room. The bronze mirror showed what I could feel, an army of pimples on the left side of my forehead. Why there, particularly? Why not just the odd red pluke with a yellow head, as on the rest of my face and back? Some faded. Others grew. I didn't know what was happening. I was puzzled. We were taught to know what was going on in our minds, but my body was doing things over which I had no control.

But Laelius suffered all these things as well. I found comfort in that.

'Stand straight when you're spoken to!' The fat jailer jabbed me in the kidneys. I winced.

'I'm sorry,' I faltered. 'I am very weak. And the light.' It was so bright after the dark.

The magistrate seemed far away, swimming before my eyes. His toga was very white, his chair and table above me on a dais. 'So, you maintain you are a teacher,' he said. 'You know the penalties for lying?'

'No, but I can imagine.'

'Don't be impertinent,' the jailer snarled, giving me another jab, harder this time.

'What is your name?' the magistrate asked.

'Bostar, sir.'

'Of?'

'Of Chalcedon. I am a Bithynian. But that was long ago.'

'Your Latin is good, certainly,' the magistrate said. He had a kind voice. I focused on him. A southerner, by his dark skin. 'Where did you learn it?'

I had decided to keep my story simple. 'I knew some before, but I learnt most of my Latin in Saguntum. I was secretary to Caius Sempronius, your envoy there, sixteen years ago.'

'Were you indeed?' Mild and measured. I liked this man. 'We can check, you know.'

'But not with Caius Sempronius, sir.'

'No? Why not?'

'Because he was killed when Hannibal captured the city.'

'And why were you spared?'

'Because Hannibal killed only Romans. He let the rest of us go free.'

The magistrate stared at me for a long time. 'Yes, I know that what you say is true.' He looked away. 'And then?'

'Then I lived for some time like the others, like rabbits in the town's ruins, until a merchant ship came.'

'What happened then?'

'Then I bought my passage.'

'Bought it? With what?'

'Sir, please may I sit down? I am very weak.'

There was a stunned silence in the court. The clerks looked up from their recording and gawked.

The magistrate sat back in his chair and stared at me intently. 'Yes, you may,' he said slowly. 'Officer, bring the accused a chair.'

I sat down. 'Thank you.' I looked up at the magistrate. 'I bought my passage with gold I had earned from Sempronius.'

'Passage to where?'

'The ship was bound for Syracuse with a cargo of the fish paste you Romans call garum. But I never disembarked — at least, not there.'

'Why not?'

'Because during the journey I began to help the merchant with *his accounts. I liked him. He was gruff, but kind. When we got to Syracuse, he asked me if I wanted to stay with him. I said I did, and for ten years I worked as his assistant. He was a fair man.'*

'Fair?' The magistrate laughed. Following his lead, so did the jailer and the clerks. Only the guards stood impassive, at attention. 'A fair merchant?' he went on. 'Now that's a strange piece of evidence. A fair merchant, that's a, a — by Hercules, what is the word for a juxtaposition of opposites?'

'An oxymoron, sir,' I volunteered.

'Yes, an oxymoron. Another word we've borrowed from the Greeks. So,' and the magistrate tugged his beard thoughtfully, 'you have Greek too. Perhaps you are a teacher.' His attention seemed to drift. Suddenly, 'How many languages do you speak?' he asked me.

'Eight or nine, sir. With a working knowledge of several more.'

'Do you now? Do you indeed?' he mused. 'And how have you achieved this? From books?'

'To some extent, yes. But books are scarce, and all the more so in the life that I have lived.'

'So how, then?'

'By listening. By ear. Languages each have their own music. If you catch it, you too can play the tune.'

'I see, I see.' He drifted off again. Then his tone changed. 'Anyway, fair or otherwise, you say the merchant "was". What became of him?'

'He died, sir, peaceful and asleep in his old age. His widow let me go. She had, she said, no more need of me or her late husband's business. She wanted to move inland, far from the stench of fish and the smell of the sea.'

'And this merchant, what was his name?'

'Publius Aponius, sir, of Brundisium — though he wasn't often there.'

'And that first ship of his was carrying garum. So he was a garum merchant?'

'Principally, yes, but anything to do with fish as well, salted,

pickled, barrelled. Sturgeon from the Caspian Sea, herring from the north, pike from the eastern lakes—' He held up his hand to stop me.

'Bailiff!' the magistrate barked. The man moved forward on crutches. No legs. A Roman veteran, I assumed. The state always tried to find jobs for those disabled in her service.

The magistrate nodded towards the door. The bailiff stumped off.

I understood. Archives. There has never been such a people for archives and records. The taxation system was the key, and there was a tax on every cargo, the rate of tax carefully written down, with copies sent to each provincial capital. I should know. I recorded enough of them. Aponius always moaned. 'These taxes,' he would mutter. 'But at least the seas are safe, despite that bloody Hannibal.'

I had changed the order of events for my own reasons, but what I had said was true. The bailiff would go to Capua's records, and check on Publius Aponius. My worry was whether the records would have been kept that far back – I served Aponius not after Sempronius but before. So I was anxious, but not surprised, when the magistrate's gavel banged and he said mildly, 'The court is adjourned.'

Words contain what we have lost. I must use them now.

For several days, the table had been out in the atrium with votive offerings to Lucina, the goddess of childbirth. Small sweetcakes coated with honey and poppy seeds, little cups of olive oil and fine Lucernian wine, all replaced each day. My mother's time was due. There would be a feast when she had given birth, and this time I was old enough to go. My newest toga was clean and ready in my room, and new sandals with straps of gold. I hoped for a brother. Cornelia I hardly ever saw. She was brought up in the women's quarters. How, I really didn't know.

I had heard nothing in the night. I woke later than usual, judging by the light pouring round the edges of the curtain. Something was wrong. What? No noise. From my bedroom you could always hear some noise, of servants stirring, of vague bangings or voices from the kitchen. That morning, it was the silence that was noisy. I sat up with a start, got dressed quickly and, barefoot, went out.

There was no one in the *tablinum*, no breakfast table. No smell of bread. I walked on. No one in the atrium. Where were the clients? It was time. They should have been mingling there, exchanging their pleasantries and gossip before they went in to my father. And then I saw it. Over the table to Lucina there was a black shroud.

A soft breeze rustled. It brought with it a sound new to me, a snatch of low wailing, a steady ululation. It came from the women's quarters across the colonnade. I remember the sweat. It started, a sticky flush, in my armpits and my groin. The fear sweat, known to soldiers since time began. I spun round to follow the sound of keening, down the atrium, into the colonnade.

In the garden, on a bench half hidden by a climbing wisteria on a frame I saw him, sitting cowering, arms over his head, afraid, alone, my father. I walked up and squatted down beside him. His eyes were wild, his face wet with tears. He sobbed, convulsively, and clenched his teeth.

'How can he weep? He is my father,' I remember thinking. 'How often has he said that men don't cry?'

So, when I was fifteen, I lost my mother, Pomponia. She died giving birth. I had gained a brother, but I never saw him feasted. For years, my father couldn't bear even to look at him. I often wonder how that rejection affected him and whether it brought about what was to come. Life is custom and habit and will, but also chance. What does the poet Simonides say?

ἄνθρωποζ ἐὼν μή ποτε φάσηιζ ὃ τι γίνεται αὔριον,
μηδ' ἄνδρα ἰδὼν ὄλβιον ὄσσον χρόνον ἔσσεται·
ὠκεῖα γὰρ οὐδὲ τανυπτερύγου μυίαζ
οὔτωζ ἀ μετάστασιζ

Being no more than a man, you cannot tell what tomorrow
will bring, nor, when you see someone doing well, know for
how long that will be. For the beat of the quick-lifting wings
of the dragonfly is not more swift than is the fate of man.

What a poet, Simonides. From the tiny Cycladic island of Ceos.
How I want to go there, and see where he was born. I want
to see if I can understand from what these Greeks drew the
quintessence of life. The blues and greens of their sea, their
ethereal light? But now, of course, I cannot travel anywhere.
I am denied those things that should accompany old age. The
peace of place, the rewards of discovery, the company of friends
and family, the consolation of a life well lived, all these are things
I must not look to have, as I wait for the verdict that is to come.
I too have known the μετάστασιζ, the overthrow, the radical
change in the haunting metaphor of Simonides and tears fill my
eyes – but I must not let myself be sombre. The verdict may set
me free. Then I shall go, in search of the spirit of Simonides.

Interesting that so much of the best of Greece came, and still
comes, not from the original city states, but from their colonies
and islands. I wonder when or if that will also be true of Rome
– and when or if we will have poets who begin to match those
Greeks.

It's not as if my brother killed my mother. But he might as
well have done, such was the price he has paid. We Romans
do not need a mother except to bear us – though one day, I
hope, that will change. I mourned my mother not for herself,
but for the love my father lost. For the hurt he then took in
on himself and out on my brother and, without meaning to,

on me. When the wings of Simonides' dragonfly danced and my mother died that night, chance shaped many lives. Few of them have moved from mourning into morning.

'I am going away, Publius.' He looked haggard, drawn. Deep lines creased his cheeks and his skin seemed grey, even in the soft early-morning light in my room.

'When will you be back, Father?'

'I don't know.' He screwed up his nose, and then scratched it. 'I'll be back when I am.'

'Where are you going?'

'To war, in the north.' He seemed almost bored.

'Who against?'

'Against whom, Publius, against whom. Didn't—' Whatever he was going to say, he changed his mind. He sighed. 'Against two northern tribes in Gaul, the Boii and the Insubres. And then I may have to go on to Celtiberia.'

'Celtiberia? Why?'

'So many questions. Still, you ought to know. Because the tribes there, like those in Gaul, are restless. There's trouble, we hear, near Saguntum. You know where that is?'

Sitting up in bed, my arms round my knees, I nodded. A Roman town, halfway up the east coast of Celtiberia, beyond Corsica and Sardinia, across the Internum and then the Massilian Sea.

'But there's more to it than that, or so we think. The Carthaginians are expanding their interests in the south. You know about Hamilcar?'

'Yes. He surrendered in Sicilia.'

'Carthaginians don't surrender, Publius. They just buy time. Hamilcar never went under the yoke. Anyway, he's dead now. But he has a son called Hannibal. I may have to go and see what's going on. I don't know why, but I have a feeling we'll be hearing more of Hannibal.' He seemed tired, old. He put his hands up to his face and rubbed it.

'Father,' I said, 'can't I come?'

'No, Publius.' He huffed. Was he angry with me? He looked away, distracted. At last, he spoke again. 'No, of course you can't come. You will stay here and work with your *grammaticus*—'

'You've found one?' I blurted. 'What's his name?'

'Don't interrupt me, boy!' he almost shouted. He sucked in air, his nostrils spreading. In a calmer voice, he went on, 'His name is Euphantus, Euphantus of Olynthus. You will start with him tomorrow. Any questions?'

'Will Laelius be with me?'

'Laelius?' He seemed almost to have forgotten. I hadn't seen Laelius for the weeks of the mourning, dark days of silent boredom in my room. 'Yes, Laelius will be with you. Work hard.' With that, he turned and was gone. I fell into a fitful sleep, remembering my father's words: 'I have a feeling we'll be hearing more of Hannibal.' A strange name: I wondered what it meant. If I was Rome's staff, what was he to Carthage?

I was marched back in. The magistrate banged his gavel. The clerks sat up at their desks, alert, styluses poised.

The magistrate cleared his throat. 'Bostar of Chalcedon, you are free to go.'

The jailer beside me snarled, 'You are free to go.'

Free? I have never understood freedom. People say that a slave, for example, is not free, but a senator is, or a ship's captain, or a merchant. Are they?

I am free, surely, when I do something I could have done otherwise. At least, I think most people would agree with that. In that sense, the slave is certainly not free. But it is not enough to say that freedom lies in the capacity for choice. What shapes or forms that capacity and those choices? What if all our actions are the effects of preceding causes? If that is so, our futures are as unalterable as our pasts, and almost none of us is free. Then the only man who is free is the man who knows he is not.

Besides, to relate freedom to choice is not enough. What is choice? It is voluntary, yet it is not the same thing as voluntary. A horse and a small child are both capable of voluntary action, but not of reasoned choice. Things we do on the spur of the moment we can call voluntary, but not chosen. So can we call them free?

The other day, I was watching one of the kitchen-girls playing with a kitten in the yard. She had a ball of string, and each time she unrolled it the kitten pounced and played. An instinctive response, in a game as old, I imagine, as man — or cats. But, I thought, what if I were standing there and someone rolled a ball of string past me? Would I jump after it? No. Simply because I am a human being I would look to see where it had come from and who had thrown it. Inevitably, we look for the cause of every event. The laws of causality, surely, are deep in our natures. So how are we 'free' to do things when, if we took the time, we would see cause behind everything we do?

Well, the magistrate said I was 'free'. I didn't agree with him, but I knew what he meant.

So I became an adult before I had finished being a boy. I suppose I have never made up for those missing years. I suppose I have never grown up, and still I wonder. I have done what I have done mostly through imbalance. Have I tried to change the world only because, from the time my mother died and my father went away, I was always uneasy with it? Perhaps. If so, I am glad. Achilles was given the choice between a short and glorious life and a long and undistinguished one. He chose the former. Would it be better to be a pig satisfied, or a Socrates dissatisfied? I have never been in any doubt.

My first impression of Euphantus was of his mildness. His hair was a nondescript, sandy brown. His features were unremarkable. Most men's faces differ, I have noticed, in the shape of their jaw and the line of their brow. It is against those two dominant characteristics that a nose stands out as small or large, wide or narrow, a mouth as tight or full, and so on. Euphantus' jaw and browline were both bland. His height was average, his woollen tunic an inconspicuous dull green. Even his sandals, I saw, were plain. I hovered in the doorway. Laelius was already at his desk, sitting down.

Euphantus was standing by the window. We looked across the room at each other. In a mild voice, firm and middle-ranged, he said in impeccable Latin, with barely a trace of accent, 'So, you must be Publius. Publius Cornelius Scipio. I see, I see.'

For some reason, I blushed.

He pursed his lips. 'Well, I shall call you Cornelius. Not Publius, for that would be too familiar. Not Scipio, for that would be too formal.' He seemed pleased, almost delighted with himself, as if he had solved the riddle of the Sphinx. He rubbed his hands together. Suddenly, his tone of voice changed. Almost sharply, he asked me, 'What is that construction?'

'What construction?' I didn't understand.

'The one I just used.'

'Oh, a um, um . . .' I stumbled.

Euphantus sat down on his stool. He looked at the ground. I stayed in the doorway, awkward. When he looked up and spoke, there was something almost tender in his voice. 'Cornelius, and you too, young Laelius, never ever "um" with me. When I ask you a question, think. If you don't know the answer, be quiet and think. Don't hurry. You cannot rush knowledge.' He stood up quickly, paced across the room, his steps neat and nimble. 'No, you cannot rush knowledge,' he went on. 'Learning is a lifetime's thing and education a leading out, not a tearing. Yes, that's it!' Again, the rubbing of the hands, the look almost of glee. 'When you do know the answer, tell me. If you don't, just say so.'

He stopped suddenly. 'So what, Cornelius, was that construction?'

'An antithesis, sir.'

'Good!' He was genuinely pleased. 'And, Laelius, its opposite?'

'A synthesis, sir.' Laelius was always quick.

'Now, Cornelius, come in, close the door and sit down. We must begin a synthesis of our own.'

I walked back to the prison. If I was free, the first thing I wanted was a bath. Was that wish free will? Yes, of course. I could have wished instead not to have a bath. But why did I want to have a bath? Because my skin was itchy, and even I could tell that I stank. Neither was a circumstance I had chosen. So was the volition free?

The jailer was far from pleased to see me. 'What do you want?' he said. He scratched his crotch. Even over my stench, I could smell his breath. It could be a new form of torture, smelling that smell, I thought. You wouldn't have to touch a prisoner, just make him breathe that smell.

'I only want my satchel,' I replied.

'Satchel? What satchel?' He belched loudly.

'The one with me when I came.'

'You had no bloody satchel, darkie—'

I moved to within the breadth of two fingers from his face. His smell was rank and sour. I looked at him, focused on his piggy, bloodshot eyes. He held my gaze. I thought he would last longer. His jaw dropped. He gestured over his shoulder with a fat thumb. 'See the guard.'

I drank Euphantus' teaching as parched ground drinks rain. His learning was prodigious, his intelligence the keenest I have known. Intelligence? What is that? Some of the most intelligent people I have known have been, in wordly terms, the most stupid. They couldn't count, or write, perhaps, or reason. What I mean by intelligence is far too hydra-headed to rest in a single word. But, in all its many forms, it rests I think in empathy.

Most people regard intelligence as an intellectual, a cognitive, skill or capacity. I think that's wrong. I think intelligence lies in people's capacity to be in equilibrium between themselves and one or more environments. And, crucially, the intelligent person has an empathy with the thing or things he or she does best. That sets him or her apart. Outstandingly intelligent people have the capacity to empathise with many different things. I had a decurion in Celtiberia who was the best man with animals I have ever known. He could almost make a mule do somersaults. But he was also a brilliant strategist, an inspired leader of his men and, from what he said, a good farmer back at home.

Anyway, Euphantus was awe-inspiringly intelligent. And curious. His mind was always open, never closed. Moreover, like all the best intelligences, his was lightly worn.

We had just read a passage of Homer's *Hymn to Demeter*. I was strangely moved by the story of her daughter, the beautiful young Persephone, carried off to the Underworld by Hades, brother of Zeus and Poseidon and king of the dead.

'Right, any general questions before we look at the grammar?' Euphantus asked.

'Yes,' I replied. 'I wonder what the Underworld's like—'

'Or whether it exists at all,' Laelius said.

I looked at him. I had been about to say the same thing.

'Yes, Euphantus' – early on, he had told us to call him by his name, not 'sir' – 'exactly. Is there an Underworld?'

Sitting on his stool in front of us, wrapped in his cloak so that only his head showed, Euphantus suddenly whipped out an arm. He raised his hand, and began stroking his beard. He didn't answer, lost in thought.

He got up and walked, or rather darted, for that was the way he moved, to the window. He stood there in silence, looking out. I looked at Laelius, he at me. Then we both looked down again at the scroll we had been reading from. I read silently. I loved – and still do – the rhythm of hexameters. There are many metres more complex and subtle, but none as pure.

Euphantus broke the silence. With his back to us, 'Is there an Underworld?' he said, almost wistfully. Then briskly, 'Both of you, come over here.'

We got up from our desk, crossed the room. Euphantus moved aside. 'Now, look out. Tell me what you see. Cornelius, you first.'

I looked. All so familiar. 'I see the garden, and the colonnade, and the fountain, and the sky—'

'And the crows? Can you see the crows?'

'Yes.' Three crows were waddling about to the right of the fountain, pecking sporadically at the ground, looking for ants, I imagined, or worms.

'And Laelius, you too can see the crows?'

'Yes, I can.'

'Good, now go back to your desk.' As we sat down again, Euphantus spun round. 'What colour were the crows?'

'What colour?' I was puzzled.

Laelius jumped in. 'They were black.'

Euphantus clapped his hands in delight. 'Exactly! They were black. Cornelius, have you ever seen a crow that wasn't black?'

'No.'

'No, of course you haven't. But does that mean that all crows are black?'

'Of course all crows are black.'

'No, no, no,' Euphantus almost shouted. 'Try harder. Let your mind go.' He leant over the desk. His eyes were bright, alert. 'Think. Could some crows be white? Although the three of us have only ever seen black crows, it doesn't mean that white crows don't exist. And that, Laelius, is my answer to your question about the Underworld. Now, back to the text.'

That is what I meant by Euphantus' intelligence. 'Keep your mind open. Never let it close,' he used to say.

I have tried.

Outside the prison, standing in a corner of the square, I opened my weathered satchel. The purse was still there. Roman justice is fair. Had I been convicted, the jailer would have taken it. A young boy was passing, pushing a barrow of oranges and melons. I was hungry. I was torn. Bath or food? Both, but which first? I felt a tickling in my groin. Lice. 'Boy!' I stopped him, 'where are the baths?'

He gestured to the other side of the market. 'Over there.'

I lay in the warm water, letting my limbs relax. The steam coiled and drifted around, and I let my mind do the same. Flickering shadows came and went, images of Sosius and death and Hannibal.

The sounds of someone else getting in disturbed me. I couldn't see him through the steam. I sat up, reached for the pumice stone and strigil. Carefully, I cleaned my feet. The skin on my heel where I had had that blister was hard and calloused. Gently, I rubbed it smooth. I sank back again, and slipped right under the water. I loved that weightless feeling. Then I felt the itch again. It had to be done.

Standing naked in the ante-room, I looked. Even my pubic hairs, I saw, were going grey. But there wasn't just a squadron of lice there. It was an army. I remembered Similce's de-lousing on the march with Hannibal and smiled. Was that the only time that Hannibal's army seemed happy, before its leader began to be consumed by his own hate?

I walked to the door. The attendant was there, in his booth. He looked up. Running diagonally across the whole of the right side of his face was a red and angry scar. Another veteran, I thought. Are they everywhere? 'A razor, please, and soap.' He nodded, and leant down.

★   ★   ★

I had almost two years with Euphantus. It should have been more. We had heard nothing from my father, though through the servants I had indirect news. He had subdued the Boii and the Insubres. He had gone, they said, as far as the Pireneos, the dark mountains between Celtiberia and Gaul. There was talk of according him a triumph. Publicly, I was proud. Privately, I was hurt. Had he forgotten me? He had lost a wife, but he still had a son. Two, in fact – and a daughter. Then the letter came.

There was a knock at the door. 'Who can that be?' Euphantus asked quietly. Then, in a louder voice, 'Come in!'

It was Festo. He nodded, bowed to Euphantus. 'Excuse me, Euphantus. But I have a letter from our master for the young master—'

'From my father!' I blurted out, half rising from my bench.

'Continence, Cornelius, continence!' Euphantus tutted. He turned to Festo. 'Thank you, Festo. Cornelius, you may take the letter outside and read it. Then come back. You may discuss its contents with me, or with Laelius, but only after class. Now, Laelius, where were we?'

Festo handed me a scroll, grey, nondescript, battered at the edges. But there was no mistaking the wax seal of the Scipios. Clear and proud, the staff of the Scipios. The staff of Rome.

Heart pounding, I caught up with Festo halfway down the corridor, the letter in my sweating hand. 'Festo,' I asked evenly, 'who brought this?'

'A centurion, young master, from your father's own guard.'

'Did you talk to him?'

'No. He was in a hurry. Other letters to deliver, urgent, he said.'

'What, he told you nothing?'

Festo screwed up his kind, gentle, simple face. Despite his age, he had hardly any lines. 'Young master, I asked him how the master was. But he didn't stop. As he was turning his horse, all he said was "*Scipio exercitusque, valemus*, Scipio and the army are well."'

'Do you think that's true, Festo?'

'I wouldn't know, young master, I wouldn't know.'

I walked a little gingerly back towards the market: I had nicked my crotch shaving off my hair. But, although my clothes were filthy, I was clean. The sun was bright, and the sky was blue.

The market was crowded and busy. The stalls sold everything. Chickens, half-trussed, flustered, flapped and struggled. Old, withered men in russet woollen gowns sold from wicker baskets gaudy, squawking parrots, their necks yellow, their beaks black, their irises flaming green, their pupils speckled ebony and orange. Goats bleated, lambs mewled, women haggled. There were stalls selling amphorae and oils, fruit and clothes, jewellery and spices from the East. I revelled in the colours and the smells.

I saw what I wanted at a stall down to my left. It was certainly not the best meal I have ever eaten. The stew was thick with blobs of grease, the meat with gristle. The man who ran the stall was surly. The bread was hard and stale. But it was welcome, and cheap. I had the money Sosius had given me, less what I had left for the olives and the two denarii for my bath. But I didn't know how long it would have to last.

'Fifty denarii,' the woman said. I had chosen a new cloak.

'Fifty? I'll give you twenty.'

'Twenty! Feel it, man. That's the finest wool. The only others you'll find of this quality will cost you more like eighty. Ask anyone. Fulco!' she screamed at the stall-holder across the narrow passage. 'Tell this fool about the cloaks that Ligurian sells.'

I paid fifty. But she gave me a new cotton shirt for nothing.

I took the letter to the garden, sat down on a bench. I breathed deeply, to try to still my trembling hands. There were dragonflies soaring and flitting, I remember, all greens and reds and shimmering wings. I broke the seal, opened the scroll. The hand was not my father's. Dictated, I supposed, to a scribe.

'I trust you are well, as am I. Only the great heat here' – here? where? – 'troubles the soldiers and the horses. I am discovering what it is to serve Rome.

'That is something you, too, were born to. You will have learnt much, I am sure, from Euphantus. It is time for you to learn things he cannot teach you. So, at the next new moon, you will begin your *triconium fori*.' What! My pupillage at the Senate? A year early! My heart raced.

'I have written to Fabius Pictor. He will have you. I served mine, as you know, with his father, and the Fabians are one of the other five great families of Rome. You are a member of one; Fabius' patronage will give you the love of a second. Through him, you will come to know the other three, the Claudian, the Aemilian and the Valerian.

'So go to Fabius. Remember you are a Scipio. Put into practice what you have learnt. Scholarship is a means to an end, not an end in itself, although as a means it is vital. Fabius, as I am sure you know, is not only a statesman but a scholar. He is writing a history of Rome. On the whole, you should keep your eyes and ears open, but your mouth shut. Not for nothing do we have two eyes, two ears, but only one mouth. By all means ask questions, but be wary of answers, especially your own.

'In the afternoons, when the Senate has risen, you will go to the school of Lanistus and learn to ride and fight. When I hear you are ready, I will send for you. Your father, Publius Cornelius Scipio, consul of Rome.'

My heart swelled. Fear, confusion, pride, excitement, all at once. I slipped the letter into my inside pocket. I went to urinate, and walked back to the class. Euphantus said nothing. Laelius went on reading aloud.

I tried to listen, but my mind was far away.

Clean, de-loused, clothed and fed. I needed one more thing, a bed for the night, or rather, shelter. An actual bed I thought I would find distinctly uncomfortable after years with Hannibal, sleeping on the ground. Still, I was not going to sleep in an alleyway in Capua. If the watch didn't find me, the cut-throats would.

I asked a melon-seller, 'Which way is the quarter for lodgings?'

He leered at me. 'Lodgings? Is it boys, or girls you're after?'

'Neither, thanks. A good roof, and a clean bed — no fleas. Know anywhere?'

He stared at me hard. I looked back. 'There's the old widow Apurnia's place,' he said at last. 'Clean, and not expensive. But not even any drink, mind.'

'That sounds fine. Where is it?'

'Over by the west gate. Above a smithy. Can't miss it.'

'Thank you.' I turned to go. 'Oh, and I'll have two of your melons, please.'

'But when will I see you?' Laelius asked. We had been playing bat and ball in the garden after class. As usual, he had won. I could hit the ball harder, but Laelius could place it far better — a lesson I was to put to use in later life.

'Well, I won't be in class with you any more, but I'll still see you when I come home from the school of this Lanistus.'

'But why should I stay on with Euphantus, in your father's house?'

'Because you haven't been told not to. Or have you? Have you heard from your father?'

'No, nothing. Neither has my mother. I hope he's all right.'

'He will be, or else you would have heard.'

'I suppose so.' Laelius took a slow drink from the cup of

lime cordial before him. I hadn't touched mine. His beard was growing thick now. So, I supposed, was mine. But I still had spots, up both cheekbones. Laelius' had gone. I had promised myself not to look in a mirror until mine had gone too.

Laelius licked his lips. He put a hand on my knee. I suppose I should admit it. I trembled.

'Well, Publius, I better be going home.'

I sat there, long after he had gone, wondering if he felt the same; if I should have discussed it with him.

I had felt the stirrings for some time, I remember. Dark longings in the night. I remember waking, wet and sticky round my midriff. The longing was in my dreams. Its evidence was real. I meant to talk to Laelius, but somehow it seemed too . . . too what? Not personal, not disgusting. Too natural, I think, in an otherwise completely ordered world. Yet here was my body behaving in a way I could not control. There was no plan for that. I didn't understand.

Her name was Hispala, as I later learnt. She was a slave-girl. I had never spoken to her, but had seen her round the house. She had an air of sadness about her, dark hair and doleful eyes. She was about my age, or perhaps a little younger.

I was lying on my side in bed one evening after supper, playing draughts against myself. Some one knocked at my door. I said, 'Come in.' The door opened. It was Hispala, with a bundle of clean clothes. She didn't speak. 'Oh yes,' I said. 'The chest is over here.' I pointed to the clothes chest beside my bed head, and resumed my game.

It was her smell, I think, a slight tang of sweat but also of woman – it reminded me of my mother – that first quickened me, as she leant forward beside me to open the lid of the chest. As she did so, I glimpsed two perfect, pear-shaped, honey-coloured breasts and little nipples, pert and red, pale raspberries. I wanted to touch her breasts, to see how soft they were, to hold their curves. I felt a quiver running down my stomach to my penis.

I pushed aside the game and turned on my back to watch. Her hair moved in dark ringlets. I wanted to bury my face in it and stroke it, smell it.

She closed the chest. As she stood up, her hair brushed my face. I reached out and took her wrist. She stood absolutely still, and looked at me, open, searching, unafraid. I watched her nostrils swelling and closing as she breathed, saw the delicacy of her neck and felt the softness of her skin.

Still holding her wrist, I rolled out of bed and stood up and kissed her. I did not know that mouths could be so soft. I felt the hardening in my groin. Slowly, I traced my hands down her sides. I felt the languor of her curves and knew I wanted her to bring the day to me.

Then with my middle fingers reaching down I came under her dress and slowly up her thighs and, shivering, to her buttocks, feeling the cheeks curve, the goosebumps swell. She leant back a little, reached down and nudged my hands away. She stepped back. Panting a little, she looked at me. Outside, an owl hooted in the dark. Crickets sang. In one swift movement, she pulled her dress up and off. I gasped as I saw her make a third triangle with her held-up arms. I had never seen anything so beautiful. I wanted to run my fingers over her body, and trace the reaching curves.

I too stretched down and up and took my nightshirt off. Taking both her hands, I sat back down on the bed and pulled her, not resisting or complying, to me. So simply was it done.

A long lane led to my left on the other side of the market. I looked up at the sun, and winced. Yes, the lane led west, to my lodging. After the market, it was quiet. A few curs snarled over scraps. Pigs rooted in the filth. Otherwise, I was alone.

I heard rapid footsteps following my own. I slowed down; so did they. I quickened my pace; so did they. I didn't dare look back. On either side, the houses were silent, their shutters barred. The jailer, or his men? Who else knew of my gold?

Well, face your fate, or it will face you. I turned sharply round. I saw a man, about a hundred paces back. He stopped, rooted to the spot.

This was no charlatan, no thief. I could see no one with him. He wore the Roman toga. I couldn't see clearly, but the cloth wasn't coarse. There was only a grunting sow between us, her teats swollen and hanging low.

'I am Bostar of Chalcedon, a teacher. Why are you following me?'

'I have a . . .' The sow's piglets were approaching. The sow ran snortling between us and past him. The man took several steps forward. 'I have a message for you,' he said.

'A message? No one here knows me. But come closer, and tell me your name.'

He walked on, stepping almost daintily around the pot-holes and the dung. I saw a high forehead, a face clean-shaved, wide cheekbones, a hooked nose, keen eyes, and that manner of moving — I shook my head. It couldn't be. That was long ago. This man's face was rather pinched. The head seemed too small for the forehead and the nose and cheeks that wanted to burst out of it. But the man looked gentle, and sensitive. Around thirty, I thought.

He stopped a respectful distance from me. 'I'm sorry if I alarmed you.'

I slept with Hispala often through that summer. She never spoke. Nor did I. She would come, late in the evening. In the morning, when I woke up, she would be gone. There would just be the slight smell of her, faint, but filling the room. And sometimes the slight stain of us, drying on the sheet. I used to kneel on my bed, and sniff it, and smile. I learnt to control the passion stronger than earthquake or tempest, the sudden, sweeping wild ejaculation of the young and, yes, sadly, of the not-so-young. I should know. I have been a soldier. I have seen it done.

I learnt to find the small hardness in her with my mouth and tongue and make it swell until, as she moaned and writhed, I felt and tasted her warm, wet, salt without the harshness of sea water, sweetness that did not cloy. I learnt the loveliness of soft caresses, like a warm breeze on wet skin. I learnt the power of a woman's warming, burgeoning and fundamental, of that home from which we all have come.

But then it stopped. A week passed, two. I was hardly in the house at all by day, so hadn't seen her there. Then, one night, the knock on my door, slightly firmer, I thought, than I knew. 'Come in!' The door opened.

It was Festo. 'Your clothes, young master.'

I was embarrassed, didn't know what to say. 'Oh yes, you, ah, you know where to put them.' At least my voice had stopped screeching like a broken lute.

'I do.' He crossed the room towards me. He stooped badly now. How old would he be? Had he ever known the gentleness of a woman's flesh, or just a grunting in the dark?

'Good night, young master.' Beside my bed, he stopped to bow.

'Just a minute, Festo. There's a girl who usually brings my clothes. Where's she?'

Festo shuffled his feet, uneasy. 'She, ah . . .' He cleared his throat. 'Young master, she is pregnant. She has gone away.'

'Preg . . .' I was a Scipio, remember. I was allowed to feel emotion, but not to show it. 'Hm. I see, Festo. Thank you. Good night.' He was almost at the door. 'Oh, Festo, by the way, what was that girl's name?'

'Hispala, young master. Will that be all?'

'Thank you, Festo. You may go.'

So did I learn her name, that of a love found and lost and never found again. Eros, erotic love, according to Plato, can raise souls to heaven. I have found that it does take us to a different country, but the landscape is old and familiar. It is ourselves.

I never saw Hispala again. I never asked.

I think of her now, if she is alive, in a colony to the north, no doubt, where the winds howl and the taxes are high, sold cheap as a pregnant slave, a vision to me when I was young become a cowled old woman crouched against the cold. I think of her now, and my eyes fill with tears. I have never mentioned her until now, and shall not do so again. But I will never forget her.

I was nervous, very nervous. The murmur of voices stopped as I crossed the hall of the Senate. I wished I had eaten breakfast: I had looked at it, then pushed it away.

The crowd of men, some young but most old, broke off their conversations and looked at me. I just walked on. They parted, white togas rustling, to let me through.

On the far side of the hall, across the black and white tiles, I saw two guards. I walked up to them, conscious of the glances from behind. 'I am Publius Cornelius Scipio,' I said to the taller of the two. 'Fabius Pictor is expecting me.'

They saluted. I could barely see their faces under their helmets' shadow for, although the morning was full outside, inside that great hall it was still half dark.

My new toga itched, especially under my arms. And it was, I felt, too big for me. 'Remember, you are a Scipio,' my father's letter had said. Yes, yes, even now I remember. But then I didn't know entirely what that meant, and we all are afraid of things we do not understand.

'Come this way, sir,' the soldier said. He turned, opened the door behind him and passed through. I followed.

'Don't apologise. Just tell me who you are, and what you want.'

'My name is Artixes, and I don't want anything. As I said, I have a message for you.'

'Yes, you said. From whom?'

'From the man I serve.'

'And who is that?'

'Labienus, Titus Licinius Labienus.'

'I know no such man.'

'Ah, but you do.' Artixes smiled. He had, I saw, a full set of fine white teeth.

'This is a strange guessing-game to be playing in an alley with a stranger,' I said. 'How do I know this man?'

'He has just set you free.'

'Ah, the Roman magistrate! A message, you said?'

'Yes. Labienus asks if you would care to sup with him this evening.'

I chuckled. From prison to dining-couch. But I have never turned from the new, the unknown. 'Please tell your master that Bostar of Chalcedon accepts with pleasure, though he will hardly be finely dressed. Where is your master's house?'

'A slave will come for you. Where will you be?'

'I am hoping for lodgings with the widow Apurnia.'

'And, my friend, I think you will find them.'

'How can you know that?'

Now he chuckled. 'Labienus said you had a quick mind. But no, I do not have the second sight. She'll take you, if only because her mother, too, came from Chalcedon.'

'Wherever her mother came from, she can't give me lodgings if she has no room.'

'She'll have room. The town is quiet, and will be until the festival in nine days. So, Bostar of Chalcedon, a slave will come for you to the house of the widow Apurnia. Go well.' With that, he turned and retraced his steps, avoiding the sow now lying giving suck in the mud and filth of the alley.

*   *   *

103

I followed the slave's torch as it gusted and flared in the blustery night. The widow Apurnia had taken me in, though she never mentioned Chalcedon. I could see her blood in her dark skin, raven hair and almond-shaped eyes. My room was small and simply furnished, but clean. A bed. How long had it been?

We walked back through a deserted market, on through the Forum. The buildings were fine and large. Money had never been a problem for Capua. Her bankers and merchants were renowned.

The street was broadening out. Blocks of insulae, *flats, became houses, standing on their own. Going the opposite way a litter passed us, carried by four slaves, and I heard its bells tinkling as it disappeared into the dark. Then, as the street began to climb, the properties became even bigger, surrounded by high walls. At the third or fourth of these on the left, the slave stopped, and knocked at a gate in the wall. A hatch opened.*

'I bring Bostar of Chalcedon, as bidden,' the slave said.

The door swung open. The slave stepped back, held the torch high and gestured to me to go in.

The corridor was long and wide, its ceiling lost in the dark. The soldier's boots rang heavily on the flags. We passed doors, and smaller corridors veering off, spluttering torches on their walls. The soldier stopped at last, and knocked sharply on a door. 'Come in!' I heard the muffled reply. The soldier opened the door, stepped forward.

'Publius Cornelius Scipio, sir!' he barked. He stepped back, saluted me, and turned. I moved forward to where he had been.

His head was huge, with the highest forehead I have ever seen. He was almost bald, but his beard was long and pure white. He looked up at me from behind his desk, and underneath the beetling brows his eyes gleamed.

'Publius Cornelius Scipio, you are welcome,' he said in a bass voice. 'Come in, and close the door.'

I spent the next ten months with Fabius Pictor. I grew in more ways than the physical. I was his shadow. I read when he read, wrote when he wrote. When he spoke in the Senate, I sat and listened, knowing what he intended to say and, because we had discussed it beforehand, how he intended to say it.

I suppose the greatest revelation for me in those first weeks was how mundane most of the Senate's work was – and is. Taxes, appointments of minor officials, water supplies, applications from property-developers, tenders from merchants to supply the army with grain, or nails, or boots, or greaves – so much went into, or so it seemed to me, so little. The broad issues were already agreed. Rome was to expand.

I have since met many people who assumed that our expansion was purely for conquest, that Rome was and is a military power. I learnt from my *triconium fori* that that is wrong. Rome expanded and expands for trade. We are a mercantile, not an aggressive, people. We fight, when we have to, as a means to that end. But our nature presupposes order.

I used everything that I had learnt from Rufustinus and Euphantus. Fabius worked me hard. I read reports and despatches and prepared summaries for him. I also spent a lot of time drafting his speeches. The first time he asked me to prepare one, we were as usual in his Senate room, he at his large desk under the window, I at my smaller one along the wall.

'I have a new task for you, Publius,' he said, breaking the silence. I looked up from my scrolls. 'I want you to draft a speech for me.'

'A speech? What on?'

'Oh, just a little idea of mine. I want to propose a courier service.'

'A courier service?'

'Yes, you heard me! Or have you grown deaf?' Fabius could be testy, as I had learnt. He expected to say something only once.

'But the private couriers work well,' I said.

'Do they? In what way?'

'Well, there are so many of them, competing with each other, that—'

'Yes, yes. That costs stay low and efficiency high. Isn't that what you were going to say?'

'Yes, Fabius.'

'Well, it's rubbish. You must learn to look below the surface of things, young Publius.' He got up, and started pacing round the room, stroking his beard. 'If I gave you a despatch now and asked you to have it taken to the city prefect's office, what would you do?'

'I would take it to the ante-hall, where the couriers wait, and have the guard call out the destination.'

'And then?'

'Then the couriers would call out their bids, and the guard would give the despatch to the cheapest.'

'Would the bids vary?'

'Yes.'

'By how much?'

'Ah, by . . .'

'Don't "ah" me. By how much. A little? A lot?'

I hung my head. 'I don't know, Fabius. I've never really followed it.'

He strode over to his desk, his sandals scuffing the floor, and picked up a despatch. 'Well, time you did. Take this. It's for the plebeian aedile, but this time listen.'

I got up and walked towards him.

'No, life's too short. I'm sorry, young man, I didn't mean to be so sharp. I'm supposed to speed your learning, so I'll save you the effort. The bids are all within a few pennies of each other. You know about the *collegia*, the trade unions.'

I nodded. Of course I did. The last four debates in the Senate had been about just that, and more particularly how to end a strike by one of them – of all things, the flute-players' union. They were refusing to play without a pay rise. The High Priest, the *pontifex maximus*, was refusing to conduct the appointed rituals without the necessary musical accompaniment. So the butchers were complaining, because the priestly college wasn't ordering the normal number of animals for sacrifice; and so it went on.

Fabius had the house in stitches when he spoke on the subject. He followed one of the Valerians, who had thundered and harangued and more or less said that all the flautists should be executed.

'This is indeed, my fellow senators, a grave matter,' Fabius said. 'It is so not least because it demonstrates one of life's immutable laws: greater fleas have lesser fleas upon their backs to bite 'em. And lesser fleas have smaller fleas and so ad infinitum.'

Sorry, Bostar. Back to the couriers. 'These *collegia* all have one thing in common,' Fabius said. 'The couriers are no different. They're price-fixers, pure and simple. That's one reason why we need a state-run courier service. Think of others, and draft me a speech.'

On my left was the porter's small lodge. I saw a glowing brazier, a chair and a small low table with a pewter plate and the remnants of a meal. 'Straight on, straight on,' the porter growled. The path was of white gravel, with a low hedge on each side beyond which shrubs and gardens, trees, ran on into the dark. Brought on the breeze I smelt the smell of an orchard, of figs and pomegranates, and it was a long time since I had felt so safe and self-contained.

Ahead, white marble columns glowed in the light of torches round the porch. I walked up the first flight of four steps, then the second.

A man stepped forward. 'Welcome, Bostar. It is good to meet on cleaner ground.'

I smiled, and looked at him. 'It is, Artixes, it is.'

A screech rang out from the garden, a horrible strangled sound that made the hairs on the back of my neck stand up. I turned, alarmed. Artixes put a hand on my arm. 'Only a peacock. They are noisy brutes, but Labienus likes them.'

'He keeps peacocks in his garden?'

'And guinea fowl, and even some ostriches, though they are in a pen. But you'll see — or may. Meanwhile, come in. Labienus is expecting you. Just follow me.'

Lamps lit the dining-room. The light was softer than that given by the torches in the atrium we had crossed. Labienus was lying on a couch on the far side of the room. He got up as I followed Artixes in.

'Ah, Bostar, welcome. It's good to see you under . . . different circumstances.'

His voice was warm and genuine, as was his handshake. He was no taller than I, though he had seemed so in court. 'Now, come over and recline beside me. Take that couch. Will you join me in some wine? And you, Artixes?'

I was being treated as an equal. What could Labienus want?

The meal was memorable, if you like that sort of thing. I don't. I find it too rich and filling. What I do appreciate is the skill of the cooks, not only in cooking but in presentation. Of both, the Romans have made a science and an art.

I had barely sat down when the slaves brought in the first course. I was expecting that: it is the Roman way. To find out what Labienus had in mind I would have to wait. When Romans of his class dine, they do not talk. They eat. No, that implies that they gorge, as pigs at a trough, but I do not mean that. They savour, and enjoy.

We were three, myself, Labienus and Artixes.

'It is a fine wine, don't you think, Bostar?' was about all Labienus said to me before the meal.

I took a sip. I have never had a taste for alcohol. It clouds my mind. 'I am not the man to ask, Labienus. It is a subject of which I know nothing.'

'*A pity. Perhaps you will learn. But begin by smell, not taste.*'
He swilled the contents of his goblet round and leant forward to smell.
Artixes did the same. '*Delicious.*' He furrowed his brow and shut his
eyes. '*I smell raspberries and blackcurrants and . . .*'

'*And vanilla,*' Artixes said.

'*Yes, exactly!*' from Labienus, who at least had his eyes open now.
'*It is a fine Falernian. I should have ordered more.*' They both sipped
and sniffed in silence. '*What do you think, Artixes? I rate this more
highly than even vintage Setinian.*'

'*Yes, possibly,*' Artixes mused. '*Though I would like to try that
Fundanian again before making up my mind.*' I thought the whole
thing almost ridiculous. '*And the Signine wine is hard to beat,*' he
went on. '*They say it's good for your bowels, too.*'

Labienus laughed. '*You and your bowels, Artixes! I'm thinking
more of my palate. Yes, this is a fine wine indeed. Ah!*'

The slaves' entrance saved me from the joys of more oenology.

'It's not bad,' Fabius said when he had finished reading. 'I can
make something of this speech.' He got up, pacing round as
was his wont. 'Yes, Publius, I like it. Well done.'

I started, I think, to blush. This was high praise.

'I like your three points of cost, confidentiality and efficiency.
One can make only three, perhaps four, in a good speech,
knowing that your audience will forget at least two of them.'
He stopped at my desk, put his hands on the edge and leant
over me. His voice was harder now. 'What will they remember,
Publius?'

'Well, if they forget at least two points—'

'No!' He was sharp. 'What will they remember?' He stared
at me. I saw the veins in the whites of his eyes, the creases in
his cheeks, the signs of age.

'I . . . I don't know.'

'Pah!' He straightened and turned. 'They will remember,

Publius, what every audience remembers. Not so much what you said, but how you said it.' He walked back to his desk, picked up my draft and turned to me with it in his hand. 'Now, what do you think are the virtues of any speech?'

'It should be clear,' I said.

'Yes, I agree. What else?'

'It shouldn't wander.'

'What do you mean?'

'It should stick to its point or points. It should not be discursive.'

'Yes, you're close. But I suppose I'm here to teach as much as you are to learn. Let me answer my own question. The virtues of a speech, Publius' – his voice was softer now – 'are three.' He cleared his throat, stood still and looked at me. I shall always remember. 'Clarity, lucidity, euphony. Repeat!' he barked.

'Clarity, lucidity, euphony,' I said.

'Yes, Publius, yes!' He chuckled. 'Come over here and sit beside me.'

As I crossed the room, he put an arm around my shoulders and I felt a warm glow. Like that, we walked to Fabius' desk.

The first course was a platter each of sea-hedgehogs, raw oysters, other sorts of shellfish and asparagus. Beside each of our couches a slave-boy squatted, with a bowl of warm water and a towel. My boy was a Moor, milky black, with a fine hooked nose. I tried to catch his eye each time I dipped my fingers in the bowl but, well-trained, he kept his eyes on the ground. No ears, no eyes: the perfect Roman slave.

From Labienus and Artixes came no sound but those of appreciation. I watched them. Artixes ate solidly, but Labienus, like me, picked and only sipped his wine.

Labienus rang a small bell on the floor beside him. Soundless, barefoot, slaves took our plates away. On a long, low table between us a different slave, an older man, the cook I assumed, carved a boar as we watched. He had great skill, I thought, but then I was hardly an adept of these things, and one by one, I first, we each had a plate of the steaming meat, covered in a distinctly greyish sauce.

'It's all in the sauce,' Labienus said to no one in particular. I watched as he tilted his plate and, with a little silver spoon, brought some sauce to his lips. 'Again, the smell, Bostar.' His nostrils arched. 'Mm. I think it may have worked, Artixes.' He put the spoon into his mouth, rolled his tongue round his cheeks. 'Yes, it has. The ligusticum makes all the difference.'

'Ligusticum?' I dared to ask.

'A type of herb,' Artixes answered. 'Labienus studies them for his famous sauces. This one will have been made with pepper, ligusticum, a pinch of asafoetida, rocket seed, ground almonds and dates, honey, garum sauce—'

'Enough, Artixes,' Labienus chided him. 'Let's eat, not talk. You of all people should know that talking disturbs the vapours in the belly.'

'Clarity and lucidity, Publius, are the easiest of the three,' Fabius said, his face only a hand's breadth from mine. 'Most orators can manage them, as you have with this speech. But euphony, that is a different matter. What do you think it is?'

'Sounding good. The prose should be constructed so as to please the listener's ear.'

'To "please"? Yes. But more than that. To arrest, to beguile. To emphasise certain points, and mask others. How do you think we might achieve this?'

'By tone and pitch of voice. By speed or slowness of delivery,' I replied.

'Good, very good. Your father would be proud of you, and he is a speaker to remember. Few can hold the house as he can. So, for a start, I want this speech of yours marked in the margin. Two thick lines in the margin where you think the delivery should be fast. One thin line for slow. Two wavy lines for loud, one for soft – at least, these are my keys, and I'm too old to change now. Understand?'

'Yes, Fabius. It seems a good system to me.'

'Well, it's simple, and the best things always are. But now comes the hard part. How much do you know about devices?'

'A little. We covered them with Euphantus.'

'Oh, yes, your *grammaticus*. I hear he's good. My cousin Marcellus had him for his sons. So what's asyndeton?'

'Not being bound – the absence of conjunctions.'

'And where would you use it? In the fast passages, or the slow?'

'The fast, of course.'

'Exactly. As in a string of verbs like . . .'

'Well, one example Euphantus gave us was: *abiit, excessit, evasit, erupit* – he left, he departed, he went away, he quit – used of someone who made what Euphantus called a quick exit.'

'I like it, young Publius!' Fabius slapped me on the back. 'And what about, say, prosopopoeia?'

I was on familiar ground. 'Personification. You use it when you address an abstraction.'

'Like?'

'Like hope, or youth, or memory.'

'Yes. As?'

'As a person.'

And so we went on, well past the ninth hour in mid-afternoon when, usually, I would go to Lanistus for lessons in riding and use of the sword and Fabius would resume work on his history.

I heard the guard change, the hours called. We covered rhetorical devices I knew, and some I didn't. We placed them, as a slinger throws his shot, in Fabius' speech until, at last, he was contented. Euphony, euphony, euphony. The word itself – long, short, short: it is, of course, a dactyl – sounds sweet.

But I learnt from Fabius that true ease in speaking comes from art, not chance.

I was full after the first course. The third, small roasted duck, potted river fish, leverets and sweet honey cakes, would have fed me for a month.

'You eat sparingly, Bostar of Chalcedon,' was the only comment Labienus made when, at last, the plates had been cleared, the wine pitcher renewed and the slaves had all withdrawn.

'So, I see, do you, Labienus.'

'Yes. I prefer the art to the eating. All the more so, now that Hannibal has gone.'

'But I heard' – I chose my words carefully – 'that Capua had sided with Hannibal.'

Labienus sat up as if someone had slapped him. His eyes narrowed. 'Bostar,' he said slowly, 'you may talk of anything in this house. But not that. Is that clear?'

What secrets had we here? Well, I would not tempt fate. 'Yes, absolutely clear.'

'Good.' Labienus exhaled, and lay back. 'Now, to business. I— No. I must relieve myself first.' He got up. 'After all, we musn't make heavy water of things, must we!' He was still chuckling at his joke as he left the room.

Such were the things that Fabius Pictor taught me in my forming, before it was time for me to do, before— Yes, what is it, Aurio? You know you're not to disturb me when I'm working. Well, don't just stand there! What is it?

A letter, master.

From whom?

From Theogenes, master, your art dealer.

Yes, Aurio, I know who Theogenes is. Then it must be important. Who brought it?

Theogenes' own body-slave.

Ah, Theophilus. Where is he?

Gone, sir. Said he had to get straight back to Rome.

All right, Aurio, you did well to bring it. Bring it here, and leave us. Bostar, I'll read it now. In fact, I'll read it aloud, so you can note down what my old friend has to say – about the verdict, no doubt. Who knows? This account I have been dictating may have to end.

Right. Let me see. Not even the usual pleasantries. And Greek, in Theogenes' own hand. Hm. Then it must be important. He likes to deal with his correspondence, I know, by dictating when in the bath. Anyway, let's see. 'It is said,' he writes, 'that the Senate voted narrowly for your acquittal. The plebs' vote for that was clear.' Please take this down verbatim, Bostar. We come now to the crux.

'But Cato applied for an appeal. His application was successful. He has demanded three things: the evidence of your friend Laelius – why, I do not know and cannot discover – that of Scribonius about his time as your tribune in Syria, and a statement from the Carthaginian Senate about your dealings with them in the war. This will all take time. Laelius is, of course, in Rome, and seeing a great deal of your brother, by the way, but Scribonius, as you know, is governor in western Celtiberia. He has been summoned. So stay where you are. There is nothing you can do. On no account come to Rome. You have many friends here, but also many enemies, and unfortunately, jealousy and hatred are more active, I have found, than the bonds between friends. I fear for your brother's safety. He clouds his days with drink and would, I think, welcome the knife of the assassin. Yes, I would not put that past Cato. The man is desperate. His hatred of you consumes him. So destroy this letter when you have read it. I risk my life, and that of Theophilus, in sending it. Or, even worse, I risk my fortune. But it comes from, truly, your friend.'

Well, well, Bostar. How I miss Theogenes, and his jokes. He probably is more concerned for his fortune than for his life, though. I had hoped to find the time to spend with him that I lacked when I served Rome. Well, that may come. So, Laelius. Not under torture, not with his dying breath, would he say anything to incriminate me – for all the many things he knows. As for Scribonius, he will not betray my secrets, and perhaps Cato will burn out, like a shooting star. Who knows what the Carthaginians will disclose? Old Hanno whom I dealt with mostly is long dead. So we have more time, Bostar, perhaps enough to finish this account. We must live on, then, in the shadow of death and the light of life. For me, that is nothing new.

Look how brightly Theogenes' papyrus is burning in the brazier. Nothing but the best from him. Now, where was I, Bostar?

You were talking about your days with Fabius Pictor.

I will write this in the margin when I transcribe my notes to fair copy. I must record my misgivings and fears. I cannot share Scipio's confidence in Laelius. Doubts come to me in the deep silences of thought. But this is Scipio's account, not mine.

Oh, yes, I remember. Those days were long, and lonely. After lessons from Lanistus, I would go home and eat, sometimes with my little brother, but usually alone, served by Festo. Then I would fall into a deep, exhausted sleep. I didn't see Laelius. I didn't hear from him, nor he from me.

What else do I remember?

One night, after supper, rather than go straight to bed I went out into the garden. I wanted to watch the stars. I lay down beside the fountain, as the frogs and crickets sang, and watched them in their silent thousands, glittering and glistening afar. A sound disturbed me, repeated. A low moan, and then another; two voices. I got up, and followed the sounds.

We had a summer-house – we had, I have, it is still there – at the back of the garden, screened by oleander bushes. There was a gap between the back of it and the high garden wall. On tip-toe, I went closer. That is where the sounds were coming from, faster, clearer, more insistent.

I knelt down and parted the bushes. Her spread legs, I assumed those of one of our slave-girls, shone as alabaster in the darkness. On top of her was a man, his tunic ricked up, his buttocks pumping up and down. He grunted, and she moaned.

I should have stood up and stopped them. Slaves may not breed without permission. Instead, I knelt there and watched and trembled. I wished it had been lighter, and they naked. I felt my penis stiffen. I loved it, thinking of his penis, head red, in her wetness. His thrusts grew faster, their moans more rhythmic. He pushed up on his arms above her, and paused, and with one last effort he came crashing down and home, and their groans became murmurs. I wanted to slip my hand inside her then, and feel what he had done.

Instead, I slipped away, conscious of a light sweat all over me. In my room, in the dark, at home but without a home, I worked myself up and down, up and down, until with a juddering shudder the semen came. I lay back on my bed, exhausted, thinking of that woman and my shame.

My tunic was covered with semen. I remember the panic. Where could I put the dirty thing? Only when I thought of a plan did I slip into a fitful sleep. I dreamed of them, thousands of them, out there, under the stars or under roofs, on ships or in cheap inns, on the ground or in beds, rutting, thrusting, pumping and crying out because, when they had finished, they were utterly alone.

I put the tunic in my bag. I left for the Senate the next morning earlier than normal, in the half-light when the world is still and the terrors of the night have given way to morning. I passed the clump of trees and bushes, wild ashes, birch, wisteria, that had grown up from the ruined foundations of the house of Vitruvius Vaccus. I stooped down, picked up a stone. Opening my bag, I stuffed the stone into the tunic, made a ball of it and threw. This was one thing, at least, I could not discuss with Fabius.

'Good morning, Fabius Pictor,' I said, as I always did, when I entered his room. As usual, even this morning when I was early, he was there before me.

'And the same to you, Publius,' he replied, turning to look out of his window. 'It is a fine one, it seems, though a trifle cold for this time of year. Now, come and sit down – oh, bring me a glass of water, will you? I have a job for you that you will enjoy.'

'What's that?' I asked, putting the water down beside him.

'Thinking.'

'Thinking? Is that a job?'

'Yes. There is none harder,' Fabius said sharply. 'Any fool can do things. Few can think.'

'If you need to go, Bostar, the latrine is through that arch and down the corridor on your left,' said Labienus as he came back in and settled down.

'Thank you, I'm fine.' I heard Artixes settle back in his couch, just as Labienus leant forward.

'Now,' said Labienus, looking intently at me, 'you probably want to know why I asked you here. Why should a Roman patrician ask you to sup with him?'

'I have, as you can imagine, been asking myself that question.'

'Of course.' Labienus sat up straight, swinging his feet on to the floor. I stayed as I was, lying back but turned on my side towards him. 'Where are you planning to go from here?' His voice was hard, inquisitorial.

'I thought, Labienus, that before Roman law I was free.'

He held my gaze, then broke off and smiled. 'I'm sorry, Bostar. I spend so much time in court that, as Artixes often has cause to remind me, I assume a forensic manner when I do not mean to.'

'I understand.'

'Of course you're free. You can go anywhere you please – although, these days, you shouldn't be surprised if you're hauled in again. The patrols are jumpy.'

'And we shouldn't be surprised at that, either,' Artixes added, 'with Hannibal around. I wonder if Scipio will prove a match for him?'

'If?' Labienus scoffed. 'Don't underestimate Scipio, Artixes. He's the greatest general Rome has ever had, in my view. And Hannibal must be tired, yes, very, very tired. What do you think, Bostar?'

'I . . . I, ah, I prefer to stick to things I understand. As I said, I am only a teacher. I know about the motions of the stars, the laws of mathematics and languages, but not the ways of men or war.'

Labienus seemed satisfied. 'Quite. Anyway, Bostar, it is to such things I want to turn. You see, with Hannibal in Italy – Artixes, how many years was it?'

'Sixteen, Labienus.'

'Sixteen! And outnumbered by hundreds to one. Astonishing! Anyway, through much of that time life has been far from normal. Disrupted trade, disrupted courts and – this is my point, Bostar – for my children, disrupted education.'

'How many children have you?'

'Two. Two boys. But the grammaticus that I had taken on was conscripted.'

'How old are they?' I asked.

'Sixteen and eighteen. But they are . . .' Labienus looked away. 'How shall I say it, Artixes?'

'Let me. They are, in a word, louts.'

Labienus became apologetic. 'I can't disagree. Their mother died twelve years ago. The damn war. I had no time. I was busy trying to keep my business going.'

'What sort of business is that?' I asked.

'I am, as was my father, procurator to the southern Roman fleet. I supply food, clothing, sails, everything. But allow me to repeat my question: where, Bostar, are you planning to go from here?'

'As I said to you, Labienus, though under different circumstances, I am bound for Rome.'

'To do what?'

'To teach. What else should a teacher do?'

'Quite so. Then, Bostar of Chalcedon, I have asked you here to put a proposal to you.' I had seen it coming for some time. 'Teach, indeed. But here. Stay here, and teach my sons.'

'What I want you to think about,' Fabius said, 'is government.' I must have looked puzzled. 'You see, I have reached the point in my history of Rome when the second, plebeian consulship is established. I want to set that in context. I want you to think of a better way to rule. How would you judge a government, Publius?'

'By its results. How else?'

'What might they be?'

'In good government, prosperity, order, equality before the law.'

'Yes, I'd agree. And in bad?'

'The opposite. Poverty, disorder, inequality.'

'And what about war?'

'That depends on what caused it. Civil war reflects bad government.'

'Yes, but if a state is at war, does that mean it is badly governed?'

'Not necessarily. We can only conduct and win wars because we are well governed.'

'Yes, I would accept that.' Fabius was up again – how I treasure these memories – pacing round, stroking his beard. 'As you know, Publius, our constitution is unique. It is in balance. Tell me what other states' governments you have learnt of and admire.'

'There are two.'

'Yes?'

'That of Minos in ancient Crete and that of Solon in Athens.'

'Good. Very good! You have been well taught.'

We talked on, right through the midday meal. I always think of Fabius when I feel tired or hungry. *Vita vigilia est*, he used to say. Life consists in being awake. We discussed Minos and Solon. I accepted Fabius' point – although he never made it directly: he led me by questions to his answer – that both their governments were flawed. Both men were benevolent dictators.

Minos died, and his successor failed him. Solon, having reformed the laws and constitution of Athens, resigned his office of his own accord. Our constitution, we agreed, epitomised the balance Solon tried to find in his – but failed, because he gave too much power to the people.

The people must have a voice. So, too, must the patricians. The people and patricians must stand equal before the law. But if you entrust too much power to the people, you give it to some who have neither the time nor ability – nor, often, the education and intelligence – to reflect upon the common good.

I was reading that section of Fabius' history in bed the other night. 'So, with the establishment of two consuls, one plebeian, one patrician, in that balance did Rome's constitution crown the world's and make possible the glory of the Republic,' he wrote. I learnt that balance from the one who first expressed

it in writing. It is something that I have fought to uphold —
with my life.

'I am honoured, Labienus, honoured.'

'Well, do you accept?'

*'I think, Labienus,' Artixes interjected, 'that Bostar — or anyone
— would want time to reflect.'*

*'Yes, yes. All right. Until tomorrow. And Artixes, please tell Bostar
of my terms. Bostar, I must go to bed now. I dislike late nights. But I
hope that you will accept my offer.'*

*'I will tell you, Labienus, tomorrow. Meanwhile, I thank you for
your hospitality.' We both got up. I took Labienus' extended hand.*

*'The pleasure was mine,' he said. 'But if you come, I think you
might prefer simpler fare.' Chuckling to himself, he left us. I liked this
man. But was mine a different road?*

*Artixes and I talked a little longer. Or, rather, he talked and
I listened. Money, duties, perquisites. 'So you will be comfortable
here, Bostar.'*

*My body, yes. But my mind? 'Thank you, Artixes. You will have
your answer tomorrow.' I got up to go. A slave was waiting in the
shadows, I presumed to lead me to Apurnia's, though I could have
found my way alone. 'Oh, by the way, Artixes. How did you come
to be here?'*

*He laughed. 'That, Bostar, is for an earlier hour. Come, let me
see you to the gate. And, whatever you decide, remember the Greek
saying: "Blame the message, not the messenger."'*

*Back at the house of the widow Apurnia — she had left a lamp burning
for me in the window — I lay down on the bed. It felt strange, after so
very long. It creaked. I turned on my side, and fell asleep at once.*

*I went first thing the next morning to the courthouse. Grudgingly,
a bailiff led me to Labienus' chambers. He was deep in documents
when I was shown in, preparing, I imagined, for a case. But his eyes
brightened when he looked up and saw me.*

'So, Bostar of Chalcedon. Forgive me, but I must be brief. Do you bring me good news, or bad?'

'I'm not sure I bring you either, Labienus. But I have made up my mind.'

'And?'

'And I accept your offer with pleasure. I will teach your sons as best I can.'

'Excellent! Excellent! I am delighted.' Labienus bounced over to me and pumped my hand. He looked, I thought, tired. Too much on the mind. 'So when will you start?'

'Artixes said last night that everything was ready – a room for me, a classroom for me and your sons.'

'So?'

'So I propose, with your agreement, to move in tomorrow and begin my lessons the day after. But I will need—'

Labienus waved a hand. 'Tell Artixes. He'll arrange anything you need.' Behind us, the bailiff coughed. 'Yes, Sentio, I am coming,' Labienus said. 'Bostar, I must go. I will see you, then, this evening.'

And that, truthfully, is how Hannibal's mapmaker became, among other things, a teacher. The teacher was Labienus' doing. The rest, as you may see, depending on the verdict, was mine.

We had spent the morning in the debating-chamber. I had just eaten my usual midday meal, soup and bread and two fresh apples, newly in season. As I have said, Fabius was a frugal man. He had picked at a pear. I was, frankly, dozing at my desk as Fabius wrote on. Lanistus had been pushing me hard. I felt tired most of the time, as muscles adjusted to parrying with shields, and throwing the *pilum*. I was half wondering, as I sat in Fabius' room, why the Roman *pilum* was so heavy. To penetrate armour, I could see that. But had anyone tried to reduce the weight, experimented? What, I wondered, about cornel wood for the shaft? Was it any lighter than the usual ash?

Did the *pilum*'s whole head have to be triangular? Why not just the point? If, because it was lighter, you could throw a *pilum* faster, would it not penetrate armour just the same?

A commotion in the corridor outside disturbed my reverie. Guards shouting. In this hallowed place? I glanced at Fabius. Even he had looked up. The door slammed open. In came – well, almost fell – some kind of soldier: he was so dusty that it was hard to see.

'What is the meaning of—' Fabius thundered, outraged.

'Sagunt . . . Saguntum, sir!' the man managed.

'Yes! What about it?'

'It has—'

Just then, two guards, their *pila* levelled, ran in. 'I am sorry, sir,' the first one blurted. 'He just burst past us, and ran. He said he had no papers, or seal.' That one moved forward quickly, blocking the way between Fabius and the man. The other guard put down his *pilum*, and drew his sword.

'Enough!' Fabius shouted. 'There will be no killing here! Soldier, move aside. You, you said Saguntum. What about it?'

'It has fallen, sir, sacked,' the man gulped.

'Fallen? Impossible! When?'

'Four days ago. Scipio said—'

'Scipio?' I said. 'My father?'

'Silence from you, boy!' Fabius roared and the look he turned on me was of fury. 'Now, soldier, calmly. What has happened?'

'Scipio sent me. There was no time, he said, for despatches or seals. I have foundered five horses to reach you.'

'For the last time,' Fabius said, almost in a whisper that was chilling, 'I ask you: what has happened? Publius, if you can't hold your tongue, at least give this man a drink of water.'

The soldier's eyes showed his gratitude. The drips from his lips cut tracks through the dust that caked his face. He licked his lips, shuddered, then stood to attention. In an even voice, he said, 'Saguntum has fallen, sir. Hannibal the Carthaginian sacked the city, after a short siege.'

'And where were Scipio and his army?' Fabius asked.

'On the east side of the Rhodanus, sir, pursuing the Insubres, who had rebelled.'

'What, again?'

'Yes, sir. We think it was a ruse. We took some prisoners.'

'And?'

'And on them we found Carthaginian gold.'

'I see. I see.' Fabius sat down again. I stood where I was. My father!

'And where, soldier, is Scipio now?'

'Moving south-west, sir. He struck camp as soon as we heard about Saguntum. He intends to scout towards the Pireneos and see if he can find this Hannibal. I am to take him the Senate's instructions as soon as possible.'

'Right. Publius!' Fabius barked. 'Go and tell my colleagues that, as father of the house, I summon a full sitting – at once, do you understand? Send out messengers. I want everyone, within the hour,' and he looked at the calibrated candle burning on his desk. 'Oh, old Claudius has gout. Send a litter for him.'

I nodded. As I was turning to leave, the soldier stopped me. 'Are you Publius Cornelius Scipio?'

'I am.'

'Then, with your permission, Fabius Pictor, I have another message for you both.'

'From?' Fabius demanded.

'From this young man's father.'

Fabius nodded. 'Go on.'

'He sends his thanks to you, sir, and hopes to give them in person another time. He says he is sure no man could have taught his son better, but that is as well, because from this day the *triconium fori* of Publius Cornelius Scipio is suspended. His *triconium militiae* has begun. Publius Cornelius Scipio, your father sends for you. You are to join him in arms, in the service of the Senate and people of Rome.'

I skipped down the corridor with my message. My heart was bursting. I was young, and the young love the thought of war.

That night, as I slept fitfully, packed and ready to leave at first light, I dreamed of war-trumpets and alarms, of marches, battles and glory. Now, when these dreams come to me, an old man, I wake up, drenched in sweat and shuddering. As you will see, if I have time, I have known the horror that is war. Lives end. Life goes on. That is a great mystery.

Proving

Par est fortuna labori.

Luck is labour's reward.
Roman proverb

Four days had passed. The message came we were to leave. So, on the fifth, I went back up to my room after a breakfast of bread and – yes, after almost forty years I still remember – cheese and figs and warmed goat's milk with a pinch of cinnamon. I reread the letter I had left on my bed for Laelius, the letter Festo was to deliver to him when I had gone. Once more, I checked my saddlebag. Frontinus, the soldier who had brought my father's message, had told me what to take: 'As little as possible.'

'Should I take my best sandals?' I asked him.

'You can take your granny as far as I'm concerned, sir, but—'

My look silenced him. I was a Scipio, born to command. He knew, and his eyes fell slowly to his feet. Then, in a quieter voice, he went on without looking at me, 'There is little ceremony in camp, sir. The best thing you can take you cannot pack.'

'And what is that, Frontinus?'

'Your health.'

The household were all outside in the street to see me off, a loose and shuffling crowd, a *familia*, as I thought when I walked through the gate and saw them, motherless and, for many months, fatherless; and now I too was to leave. I felt a gnawing in my stomach.

I looked around for him. I saw his nanny, wrapped in a shawl against the early-morning cold. He was, I had heard from Festo, learning to talk. Lucius, my almost unknown baby brother, was playing with pebbles at his nanny's feet. I squatted down beside him. He looked up, and shrank from me, then put an arm round one of his nanny's legs. I reached out to him. He wriggled away. 'Goodbye, brother. I will . . .' What would I do? 'I will bring you a present from across the sea.' Snot was running from his nose. Lucius licked his lips, and looked steadfastly at the ground.

My sister, Cornelia, was standing at the front of the crowd, calm, reserved. She always had an air of self-possession on the rare occasions when I saw her. I looked at her. Her hair was thick, and had, I thought, some of our mother's lustre. 'Goodbye, sister,' I said. She nodded, and smiled, not just with her mouth but with her eyes. How many women of the *gens* Scipio, I wondered, had stood so and seen their men off to war?

Behind me, I heard steps. I turned. It was Festo, holding out a plain bag of kid leather. 'This, master, is for your journey.' I noticed that he had dropped the 'young' from 'master'.

'What is it, Festo?'

'Just food. For you and the soldier. I hear the inns along your way are poor.' He knew where we were going, and probably why. They say wind is fast, but so is news. Always the same: if you want to know what is going on, ask the slaves in the house of a patrician.

I took the bag, and slung its strap across my chest. 'Thank you, Festo. I . . .'

There was an expectant hush, all eyes on me. I had given no thought to this. Festo and Quinta and all the slaves and servants, the ostlers and gardeners, laundry maids and servers, most of whose names I never knew, all gathered there because another Scipio was going to war.

I cleared my throat. '*Familia*,' I began, 'I—'

I still wonder what I would have said. This was a rite of passage, and I knew it. The sound of two horses' hoofbeats, one heavy, one light, meant the moment was lost. On a white charger, and leading a grey gelding, Frontinus appeared. So was the world spared yet another speech. Frontinus slipped, cavalry-style, off his horse by sliding over its neck and head, and walked to the gate where I had left my saddlebag. In silence, he carried it to the gelding and secured it over the horse's back. The gelding, protesting at the strange weight, shied and bucked. Alarmed, the crowd moved back.

Frontinus looked at me. We mounted.

In a lazy coil, smoke drifted up from the kitchen fires of my home. It began to rain, a steady drizzle. All eyes were on me.

'*Valete,*' I said in a steady voice, 'Be well.'

As I turned the gelding's head, I heard the ragged reply, using the familiar personal pronoun, as was allowed on such occasions: '*Et tu, vale.*'

I woke to the smell of cooking, stew, perhaps, or soup, and the sound of hammering from the blacksmith's forge below. The sun was up, and shining. My back was stiff from the strangeness of a bed. Under it, I found a chamberpot. My urine was very yellow, I imagined from the wine I had drunk the night before. 'You are what you eat,' say the Pythagoreans – and drink, I thought. In the corner of the room there was a washstand. I washed my face and, with the heels of my hands, rubbed the sleep from my eyes. I tied back my hair, and walked out of the room towards the smell. It was strange that after so unaccustomed and large a supper I now felt hungry.

The widow Apurnia looked up from the hearth as I came in. She gestured towards a chair. 'Sit over there.' Her Latin was fluent, but her voice was clipped. As she walked towards me with a bowl of stew, I saw her face clearly for the first time. She wore hardship like a mask, in the tight lines around her eyes and mouth. Her face was the face of one who has journeyed long, but never arrived. 'Do you want bread?' she asked.

'Yes, please.'

She took a loaf from the oven above her hearth and brought it to me with a knife, then walked back again to her hearth and sat, her back to me, on a stool. 'Eat, stranger, eat,' she muttered.

*I cut some bread, dipped it into the bowl and sucked. 'Delicious,'
I said.*

*'Plainer fare than you would have had last night,' she gave back,
now stirring the pot before her with a long wooden spoon. I continued
eating. The stew was delicious. Goat, but not too strong and delicately
flavoured with, I thought, cardamom. The last time I had eaten such a
thing had been long ago. It was a great skill of my mother's, cooking, and
I paused between spoonfuls and remembered with that strange longing
we feel for something we have lost and cannot find again. Or does its
only value lie in the fact that we have lost it?*

*'How long are you staying?' Apurnia asked me suddenly, sharply.
'There's a fair in three days. I'll need your room.'*

'I know about the fair. I will leave this morning.'

'So you've taken the job, then?'

'How do you know about the job?'

*'How?' She scoffed. 'This is Capua, stranger. People know what
you're going to do before you've done it. There's a joke that in Capua
a secret is something you tell only one person at a time,' she said with
something approaching bitterness. 'More stew?'*

*'No, thank you. That was more than I'm used to. And very good,
by the way.'*

*'Hm. Men. Compliments. But when they've had their fill, of one
kind or another . . .' She turned towards me, scowling. But then her
look softened. Or was it a trick of the light? 'Where have you come
from? You're from Chalcedon, I hear.'*

'And so, I hear, are you.'

'I was born there, that's all. I've spent my whole life here.'

'How's that?'

*'You mean you haven't heard? You must be the only person in
Capua not to know. I came here as a slave. Or, rather, as the daughter
of a slave.'*

'But now you are free. This house—'

*'Free!' There was anger in her voice now. 'Free? To have a husband,
to rear two sons?'*

'Where are they?' I asked gently.

She banged the spoon on the rim of the pot, shaking off the gravy. 'They're wherever men go after this life.'

'You mean they're dead?'

'Yes, they're dead, stranger, all three, all killed fighting for Rome.' She stood up, wiping her hands on the leather apron round her waist, and turned to me. 'Now, leave your money, and go.'

I stood up too. Then I saw what was so strange about her face. She had a high forehead, but her hairline ran very low – at the sides, almost to her eyebrows. 'What are you gawking at?'

'I'll just get my bag from my room, and be on my way.'

'Do that.'

'But one thing. You said you came here as the daughter of a slave. But now, obviously, you're free. How—'

'How did that come about? None of your business. Or, if it is, it shouldn't be.'

I went and got my bag, leaving more money than she'd asked for on my bed. I thanked Sosius for his gold. He had given me freedom, to work for Labienus, or go. I climbed down the stairs and was outside in the street, a few steps away, when I heard a door open behind me. I turned. It was Apurnia.

'Since you're going there, stranger, you may as well hear it from me. It was Labienus who bought me my freedom.'

I walked back towards her. 'You may hear that it was for' – she hesitated – 'for services rendered.' She said those three words carefully.

'And it wasn't?'

'Not the way most mean,' she said, this time with passion in her voice. 'It was for— Never mind. You'll find out when you've been there a while.'

'You make it sound a strange house.'

'A strange house?' She was almost wistful. 'No, but stranger than it seems.'

I turned to go, and bumped into a stocky boy of, perhaps, twelve, who was making for Apurnia's door. 'Sorry,' he said.

'No, it's my . . .' My jaw dropped, and the blood drained from my face. He had to be. It could only be. The look was too peculiar, the hair that same coal black, the fine, hooked nose, the same wild, piercing eyes. But it couldn't be. That was impossible.

'Come in, Hanno,' Apurnia said softly. 'You're late.'

With that same urgency of movement that I knew so well, the boy squeezed past her, and through the door.

'Hanno?' I asked her, composing myself. 'A Carthaginian name.'

Apurnia nodded. 'Yes, it is. But there are many races in Capua. Go well, stranger.'

'Might I . . .' I rubbed my face. It couldn't be. It could. I had to ask. 'Might I ask you who the boy's mother is?'

'His mother?' She bit her lip. 'Since the whole city knows, I may as well tell you.' She straightened. 'I am.'

'But you said . . .'

'That I had two sons, both killed?' I nodded. 'That's right. They were the sons of my marriage. After that, I bore Hanno. But he, as anyone will tell you, is a bastard.'

'But he had a father.'

She sneered. 'Well, well. You know a lot.'

'Who was he?'

She stepped forwards from the doorway. 'Stranger, that is one secret in Capua that is, and will stay, safe with me. Now go.'

I have never enjoyed riding; I much prefer to walk. Lanistus had taught me well, but I think to be a true horseman you need to be brought up with the beasts. I had learnt to ride, true, but as a technician. I lacked the sense of ease, of empathy, that true horsemen have. Riders such as I are like our Roman potters, who copy Greek vases. They can copy, but they cannot paint or pot. Such skills, like riding well, you are born with, or must learn young.

Uneasy on my gelding, I followed Frontinus as he rose and fell, rose and fell. We crossed the Forum, still almost deserted, shrouded in a gentle light that shone through the drizzle and under which the water glistened on the flagstones as our hoofbeats sounded loud. My horse was settled now, sensing, I suppose, that I was more a passenger than a rider.

Just as we left the Forum and entered the narrow lanes of the weavers' quarter, I looked back. I could see the houses rising up the Palatine Hill, the newer blocks of *insulae*, apartments, at its foot, then, as old as Rome itself, the temple of Jupiter Capitoline across the Forum, and the lake of Curtius. I took it all in, food for my journey, not knowing when I would see it again, and I remember thinking how I loved the variety of old and new, of functional and religious architecture. Rome's buildings are as varied as men's lives.

I had heard of the building of the Via Flaminia, Rome's new road to the north. Fabius had told me all about it. Its builder, the censor Gaius Flaminius, was a friend of his – even though Flaminius was, like Laelius' father, a *novus homo*. Fabius had steered the bill for the new road through the Senate, a task, he often joked, that was harder than building the road would be. As usual, there were questions of land ownership to be settled, and wayleaves, compensations, laws.

Nothing of what I had heard prepared me for what I saw as we rode out through the Capena gate. Straight and far, the road ran north, its flagstones glinting in the sun and slanting rain. Off to its left was the old road, the Via Salaria, used since time immemorial for transporting salt. But the Via Salaria was unpaved and full of holes. Flaminius – and the Senate – had wanted a new road so that we could get our soldiers north in a hurry if there was trouble from the Gauls. At least, that was the official reason. I'm sure there were others, but I don't know what they were.

Frontinus, ahead of me, had paused. 'No need to look now, sir. There'll be time enough on the road,' he said as I rode up beside him.

'It's amazing, Frontinus.'

'And just finished,' he said proudly. 'One of my cousins was assistant to the engineers.'

'How far does it run?'

'As far as Ariminum, through Narnia, Mevania and Nuceria. Nuceria's where we'll have to turn off, though, and take the old salt road.'

'Is that bad?'

'Yes, sir.'

'Why?'

'Because the riding will be rough, and slower. I should know. I almost broke my neck on several occasions coming south. But we can't afford to walk the horses.'

'No? Why not?'

'Because your father's instruction was to make all speed. We are to go to Massilia, and find out there where he is. To do that quickly means going by sea, not road. So we'll stop at Populonia, and if there's no ship there we'll try again at Pisae. Right, let's check your saddlebag ties. Then, sir, we ride.'

It was the passivity I enjoyed. All I had to do was sit there, and be still, and try to forget the boy I had seen. The barber tried his usual banter, gossip, but when I didn't respond he soon gave up. For the first time in many years, I was having my hair cut. The Romans have a profound dislike of long-haired men. It must come from their deep-seated fear of the Gauls, who never cut their hair or beards and have been for so long the only people to withstand Rome. They call Gaul 'Gallia Comata, Long-haired Gaul', or at least they used to, and no doubt nannies still scare children with tales of the Gauls of the long hair, coming to murder them in the night.

I saw the hanks of my black hair lying, tinged with grey, and smiled. I liked the thought that not only the pubic hairs I had shaved off were grey.

★ ★ ★

From a walk, we moved to a trot and then to a canter, just as Lanistus had taught me. But my schooling had been on sand. Here, on stone, my bones jarred. My horse was just following Frontinus, running, not being ridden. I tried to loosen to the rhythm of its stride. I suppose it is a song that horses sing, but those first hours were uncomfortable, afraid.

I felt fine when we stopped at the first inn and dismounted, after a long unbroken trot. 'Only water for the horses,' Frontinus said, 'and a little hay.' When we re-mounted, though, I felt the soreness.

Frontinus noticed my grimace, and smiled. 'If you don't mind me saying so, sir,' he said as we rode on abreast, 'it's in the legs. Tight on the up, but relax on the down. You're tight on both.'

That whole first day I hardly spoke to him. As I worried less about the riding, I wanted to think. That seemed to suit Frontinus, who didn't try to engage me in conversation. Anyway, that would only have been possible during the times we slowed the horses to a walk. So, as we rode on up the Via Flaminia, I thought of all the little things that had prepared me for what had just begun, the many people, factors, influences, that had made me what I had become. Rufustinus, Euphantus, my love of light, Quinta and her kindness, Lanistus – one life from so many parts. Hispala crossed my mind. I pushed the thought away. I was riding to war.

We changed horses at a posting-station, a huddle of mean huts and corrals by the road. The stable-boy was surly. 'What's wrong with him?' I asked Frontinus when the boy had stomped off to see, he said, his master.

'He expected cash, and a fat tip.'

'But we'll pay him, won't we?'

'Yes, of course, but not the way he wants.'

'How, then?'

'We'll pay, sir, with this.'

On Frontinus' outstretched hand there was a small rectangular piece of white marble. I could just make out the words inscribed on it: *senatus populusque Romanus*.

'What is it?' I asked.

'A pass, a *tessera*. From the Senate itself. Apart from anything else, we – or, rather, I – am,' and he patted the small leather satchel that hung across his chest, 'the Senate's messenger, with despatches for your father.'

'And the pass?'

'That means that this inn must send its bill to the Senate.'

'Which means they will be paid.'

'Yes, but not for a month at least. And the taxman will have his share. Two good reasons for them much to prefer cash. But come on, sir. Water and some food. We've some hard riding ahead. I'll join you inside. I'm just going to the latrine first.'

After the barber, I wandered round the market for a while, looking, listening. It was good to see life go on. Normality, whatever that is, was there. I was surprised by the variety of the produce for sale. But then it was six years since Hannibal had burnt the fertile lands around Capua. More than enough time for them to recover, and I thought of old Sosius in shabby Secunium, hoeing his beans because, whatever happens, like the seasons life goes on. Winds will always blow, rain fall, men be born and die. If Sosius, broken, put down his hoe and starved, someone else, somewhere else, would pick it up again.

I was struck, too, by the variety of imported goods. Rome's trade, it seemed, had gone on uninterrupted. So much for Carthage's great fleet. What stopped them disrupting Rome's trade? They could have done that with little danger. Twenty or thirty semi-official pirates would have been enough.

And then I found what I'd been looking for, my one preparation for the house of Labienus. In a corner of a spice stall, vivid with the colours of cassia, cloves, ginger, nutmeg, mace, turmeric, cardamom and cinnamon, I found a grey block of bdellium, of gum. I bought it — I would cut it into strips myself — put it into my satchel, felt with my hands the strangeness of my short hair, and walked on.

We rode on, through rolling hills now. The roadside was alive with weeds and flowers. I saw many that I recognised, hemp agrimony, ploughman's spikenard, pale toadflax, snapdragons, burnet saxifrage, bearded bellflower and wild leeks, but many more that I didn't. I almost stopped Frontinus to ask him if he knew, but, even if he did, this was not the time for botany lessons. Then I thought of Laelius, and my letter to him. I felt sure he would have read it by now, or even be reading it as we rode. I suppose it isn't important to my story, but it felt so then. That letter was the only anchor I had left behind. I had left Rome and my childhood, and in leaving I had left a friend behind.

The letter was short, the first I had ever written. I told Laelius I was sorry not to have seen him for so long. I told him I was going to join my father and, for that matter, his, and that I hoped that he would join me. I would ask my father, and then send for him. I pondered over how to end the letter. I both wanted and didn't want to show my feelings. So in the end, I signed myself 'Your dear friend', though I thought the letters looked awkward in the wax.

At the next posting-station, Frontinus stopped again and slipped off his horse.

'The horses can't be tired yet, Frontinus,' I said. 'We haven't even cantered them.'

'Horses are like people, sir. No two are the same. Mine's all right, but look at yours.' As I sat there, in a cloud of buzzing flies, my mount, a mare, shifted her weight testily from leg to leg. 'That shows she's tired,' Frontinus said. 'It's her feet. This new road may be good for marching men with boots on, but not for horses. I don't want to founder her and have to use our legs instead, so we'll change here.'

We rode on into a glorious golden dusk, the sun setting to our left, and I felt my cloak drying from the drizzle of the morning in the breeze. We slept on mattresses of straw on the floor of a poor inn. 'Thank you, Festo,' I said under my breath as I pushed the plate of rank and stinking barley gruel away from me in the half-light of the following early morning and took from the bag that he had given me an apple and some admittedly sweaty cheese. 'Would you like some?' I asked Frontinus.

'No thank you,' he replied, swallowing a spoonful of the gruel. 'I've eaten better, but I've eaten worse. How are you this morning, sir?'

'Stiff, Frontinus.'

'That'll get easier. We'll make a horseman of you before we get to your father.'

'When will that be?'

'I don't know, sir. That depends on where he is.'

I knocked three times at the gate of Labienus' house. I heard bars being drawn, and latches turned. No hatch this time. The door swung open. I stepped in. The porter came out from behind the door. He was old and stooped, a different one, the day porter, I presumed, his face almost invisible behind a huge grey beard and shaggy hair. Labienus gives his slaves more liberty than many, I thought. But this man's clothes were clean, and he didn't smell.

''Ood 'orning. You're 'spected,' he said in that strange Capuan dialect which seems to take its consonants on the run. 'I'm 'Ulvio, the 'ead 'orter.' He smiled at me, toothless but friendly.

'And I am Bostar of Chalcedon,' I replied.

'I 'now 'at. Master 'old me 'isself. Sis mornin, that 'e did. Said yo'd be 'oming, so I wiz 'spectin you, so I wiz,' and Fulvio muttered away beneath his beard. 'No 'ags?' he asked me.

'Sorry?'

'Dun't ye no 'av no 'ags?'

He looked around. I understood. 'Bags? No, none.'

He belched, and held a gnarled hand over his mouth. The knuckles were red and sore and swollen. Arthritis. Perhaps he'd let me try a cure. 'Then 'tare,' he gestured up the path towards the house. ''Tixes 'spectin you. Te 'aster in't in. Out. 'ourts, so 'e be . . .' Still muttering, Fulvio shuffled into his little lodge and I took the path I had been on twice before.

In the daylight this time, I saw the house was huge, all stuccoed white. Around it on three sides, the garden stretched away beyond my sight.

On the second day we had to ride more slowly, mostly at a walk and never at a canter. The road was not yet flagged, and the loose stonework was a poor surface for horses' hooves. Along the roadside, piles of flagstones stood ready to be laid, and there were mounds of left-over sand and hard-core still to be taken away.

'Why is this section still unfinished?' I asked Frontinus.

'They were working on it when I came south,' he replied. 'But I brought a despatch from your father to the Senate, asking for more men. I should think those who were working on this stretch are at muster right now, preparing to march.'

'More men? How many did my father ask for?'

'That I don't know, sir. I am a soldier, not a general.'

'How many does he have at the moment?'

'Well, when I left, three legions of thirty maniples each, although a few of those are under strength: there's been a lot of fever about. But there's the other consul, Sempronius, in the south, in Bruttium, I think. Maybe the Senate will send for him. What I do know is that, as I was leaving, so was another messenger from your father to your uncle and the garrison at Placentia, asking him to come west. So that would make at least four legions.'

'Or twenty thousand men, in a hundred and twenty maniples.'

'Less what your uncle leaves behind to hold Placentia. But then more, sir, with the auxiliaries. Your father had been levying them.'

'What, Celtiberians?'

'No, Gauls, from the loyal tribes.'

'I didn't think there were any.'

Frontinus looked across at me, and smiled. 'There are some when we're winning, and they're being paid. But your father also has at least one troop of Baliaridean slingers, and your uncle, I heard, two more.'

'So this is real war!'

'No, not yet. At least not officially. Hannibal may have sacked Saguntum, but it is not a Roman city, remember, at least, not officially. So, of itself, that is not a *casus belli*. The Senate will not declare war for that alone – at least, I don't think so.'

'What will they do?'

'I don't know yet, sir. Though I imagine the answer to your question is in these despatches for your father. I should think they will protest to the Carthaginian Senate, and demand that Hannibal sticks to the treaty.'

'The one confining Carthaginian influence to south of the River Ebro?' Thank you, Fabius, I thought. I have been well taught. 'But Saguntum is well south of the Ebro.'

Frontinus looked impressed. 'Yes, sir, you're right about the treaty, and Saguntum. The point there is that it's a Roman ally, a *socius*, even though it's south of the Ebro and therefore in Carthaginian territory. So Hannibal should have left it well alone. But this is all theory.'

'What do you mean?'

'Well, treaties and alliances are what's supposed to happen. But I talked to some of the Spanish levies under your father's command. This Hannibal, it seems, is no mere brigand: he routed several of the important Spanish tribes. His army is incredibly well-trained, and doesn't rely on its elephants. Hannibal has a nickname in the Spanish tongue.'

'Oh yes. What's that?'

'"El Inesterado", sir.'

'What does it mean?'

'It means "the Unexpected One". He always does the unexpected, they say. Sir, I'm only a soldier, obeying orders, but it seems to me we don't know what this Hannibal is up to. What's he doing so far north? He's miles and miles from the new Carthaginian settlement at Carthagena, let alone from their silver mines near Gades. But what really puzzles me is that he can't go anywhere. The coast is covered by our fleet. And even if he crossed the Pireneos and got past your father's army, then your uncle's, he'd be trapped.'

'Trapped? By what?'

'By our armies behind him and the Alps ahead.'

'Couldn't he cross the Alps?'

'Excuse me, sir, but that's impossible. Cross the Alps? Just you wait until you see them. No.' Frontinus laughed. 'No, it can't be done – except by a wizard, or an eagle.'

We fell silent. I wondered what the unexpected one was like, and what he would do next. We rode steadily on.

Artixes met me, once again, on the porch. His smile was warm, and genuine. In the light of day he looked even younger than I had thought, perhaps thirty. 'Welcome, Bostar of Chalcedon. I am very glad you've come. Labienus told me of your decision.'

'Well, I'll try those boys of his for a term at least — and they, of course, must try me. Where are they? I'd like to meet them.'

Artixes looked embarrassed. His gaze faltered. 'Ah, I'm afraid, Bostar, that they're asleep. They get up late, you see, because . . .'

'Because they're out all night?'

'Exactly. Boys will be boys.' *He gave a rather hollow laugh.* 'But they should be up for the midday meal. You'll meet them then. In the meantime, let me show you to your room.'

'And, please, to the classroom.'

'Of course. Now where are your things? Is Fulvio bringing them?'

'My things, Artixes, are here.' *I spread out my arms.*

'You have no books, no charts, no other clothes?'

'No, but there are a few things I should like you to buy for me before I start teaching tomorrow. Labienus said you would see to it.'

'Of course. New sandals, shirts?'

'No, no.' *I laughed.* 'I am a teacher, not a tailor. Just a few tools of my trade.'

'Were you comfortable at the house of the widow Apurnia?' *Artixes asked me as we walked through the house.*

'Yes, very. She is a strange one, though.' *I felt Artixes stiffen as we walked. I stopped, and looked at him.* 'She has a son called Hanno.'

'Oh, yes. The bastard.'

'What do you know about him?'

Artixes blushed and cleared his throat. 'Bostar, that is one subject you should not raise in the house of Labienus.'

'No? Why not?'

'Because . . .' *He tugged his beard, nervously I thought.* 'All right, I'll tell you, but never talk of it again. Apurnia was in service here. Her bastard, Hanno, was conceived in this house. Then she, ah, left, to do what she does now. Does that answer your questions?'

'Almost. How old is the boy?'

'Twelve, if you must know.'

'One more question. Who was the boy's father?'

Artixes looked startled. 'Why do you ask?'

'Because he reminds me of someone I knew once.'

'Really? Well, I can't help you there.'

'Why not?'

'For the very good reason that I don't know. Now, shall we move on?'

We did, but I knew he was lying.

The second day passed, and the third. We stopped at Populonia, but found no ships, nor news of any. 'But there must be someone due,' Frontinus demanded of the harbour-master.

'You know what it's like,' he replied. 'When merchants hear there may be a war, they make themselves scarce.'

'A war? Who says that?'

'Who doesn't? It's the talk of the town.'

'And our fleet? No sign of it?'

'Across the sea, young man, when last I heard, patrolling – or should I say observing? – the coast from Emporiae down to what's left of Saguntum. Bloody Celtiberia. Never been anything but trouble, if you ask me. And these old bones of mine feel more coming on.'

We ate and drank and went on. I was easier on horseback by then.

'Tell me, Frontinus, where are you from?' I asked as we rode.

'From a small village south-east of Rome, sir. You won't have heard of it.'

'And your people?'

'Farmers. Olives, mostly, and a few goats. But I was the youngest son of six, and so I couldn't see much future there.

One day, the recruiting party came. I had just turned seventeen, so I joined up.'

'How long ago was that?'

'Seven years ago, sir, so I have nine to go.'

'And then?'

'Then I'll take my gratuity, and my pension, and buy myself a little plot of land.'

'And do anything in particular?'

'Well, I'd like to marry, of course, and have children. I'll still be young enough and, Jupiter willing, able. And I'd like to keep bees.'

'Bees?'

'Yes, sir. I love them. Ordered, industrious . . .' There was real life in his voice. And as the sun strengthened on our backs, Frontinus told me about bees. I have rarely met a person who did not have some passion or other. You have only to keep asking until you find it. Frontinus had, it seemed, not only a passion but a special gift. Others wore gauze and masks and gloves and hats when bee-keeping. Not Frontinus. He had discovered as a young boy that bees didn't sting him.

We stopped to rest the horses, and ourselves, in the shade of an old oak tree, its branches spreading like years. 'And so you joined, Frontinus, as a legionary.'

'That I did. Two years as a *hastatus*.'

Of course I knew the three ranks of Roman soldier, reflecting our standard three-line battle formation, the *triplex acies*. *Hastati*, the youngest, formed the front row, armed with the Roman spear or javelin, the *pilum*. Then came the *principes* and behind them the most experienced troops, the *triarii*. The theory was that the *hastati* took the brunt of the attack, but had the steady *triarii* behind them, literally pushing them and the *principes* on. If the *hastati* broke, the *principes* fought; they had no need of *pila* at such close quarters. If the *principes* broke, then, as the Roman proverb says, 'It has come to the *triarii*.'

If they broke? It had happened only once, two hundred years

ago, when the Gauls broke our last line at the battle of the Allia and then sacked Rome. Since then, the Roman army had been invincible – well, apart from Pyrrhus, but it was his elephants that broke our line and still we fought on. The whole world, I had been taught, knew a Roman army could not be beaten. So what was Hannibal doing? I pushed the thought away. If he was going to move north, he would meet our army and, like many, be lucky to escape the way that he had come.

'Why didn't you join the cavalry, Frontinus? You must have been reared with horses.'

'For a start, sir, because it wasn't offered. Secondly, if you'll forgive me, because we don't take the cavalry seriously. Only three hundred to a legion, hanging around like a bad smell. They're only used as scouts, really.'

'Perhaps that's what they're good for.'

'I don't think so, but it's not for me to say, sir. You'll soon see for yourself.'

'When did you first see active service?'

'At the battle of Telamon, against the Gauls.' He spat. 'There were hordes of them, savages, Gaesatae and Insubres, Boii and Taurisci, most of them naked and covered in bright paint . . . Ugh.' He shuddered.

'You don't seem to like the Gauls, Frontinus,' I said. 'I was taught by one. Well, a Celt, actually.'

'Like 'em? No disrespect to your teacher, but they're animals, *animals*. They're bred for war. Every Gaul drinks the blood of the first man he kills in battle. Afterwards, they take to their king the heads of all the men they've killed. No head, no loot. Then they cut the skin off the heads and dress them, as we would leather, and hang them on the bridles of their horses. Why, any Roman soldier would rather fall on his sword than be captured by the Gauls—'

'But come, sir. I've said too much. We'd best be getting on.'

*   *   *

The room Labienus took me to was large, and light and airy, the walls whitewashed, the floor of terracotta tiles. It was at the back of the house, down a long corridor that ran off to the right of the atrium, and its window looked out over an ornamental pond, covered with lilies and hornworts and purslanes with their reddish stems and dainty oval leaves. Fireflies were dancing over the water, and butterflies dropped and soared. It was charming, and I said so.

'I'm pleased,' Artixes replied. 'But there is a problem.'

'Oh, what's that?'

'The peacocks, I'm afraid. They love to come and drink here. I noticed the last time you were here that you found their screeching unpleasant.'

'Blood-curdling, more like!'

'Anyway, I've spoken to the head gardener.'

'The head gardener? How many are there?'

'Oh, ten or so. But it's a big garden. You'll see. Perhaps you'll even teach in it, like – who was that Greek philosopher?'

'Epicurus.'

'Yes, Epicurus, who taught in a garden. Anyway, the head gardener said he could and would fence off this part of the garden, but that it might take a few days. The brutes can fly, you see, after a fashion, so the hurdles will have to be high.'

'That's very kind of you, Artixes. In the meantime, I'm sure I'll survive having my blood curdled for a few days. The opposite of blood-letting. Who knows, it might even be good for me.' We both laughed.

'I'll let you settle in. There's a washroom first on your left. I'll wait for you in the atrium, and then show you where you are to teach Labienus' boys.'

I had a bed, a chest, a table and chair, plenty of lamps and candles, curtains. There was even a bronze mirror hanging on the wall. I had, it seemed, a job. And I had plans of my own. I squeezed my eyes closed and thought of Hannibal. Was his destiny unfolding too? Where was he, and how?

PROVING

I sat down on the bed and bounced gently. Not your standard Roman bed of a frame with leather straps and a mattress of straw on top — which simply slipped in lumps between the straps, as I had found out last night at Apurnia's. Extraordinary that the Romans design fleets and roads and armies and great public buildings but cannot make a bed. This, though, was a bed of solid wood, its mattress of wool. I could, I thought wryly, get used to this.

'Tell me more about the battle at Telamon,' I asked Frontinus as we rode on, passing for the first time a group of wagons going south.

'It's simple, sir. We won.'

'You know, I heard something similar from my father once! What I mean is, what was it like?'

'I'm the wrong man to ask. You'd be better speaking to one of the officers who were there. There are several with your father.'

'But I want to hear it from you.'

He shook his head. 'You'll find out, sir. You see, a soldier doesn't know what's going on. All you're trying to do is stay alive. It's smell and sweat and blood and screams and unbelievable noise and you stab and hack and slash at the man in front of you, then the next one and someone tries to break in at your side and your arms ache and your head pounds and you can't even see clearly because of the sweat pouring into your eyes under that damn helmet and the battle passes in a frenzy.'

'But surely you must know if you're winning or losing?'

'No, at least not at the time. Your maniple might not break. It might even be advancing, but you still haven't got a clue what's going on in the other maniples, elsewhere along the line.'

'You haven't?'

'No disrespect, sir, but you've got a lot to learn. In battle, your whole life is simply an arm's length around you. At Telamon, I was on the right flank. I didn't have any idea what the centre was doing, or the left. Only when the Gauls in front of me started to turn and run did I realise we might be winning.'

'So you'd broken through their line?'

'No. We just held them. I found out only later why they turned. It was our left flank that broke them, about a stade away from me.'

'And then the Gauls could see they would be encircled, so they ran?'

'I suppose so, sir. But that's what I meant when I said you should ask a staff officer. They stay out of the fighting, or try to. They see what's going on.'

'And they issue orders, move up reserves, or cavalry?'

'Again, they try to. But you wouldn't believe the noise. Can't hear a thing. At Telamon it was very windy, and that made it even worse. The only trumpet-call I remember was the one to sound the advance.'

You see, I was learning. Here, already, was much food for thought. Cavalry, and orders. What else had to change?

'Anyway, Frontinus, we won – and you survived.'

'I did, sir, though only just.' I was riding on his left. He tugged his singlet up to expose his left thigh. Just above the knee ran a long, red scar. 'See? Damn Gauls. They went for our hamstrings. Face up to you with a sword, then duck and reach behind and snip you with a dagger. If this,' and he nodded towards the scar, 'had been a hand-breadth lower, I wouldn't be here to tell you about it now.'

'But a cut hamstring, surely that wouldn't kill you?'

'If you go down in battle, sir, whether it's hacked or stabbed or pulled, believe me, you're dead.'

Yes, I had much to learn.

* * *

The schoolroom, in an outhouse at the back, was more than adequate, well-lit and simple, with a table and chair for me, a larger table and two chairs for my pupils, a blackboard on one wall and an ample supply of chalk. Artixes went off to get the other things I needed. I sat in the schoolroom, and thought about the curriculum I would follow and, I hoped, my charges too. The balance must lie in learning as I taught.

The sound of a great gong disturbed my meditation. I got up, and walked outside, to find Artixes coming down the path towards me. 'I'm sorry, Bostar, I should have warned you,' he chuckled. 'It's simply the gong for lunch. Are you hungry?'

'Well, yes, but . . .'

'But what?'

'I don't feel I could quite manage sea-hedgehogs and oysters.'

Artixes laughed, and those fine white teeth glistened in the light. 'Don't worry! We usually have just soup and bread and cheese, and some salad.'

'That doesn't sound right for Labienus.'

'No, he probably wouldn't enjoy it much, though actually, as you may have noticed the other night, he's quite a frugal eater. Quality, not quantity, is his thing.'

'And yours?'

'Ah, mine!' He laughed again. 'What does the Delphic oracle say? Μηδὲν ἄγαν: nothing in excess. I'm like the man in Labienus' favourite story about the distinguished magistrate who always tried, he said, to steer the narrow line between partiality, on the one hand, and impartiality, on the other.' I chuckled. 'Anyway, come in. Your pupils should be up now.'

'And will join us?'

'They usually manage lunch. All sorts of, ah, activities need the energy that eating brings.'

'What about Labienus?'

'No, he eats in his chambers. He has two private rooms. You won't see him until this evening.'

*   *   *

'And so, Frontinus, you served your time in the *hastati*?'

'I did, though fortunately there were no more pitched battles against Gauls. Well, there were a few skirmishes after Telamon, but I wasn't there.'

'No? Where were you?'

'In hospital, and then at home.'

'Of course. Recovering from your wound.' I was embarrassed to realise that I didn't have the faintest idea how long it took to recover from such a wound. 'And then?'

'Then I rejoined the legion, and the following spring I moved into the *principes*.'

'Where were you stationed?'

'At Placentia. Our job was to guard the River Po.'

'Which you did?'

'No, not really. Publius Furius and Gaius Flaminius were consuls that year. They had had enough of the Gauls' raids. Our settlers kept complaining about burnt farms, stolen cattle. The tax-collectors kept complaining that, as a result, there was no money to collect as we drilled and marched and schooled behind the walls of Placentia.'

'And so?'

'So we marched west, and crossed the River Clusius, and routed the Cenomani, and then burned the farms of the Insubres at the foot of the Alps.'

'You make it sound simple.'

'It was. We got the measure of the Gauls. All you have to do is withstand their first charge. If they don't break your line with that, they give up and drift away.'

'And how did you manage that?'

'It was the consul Flaminius' idea, sir. Instead of the *hastati* using their *pila*, when the Gauls charged he had them kneel down and lock their shields. The Gauls ran into a wall of shields, and the *principes* speared with *pila* over the *hastati*'s heads.'

'It sounds brilliant.'

'Well, it worked – for a while at least.'

'Until?'

'Until the Gauls learnt to stop their suicide runs. Then they just sniped at us. Our scouts would report a war party, we'd form battle order, but instead of charging they'd pick off a few men at flank or rear and then disappear.'

'I see.' I had thought of war, insofar as I'd thought of it at all, as static, played by the rules and the tactics of the military manuals. But here, it seemed, the rules and tactics were changing. Good for the consul Flaminius. I wondered what my father's reputation was. I dared not ask. 'And now you're on my father's staff, Frontinus. How did that come about?'

'I'm not just on your father's staff, sir. Remember we get a new commander, a new consul, every year. I'm attached to the staff of whoever is in command as consuls. That's why we're known as "cocks".'

'Cocks?'

'Yes, sir.' He laughed. 'Weathercocks. The consuls take overall command on alternate days – assuming their two armies are together. So we on the staff have to get used to the ways of two men, not one, and spin with the breeze.'

'I see. But who decides who is to serve the consuls?'

'All the senior centurions, sir. They decide together, and nominate two of their number. A sort of bridge, really, between the standing army and the commanders. As you know, each consul brings his own legate and tribunes and other officers.'

I didn't know, but I felt I should have. Perhaps if I'd had more time, been warned that I was about to begin my *triconium militiae*, I'd have been taught these things. As it is, I have had to learn them, and many like them, at first hand. Whether that is better or worse, I do not know. It has made me what I have been – and, for a while longer at least, depending on the verdict, what I am.

'So you had become a senior centurion, Frontinus?'

SCIPIO

'That I had, sir,' he replied with warmth and pride. 'Worked my way through the ranks, through the *triarii*. In fact, I was *primus pilus*, senior centurion, before I took my present job.'

I thought quickly. Thirty maniples of a hundred and sixty-six men each make up a legion. Two centuries make up a maniple, and each of those has a centurion in charge. So sixty centurions to each legion. To be the senior one, the *primus pilus*, was quite an honour. I looked at Frontinus, who was still only in his mid-twenties, with new eyes.

'By the way, Artixes, what are Labienus' sons called?' I asked as we walked into the dining-room.

'Oh, yes, I'm sorry. I should have told you. Corbullo and Rullus. They should be here soon. Anyway, let's start.'

No couches, this time. A long, narrow table of beech, with a bench along each side. I sat next to Artixes. A slave brought a bowl of warm water, and a towel. First Artixes, then I washed and dried our hands. We had just started on our soup when a gangly, lanky youth walked in. His brown hair was dishevelled, but his toga clean. He had, I saw, dreadful acne. Diet? Age?

'Ah, good morning, Corbullo. I was wondering where you were. This is Bostar, your new teacher,' said Artixes.

'Yeah, yeah, Father told us about him.'

'Him, Corbullo?' I said quickly, evenly. 'Do you mean "him", or me?' He stopped, awkward, halfway across the room. He blushed slightly. Good. Unruly, but malleable. 'I'd rather you addressed me in person hereafter.'

'All right, all right,' Corbullo said, and came and sat down opposite me.

Artixes was looking at me, eyebrows raised. I looked back at him, and winked.

Rullus was next. He wasn't as tall as his brother, but he was heavier. His beard, unlike Corbullo's, was almost fully grown. He was much

154

the more handsome of the two, with high cheekbones and, unlike his brother, well-spaced eyes. At least he had the courtesy to address me as he sat down, rubbing his eyes. 'Morning. I suppose you're the new teacher. What's your name again?'

'Bostar.'

'Oh yes, Bostar. Funny kind of name. Sling the bread over, Corbullo.'

We had our first lesson that afternoon. I shall never forget it. I taught nothing, but I learnt much. The boys were both late. So when they came in and sat down, I stayed exactly where I was, at my table, looking out of the window. I heard the odd whisper, their chairs scratching on the floor, a yawn.

Eventually, Corbullo said, 'Ah, we're waiting, Teacher.'

'Waiting?' I replied, without turning round. 'Parse that for me, please.'

'What?'

'Parse "waiting" for me.'

'"Parse"? What does that mean?'

'It means define the part of speech. What is "waiting"? A verb, a noun or an adjective?'

'It's a verb,' said Rullus.

'Good!' I said, turning round to face them. 'What part of the verb?' Silence. Rullus scuffed his feet on the floor. 'Is it, for example, an infinitive?'

'You're wasting your time, Teacher. We don't know that sort of stuff,' said Corbullo.

'What do you know, then?'

'Well,' Rullus sniggered, 'we can tell you where to find the best bookie in town.'

'And the best brothel,' Corbullo added. 'There's one just by the western gate with black girls. Some of them have the biggest tits you'll ever see, eh, Rullus?'

'So,' I said, 'gambling and brothels. Good old Capua. Let's start with gambling. What do you know about it?'

That puzzled them. 'What do you mean, know about it?' from Corbullo.

'When did it start? Why do people gamble? What do they gamble on? That sort of thing. Just tell me anything you know.'

So passed my first session as a teacher in Capua. My pupils proved remarkably well-informed. It was an interesting afternoon.

At Pisae, we were lucky, not only in finding a ship, but in the tide. Both were ready, even if the ship's master was hostile at best. He was a Sardinian, out of Tharros, where he was bound with a cargo of wine. 'And Tharros, if you didn't know it, is not exactly Massilia. But I'll take you there. And keep your damned *tessera* in its pouch, Centurion – or whatever you are. I won't be sending in a bill. I've been paid by Rome before. First the money, then, before you know it, the inspectors.'

Frontinus shrugged. 'As you wish.' We went below, and sat on the floor between coils of rope in the strange smells of salt and caulk and sea. 'You won't have been at sea before, sir.' A statement, not a question.

'No, I haven't.'

'Well, at least it's autumn. The passage shouldn't be too bad. Might be a bit rough, though, once we're past Corsica. But if you start feeling seasick, best get up on deck. Breathe deeply. Now, if you'll forgive me, sir, I'm going to sleep. A soldier's law, sir: sleep when you can.'

My mind was in turmoil: so much to take in. And I was going to join my father! Always, though, my thoughts kept coming back to the army, and to what I had learnt from Frontinus. What did I imagine? I suppose, a short campaign against this Hannibal, full of order and clear commands and men like Frontinus who followed them unquestioningly. Then, with my father, I would return to Rome. Then more of my *triconium fori*, and then complete my *triconium militiae* as others did, somewhere in Italy . . . The ship creaked and rolled, moving westwards through the night.

'Tell me, Frontinus, what's the most important part of a legion?' I asked him next morning, over a breakfast of dried fish and bread and figs and brackish water.

His answer was quick, and firm. 'Its spirit, sir. No matter how well trained a legion is, its spirit must be right.'

'You mean it must want to fight?'

'No. Of course the legion wants to fight, when it must. Haven't we all taken our oath to the Senate and people? It's how it fights. It must do so as one man.'

'But you said that at Telamon you felt completely alone.'

'You are and you aren't. Remember the shields, sir. Each line of the *acies* is locked together. Your shield protects you, but also the right side of the man to your left, just as your right side is protected by the man on your right. You fight as individuals, but as one line.'

'And if someone in the front line falls?'

Frontinus laughed. 'If! When, more like! It's hard to keep on your feet alive, let alone wounded – or dead.'

'Why's that?'

'The blood, sir. At Telamon, it wasn't long before we were fighting up to our ankles in blood. It gets everywhere. Down your arms and up your nose. You get so much on your hands that your sword slips. Why, we were three full days after Telamon cleaning up.'

I had never thought of that. A man contains, they say, around ten *heminae* of blood. Twelve *heminae* make a *congius*, and eight *congii* an amphora – like the amphorae that stood in ghostly rows on this ship, as tall as a man and broader. The Gauls lost, Frontinus had told me, nine thousand men at Telamon. Say each of the dead lost only half his blood as he lay dead or dying. That would be forty-five thousand *heminae*, or three thousand seven hundred and fifty *congii*, or just under five hundred amphorae of blood, spilt on a small area.

Frontinus was sitting sharpening his dagger on a small whetstone. 'Frontinus, is this a big ship? I mean, it seems it to me.'

'About as big as you get – although I'd say this one was near to overladen. That's a Sardinian for you. Heavy stuff, wine. Let's hope we don't get any rough weather.'

'And how many amphorae do you think it's carrying?'

'Oh, I don't know. Sixty, perhaps seventy. No more, or she'd sink. Why do you ask?'

'It doesn't matter.' I smiled at him. 'Just a thought. Your whetstone when you're finished, please.'

That night I dreamed of five ships, each carrying a hundred amphorae. Their crews took them to the harbour wall at Pisae, but the tide was out and the harbour was dry. One by one, they emptied out the amphorae, and soon the whole harbour was a sea of blood. The blood of Telamon. I wonder how many oceans my life has filled.

I was in my room, writing up my notes on that afternoon's – I won't call it teaching – work. As I've said, I learnt. There was a knock on the door. 'Come in!' I said.

It was one of the slaves. 'My master asks you to come to him. He wants to speak to you alone. He is in his study.'

'Where is that?'

'Follow me.'

I knocked at the door where the slave left me. Labienus opened it. He looked flustered, angry. 'Yes, Bostar,' he said at once. 'Now look here. I've just spoken to my sons. They said you spent the afternoon discussing gambling. Is that true?'

'It is, Labienus.'

'Then you'd better explain yourself. What are you up to?'

'Just something I learnt from the best teacher who ever lived.'

'Who was that?'

'Socrates, of course.'

'You're not trying to tell me that Socrates taught gambling!'

'No, I'm trying to tell you that Socrates always began his teaching with what people already knew — or thought they did. I have no idea what your sons know about mathematics, or astronomy, or rhetoric.'

'That's exactly what you're supposed to teach them!'

'Yes, Labienus, and no. Teaching should be a leading out, not a cramming in. It is a conversation, not a lecture. Your sons are far too old to be lectured to, anyway.'

'Perhaps, but still, why gambling?'

'For two reasons. First, because I wanted to begin with what your sons know. Maybe they shouldn't know about gambling, but they do. It has a history, and teaches many important lessons.'

'And the second reason?'

'Your sons and I, Labienus, will have to get on if they're to learn anything from me. They don't have to like me, but we will have to get on.'

'So you thought you would begin by sharing one of their interests with them?'

'Exactly.'

'Anything else?'

'Yes, Labienus. My interest is much more in how *people think than in* what *they think about. I'll succeed if I can help your boys to think about things, anything, in the right way.'*

'What way is that?'

'With clarity, consistency and honesty. With minds open to what lies behind things, rather than what they seem to be. With, I suppose, curiosity.'

'And what, Bostar, about facts? I am a magistrate. Laws are facts. I give judgment in accordance with the laws, not my opinions, or my' — he said this with heavy irony — *'curiosity. How you calculate*

circumference, for example, or density: these are facts, and I want my sons to learn them.'

'And I will teach them what I know of these things; when they are ready.'

His anger evaporated. He looked, as always when I had seen him, tired. 'I see, I see.' He broke off, and walked away towards his desk. There, he stopped, and turned round again to face me. 'You know, Bostar, you are a mystery, an enigma. I don't know anything about what lies behind you, and little enough about what you seem to be. Have I been rash, or foolhardy or' — he snorted — 'plain curious?'

'That's not for me to say, Labienus. But if you want me to leave, I will go.'

We looked at each other across the room, different people, different races, different lives, brought together by chance.

'All right, Bostar,' and this with a smile, 'but I don't want my sons taking you gambling — nor you them. You have your methods, obviously. Unconventional, but so are the circumstances. I'll give both time to work; or fail.' Then his face brightened. 'Let's put this behind us. I made a decision, and I'll back it. I'll see you at supper.'

Massilia's harbour was huge, and alive with ships as we sailed in. Merchantmen like ours, with two sails, skiffs and barques, barges, punts, cutters, lighters like the ones I had often seen at home on the Tiber, coasters and coracles, bobbed and tossed at anchor or glided on their way. Around them all, boys rowed in little dugouts, selling fruit and flowers, shirts, sweetmeats, honey-cakes, wine. And then, moored to the quay, I saw them, two Roman galleys, sleek and long and sinister, on their poopdecks, shining in the sun, the skins of the great drums that gave the rowers the timing of their strokes.

'Excellent!' said Frontinus beside me, leaning on the thwart.

'What is?' I asked.

'The galleys, sir. They'll have told the prefect exactly where your father is. Or at least to within a half-day's ride.'

'How's that?'

'Because the fleet and army work together, when they can. The ships carry supplies for the soldiers, and the soldiers man the ships if there's to be an engagement.'

'The soldiers do? What about the rowers?'

'The rowers, sir, row. They're slaves, not soldiers.'

'And what if the galleys have no time to pick up soldiers for a fight?'

'Their standing orders are to run. But if they can't, they ram, and hope for the best.'

'I thought galleys always rammed each other anyway?'

'That's right, sir, they do in an engagement. But see that high raised walkway, midships on both galleys?'

'Yes.'

'Well, that's the *corvus*, the crow. When we get closer, you'll see that each *corvus* has a long metal spike on each tip. And the whole walkway is hinged. When the galleys have soldiers on board, they ram the enemy ships and then drop their *corvi*. With a bit of luck and good judgment, the spike sticks firm in the enemy deck. Then the soldiers charge across, and they fight—'

'As if they were on land!'

'Exactly, sir. We copied our galleys, of course, from the Carthaginian ships we captured in the last war. But the *corvus* is an entirely Roman invention, I think of our admiral Regulus.'

'Yes, I've heard of him. He was captured by the Carthaginians, but sent to Rome with their terms for peace. The Senate said they hadn't any, and Regulus took that message back to Carthage. When they heard it, the Carthaginians cut out his tongue, and his eyes, and sent him back to Rome.'

'That's right. But do you know who cut his tongue out?'

'No. Who?'

'Hamilcar.'

'Oh yes, the Carthaginian leader. I've heard of him. My great-uncle Cornelius was consul and our commander in Sicilia when Hamilcar surrendered, and ended the war.'

'Surrendered? He didn't surrender, sir. He left. He never went under the yoke. But that's not the point. Do you know who Hamilcar's son is?'

'No, tell me.'

'His son, sir, is Hannibal.' Frontinus was looking straight ahead, towards the quay. 'Now, as I said, I'm only a soldier, but any son of Hamilcar will have an uncommon hate for Rome.'

'But surely, Frontinus, the sack of Saguntum isn't war?'

He was grave. 'Maybe, maybe not.' He turned to look at me. His voice was lighter as he said, 'Who knows? Perhaps it's just my peasant blood, but my scar feels sore today. Come on, sir, we must get ready to disembark.'

A little bleary-eyed, perhaps, but both Corbullo and Rullus were in the classroom at the appointed hour the next morning. That was a quiet victory, one Labienus would note. Such formal signs mattered little to me, but much to him. Most men live and die for such things. I was no better; I was merely different.

I had the subject of our lesson planned: prostitution. Education, after all, concerns itself with human beings. There are few professions more human than the oldest in the world.

After the usual niceties, I announced my subject for the lesson and – quickly, I admit, as their jaws dropped – began, in the best Socratic manner, with a question: 'Why, gentlemen, do you think there are prostitutes?'

'Why?' This from Corbullo. 'Because of horny goats like him!' and he dug his brother in the ribs.

'Good!' I said. 'The male urge. Sailors, for example, who spend months at sea and then need to spend their fluid. Men' – I used

the word advisedly − 'like you, who are patricians, and have heavy
responsibilities ahead of you but who are still men. Yes?'

They both nodded appreciatively.

'But is that all? Couldn't there be other reasons?'

'Like what?' asked Rullo. I had their attention, certainly.

'Well, what about religion?'

'Yes!' Rullo again. 'I hear that those Vestal Virgins are hot! I
heard that, for the right price, you can have 'em—'

'What, all of them?' said Corbullo.

I had to move things on. 'Gentlemen, consider that in Egypt,
Phoenicia, Assyria, Chaldea, Caanan and Persia, the worship of Isis,
Moloch, Bel, Astarte, Mylitta and other deities involves prostitution.'

'Whoh! That's a lot of cunt!' said Corbullo.

'Please, I'd rather we didn't use the, ah, vernacular in this room.'

So the morning advanced, slower, in the sense I wanted, than the
sun. Such was the slow learning I began in the house of Labienus.
But my way had begun.

We found the prefect's office easily, in a little house just above
the harbour. The fat, bald, sweating clerk seemed scared.

'Well, where is he, then?' Frontinus demanded.

'He's, he's gone to Rome,' the man stammered.

'On whose authority?'

'No one's. At least, I don't think so. There was no one
to ask. The reports from Saguntum have been terrifying.'
The little man leant forward over his desk and looked at us
intently. 'Do you know, they say Hannibal isn't a man at all,
but a—'

'Shut up, you fool!' Frontinus shouted. I was seeing some of
the qualities that had brought him to be *primus pilus*. 'With or
without your prefect, I need horses, food, clean clothes. And
more than that, I need to know where Scipio is!'

The clerk twisted the stylus in his hand nervously. 'Of course, sir, of course. Just help yourself to anything you need. The store-house and stables are out the back.'

'And Scipio?'

'Forgive me, sir, but which one?'

'Idiot!' Frontinus yelled. I thought he was going to hit the clerk. I reached out, and touched him on the shoulder.

'Actually,' I said quietly, 'it's a fair point, Frontinus.' I took a step towards the man's desk. 'Clerk, I am Publius Cornelius Scipio.' The man gulped, and looked even more alarmed. 'We've come to join my father, of that same name, not my uncle, Gnaeus Cornelius. Where is my father?'

'Well, sir, I can help you. For a start, the two are one.'

'Speak in plain Latin, clerk, not riddles!' barked Frontinus.

'You mean,' I said, 'the two armies have joined?'

'Exactly, sir, exactly.'

'But exactly where?'

'We had a despatch this very morning, sir, from the galleys that you saw, no doubt, in the harbour. Fine ships, wouldn't you say—'

I leant across until my face was a handbreadth from him. 'Where?'

'Your father, the consul, and your uncle, sir, the legate—'

'We know their ranks, you fool!' Frontinus hissed.

'Your illustrious relatives, sir, are near the mouth of the Rhodanus.'

'By Hercules, they've moved fast!' Frontinus exclaimed. 'On which side of the river-mouth?'

'The east.'

'And our fleet?' I asked.

'Half with your father, sir, half standing off Saguntum.'

'Then we must hurry,' said Frontinus. 'Come, sir, come.'

We covered the religious aspects of prostitution. I told my charges, for example, of the great gardens round the temple of Bel in Babylon and how each and every Babylonian woman, whether high or lowly born, must lose her virginity there and be paid by the man who has her, before she can marry. This, I explained, was ritualised prostitution, but religious. Because it takes place in the gardens of the god, it means that the god has had the woman first and so will not be jealous but bless the marriage.

As I had hoped, this interested the boys. We had an interesting conversation. They were thinking of something other than their own pleasure, at least.

'Does every woman find a man?' Rullus asked.

'They must,' I replied.

'Why's that?' asked Corbullo.

'Because to marry they must have a certificate of de-flowering from a temple priest.'

'You mean the priests inspect them afterwards?'

'They do.'

'Or do the job themselves, no doubt!' said Rullus.

'No doubt, at times,' I granted.

'But what about the ugly ones, the real bags?' Corbullo was the more thoughtful of the two.

'I don't know,' I answered. 'Perhaps they have to pay to get someone to, ah, oblige before they themselves receive a token fee.'

'Or perhaps,' Corbullo added, 'they bribe the priests for a certificate.'

And so we went on, for several days. From the religious aspects of prostitution, we passed to the legal, and finally to the medicinal. Neither of them, or so they said, had ever caught the infirmitas nefanda, *venereal disease; perhaps I saved them from that, at least. So, in a few days, through the subject of prostitution I had introduced religion, law and medicine to an unconventional but, I hoped, effective curriculum.*

The prefect's store-house was large and well-stocked. There were racks of cheeses, hams hanging from the rafters, huge amphorae of, I assumed, wine.

'See if you can find any biscuits, sir,' Frontinus said as we stood, our eyes adjusting to the lesser light. 'I'll look that way,' gesturing to his left.

'Biscuits?'

'Yes, sir. Standard rations. Barley cakes, perhaps, to you.'

'But we could get bread in the market—'

'No time for that, sir, nor a change of clothes. A ham, a cheese, some biscuits, then we go. Oh, and we'll need a water-skin each. I can see some over there.'

'You make this sound a hard journey, Frontinus.'

'Hard, sir? No. But hurried. And this is Gaul: we'll find no posting-stations here.' With that, he disappeared down an aisle between the rows of shelves.

Back outside, I screwed up my eyes against the bright light. From below, the sounds and smell of the harbour were carried to us on the breeze. The satchel Festo had given me was full again, and Frontinus' saddlebags.

'Now, the stables. Here, sir,' said Frontinus, digging into his bags. He handed me a rectangular biscuit, brown and hard. I put one end gingerly into my mouth. 'No, not like that, sir!' Frontinus exclaimed. 'You'll break your teeth. We have a joke that they use these things for ballast. Suck it, don't bite.'

So, each sucking on a biscuit, we walked further up the hill towards the stables. There were twelve horses in the stalls. I stood in the doorway as Frontinus walked to each stall in turn and looked carefully at its occupant. Turning from the last stall, he spat, hands on his hips, and shouted to me, 'No good, sir. Bloody prefects!'

'What do you mean, Frontinus? They all look good to me.'

'Good, yes – for a parade ground.' He was back beside me. 'These are fancy brutes, sir, ideal for prefects, or tax collectors, or merchants, putting on a show. But they haven't got what we need.'

'What's that?'

'Strength, sure-footedness. These are bred for their looks. Their legs, for example. Like needles. They'll break on the first rough ground. And their feet will be soft from all that straw they're bedded on. No, sir, these are no use to us. Be quicker to walk the whole way. But I know what we need.'

'What's that, Frontinus?'

'Mules, sir, we need mules.'

In a field behind the stables we found some, cropping at thin grass.

'You see!' said Frontinus angrily. 'Look at that, sir. The water-trough is dry. They give their fancy horses straw and hay and oats, but they can't even be bothered to water the mules.'

He leant over the fence and poured the contents of his water-skin into the trough. The five mules came running, pushing. 'We'll take the two that get here first, sir. Now, your water too, please.'

As he left to refill our water-skins, I watched the mangy mules, flicking at flies with ears and tails, drink. Another lesson, a new learning. It wasn't, I thought, Frontinus' peasant blood that made him side with the mules. It was the practice of survival, and war. I would raise the question of the prefect's stables with my father.

'The mule, sir, or the hinny?'

'Sorry?'

'Which of the two do you want to ride?'

I was puzzled. 'They look the same to me.' They did. Both bay-brown, now grazing again, their heads short and thick, ears long, limbs thin, manes short. 'What's the difference?'

'The one on the left's a hinny, the one on the right a mule.'

'But mules are mules, aren't they? What's a hinny?'

He smiled at me. 'No disrespect, sir, but what do they teach you patricians in Rome? A hinny's sired by an ass to a mare, a mule by a stallion to an ass.'

'How can you tell the difference?'

'Look at the line of the neck. See the hinny? Much squatter, straighter. See what I mean?'

'I can't say I do, Frontinus.'

'No matter, sir, you'll learn. Well, I'll ride the mule. I'm heavier than you, and they're stronger. Though I'm a hinny man, myself.'

'Why's that?'

'Ask any muleteer. Tremendous stamina. They never give up. They'll work until they drop, hinnies. You can't push a mule as hard. He'll lock his legs when he's tired and only a fire under him will move him. But come on, sir. We'd best be moving.' He looked up at the sun. 'We'll get a good way towards your father today, if we hurry.'

So, on what were still to me two mules, we left Massilia. As we rode abreast along the town's main street, heading west, the people stared. Smiths stopped their hammering, stallholders their haggling; children stopped their playing in the street.

'These people don't seem to like us much, Frontinus,' I said.

'They've no cause to,' he replied.

'Why? We've never fought Massilia.'

'Massiliotes never fight anyone. All they want is money. Why, they'd trade with Pluto himself, if they could do so at a profit.'

'But Rome brings them trade. We're in alliance. So why should they be hostile?'

'Because we're soldiers. We bring war, more often than peace, and war is bad for most people's trade.'

'Most people's?'

'Well, the merchants supplying the armies and fleets do well, of course. But no one else.'

'Who says we bring war?'

'Perhaps they don't say it. They're sailors. They feel things, as I do.'

'Well, I'm sure that Hannibal will be long gone, back down south. You'll be back in your garrison at Placentia within the month and I'll be back in Rome. Who knows, if I get back to my riding-school, I might even learn to ride.'

It was, I suppose, a thin joke. One sense Frontinus did not have in abundance was humour. I have always loved laughter. Now, it is leaving me, under the shadow of the verdict I am waiting for, as in autumn the light lessens. When will we hear?

'Best way to learn, sir, is to do it. You're doing fine. Right, we're almost out of the town. Ready to trot?' I nodded. 'Anyway, I've a funny feeling you'll get more practice than you bargained for.'

From Massilia, the road was of dirt but good. We rode on steadily, unspeaking. I grew accustomed to the soporific rhythm of my mule. The countryside was scrubland. Here and there, a plume of smoke or the faint yapping of dogs betrayed a village or a hamlet, but we saw no one. To our left, the saltlands reached out to the sea, their reeds shivering in the breeze. We followed the sinking sun.

Ahead of me, Frontinus reined in and dismounted. 'We'll stop here for the night, sir,' he said as I rode up.

'But there's at least an hour of daylight left, Frontinus. I thought we were in a hurry.'

'Yes, sir, but you won't see another of these tomorrow.' I followed his pointing arm and saw the spring. 'Last good water before the Rhodanus. And our mules need a good drink.'

'How can you tell?'

'Look at the flecks of white round their muzzles. Means they're very thirsty. No point in going on. Even mules founder, sir. We'll water them, and let them graze, and eat and sleep ourselves, and leave at first light. We should be with your father by mid-morning, if he's where I think he is.'

A nudging in the night half woke me. Then another, and I opened my eyes. The stars were bright, the breeze cool. Then I felt his hand, squeezing my arm. I looked over, and could just see Frontinus' face on the ground where he had gone to sleep beside me. With his free hand, he pointed to the stand of young eucalyptus trees where we had tethered the mules. I saw the shadows that the trees cast, and heard the leaves rustling in the breeze, the spring sounding behind us, nothing more.

I opened my mouth to say, 'What is it?' but felt, as much as saw, the intensity of his finger on his lips. Still, I was about to say something when, in one spring, the cloak under which he had been sleeping fell to the ground, and he was up and running forward. Beyond me, in the darkness, I heard a grunting, then a muffled shriek of pain and I too was up, bewildered, running forward to the trees and the noise. Something tripped me, and I fell. I reached out. I felt a man's beard and recoiled. My hand came back sticky. I touched the wetness with the tip of my tongue. Salty: blood. I shuddered, got to my knees and ran on.

I heard Frontinus say, 'Who are you?' I was blundering, breathless, heart pounding, through the trees. Then again, louder: 'Tell me – now or never.'

Then I stumbled on them, in a little clearing. In the starlight, I saw a dagger glisten at the man's throat and, as I came forward, he fell towards me, eyes bulging, astonished, open, blood flowing down his chest. He slumped down on to his knees, then slowly forwards, falling to the ground.

Frontinus stepped forwards. 'Are you all right, sir?' He hunched over and wiped his dagger on the dead man's back.

'All right? I'm . . . What happened?'

'Robbers, sir – or worse.'

'Worse? What do you mean?'

'Well, we'll never know now. But they could have been spies, or—'

'Spies? Wanting what?'

'This, sir.' Frontinus put his right hand on the satchel at his side. The despatches from the Senate for my father.

'Or?'

'Sorry, sir?'

'You said "or".'

'Or assassins.'

'Assassins? But why should they want to kill us?'

'Us? You're right. Not us.'

'Who, then?'

'You, sir. Is your name not Scipio? Now, get your bag, and mine, please. I'll find the mules, and then we'll ride.'

'But it's still dark.'

'If it's light enough to kill, it's light enough to ride. I wouldn't chance it on a horse, but mules are very sure-footed.'

'Why don't we wait until daybreak?'

'Because trouble, sir, is like the thistle. It comes in crops.'

So, under the starlight, we rode on, side by side. I was hungry and thirsty, shocked. The road led inland. It began to rise and fall, the trees alongside to encroach and threaten in the dark. Frontinus stopped. I did too.

'I don't like this, sir,' he said softly. 'I'd forgotten this section was so wooded. What we need is open ground.'

'You really think there could be more of them?'

'Maybe, maybe not.' A favourite phrase of his. Under his breath, he whistled gently. 'Right, we'll have to risk it. We're going to canter, not walk. Stay behind me. Any trouble, gallop, sir, break through and ride on. Don't stop or wait for me if we're separated.'

'Ride on? Where?'

'Just follow the road. It leads to the Rhodanus. Your father's camp should be by the river-mouth.'

'How far is that?'

'Two, perhaps three, hours' steady ride. Right, sir. First, I want you to take this.' Frontinus took off the satchel he carried, and handed it to me. I slipped the strap over my head and across my chest. 'Remember, sir, that's for your father's eyes only.' I nodded. My mule shifted uneasily under me. 'Second, we must both eat and drink.' He reached behind him to a water-skin, uncorked it, and took a long drink before passing it to me. The water was cold on my teeth and I shivered. It didn't stop the dryness in my mouth. People trying to murder us, and here I was on a mule in the middle of the night . . . Frontinus handed me a slab of cheese. I bit into it, but suddenly had no appetite.

'I can't eat this, Frontinus.'

'You must. I said before that soldiers sleep when they can. Same goes for eating,' he said as he chomped.

I tried again. My mule defecated, and we heard the plop, plop as its turds hit the ground.

Frontinus laughed quietly, 'You see, sir, life goes on. Take your lesson from the mule.' He patted the neck of his. 'Life goes on – though it helps if you want it to. Where's your dagger, sir? I assume you've got one?'

'It's in my saddlebag.'

'Then get it out.'

I did, and felt the handle of my first Saturnalia's dagger cold in my hand, and remembered my father's words when he gave it to me. I didn't know where to put it. Frontinus saw. 'Like this, sir,' and he hitched his tunic up to his thigh. In the dim light, I saw an unsheathed dagger, strapped to his right calf, just above his boot. 'Put the sheath back in your bag.' In the still air, the sound of the tearing was loud as Frontinus ripped a piece off the bottom of his cloak. He handed it to me. 'Now strap the dagger on to your calf, like mine. And in a fight, sir, leave it there as long as you can.'

'Leave it? But I thought—'

'Most people are off their guard when they think they're dealing with an unarmed man.' He smiled; I saw his teeth in the half-light. 'Don't look so worried, sir. We'll be fine. Just taking precautions. Why, we'll be with your father for the midday meal! Ready?'

I rubbed my face with my hands. 'Just one thing, Frontinus.'

'Yes?'

'This dagger.' It felt uncomfortable on my leg.

'What about it?'

'I only learnt about the sword and *pilum* from Lanistus. How do you use a dagger?'

'Any way you can, sir. Hamstring, throat or heart is best. But wait for the moment. Against a sword, that's just after the swing. Duck or swerve the swing, then in close, quick.'

'Will you show me?'

'I'd be glad to, sir – in camp. Now,' he said, placing his sword across his lap, 'let's ride.'

I waited until I couldn't see Frontinus in the dark, until I heard his mule move from walk to trot to canter. Then I heeled mine on and did the same. The trees cut out the starlight almost completely, but the night air was cool and welcome on my face, and the rhythm of riding soon became my own.

I heard the noise of steel on steel before I saw the shapes, and my mule, checking, brayed in alarm. Actions are so fast, and I must search far to remember them. My mule was slowing. I saw two men on shaggy garrons, swords drawn, wheeling around Frontinus on the road. I remember that my jaw dropped, that I felt the cheese I had eaten rising up my throat. I was dreaming. Frontinus' scream woke me, saved me. 'On, sir, ride on!' I kicked my mule with fury and it reared and brayed and changed its movement so suddenly that it almost threw me and I went backwards, forwards, squeezing with my thighs to stay on, dropping the reins, kicking, clinging to the shaggy neck.

We raced towards them, we were upon them, and one of them, shouting, wrenched his pony across my way. I passed so close to him that I could smell him, and my left leg grazed his pony's rump. I half heard cries, lost in the rushing wind.

The pain was quick and sharp and short and stinging. I was still leaning right over my mule's neck and something, a *pilum* I half presumed, grazed my left shoulder-blade, cutting through my cloak and shirt, and I think I heard it crash into the trees behind me as I passed, racing on. On I galloped, my head swimming, spots before my eyes, on and on as the dark lessened and the trees gave way to light, I not riding but being taken by the sureness of an animal's ancient wisdom that says run from fear.

It was only the soreness in my fingers, clenched in the mane, that stopped me, and the mule's laboured, rasping breath. Gallop slowed to canter, trot and quickly to walk. My shoulder burned. I straightened slowly, put up a hand to my face and felt it wet, soft and sticky. I looked at my hand, amazed. Mule's phlegm, its tiny bubbles bursting in the light. I reached across my chest with my right hand to my shoulder. It came back red. I remembered, my gut churning, my mouth so dry that I thought I would choke, I must ride on – what if they were coming after me? – and again and again I kicked with my heels. Reluctant and unwillingly the mule moved again to trot, then slowed and I kicked again, again, again.

I was half asleep. The road was clear and empty. We were walking, I lying on the mule's warm, scratchy, sweaty neck. I felt the sun on my back, heard the flies buzzing round and on me. The mule faltered and I kicked it, knowing nothing but the will to ride on.

I checked that the lamps were full of oil. One stood on my table. I moved another there, and turned up the wicks on both. I unpacked the box of things Artixes had bought for me. Dividers, set square, styluses, the finest beeswax tablets, five scrolls of vellum, five quills, a small round pot of ink, cork-stopped. I had specifically asked for sepia, the black liquid of the cuttlefish. The cheaper inks, usually based on charcoal or soot, I knew all about. After a few years, they fade – which is why merchants, who can hardly be taxed on accounts no one can read, prefer them. I unstopped the pot, and held it to my nose. Yes, sepia, the only smell stronger than that of the garum which had filled my nostrils all those years I was with Publius Aponius. As I have said, he was an honest man.

I checked the wax on the tablets carefully for impurities. There were none. I closed my eyes for a moment, and the image of Apurnia's boy, Hanno, filled my mind. Could it be? I pushed the thought away. I was ready to begin.

The idea had come to me as I was riding – being conveyed – to Capua under arrest. My hands were tied, so I didn't hold the reins. But I had watched the Roman cavalrymen around me. They controlled their horses, of course, through the reins. And the reins led to the bridle, and on to the bit. So what, I asked myself as we rode, controls the horse? It is not, I thought, the reins, the bridle or the bit. It is the precise angle of the rider's arm in play with reins, bridle, bit. Underlying all is angle, and it was this I wanted to explore. The angulation of the bit to the bridle, the bridle to the horse's jaw and neck, of the rider's forearm and biceps. What seemed is not what was, and I was returning to geometry, a study of my childhood, a passion of my father before the—. I should tell of this, I suppose. In time. Now I shall just say: before they came, and took me away.

I sat down, settled in my chair. It had a comfortable, padded seat of horsehair, overlaid with leather. There was much comfort in the house of Labienus. There was a polite, soft knock on my door. 'Venite. Come in,' I said loudly, turning round.

It was Artixes. 'Ah, you are working, Bostar.'

'No, about to, Artixes. But come in. Sit on the bed.' I got up, and turned my chair towards him.

'Thank you. I just came to see how you were. I'm sorry I missed *you at supper. But you had your pupils for company?'*

'Yes, and Labienus.'

'Did that go well?'

'Very. The boys entertained their father with tales of prostitution.'

Artixes gave a gentle chuckle. 'Well, I'm sorry I missed that.'

'Oh, I'm sure it's a subject Rullus and Corbullo will revert to. But where were you?' I asked.

'Out.'

'Out? That's rather mysterious, Artixes. The riddles of the house of Labienus grow.'

'Not as far as I'm concerned, Bostar. I was out seeing a patient.'

'You're a doctor?'

'I am. Or so they call me. I treated Labienus for gout some years ago, and then he asked me here.'

'And who was your patient this time?'

'A tailor. Labienus', among others. He has good clients, and works hard — or did.'

'Did?'

'Yes. He hasn't worked for several weeks now.'

'Why's that?'

'A case of much from little. So common, I'm afraid. A needle through his left index finger, but the wound turned septic and now his blood is poisoned. He's very ill.'

'Feverish?'

'Yes.'

'Hallucinating?'

'Yes.'

'How are his irises?'

Artixes smiled, and shook his head. I saw it turn, in and out of the shadow of the lamp. 'Well, there's even more to you than I thought, Bostar of Chalcedon. So you're a doctor as well as a teacher?'

'No, but medicine interests me. I have seen much illness, of the body and the mind, in the life that I have led.'

He was about to reply, then changed his mind. He yawned,

and rubbed his eyes. 'I'm sorry. I'm tired. We must continue this conversation in the morning. Anyway, you have all you need?'

I stood up. 'Thank you, Artixes. All I need, and more. Good night.'

'Until tomorrow, then. Good night.' He smiled, got up, went out, and softly closed the door behind him. He was a man about whom I wanted to learn more. Do humans also approach each other through angles? I wondered. A fancy. I would begin with more staple fare.

I felt the drumming coming through the earth towards me. Hide. I must hide. The mule needed no encouragement to stop. I slipped off, fell, tottered to my feet. The sound was closer now, coming from the west. I took the mule's bridle, and tugged. There was a bed of reeds, just off the road; we would hide there. The mule locked its legs and brayed quietly. Then, pulling me, it lay down, panting in short, laboured bursts. I – couldn't I too lie down, and sleep, and dream, and be back in Rome, and be back in Hispala, up and down, soft on soft? I felt tears welling up, of frustration, weariness, confusion, pain.

'Remember, you are a Scipio.' My father spoke to me. To this day I am sure he did. There was no sympathy: just fact. I was, and I am, a Scipio and as now, I await the verdict of the Senate and the people of Rome, so then did I assume what I am in my being and my blood.

I shook myself. I took a water-bag from the mule's bag, checked I still had the satchel of despatches, felt the dagger strapped to my calf. Unsteadily, I walked into the reedbed as the drumming of the horses' hooves came closer and, looking back, I could see the shifting cloud of dust they raised as they came on.

Lying from long ago there was the bole of an old oak tree,

half-sunk in the mud. I squatted down behind it, feeling my shoulder's pain. I could not run from men on horses. Where was Frontinus, alive, wounded or dead? Disordered thoughts and images floated round my brain like refuse on the Tiber. The long, straight Via Flaminia. The amphorae on the ship that took us to Massilia. Blood. Men drowning in blood at Telamon. Euphantus' fastidious fingers, writing on wax. I concentrated on the road. The shapes I saw swam away before my eyes. I hauled them back again. I saw their colour. They were cavalry of Rome.

I stood up. 'Here!' I tried to shout, but could only croak, for my throat was dry. My lips cracked; I licked them. 'Here!' I managed, waving my right arm.

I don't suppose they heard me, but they saw. The *turma*, thirty horse and thirty riders, stopped. Their dust billowed round them, their armour shone in the sun as I half walked, half ran back through the reeds and the ground squelched under my feet.

Two ran towards me, taking off their helmets as they came. 'Are you Scipio minor?' called the taller of the two.

'I . . .' I stammered. 'That is who I am.'

They were beside me. 'I am Sulvio, sir, decurion in the army of your father. He sent us to find you.'

'How . . . how did he know?' I managed.

'Prisoners, sir. They told us. But your father will explain. Can you ride?'

'Yes.'

'But you're wounded.'

Gingerly, I felt my shoulder. 'A scratch.'

'Where's Frontinus?' the second cavalryman asked brusquely.

'I don't know. Back there.' My head was spinning. 'There was a fight, a second ambush—'

'A second!' Sulvio interrupted.

'Yes. Frontinus told me to ride on. I burst through.'

'This is bad, Antinus,' Sulvio said to the second cavalryman. 'Take ten men. Go back, and see if you can find Frontinus.' Antinus turned. 'But be careful.'

'I will be. Don't worry.'

Sulvio put an arm round me and began to lead me towards the waiting troop, ten of whom, with Antinus, were already turning back east, churning up the dust. 'Right, sir. Let's get you to camp. Can you ride?'

'Yes. But my mule, it's very tired.'

'More than tired, I think, sir, from what I saw. We'll ride two up. How's your shoulder?'

'Aching.'

Sulvio stopped, and inspected the cut through my cloak, tunic and singlet. 'You're right. A scratch. But it'll need careful cleaning, or it'll fester. We'll see to that in camp.' He reached up to his forehead, and wiped away the sweat. 'Oh, one more thing, sir. Frontinus had despatches for your father.'

I patted my side. 'Here. Under my cloak.'

Sulvio sucked in his cheeks and nodded. 'Then your father will be doubly pleased.'

Back on the road, the other riders were waiting. They looked at me impassively. To one side was my mule, now lying on its side, panting hard, desperate to breathe. I moved towards it. Sulvio put a hand on my shoulder. 'No point, sir. I'll see to it.' He took three steps and knelt down beside the mule to which I owed my life. So quick, everything was so quick. The white flash of a dagger, the sudden spurt of blood and as I was helped on to Sulvio's horse I saw the poor brute twitching, its life leaving as the red blood from its neck stained the ground. Was Frontinus' blood, I wondered, doing the same?

We trotted steadily, three abreast. I think I dozed, my arms round Sulvio's waist, the scabbard of his sword rubbing and dancing on my thigh, my saddlebag on the back of the horse beside. We stopped once, and each man drank from his water-skin and ate dried beef and the barley cakes Frontinus had introduced me to. I walked off to some scrub to urinate. Sulvio joined me. 'Not far now, sir' was all he said as our urine spattered the dried and crackling leaves. Remounted, he looked back. I tried to too, but my shoulder screamed.

'Antinus?' I asked.

Sulvio shook his head. His face was set and glum. 'I wish I knew what by Jupiter is going on. Troop,' he shouted, 'ride!'

The air was salty now. The land to our left ran in a flat and featureless plain towards the sea. Here and there, abandoned saltworks stood out white. Gulls soared and squawked in the shifting wind. We climbed a steady rise, walking now, and Sulvio turned his head and said, 'Now, sir, you'll see.'

Across a low valley, shining, almost blinding in the sun, a wide white ribbon seemed to lie across the earth. It was enormous, reaching north as far as I could see.

'The Rhodanus?' I asked Sulvio.

'Yes, sir. And there' – he pointed with his left hand to the river-mouth – 'is your father's camp.'

I saw it, standing proud on the plain. A perfect tiny square, it seemed. I could make out the grey-white canvas of tents, and rising from it the smoke of many fires. Just beyond it, where the huge river yawned into the sea, I could see ships – or were they galleys? – that looked like floating leaves.

Against the pain I turned my head north and east again. Something shone and burned in the light. I rubbed my eyes, and looked again, this time sure I saw them, great white shapes dancing, gleaming, returning the light's reflection, high above the blue sky in the clouds. No wonder, I thought, that we call them 'the White Ones'; white for the priests, white for the gods, white for these mountains, which, too, lie beyond.

Sulvio noticed me staring. 'First time you've seen 'em, sir?'

I nodded. 'Yes, they're quite a sight, those Alps. They say this river rises there, sir, fed by all that snow. Doesn't look to me as if any of it ever melts, though.'

'Have you ever been there, Sulvio?'

He spat. 'No, sir, thank the gods. Don't want to, either: freeze your balls off. It's only crazy Gauls that go there. No wonder they have so much hair. But the Alps have their purpose, that's for sure.'

'What's that?'

'They keep Rome safe, sir, from the west, better than a wall and gate and key.' He turned in his saddle, and looked up and away towards the Alps. Under the nose guard of his helmet, I saw him purse his lips and frown. 'So what's that bloody Hannibal up to, then?' he muttered, almost to himself.

'What do you mean?'

'You'll hear more from your father, but those men who ambushed you . . .'

'Yes?'

'He sent them.'

'But that's impossible!' I exclaimed.

'That's not what we learnt from those prisoners we took. He's got a whole network of spies and informers, right across northern Celtiberia and Gaul. And he pays them well.'

'But for what?'

'Exactly! You tell me, sir. You've seen the Alps now. He's got nowhere to go but south again. He hasn't even got a fleet. Our galleys have scoured the coast, right down to the Pillars of Hercules. So what's it all about?'

'I don't know, Sulvio. You tell me.'

'Me, sir? What do I know? I'm just a decurion — and one who was sent to bring you to your father, not to talk about things I don't understand.' He cleared his throat, turned round, and took up the reins again. 'Troop, to camp, at a canter!'

In theory I knew what to expect. First the ditch, then the rampart wall, made of the soil from the ditch and reinforced with sods of grass and wooden stakes. As we approached, I saw both those things, and beyond the wall, between the camp and the river, I saw the mules and horses, the cattle grazing. It seemed a perfect site. Grazing, water, and clear ground for miles around, with no cover from which an attack could come. As we rode up, a flock of storks, disturbed, rose up from the edges of the river-mouth beyond us and flew ponderously away.

Trumpets sounded. The camp gate swung open. We rode in. What I was not prepared for was the order. In front of me ran a main street, with avenues leading off it. The tents stood in neat rows. To my left was a parade ground, clear space between the rampart and the tents. No fire-arrow or javelin could cross it to the tents. I heard the sound of a smith's hammering on an anvil, fixing weapons or tack. To my right, again in clear ground, I saw what I assumed were the kitchens, judging by the spits and water-barrels outside the long, low tent. This was order, peace. This, I thought, is where my father is.

So, angles. But to angles we give numbers, and it was on those that I began to work that night. I wanted to try to move beyond the simple quantity of numbers to what I thought of as their quality. We can talk of five apples and three pears. But what are five and three, apart from the apples and pears?

That, I thought and think, is what Pythagoras meant when he said, 'All is arranged according to Number.' Yes, 'twoness', 'threeness', 'fourness' and so on are composed of two, three and four units. But they are also wholes, unities in themselves. So a right angle, for example, we describe as one of ninety degrees. That is its quantity. What is its quality?

Consider a revolving sphere. When we see one, we think instinctively of its axis. Through that sphere there runs a line with no objective existence, but one which is no less real for that. We can determine anything about that sphere, such as its inclination, or speed of rotation, only by considering this non-existent line. The quality of number, then, is analogous to that immobile, unmanifest axis. What is not, is.

Apply this analogy to the two-dimensional plane. Take a circle and a square. Give the value 1 to the diameter of the circle, and also to the side of the square. The diagonal of the square will always be a number without finite quantity. But it, too, is no less real for that. And in the case of the circle, if we give the value 1 to its diameter, the circumference will always be an infinite number. That is why the Greek mathematicians give it not a number, but a symbol, π.

So in Capua I studied numbers. Everything must have an opposite. There would be no cold without heat, no something without nothing. What is the opposite of the number 1? No people that I know of have the answer. The Egyptians, the Babylonians, the Chaldeans, the Carthaginians, the Greeks, even the Assyrians and Hittites, all had numbers long before the Romans, but all begin with 1. What, though, is 'not 1'? Perhaps 'not 1' cannot be. Why not?

But these are subjects for a treatise, not the biography of Publius Cornelius Scipio Africanus, the greatest Roman, I believe, ever to have lived. Anyway, his account is developing an urgency of its own which is ill-served by my enquiries. Let those to come who may read this account think of me for the next few years settled in Labienus' house in Capua, teaching Rullus and Corbullo, working out my numerical and geometric theorems, and coming to practise medicine with Artixes.

There are other matters worthy of record: those concerning the widow Apurnia, for example, and her son, Hanno. There may be time for that, there may not. And although important, the next few years were for me full of ordinary lives. You will find them, differing as to form but never as to substance, in any town, anywhere in the world, now and in years to come. The life of Scipio, though, now began to shape the world. So, also because I do not know how much more time we have, let Bostar of Chalcedon be silent for the most part, and leave Scipio to his memories.

Besides, Scipio no longer goes round the estate. He used to dictate to me for two or three hours a day; now it is for seven or eight. My fingers were sore at first from so much writing, but they are used to it now. There is a desperate urgency in Scipio that moves me, a deep sense of an end. No longer does he seem to need contemplation, as a silver moon rests reflected on a silent pond. And yet in all these battles and politics, I cannot hear or feel the warmth and kindness of the man I love. That may come. We shall see. Besides, when two ride a horse, one must ride behind. So, be silent, Bostar, say little and be carried. Journeys contain their own ends.

Sulvio reined in, dismounted. I did the same. 'Right, sir. I'll take you to your father.'

I followed him, my thirst and stiffness forgotten, my heart pounding, up the main street. It had to be the consul's tent, by far the largest, set apart, a blue consul's colour flying languidly from a spear-shaft in the ground. We were almost there when the tent flap was jerked open. Sulvio stepped aside.

He came out, in armour; his hair was greyer, his beard streaked with white. He took one look and held me with his eyes before taking three quick steps forward and he reached out, a hand on each of my shoulders, and saying softly, 'Welcome, my son.' I flinched. He saw. His face tightened with concern, and he said, 'You're wounded!' Then 'Sulvio!' he barked.

Sulvio snapped to attention. 'Sir!'

'What's been going on?' my father demanded

'Sir, this is how we found him.'

'And Frontinus?'

'We don't know, sir. Antinus is looking. There was an ambush.'

'An ambush! Where?'

'In the woods after Massilia, sir. But you'll have to ask—'

'It's all right, Father,' I interrupted. 'I can tell you. But first, you must read these.' I reached under my cloak, felt for the strap and with my right hand lifted the satchel over my head.

His eyes were intense, clear. 'From the Senate?'

'Yes, Father. Frontinus had them. But . . .'

'Never mind. This is a poor welcome for my son.' He turned again to Sulvio. 'I want a full report. By the next watch. Now go and get the bath slaves, and the doctor. Then see to your horses.' Sulvio saluted, turned. 'Oh, and Sulvio, I want to see Antinus the moment he gets back. Send him straight to me.'

'Yes, sir.'

'Now, Publius.' My father smiled at me. 'Goodness, you've grown into a man since last I saw you. Come in.' As we walked into the tent, the two guards on either side of the entrance didn't move. They might have been made of stone.

The tent was cool and airy. I saw a chest that I recognised from our house in Rome, a low bed, a washstand, a table and four chairs and, in the far corner, swords and armour, *pila*, a pile of bridles and reins. But most of all, I saw my father.

He led me to a chair. 'Now, sit down, Publius. Let's look at that shoulder.' He leant forward to take off my cloak.

'It's all right, Father. Shouldn't you read the despatches first?'

'And ignore a wounded son? Come on, now your shirt.' He peered at the cut intently for a moment. 'So, Fortuna has smiled on you, Publius Cornelius Scipio. A graze. No harm done, but it does need cleaning. Where's that doctor? He's a Cretan, I think. They're always late, Cretans. Always praying to some god, or making potions under a full moon. Still, he's good. What was it? A *pilum*?'

'Yes. But it was dark. It all happened so quickly. I think Frontinus saved my life. I just rode,' I blurted out.

'First things first. Hasten slowly. A drink, food, a bath and the doctor. Then we'll talk. There's no sign of that brigand Hannibal. We'll have lots of time to talk before we're called back to Rome.'

At the washstand, from a bronze pitcher, my father poured

water into a heavy gold goblet and handed it to me. He walked briskly to the tent flap, and stuck his head out. 'A plate of stew,' he said. 'And some bread. On the double.' Back facing me, he grinned. 'It's good to see you, Publius. I want to hear all about your time with Fabius, and your trip.'

'But what about Hannibal, Father?'

'What about him? As I said, disappeared. I admit, I was very worried when I heard about Saguntum. But he's gone. Your uncle and his army have been looking for him for days: nothing. Probably gone back to Gades, or wherever he came from.'

'But we heard Uncle Gnaeus was with you.'

'That's right. He was. He force-marched from Placentia, and as soon as he arrived I sent him out to scout – for nothing, it seems.'

'But the ambush?'

'Gauls, I should think. They'll do anything for gold.'

'You caught some?'

'Yes. Under, ah, persuasion, they told us all about it. That's why I sent Sulvio to find you.'

'But didn't Hannibal pay them?'

'He did, but that needn't mean much.'

I took a sip of water. 'Then what was he up to, Father?'

'This is border country, Publius, bandit country. Someone's always stirring up trouble. If it's not the Celtiberians, or one of their interminable tribes, it's the Carthaginians. If it's not the Carthaginians, it's the Gauls. Youthful high spirits. That's all I think Hannibal's been up to. I've probably stirred everyone up for nothing. His sack of Saguntum was probably just a prank. He's young. He'll settle down, and get back beyond the Ebro, and we'll get back to Rome. We settled all this, remember, after the last war. There's a treaty. Hannibal will keep it – or else.'

Two slaves came in carrying large bowls of steaming water, then a third with a shallow tin bath. They crossed the tent and went behind a cotton screen.

'Good,' my father said. 'It's not exactly what you're used to, Publius, but it'll do. Get in. I'll read those despatches while you wash. Try and get the worst of the blood off your shoulder. They'll help you.'

I was sitting, mildly embarrassed, in the little bath, one of the slaves gently washing my shoulder with a cloth, and watching the light through the canvas dapple the grass. So much to come to terms with, to try to understand.

My father shouted, 'Great gods! Publius, I don't believe it!' and came behind the screen. In his hand, he held a scroll of finest vellum. At once, I recognised the careful writing of Fabius Pictor. I struggled up. A slave wrapped me in a robe.

'What is it, Father?'

Until I die I shall always remember how, standing dripping in a cheap tin bath inside a tent beside the mouth of the Rhodanus, I heard the news that has shaped my life.

My father was intense. His voice was clipped, his face tight. 'It is simple, Publius. It is war. We have declared war.'

'On Hannibal?' I asked. 'Or on Carthage?'

'Both. My orders are to find his army, wherever it is, and exterminate it. Meanwhile, the Senate plans to launch an attack on Carthage from Sicilia, under my colleague Sempronius.'

'But why? I don't understand.'

'We'll talk on the march.'

'We're striking camp?'

'Within the hour. Get dressed, Publius. There are clean clothes in the chest. Oh, and you'd better put on some armour, once the Cretan's dressed your shoulder. And eat. I'll be back for you shortly.' He turned and went out of the tent; I heard his footsteps fade away.

On the table, he had left the despatch from Fabius. I picked it up. I would, I think, have read it; but just then the doctor came in.

I was buckling on a breastplate when my father came back

with two men, both in armour but without helmets, sweating, looking, I thought, worried. 'Ah, good, Publius. How's that shoulder?'

'Better, Father. The doctor says it'll heal quickly.'

'That's a blessing. I feel everything's going well, Publius. If Fortuna keeps smiling, we'll soon have Hannibal sorted out, won't we, Priscus? Oh, forgive me. You haven't met my son. Publius, this is one of my tribunes and clients, Priscus Laelius.'

'I'm pleased to meet you. Your son is my friend.'

'Yes. I know about your lessons with Euphantus,' Priscus said, uncomfortably, with a hollow and forced laugh. He was short and squat and quite unlike Laelius. His nose was splayed, his nostrils wide, his eyes too close together, his forehead low.

'And this, Publius, is my first tribune, Scribonius.'

'Welcome to camp, sir,' Scribonius said.

'Thank you,' I replied. I liked the look of him: blond, with clear blue eyes that looked straight at you, and fine skin. There was a mottled scar across his brow. Sword, I wondered, or *pilum*?

'Right,' my father said. 'There'll be time enough for pleasantries when this jaunt is over. Scribonius, how soon can we leave?'

'The vanguard right away, sir. The rest of the army by the fourth watch.'

'So we can get to the ford upriver by late afternoon?'

'Yes, sir.'

'Good. See to it, Scribonius. We'll camp there, and cross in the morning.'

'But why don't we cross by ship?' asked Priscus.

'Because, my friend, of time. Remember, half the fleet's standing off Saguntum. No, we'll use the ford. Anyway, I've just sent a message to the admiral, telling him to make all speed for Sicilia. Sempronius'll need all the ships he can get his hands on. Scribonius, send the camp surveyors on ahead. Nothing fancy tonight. No ditch. Just a palisade, if the ground's right. And I want a messenger to find my brother and his army. They should only be an hour or two's ride north. Tell him to join me. We'll be heading south.'

'South, sir?' There was astonishment in Scribonius' voice. 'But the last we heard of Hannibal, he was north-west of here.'

'And since then, what have we heard, eh?' Both Scribonius and Priscus looked at their feet. 'Exactly. Nothing. Where would you go, if you faced being caught between a Roman army and the Alps? No, he'll have turned south. A few more of our allies to burn on his way home. We'll catch him.'

We heard angry voices raised outside the tent. '. . . Told to report . . .' 'You can't. Council . . .'

My father went to the flap. 'Ah, Antinus. It's all right. Let him in.'

The cavalryman Antinus came in. 'Sulvio told me to report, sir,' he said. His jaw was set. His eyes were flaming. I felt anger in him, pain.

'And?' my father said.

'We found this, sir.' From behind his back, Antinus held out a broken sword. 'I know it, sir. It's Frontinus'.' His voice was clipped.

'Is that all?'

'No, sir. We found one dead Gaul, a horse with a broken leg, and blood along the road, leading into the trees.'

'Did you follow it?'

'As far as we could, sir. But the undergrowth became very thick.'

'I see. Right, dismissed. You too, Priscus and Scribonius.' As Antinus left, he looked at me. And for the first time in my life, I felt someone's hate.

When they had gone, as my father was buckling on his greaves, I said, 'Father, Antinus seemed very upset about Frontinus.'

'Yes, he did, didn't he? But then, so he should.'

'Why's that?'

'Because Frontinus, Publius, is his brother. Or perhaps I should say, by the sound of it, "was".'

He on a roan gelding, I on a bay mare, my father and I sat ready to lead the vanguard from the camp. I was amazed at how quickly and quietly the tents had been taken down, the wagons loaded, the beasts corralled, marching order assumed. In row after row behind us, in the now tentless square, fifteen thousand Roman soldiers stood impassive in the autumn sun, each carrying his weapons, a pack, a stake for the palisade, a spade. Behind them, against the back wall of the camp, the *turmae* of cavalry were mustered, ten to each legion, nine hundred horsemen in all. I thought of what Frontinus had said. Just for scouting, that was ample. For anything else, was it enough?

Nearest me, standing apart in five maniples, were the strangest men I had ever seen. Their skins were almost black, and their hair was short and curly. They wore no armour, but leather jerkins and a kind of skirt of animal skin; no boots, but thick leather sandals. Each had round his waist a belt and a pouch, and in his hand what looked like a leather strap.

My father saw me looking. 'Yes, they're quite a sight, my Baliaridean slingers. But wait until you see them in action, Publius. They've routed Gauls for me without our throwing so much as a single *pilum*. With those slings of theirs, they can split open a man's head from three hundred paces. Incredibly accurate – though they take for ever choosing the right stones for their pouches. They drive Scribonius mad.'

'But look at the rest of them. Even after twenty years it still thrills me, Publius. No wonder men fear Rome.'

'How can so many men get ready so fast?'

'I thought this was a trifle slow, actually – but then, it was unexpected. But they're fast because they're practised. Did you notice how silent the camp was? How few orders were called?'

'Yes, Father, I did.'

'That's how it should be. The Roman army always knows what to do – as Hannibal will soon find out.'

'How's that, Father?'

'Again, practice, drill, exercise. That's what we take the word for "army" from, after all. Why, didn't Euphantus teach you any etymology?' He smiled. I blushed a little. I did know, but I'd forgotten.

Yes, I know, Bostar, that again. But there is no time now for digression. Who knows when the verdict will come? So let me hurry, as what happened then was hurried.

My father raised his left arm, then kicked his horse forwards. I was riding, beside my father, with fifteen thousand men, to war and—

'Blast!' my father said beside me.

'What is it, Father?'

'I forgot the libations. Should have let the priests do their stuff. Oh well. You remember the story of your maternal great-great-uncle in the first Punic war?'

Of course I did. Before the great sea-battle of Ecnomus, Manlius Vulso had, as custom demanded, consulted the sacred chickens on his deck. They were thrown barley. If they ate it, that was a good omen, and he should attack; if not, not. The chickens wouldn't touch the barley. My uncle had them thrown overboard, saying, 'If they won't eat, let them drink.' He attacked.

'He won the battle, Publius,' my father went on, 'and we won the war. Even so, the legionaries like the omens to be taken – especially when they're favourable. Remember that.' I did.

The column stretched behind us in the weakening autumn light. 'Father, what did the despatches say?'

'I told you. War.'

'Yes, but why?'

191

'Apparently the Senate sent envoys straight to Carthage from Ostia by fast ship.'

'Fast, Father? How long does it take?'

'So many questions!' He laughed. 'It takes, Publius, a day and a night, perhaps a day and a half, if the winds are right and the rowers strong.'

'I see. So that's why I waited for four days.'

'What's that?'

'Nothing, Father. You were saying . . .'

'Yes.' He looked at me strangely, then went on, 'The Senate told our envoys to offer the Carthaginian elders peace or war. There has been so much trouble like this. Illyrians, Gauls. We had to make an example of Hannibal. By peace we meant restitution for Saguntum, a new treaty and Hannibal in chains. Well, the Carthaginians chose war. Simple as that.'

'But what about the peace treaty after the last war?'

'Not worth a thing. The Carthaginians never kept to it, anyway. They're trading on all the routes they agreed not to. In the east, particularly, their pirates have been troubling our merchant ships, and we've been protesting for years.'

'The Carthaginians have been attacking our ships?'

'No. At least, not yet. Demanding harbour dues, that sort of thing. That's the key to Carthaginians, Publius. Their only interest is in trading, and making money. I for one have been thinking for some time that we should act. I'd have said so in the Senate, if I hadn't been tied up with the Illyrians, and then the Insubres.'

'Act, Father? What do you mean?'

'I told you this was bandit country. High time we made a province of it right down to the Ebro, and maybe beyond. Fine ground, too, there. Grows good grain. So, thanks to the Carthaginians we can now claim southern Gaul and northern Celtiberia and make provinces of them, get some order – once we've dealt with Hannibal and his so-called army.'

'Why "so-called", Father?'

'Because it'll be just another Carthaginian mercenary rabble. No discipline, no tactics. We learnt in the last war how to deal with them.'

Because my father was looking over his shoulder at the column we were leading, it was I who first saw the horsemen coming: two of them, at the gallop, cloaks streaming, *pila* bobbing as they rode.

'Father, look!' I called out.

'Ah, scouts! I wonder what they've found.' They rode straight towards us across the grassy, marshy plain. Ducks burst up beside them and squawked away, dropping their dung. My father raised his right arm high in the air to stop the column. My mare shifted on her feet.

'*Salvete*, consul. And you, sir,' the first of the two said, slipping over his horse's neck to the ground.

'So it's you, Calvus,' my father said. This was the father I knew, always remembering people's names. 'Publius, this is Calvus. Best scout we've got.'

'Thank you, sir.' Calvus was grinning broadly. He was so covered in dust, he looked almost black. He was slight and short, with a small, fat nose, hardly any older than me.

'Right, Calvus. What have you got for us?'

'The camp, sir, the camp!'

'Whose?'

'Hannibal's, sir – well, it could only be. We saw elephants, and heard them.'

'Where?'

'Across the river. Three hours' ride north of here, sir.'

'North!' my father exclaimed. 'Damn. How many, would you say?'

'Hard to tell, sir. The camp's on a rise. We couldn't get very close. No cover, either.'

'No matter. If they do outnumber us, it won't be by enough.

Right, Calvus, change horses. Go and find my brother. Tell him to meet me there. Tell him I want him to approach the camp from the north. And you,' he asked the other scout, 'what's your name?'

'Marcus, sir.'

'Right, Marcus. You'll show us.' With that, my father turned to his staff behind us. 'Trumpeter, sound "Forced march". Priscus, fall back with two maniples and see to the wagons, beasts, followers and sick. How are those men with fever, by the way? Never mind. Wait for us at the ford. I dare say we'll be back tomorrow night.'

We crossed the ford and marched on. There was no noise, only the susurrating tramping, almost running, of many men, fast enough to keep our horses at a brisk walk. No talking, no singing. This was a machine.

My father rode up and down the line, encouraging, cajoling. Scribonius and I rode abreast through the silent, eerie hills. We didn't talk. High above us, buzzards soared and dropped. The rock and earth around us were dark red. As we moved further from the river, the land became parched and hard. There was little vegetation, and what there was was bleached and barren from a summer of harsh sun.

The light was turning. My father rode up at a trot. 'Right, Scribonius. That plateau ahead will have to do, even if there isn't water. We'll camp there for the night.'

Scribonius nodded. 'I'll pass the word.' He wheeled his horse away, leaving me and my father again in the van.

'Forgive me, Father, but you said "camp". Shouldn't we keep marching, and then just bivouac for the night?'

'What!' He slapped me on the back. My shoulder twinged; I hope I didn't show it. 'You saucy pup, Publius!' he laughed. 'Still, it shows you're trying to think. That's what Fabius was supposed to instil in you.' He looked round, and back at me again. 'No, we shouldn't keep marching. Understand this,

Publius. Standing orders: every Roman army always makes a proper camp when on the march, each and every night. Remember that.'

'I will, father. But . . .'

'But what?'

'Doesn't that slow it down a lot?'

'It does, but that doesn't matter. We get there in the end, as we will to Hannibal and his rabble, and our men will feel rested and secure. We're not Gaulish bandits, you know, or Carthaginian brigands skulking around. You may not have a tent tonight because of this forced march, but we'll be in a proper camp. Now come on, I'll race you to the plateau.'

I sat and watched the camp form around me. A piece of Rome on a plateau above the Rhodanus. First the soldiers built a palisade from the stakes they each carried and such brush and wood as they could find. My father spared them, at least, the ditch. Next they dug the latrines, and screened them. Then the tribunes and the centurions marked out the sections of the square, one for each maniple, and the decurions of each cavalry *turma* set up their horses' picket-lines.

The men laid out their bedding-rolls beside their packs, took off their armour and, as the day died and the light lessened, the cooking began.

I wondered about the fires. I thought of Frontinus and his barley biscuits. Would they not have done, or was a hot meal more important? Anyone for stades around would now know where we were. Did that matter, when we had a palisaded camp? But at what cost of time? The Roman army worked as it had done for centuries: was it time to change? Seeds were forming in my mind.

My father and I sat together that night for the first time in almost a year, round a fire, eating first some kind of stew (I did not ask of what), and then dried figs, and drinking from our water-skins. What one ate, all ate, I saw. This was the army of Rome.

We talked, about Rome, and our home, and my brother, and my sister, and Fabius and other things that do not matter now. Of my mother, and her death, we said nothing. Even now, thirty-seven years later, when I have seen and known almost everything there is beneath the sun or in the restless heart of man, the loss of my mother is something of which I do not know.

'Come on, sleepyhead!' I heard my father's teasing voice, and felt his gentle kick. I opened my eyes, sat up. Everyone around me was dressed, in armour, most round their cooking-fires, on which iron pots of porridge steamed in the chill morning air.

'How's that shoulder today?' my father asked.

'Fine,' I said, rubbing it. The truth is that it ached and throbbed, more, I think, from sleeping on the stony ground than from the wound. I threw off the cloak under which I had slept, and pulled on my boots. I stood up in my tunic.

'A great day to be alive, Publius!' my father said. 'Today, you'll see the might of Rome, led, as so often, by a Scipio. Now, porridge?'

'In a moment, Father. I'll just go to the latrine.'

The soldiers I passed eyed me with curiosity. Near the latrines, they were already taking their stakes from the palisade. The sun had yet to rise over the eastern hills, but Rome's army was almost ready to march.

The forced march was harder that morning, at least for the legionaries. The ground was much more uneven and, to pass the clumps of stunted holm-oaks spread across the hills, the ranks often had to break.

My father grew impatient. 'Go and sort them out, Scribonius!' he shouted over his shoulder. 'Change order to file!' I looked back.

Scribonius heeled his horse forwards, and came abreast with my father. 'File, sir?' he asked.

'You heard me!'

'But that will lengthen the column to—'

'To around three stades, I should think. It doesn't matter. At least we should get there this morning, and not in time for next year's Saturnalia! Our van alone will sort Hannibal out. Move the maniples of *principes* forwards. They'll deal with mercenary rabble on their own.'

Did I detect a raising of an eyebrow on Scribonius' handsome, blond-bearded face? 'Yes, sir,' he said, and wheeled away.

'Why, Father, did Scribonius question your orders?' I asked as we rode on.

'Oh, ambush. A long, thin line is easily broken. That's why we usually march ten abreast. But not in this damned country. Look over there!' I followed his nod and, below and beyond us in a clearing, saw a huddle of rough huts, their sides of wattle, roofs of sod and, on their right, what looked like charcoal pits. 'These people couldn't ambush a baby,' he went on.

'But there don't seem to be any there.'

'What, babies?' We both laughed.

My father scanned the hamlet, and the surrounding trees. 'No, there aren't any people. Scared away, I should think. Ah, look, here comes Calvus!'

Down the hillside ahead and to our right, Calvus and two others were picking their way, their horses stepping carefully, reins loose on their necks. My father reined in, stopped the column. A thick cloud of flies descended on us, as we waited for the scouts.

'See that?' he said, shooing the flies away. 'Great horsemanship. On a rough slope like that, Publius, just give your horse its head.'

Calvus' face looked pinched and worried as he trotted the last few strides towards us, his colleagues behind.

'Well, Calvus?' my father demanded.

Calvus shook his head. 'Gone, sir.'

'Gone? What do you mean, "gone"? They can't have gone!'

'They have, sir. They've struck camp and gone.'

'Where?'

'North, sir. We followed their trail due north. But the ground gets very broken. They crossed and re-crossed many of the streams that feed into the Rhodanus.'

'So you lost them!' More an angry statement than a question.

'No, sir, but I thought it best to turn back and report.'

'You . . .' For a moment, I thought my father was going to lose his temper. But he took a deep breath, exhaled. 'You did well, Calvus – and you other men. But we'll catch them. They can't have been gone for long, two hours at most.'

'More, sir, much more,' Calvus said, his voice earnest, his Latin to me rough and guttural and strange.

'What do you mean?'

'The fires were well out, the embers completely cold. And . . .'

'And what?'

'And the, the dung, sir.' Behind Calvus, one of the other scouts sniggered.

'Shut up, you, or you'll be on latrine duty for the rest of your service!' my father snapped. More calmly, 'What about the dung?'

'Even the elephant turds, sir. Great big things, the size of a man's head.'

'What about them?'

'They were cold, too. So I'd say—'

'You'd say they left eight, ten hours ago?'

'I would, sir.'

I almost added, 'While we were safe in camp.' But eyes and ears open, mouth shut. I was there to learn.

'In the middle of the night, they broke camp? And what in Juno's name are they doing, heading north? Right. We'll catch these skulking cowards. We've got them in a net.' My father turned in his saddle, and nodded to Scribonius to come up.

'One more thing, sir.'

'Yes, Calvus?'

'I can't be sure, but I think we were being watched – probably are being now.'

'You've seen their scouts?'

'No, sir. Felt them.' He looked down at the ground, and almost muttered, 'Just a sense.'

'Calvus, Calvus,' my father tutted. 'You should know better. I want more from you than senses. I want,' and he shouted, 'facts!' He turned away. 'Now, Scribonius.'

He gave his orders quickly, clearly. All but five *turmae* of cavalry, forward. All troops to eat, drink and relieve themselves. Scribonius to take command of the main force, and to follow us as fast as he could. Calvus to lead us, the other two scouts to stay with Scribonius. Half a *turma* to go back to the ford, and inform Priscus Laelius. He was to strengthen his camp, and enlarge it for prisoners.

'Prisoners, sir?' asked Scribonius.

'Yes, of course. I intend to take this upstart Hannibal and some like him back to Rome. They'll make quite a show. Right, any questions?'

Scribonius shook his head. 'Seems clear to me, sir.'

'Good. Oh, Calvus, one more thing. Any sign of my brother and his legion?'

'No, sir. Not a thing.'

'Strange. I wonder where he is. Not beaten me to the Carthaginian, I hope. That would be a pity. Yes, that would spoil my fun.'

We rode on through midday, slowing as the ground rough-ened, galloping when we could. But past what Calvus said had been the camp of Hannibal, though I can't say I saw it, the land changed to outcrops of craggy granite, crossed by bursting streams. Our passage slowed. We were picking our way, Calvus pointing regularly to some dried horse dung, or a boot-print. As the sun crossed the sky, the way between the rocks grew even harder, and we dismounted.

'We'll have to walk the horses through this, Calvus,' my father said.'Don't want 'em going lame.'

'It's easier beyond that point ahead, sir,' Calvus replied, pointing up the hill to a jagged cylinder of granite, round which ravens croaked and beat their wings.

Up and on we went. Suddenly, ahead there were meadows and grasslands. 'A bowl, sir,' said Calvus, 'then another climb.'

It was a climb after that gallop, then another, steeper, then another just the same. The water of the many streams we crossed was freezing. My feet were sore, my eyes stinging from the sweat flowing down my forehead as we struggled up and on. Far away, westwards, beyond us, the Alps shone in the sky.

'He's leading us a merry song and dance,' my father panted when we paused for breath at the top of a rise. 'I'm getting too old for this, Publius.' He wiped the sweat from his face with the back of his hand.

Below us, straggling, sprawling across the hillside, I saw the rest of our column, coming on.

'I don't like it, sir,' Calvus said, squinting into the sun.

'Don't like what?'

'It's too quiet. Not even any birds.'

I looked around. Calvus was right. I hadn't noticed. There had been through the long afternoon buzzards or ravens, vultures or even pigeons, in the sky. Around us as we climbed, finches had darted from rock to rock, blackbirds had scurried away. Now, nothing. Even the signs of Hannibal and his army had been growing thin and faint.

'And look at the horses, sir. Their feet should have been

curried for weeks before this sort of ground.' He pointed down at the approaching cavalry, and I saw that at least half of the horses were limping.

'Nothing else for it.' My father walked ahead, stopped, and scanned the ground. 'At least there's plenty of water,' he said, almost to himself, when he came back, 'though fodder's short. Still, it'll have to do. Right, Publius, Calvus, just ahead, and west, there's a rise with a flattish top. We'll camp there for the night.' I was, frankly, too tired to care.

The next day was much the same. Climbing, scouting, sweating. I learnt that day the value of barley biscuits sucked soft. My father said less and less. He went to sleep that night beside me with just a curt 'Good night'. It was cold. The rows of sleeping men tossed and turned and muttered, like me pulling their cloaks tight round them through the bright, star-burning night.

The gong, gong, gong of sword-haft on shield woke me in the half-light of the morning, then the squealing of startled horses, tethered in a line. By instinct, I was up, my father so already, moving towards the sound of human voices, the shouting echoing across the hills. I followed him to the edge of the rise, and heard the voices clearly: '*Romani sumus*. We are Romans, of the legion under Gnaeus Cornelius Scipio.'

We waited, shivering, the men huddled and nervous. So, on a hilltop in southern Gaul, I met my uncle again as the sun rose, turning the white Alps in the distance into the glowing red of fire, and of pain.

'We meet again under, ah, unusual circumstances, Nephew,' he said with a thin smile. That is how I remembered him from my childhood: measured, careful, almost pompous. He had lost all his hair since I had last seen him, and the beads of sweat that came from his brisk climb shone on his bald head.

'I would have preferred it, Brother, if you had been Hannibal,' my father said – or joked? – as the three of us walked towards the fires, 'and not an uninvited guest. Anyway, what news?'

'None, bar foundered horses, and tired and hungry men.'

'You mean, no sign of him?'

'Yes, Brother,' my uncle said dryly, 'that is exactly what I mean. And, frankly, this has been like one of our childhood games when you sent me with a message for someone who was not there.'

'What are you doing, then, wandering around in the night with one of my legions?'

'The horses were nervous. We couldn't camp, or sleep. I thought—'

'So the actions of a Roman army are dictated by horses!'

'I'm your legate, not your servant, Brother!' my uncle gave back angrily. 'I haven't slept properly for days, or eaten – nor have my men. You see things in those high hills. Or rather, you don't. You hear voices, see strange shadows—'

'Well, dammit, Brother!' my father shouted. 'By all the gods, where has he gone?'

My father sent my uncle's legion, bar its three hundred cavalry, back down. When they met Scribonius, they were to build a proper camp and forage for food.

'Food, Cornelius?' my uncle asked. 'Have you seen any game?'

'No, Gnaeus, I haven't. But I've seen plenty of rabbits, and hares; they'll do. I want your soldiers' dried rations re-distributed among the cavalry.'

'You mean we're going on?'

'Of course we are. I have my orders. I've never failed Rome before.'

So we went on, two days of heat and soreness, two nights of cold. On the second, my father divided the force. 'He must have slipped past us. We're going south again. Gnaeus, I'll stay in the centre with five *turmae*. You fan out to the east, Scribonius to the west. We'll find him.'

We never did. He had disappeared. We came to the camp

that Scribonius and my uncle's legion had made. How could Hannibal vanish, and with elephants? I had seen elephants in Rome, used by builders for moving materials. Men could hide in clefts or hidden valleys. But elephants?

The mood in camp was anxious. Food was scarce; for us, certainly, but even more so for the horses. Supper was a little barley gruel in the bottom of a bowl, thickened with a pat of gravy from hare stew. Walking along the picket-lines to go to the latrines, I saw the horses had only some musty dried grass, thick with thistle seed.

That night, it snowed. We woke to a covering of it on our cloaks and the ground. Round the cooking-fires, men stamped their feet and beat their arms. The wind came searching from the north, and cut through clothes to bone. Still the sun shone on the white vastness of the Alps.

The council of war was brief. 'I'm sure of it,' my father said. 'We've missed him. The move north was a feint. He'll have turned, avoiding us, and be heading back towards the Pireneos.'

'How can you be so sure, Brother?' my uncle asked.

'He needs to winter somewhere, doesn't he?' my father returned sarcastically. 'Look around you. This is hospitable, compared to what's to come. No, I think he'll make a run for it before the real snows come. He'll zig-zag down the coast, and spend the winter in Carthagena. Don't you agree, Scribonius?'

'That, sir, is what I would do,' Scribonius replied; guardedly, I thought.

'Right, then. Strike camp. Back to Priscus Laelius, and a proper camp.'

'And from there, Brother?' my uncle asked, hunched against the cold.

'I'll consult the Senate, but in my book back to Placentia for the winter. From there, I'll be advising the Senate to let me lead a full attack on Celtiberia in the spring. Take the fleet straight to Carthagena. Do this thing properly, once and for all. The brothers Scipio attack in Celtiberia, and Sempronius in Africa itself. Brrr, it's cold. On second thoughts, I'll swap places with Sempronius for a bit of African sun. Any takers?'

No one laughed. We went slowly back the way we had come.

It was getting dark. 'Less than an hour to go, Publius,' my father said beside me. 'Then a hot bath, and a proper meal, and a bed in a tent. Priscus is tremendously good at that sort of thing. Best quartermaster I've ever had.'

We were in a dip. 'From the top of the next rise, if I remember right, we'll see the ford and the camp. I could do with soaking these old bones. And,' he went on, rubbing a hand across his lips, 'I can taste that goblet of wine already!'

We reached the top of the rise. Below, the river gleamed in the last of the light. But above it hung a thick, dark, coiling pall – of cloud, I thought at first. Then an acrid, bitter smell filled my nose and mouth.

My father stiffened, sat up on his horse. 'By all the gods!' he said with slow venom. He looked round wildly. 'Scribonius! Ten maniples to follow me! On the run!' He heeled his horse viciously, and was away, galloping down the hill.

I went after him, more slowly. I found him, still mounted, by the ford. Between us and the other bank, the river flowed, menacing and dark. The light had gone from the water. Like my father, I looked across to what had been our camp. All that was left was part of the palisade. Here and there, patches of white from the ruined tents shone out, and red tongues of flame still flickered from the group of blackened wagons. From further away I heard the sound of cattle lowing and another sound, that of animals in pain.

Behind us, I heard the quick tread of the maniples coming. My father turned towards them. Perhaps it was the failing light, but his face looked ashen and weary. 'Right, men,' he called out. 'Two maniples stay here until the others are across. The rest of you, get going. Then form up on the other bank, three deep. Who's senior centurion here?'

'I am, sir,' a voice called out.

'Then go back. Get the slingers. I want them halfway down the hillside, covering our advance, and the . . . and' – he faltered – 'and the camp.'

We urged our horses into the water, the soldiers following. The camp, or what was left of it, lay perhaps a hundred paces beyond the further bank. But the first bodies were much closer than that. They seemed peaceful, I remember thinking, lying on their sides or fronts or backs, and around their necks or chests or middles oozed the dark stain of their blood, darkening the grass and soggy ground.

In a chilling silence, we rode into the camp. In the centre, against the burnt frame of a wagon, we saw a man tied. My father stopped. 'It's Priscus!' He kicked his horse forwards, and was off it and running, slipping on the bloody ground. I dismounted, and walked slowly forwards, feeling empty, angry, lonely, sick. I stepped over the body of a dead soldier, then another, unarmed, I saw, still in his tunic, his beard barely grown, but his intestines lying across him, spreading on the ground.

My father squatted down, and reached his head out, beside the charred wagon wheel. Behind me, the soldiers formed an uncertain half-circle.

'Father, what is it?'

He began retching, puking. I waited. He stood up, and looked at me with wild eyes. He sheathed the sword he held in his hand. 'Priscus,' he said softly.

'Yes?'

'Come closer, son. They cut out his eyes, and tongue.'

I didn't. I couldn't. From four, five paces back, I could see the blood, the sheet of red and brown that once had been the father of my friend.

Like a dog after water, my father shook himself. 'Trumpeter, sound the advance to the rest of the army. You men, one maniple on sentry duty. The rest of you, dig.'

And that is what we did, dig great grave-pits just beyond the palisade and carry the dead there, through the evening and into the night. I helped. No one commented. The feeling from the men was of routine. Romans had been killed, ambushed and murdered since the day Rome began.

My father, I knew, had gone down to the river-mouth to talk to the admiral of the fleet, to make plans, he had told me, to embark. I just worked on.

At last, hungry, thirsty, aching, the many bodies buried, I lay down to sleep, on bloody ground, no doubt, but at least the blood was dry. All round the perimeter of the palisade, bonfires burned into the night, fuelled by the remains of many wagons, and sentries called out passwords and the hours.

It seemed I had hardly been asleep. I half opened my eyes. A soldier was standing at the feet of my father beside me. It was almost light.

'Sorry to wake you, sir. Men coming, from the east.'

'Men? How many?'

'Six, sir, walking.'

'Armed?'

'No. Sir, I think they're ours.'

So returned the survivors of the camp at the Rhodanus, two cooks, a smith, three muleteers. They were cold, hungry, confused. My father's interrogation was gentle, almost distracted.

The attack had come in the middle of the previous night, fire-arrows first. They had been outside the camp, on sentry duty with the cattle, sheep and goats. When they saw the flames and heard the noise, they ran.

'But, looking back, I see'd 'em, sir,' said the smith, a thick barrel of a man, with almost no neck and stubby, bandy legs. 'I see'd 'em, against the light of the fires.'

'Yes, man,' my father asked patiently, 'but who did you see?'

'Gauls, sir, they was. Almost naked, lots of hair and those strange painted shields. Just like those ones you was fighting around Placentia – the Hinsi, the Hinsibres.'

'Insubres, Flaccus.' The smith was startled to be called by name. 'Yes, I know you.' My father yawned. The bags under his bleary eyes were almost black in the unforgiving light.

'How many, Flaccus? Did you see that?'

'No, sir. Sorry. Just took one look and made for those far rocks.'

'Thank you. That will be all.' He sat with his chin in his hands, looking far away.

'Will we pursue them, Father?' I asked.

'What?'

'Will we chase these Insubres?'

'No point. Never catch them.' He stretched, got up. 'I'm going to what's left of the latrine. Scribonius, muster the men.'

'For what, sir?'

'For embarkation. We're going back to barracks in Placentia. This hide-and-seek tomfoolery has already cost too much. See to it.' With a curt nod to us, my father went.

Scribonius turned to go. 'Scribonius, would you go after the Insubres?' I asked him.

'Would *I*, sir? That's a strange question, begging your pardon. I follow orders. But since you ask, no, I think your father's right. I wouldn't follow them – if that's who they were.'

'If? What do you mean, "if"?'

'I've soldiered hereabouts for fifteen years, sir. Strange country. What you think you see isn't what it seems. Now, if you'll excuse me, I'll be mustering the men.'

The journey by sea was straightforward. We followed the coast; I was glad of that, for out to sea we saw savage storms scud across the sky. Once, one came towards us, but the whole fleet hove to in the shelter of the Stoechades islands until it passed. Only the crowding was unpleasant, what with all four legions, horses and – no, there weren't any followers left, bar the six that we had seen – on ships designed to carry half that number. The rest of the fleet was still patrolling the coast of Celtiberia, and was to winter at Massilia.

At times, in light winds, when the sails were furled and the rowers took over, the smell of so many men was overwhelming. So I learnt through the long days to find privacy in myself. My father and my uncle and I talked sometimes. But mostly, we were each alone. I found peace standing at the thwarts and looking for hours at the searching, shifting, soothing sea. I heard the men gossip about Hannibal. Most were sure, as we were, that he had slipped south but that we would find and beat him in Celtiberia in the spring. Most of the talk was of Placentia, and leave, and brothels, inns. They might have buried brothers, cousins, friends at the Rhodanus, but soldiers just go on.

We landed at Pisae, and marched across the plain of the River Po. If I say little of the winter at Placentia, it is because that is what I remember. Cold and grey and rain. I remember sleeping a lot, drill and more drill, exercising horses in the rain, despatches to and fro, between my father and Rome. His declared plans were, it seemed, the Senate's. And in the spring, as he had expected, Sempronius and his two legions were to invade Africa. We all had just to wait, as I am doing now for the verdict that, day after day, does not come.

I talked to my father sometimes, mostly about his military plans, but also about what he would do, next summer, when his consulship was over. I didn't get to know him any better. He was my father, I his son. We were both Scipios, who served Rome. That was all. This superficiality was normal, I supposed.

I improved with sword and *pilum*; I learnt to mount a running horse; I played a great deal of chess. I thought at first of writing to Laelius, to tell him about his father, to say I was sorry. But I knew he would have had official notification. I didn't know what I could add. Death is a thing at which words strain, and fail to flow.

Placentia was, and no doubt still is, a dull town, little more than a collection of huts and barracks behind its mighty walls. Only the prefect's house was built of stone. We were quartered there. The prefect was a furtive, weaselly man, sycophantic to my father and my uncle, and a great drinker. I avoided him as much as I could – which, unfortunately was not at meal times. It seemed that what we ate was, like Placentia, always grey.

Even the market was drab and squalid. The people said that only summer brought trade to them. I went once to a brothel with my father and uncle. They both retired to private rooms. The girl assigned to me reeked of musk and scent. Her face was painted like a childhood doll, her lower lip hung down, and her gown had spots of fat on it. I was disgusted. I pushed her away, and walked back to my bed through the rain.

Spring's coming was slow but sure. Each day, the darkness of the morning lessened. I began to hear the birds sing. Outside the prefect's house, the buds of the cherry trees swelled red and full. The chestnut trees round the squelching mud of the parade ground became lustrous with new green. The sap was rising. Each day, from the stable yards, I heard the stallions' neighing and the whinnies of the mares. We still had violent thunderstorms and, one midday, even a fall of snow, but the smiths' forges were busy, making or repairing spades and ploughs and hoes.

One morning after breakfast of grey porridge, followed by apples that were wrinkled, sour and old, my father said, 'Well, Publius. I see the sun is warm on the ground. *Exercitus* for exercise, remember? I think it's time we started that, don't you?'

'Yes, Father. When?'

'Today, I think, if the weather holds. We should start with the cavalry, then the men. We've got forty *turmae* of cavalry, more or less. We'll take twenty out today, and try the ground; don't want them up to their hocks in mud. Go and tell the decurions to get ready, Publius, please.'

I sprinted, delighted, to the stables. Most of that day we rode and wheeled across the grassy plains. The River Po was in spate still, swollen, angry, grey, but otherwise the world was wonderful, green and clean and bursting into spring life.

So the next day. On the third, we took all forty *turmae*, twelve hundred men. We stopped for the midday meal, cold rations from our bags. My back was against the bole of an oak tree, and my father was nearby.

'Time you saw more of the country, Publius, and I want the horses to get used to harder ground. See the hills to the north? Take half the force, and reconnoitre. Not that you'll see anything much, but I want you to learn to use your eyes as scouts do. When you come back, I'll ask you how many possible campsites you saw, and to describe them. Take care, though. I know the ground well. We'll ride west a little, as far as the River Ticinus, and see you back here.'

I was hugely excited to be leading a Roman squadron. It was my right by birth and name, but even so it is a moment that defined me, not least because of what followed.

We reached the hills at a steady canter. Slowing down as we approached the rocks, I looked back south and west. I saw a sudden glinting, as of armour in the sun, over in the west where my father had gone. To this day I do not know what moved me, but I wheeled my horse and shouted, 'Squadron, gallop, with me!' rushing on a diagonal across the way that we had come.

The ground, still grass, was falling away towards the Ticinus, a tributary of the Po, when I saw them. From full gallop, I pulled my horse up savagely, and round me the other riders did the same. What I remember is the squeals of protesting horses, but above all the astonished gasps, the oaths of six hundred serried men. I rubbed my eyes, and looked again. Impossible. Fantastic. It had to be a dream.

On the far side of the Ticinus, on the plain many stades away, coming towards us in ten columns – it was, and remains in my mind, incredible – was an army of many, many thousands, marching ants that coruscated, shifting hues and shapes and colours in the sun against the green grass over which they moved. What did I think? Not Insubres or Boii. Not all the Celts or Gauls that ever marched were as many as that host. Thoughts streaked and raced and muddled, like dreams in the night. I remembered Scribonius, his implied doubts, my father's disdain. This, I knew, was the army of Hannibal, the Unexpected One, which had not slipped south but had crossed the Alps, in mid-winter, and was now in Italy, unimaginable, inconceivable, but real.

On our side of the river, well ahead of the main army, between it and my father's squadron, a huge mass of cavalry was walking on. I looked at the square my father had formed: six hundred men. Hannibal's force was four or five times that, I thought. What could I do? What should I? A chill started at my penis, and ran up to my brain. Placentia. Should I race back to Placentia, call out the legions? Why hadn't my father turned, and done the same?

As my horse moved testily from foot to foot, I saw an extraordinary thing. As one, the Carthaginian cavalry stopped. Only the first two ranks came on, the same number as that commanded by my father, or even less. Perhaps a thousand strides lay between the two forces as the Carthaginians, still walking on, before my eyes moved with perfect precision from one line into an arrowhead formation and broke from walk to trot to canter. At their point, I saw a man dressed all in black, small on a huge white horse. If he wore armour, it was a cuirass also of black leather, and in vivid contrast to the gleaming armour of those he led.

I saw my father's right arm rise and hang and fall. His squadron moved forwards in standard, straight formation, three lines deep, walk to trot. Both forces moved to gallop, my father's colour streaming in the wind. In these words I use, what happened seems to have done so slowly, but what I remember is its speed.

Moments before the two forces clashed, the man in black stretched out his left arm and as a bird soars, with the ease and beauty of a rainbow, his arrowhead spread out to form a single, enveloping line. 'Surrounded, Father, look out!' I think I screamed in warning, but as I did so I saw the man in black bear straight down on my father and duck under his levelled *pilum*; I saw the sword flash and swing, my father fall, and I kicked and kicked my horse and let its reins go and for the first time I was really riding, floating down the hill and I felt I was the wind rushing towards my fallen father and his colour and three men, now four, now five, dismounted, round him, defending, jabbing, thrusting with their *pila* as spears.

The fight of twelve hundred had become one of knots of tangled twos and threes, some still on horseback, others dismounted and fighting from the ground. Three times as I approached I saw the man in black, still mounted, attack the group round my father. Three times I saw the stabbing spears make the man I knew must be Hannibal veer and turn away. And then as I was there and off my horse I sensed the others with me, joining the circle, their *pila* planted in the ground. I knelt beside my father. His eyes were misted and blood streamed from his side. Somehow I raised him, someone helped me, and we laid him across my horse's back and I remounted, fumbled for the reins and kicked and turned.

From the corner of my eye I saw the man in black, dismounted now, two dozen strides away, his sword held double-handed high above his head and he shouted, 'Bar-ca, Bar-ca!' and his fighting men took up the chant and he came on towards us, his shouts of 'Barca, Barca!' beating like a drum. With one great upward sweep of his sword, he felled the cavalryman who blocked his way. To swelling, growing howls of 'Bar-ca, Bar-ca', I broke, I think three riders with me, and rode and fled away.

I remember my father groaning. Only once did I look back, and I saw the red line of his blood in the grass behind. There was no one coming, only the riders with me. In through the gates of Placentia we galloped, I screaming, 'Close them, close them!' to the startled guards.

He was still breathing. 'The doctor! Help me carry him to the doctor!' I shouted to the men by my side. The Cretan who had tended me had died at the Rhodanus. This doctor was another Greek, small and doleful, kindly-eyed.

My father's breath was fast and rasping. Flecks of blood bubbled on his lips.

'*Vitabitne*? Will he live?' I asked the doctor.

'Live?' he replied. 'Ask me later in the day.'

I leant on the parapet of the central well, splashing and splashing water from the bucket on to my face. From far away, it seemed, I heard a voice: 'Publius, Publius! What's happened?' I turned, the water running down my front. It was Uncle Gnaeus.

'H . . .' My voice wouldn't come. I tried again. 'Hannibal.' I suppose my eyes were staring, wild.

'Have you a fever, Publius? Hannibal! Don't be ridiculous. What's happened to my brother?'

'I'm telling you, Uncle, it's Hannibal. Is his family name not Barca?' The chant still sounded in my ears. 'I heard him, saw him with my own eyes! Do you understand? Hannibal Barca!'

I screamed. I felt weak. I sat down on the step of the well. 'And a huge army,' I went on, quietly.

'Where?'

'Just west. By the Ticinus.'

The colour drained slowly from his face. 'It cannot be. It is impossible,' he stuttered, distracted. 'If it's him—'

'Look, Uncle!' I was angry. 'If? I'm telling you, it's Hannibal. A huge army with him, more men than I have ever seen.'

'But the Alps? And in winter! How—'

'Don't ask me how he did it, but he did.' Such disrespect was my beginning, I see now, to become a man.

'What are we going to do?'

'We? I thought you were legate here. One, I would sound full muster. Two, I would send word to the Senate. Three, I would ask them to send Sempronius and his three legions here.'

'Sempronius! Don't get carried away, Publius. Hannibal may have crossed the Alps, but we have four legions here.'

'And he has double that, I'd say.'

'Fifty thousand men, across the Alps? Preposterous!'

'Preposterous, but true, I'm telling you!'

'Right, I'll go and see for myself. West, you say.'

'Yes, not half an hour's ride.'

'I'll take one legion. You see to your father.'

My father was asleep, breathing fitfully. Across his chest the bandages were red from blood, and yellow from the poultices underneath. The doctor waved me away. I went to my room, took off my cuirass, changed my tunic, put the cuirass on again, walked back to my uncle, who was now mounted in the parade square, ready to leave.

'I'm coming with you,' I said.

'Your father?'

'Alive. The doctor's there.'

'All right. I'll leave Scribonius in command.'

My uncle was a cautious commander. On this occasion, he had

cause to be. We had no scouts, no cavalry. None had come back from the Ticinus. Why hadn't they followed me? Where were they? My uncle used the slingers instead. Each ten minutes or so, he called a halt, and waited for the slingers to come running back. Each time, their message was the same: nothing to report.

We came to the rise from which I had watched. They lay where they had fallen, forty *turmae* of Roman cavalry, my father's twenty and my own, tangled bodies, some still bleeding, the ground between the bodies red, the Ticinus running red along its near bank from the bodies piled there. My uncle and I picked our way in silence through the carnage, through the buzzing, languid flies and, already, the beginning of a sweet, cloying, sickening smell.

There were no wounded. Those cut or slashed or stabbed on leg, face, shoulder or arm had had their throats cut. There were no horses except dead ones. I presumed he had taken the living. There were no swords, or shields, or *pila*, or helmets, except bent or buckled ones.

My uncle turned, his face grey and set. 'I want to see no more.'

Halfway back up the rise, the maniples had formed defensive squares. 'Ten maniples, dig and bury,' my uncle ordered. 'Ten, take up position on the further bank, and ten, back above the rise. All of you, eyes open. Any sign of anything but a rabbit, let the trumpets sound.' He spoke so quietly that only the first few ranks, I should think, could hear. But perhaps they knew what to do. It was not, I thought, the first time Hannibal had stung Rome. It had been he, I felt sure, at the Rhodanus. Surprise attack, then gone, as here. Gone. I asked myself, gone where? And, with around a thousand fresh, rested horses, and good weaponry, for whom?

For weeks, the only people who left Placentia were scouting patrols and messengers, the latter always by night to reach Pisae and be aboard ship for Ostia by dawn. The patrols found nothing, the messengers brought first incredulous, then increasingly exasperated, despatches from the Senate. The first pointed out that it was impossible for an army to cross the Alps, let alone in winter. Were we sure this was Hannibal the Carthaginian? My uncle replied patiently. I added a note to Fabius Pictor that I had seen Hannibal with my own eyes.

Our soldiers in Placentia were withdrawn and surly, though we kept them at drill. I heard talk of magic, and saw how, at the name of Hannibal, men made the sign against the evil eye. Slowly, we came to accept that he had done the impossible. That didn't stop us wondering where he was now, and what he would do?

My father's wound was healing, though he was still bedbound and had developed a deep and hacking cough. His fellow consul, Sempronius, had turned back from travelling to Sicilia, and with his three legions would soon be here. New cavalry had already come from Rome, having seen nothing of the Carthaginians on their way. Wherever Hannibal had gone, it wasn't south.

I asked Scribonius about this when we met one morning in the officers' mess.

'He will be resting, I think, in the hills north of here,' he said.

'But why the feint at Placentia?'

'Exploratory, no more. See what he was up against. Oh, and then there's fear – as we are finding out.'

'What do you mean, Scribonius?'

'He already has the advantage. He has already done what no man dreamed possible, and then he stings and disappears. Our soldiers fight men, not wizards, sir. You've heard the men. Hannibal scares them, because he is something they don't understand.'

'Then why doesn't he press his advantage? I don't understand why he didn't attack us here, for example.'

'Whatever else he managed to bring across the Alps, it won't have been siege equipment, sir. And anyway, however he got across, his losses must have been huge. He and his men and animals must be weary, very weary. Tired men don't fight unless they have to.'

'So we should attack him now?'

'Yes, probably, once Sempronius gets here.'

'You'll advise that?'

'If I'm asked, sir, yes. But first we'll have to find him. That shouldn't be too difficult, but it doesn't mean he'll fight.'

'Why not?'

'Well, I don't know, sir. But in my book this Hannibal won't fight on ground of ours. He'll fight on ground he's chosen, or not at all.' Just then, a trumpet sounded from the parade ground outside. 'Excuse me, but that's my watch. But, by the way, sir, I've heard about the Ticinus.'

'Heard what? What do you mean?'

'How you saved your father's life. The men say you deserve a civic crown.'

I was embarrassed. 'Hardly that, Scribonius. An instinct, that was all. Anyway, if my father owes his life to me, I owe mine to Frontinus. I wonder if he's still alive?'

Scribonius looked at me as he turned to go. Was there perhaps a new respect in his eyes. 'Frontinus? So do I wonder, sir, so do I. Jupiter knows Rome needs such soldiers as him.' He saluted, and left.

When they came the next day, the Senate's orders to my father were straightforward. As soon as he was fit to travel, he was to return to Rome to recuperate – and for council. 'And Publius, I want you to come with me,' he said, when he had read the despatch.

'But, father—'

He coughed deeply, and held up a hand. 'Publius,' he croaked, 'I owe you my life. Now more than ever I would do anything for you. But Sempronius and your uncle will destroy Hannibal before the moon is full. It won't be a battle, it'll be a rout, and the real decisions will be made in Rome. We'll be there.'

'If Hannibal will be so easy an enemy, Father, why was it his sword that cut you?'

'Don't!' He coughed again. I gave him water from the flagon beside his bed. 'Thank you,' he said as soon as he was able. 'Don't mention that again, Publius. I thought you saw. He simply ducked under my *pilum* as if it wasn't there. That's not a soldier, that's a coward.' As I left him to sleep, I was not so sure.

Sempronius and his legions arrived the next afternoon. The whole town rang to the trumpets' blare. My father was asleep. I sat on a stool at the foot of his bed, hoping the noise wouldn't wake him. He was tossing, muttering, feverish, and I saw beads of sweat forming and dying on his forehead.

The door was thrown open. I knew who it was as he came in. Tall and thin, he had long, lank sandy hair. His nose was long and narrow, his eyes too small for his head. 'Longshanks', the soldiers called him. I could see why. His legs seemed to end halfway up his chest, which stuck out like a cockerel's. 'So, here's my heroic wounded fellow consul,' he said, crossing the room. His voice was high and nasal, tight. 'And you—'

'Please,' I said, standing up. 'He's sleeping.' Sempronius stopped. He cupped his chin in his hand. He looked like a stork, like the ones at the mouth of the Rhodanus. 'You must be his son, of the same name.'

'I am.'

'And I hear even the renowned filial piety of the Scipios excelled itself some weeks ago,' he said with heavy irony. 'Do you really believe you rescued your father from the sword of Hannibal?'

'Believe? No.'

'What then?' He looked arrogant, amused.

218

I held his eyes. 'Sempronius, I know.'

'Know? Know what?'

'That it was Hannibal.'

'As, Sempronius, do I,' said my father from behind me. I turned. He was sitting up in bed. A shaft of sunlight caught his face and I saw how old he looked now, how deep the lines were on his forehead, round his eyes. 'And, esteemed colleague, I don't want you interrogating my son as if he was one of your slaves.'

'Well, well! You are on the mend, colleague.' Sempronius wore a supercilious smile as he walked over to my father's bed. 'Anyway, whoever he is, I'll sort him out, and then get on my way back to Sicilia. We've got quite a fleet there, you know.'

'Yes, we've heard,' my father said weakly, leaning back on an elbow.

'In fact, I'd be in Africa by now, crushing Carthage, had it not been for this, ah, diversion.'

I saw my father's lips tighten. 'This, Sempronius, may prove more than an outing to your country estate,' he said.

'We'll see. But right now I need something to eat and drink. Young man,' he went on, looking at me, 'kindly get me whatever this miserable place can provide.'

I went to the door, which Sempronius hadn't closed, and called, 'Casca!' She must have been sitting in the corridor outside, because I had taken only a few steps back into the room when I heard her come in behind me.

She was a good maid, Casca. I had grown fond of her over the months we had been in Placentia. But she was very short, almost a midget, and fat. One leg was shorter than the other, and club-footed, and she dragged it as she walked. Her lower lip was deformed, and hung down, and as a result she drooled. Her upper lip was hairy, and her eyes were sunk in her face.

I watched Sempronius when he saw her. 'Who's this freak?' he sneered. 'This is meant to be a garrison, not a circus.'

Casca froze. I felt anger, a warmth rising to my cheeks. Whatever she looked like, this 'freak' had tended my father with tenderness and patience, changing his dressing, emptying his chamberpot, feeding him with a spoon. At the beginning, she had slept in a chair by his bed.

'This, Sempronius,' I said carefully, 'is the woman who has nursed my father. Rome is in her debt.'

'Hah!' he said, dismissively. 'Still, if I was being nursed by someone like that, I'd want to get better soon. Very soon.' He crossed to a chair by the bed, and sat down. 'Now, we've work to do. I want your maps, Scipio, and a description of the lie of the land. I've come a long way, fast. I want to deal with this Hannibal, or whoever he is, and be in Sicilia before the month is out.'

'Casca,' my father said evenly, 'bring my colleague his meal. Publius, please go and find my brother. Ask him to join us.' As I closed the door, I heard Sempronius' high-pitched voice running on.

We left Placentia the next morning, my father carried in a litter by six slaves. I rode beside him. In front and behind us marched two maniples, ordered to see us aboard ship at Pisae and then return. On each of our flanks, cavalry scouted. My father had assigned two *turmae* to form message chains, and at Placentia my uncle was ready with two legions to march to us at the first sign of trouble.

Everyone was tense and nervous. The rolling plain towards the coast seemed threatening and vast. The weather was sultry, airless and heavy. We marched on.

At sea, I looked back towards Placentia. I remembered those calls of 'Barca! Barca!' which had never left my dreams. I shivered as the ship's oars splashed to the deep drumbeats.

I went to join my father on the foredeck. The sailors had

rigged him a canvas shelter from the sun. 'It'll be a slow passage, Publius, if we don't get any wind,' he said, looking tired from the journey.

'Yes, but we're not in any hurry, Father.'

'No, that's true.' He sat up, and coughed. 'I wish the same could be said of Sempronius.'

'What do you mean?'

'You've met him. You must learn to judge men, Publius. Sempronius always was a hot-head.'

'You think he'll make a mistake?'

'I'm sure he will. Many. Didn't you feel we were being watched on the journey to Pisae?'

'Yes, I did, Father. But that's impossible. The scouts reported nothing.'

'Impossible? So was crossing the Alps.'

'Do you think Hannibal will fight Sempronius and Uncle Gnaeus?'

'Yes, I do. I think he knows exactly what's going on.'

'And win?'

A small smile crossed my father's lips. 'Win? No, Publius. That is impossible. With the legion that joined him as he marched, Sempronius has five. They're experienced, fit and rested men.'

'Yes, but how's their spirit?'

'Their spirit, Publius?'

'Just something Frontinus taught me. I wonder if he's still alive.'

'If anyone could be, he will be. Best soldier I've known.'

'I owe my life to him, Father.'

'I know that Publius, I know.' He reached out and took me by the arm. 'As I owe mine to you.'

As our eyes met, a breeze stirred the air. The moment of closeness passed. My father's tone changed. 'Now, the Greek doctor said I should let the sea air at this wound of mine.' He rolled up his shirt. I hadn't seen the wound for several days. Right across his stomach the scar ran, red and angry, ragged. Here and there along it, yellow pustules protruded. We both peered. 'Hmm. Still infected. But it's getting better. We might have to lance the pus, once we're back in Rome.'

He lay back on the deck. 'I'm going to doze now, Publius. A bit more breeze and we might soon be under sail.'

'Can I bring you anything?'

'Yes. Some water, thank you. Then go and look out for dolphins. They're a very good omen. There are usually plenty along this stretch of coast.'

I did as I was told. I looked for dolphins. There were none. Only languid clumps of weed drifted on the sea.

At home, my life resumed as if I had not been away. Perhaps that is what home is, a place where things remain the same. I remember the peace I felt, the safety from being again among the same furniture, the same servants, the same rhythm I had known. And the same friend.

I went to see Laelius the day after we got back. He was reserved at first, and shy. He looked exactly the same, although his beard was fuller. So, I supposed was mine.

'Laelius, I'm sorry,' I said, standing in the atrium of the house that had been his father's and was now, I assumed, his.

'What about?'

'Your father.'

He bit his lip. 'Oh, that. The Senate has awarded us a pension, you know. And, it seems, I'm now rich. My father left a great deal of money. I had no idea how successful his investments were, or how many. But what about you? I hear you saved your father's life. How is he?'

'On the mend, thanks. He should be back to normal in a week or so. The wound has almost healed.'

'And they say you saw Hannibal. Is that true?'

'Yes, it is.'

'What does he look like?'

'I . . . I don't really know, Laelius. It all happened so fast. I . . .'

'Come into the garden. Let's sit there, and talk.' We did, for hours.

When I got home, I went to see my father in his room. He was sitting up in bed, reading through scrolls of listed numbers.

'What are you reading, Father?'

'Oh, just accounts. Festo has done a good job while I've been gone. And you've seen Laelius?'

'Yes.'

'How was he?'

'He seemed fine.'

'Not upset about his father?'

'If he was, it didn't show.'

'Good. A true Roman.'

'Father, there is one thing we talked about.'

'Yes?' he asked, putting the scrolls down on the table by his bed. 'What's that?'

'Laelius and I discussed it. I said I'd ask you.'

'Ask what?'

'Well, I assume I'll be resuming my *triconium fori* with Fabius.'

'That's right. Remember, we agreed that on the ship. What about it?'

'Well, Father, could Laelius join me?'

'I . . . But he's not even an equestrian. I don't know how Fabius would feel.'

'Fabius taught me, Father, to judge something by its substance, not its form.'

My father stared at me intently. 'All right. You have my permission to ask Fabius. I owe Priscus that at least. Anyway, I mean to ask the Senate to elevate the house of Laelius. Priscus' death has earned them that, and more. You can tell Fabius what I'm intending. You'll be going to the Senate tomorrow?'

I nodded. 'Then give Fabius my regards.'

'I will, Father, I will.'

So it was that Laelius came to join me each day at the Senate. We kept our distance from the others doing their *triconium fori*. I saw the looks of curiosity we got. But my standing was high – I had saved my father's life – and for Laelius there was the respect due anyone whose father has died for Rome. That respect may have been grudging in his case, but it was there. Then, when the Senate passed the decree ennobling the house of Laelius, there were titters and smirks.

I pointed out that this was only to be expected. After all, I said, it must have happened when the first Scipio claimed the honour. All noble families start somewhere.

'I suppose you're right,' Laelius said casually. 'It's just taken mine about three hundred years longer than yours.'

I have to interrupt, despite my intention not to. I have to record what seems to me the importance of what Scipio has just dictated. He does not know it. He did not see it then. He does not see it now. But the jealousy began then. I fear for the fruits it may yet bear, in Laelius' evidence.

So our lives went on. My father was well again, and in the Senate every day. His late afternoons were spent with a trainer, rebuilding the muscles that had wasted away. Laelius and I spent all our time together, in the Senate or with Fabius, or in the baths, or training with Lanistus. He remarked that at least I had learnt to ride while I was away. And we waited. Sempronius' despatches, read out every morning in the Senate chamber, were brief, sure and consistent. He was 'looking for the enemy' – he never named Hannibal – and was 'confident of victory any day'.

In the Senate, the business was of money. Gold was flowing to Sicilia, for the equipment – onagers and rams and towers and ladders and ballistae – being built there to be shipped with the fleet for the siege of Carthage. King Hieron of Syracuse was, it seemed, being a true ally. The Senate had even taken a loan from the private bankers, certain – so even Fabius argued – that it would be repaid many times over when either Carthage was sacked, or peace and reparations were concluded. The mood of the Senate was purposeful. Incredulity at Hannibal's crossing of the Alps had given way to action.

At home, in the evenings, my sister Cornelia started to have supper with my father and me. She had grown tall, and had the body of a young woman, not a girl. Her breasts were pert now, I noticed, her waist pronounced above the fullness of her hips. There was a shapeliness to her shoulders I had not seen before. But most of all I thought her hands were beautiful, her fingers tapering and long. Her nails were clear and filed and utterly entrancing. I used to watch them as we ate. Once, when I looked at her, she gave me a shy smile. Her nails also shone. Some polish or varnish, I assumed. I always meant to ask her how it was done. I never did, and now in the autumn of my life, perhaps even near its end, if Cato fills his hatred's maw, I think how strange it is that I have never found out how women polish their nails, why birds sing, why the moon waxes and wanes, how fish breathe under water. There are many mysteries in simple things, and we live too much in the hybris of the light. I have learnt to look in the shadows, to see a tree, for example, in terms not of its branches, but of the spaces between them. All right, Bostar. Before you cough, I will get on. But I am weary, and cold, and drawn to the darkness of things. Shall I live to see another spring?

The management of the household was something that

Cornelia had assumed in the months I was away. Not the accounts, or the dealings with merchants and tradesmen – Festo did that – but the servants, and the overall order of the household. She was as a noble Roman woman is born to be.

These were settled days, and good, and long. At first, when we got back, I had strange dreams of Hannibal, not as a person, but as an energy. These dreams passed as time went on. All was well for me and mine – apart from my brother Lucius.

One evening, my father and I came back together from the Senate, to which he had returned after his session with his trainer. The world was suffused with light, and we agreed to sit in the garden before supper.

'Festo,' my father ordered, 'bring us some wine. Chian, I think.' We were walking to a bench under a spreading clematis when I saw Lucius, his back to us, sitting on the ground beside the fountain, utterly absorbed.

'Look, Father. There's Lucius.'

'Lucius? What's he doing up? He should be in bed. Lucius!' he shouted. No response. We walked up to him. 'Lucius!' my father said again, sharply. My brother ignored us, and went on with whatever he was doing.

I took a step round, and saw. In his lap there were three starlings, fledglings. He held a fourth in his hands, and was carefully, meticulously, tearing its wings off, as from its bobbing beak it screeched and gasped for air. I swung instinctively, disgusted, and hit him on his left shoulder. The eyes he turned on me were chill and cold.

'Look, Father. He's torturing these birds!' I said.

My father reached down and grabbed Lucius by his tunic, hauling him to his feet. 'You disgusting brat!' he whispered. He turned my brother round to face him, and once, twice, slapped him in the face. 'Now go to bed. I don't want to see you for a few days.' With that, he pushed Lucius towards the house. My baby brother took three steps, four, then stopped and half turned back towards us. His look was baleful, sullen. Then he sneered, and ran away.

'Strange, strange child,' my father said. 'Publius, go and tell Festo I want Lucius kept in his room. Locked, if need be. I'll see to him when we have the Carthaginian expedition settled. Oh, and ask Festo to clear up these birds. Burn them or bury them, I don't care. Now, where's that wine?'

Fabius' history was progressing. But his eyesight was failing, and each day Laelius and I took turns to write down his dictation of the work, or read to him from Herodotus or Thucydides to improve, he said, his style. I remember I was reading from Pericles' funeral oration when there was a sharp knock at the door.

'Come in,' Fabius said. 'Who is it?' he asked as the door closed.

'The usual courier from Sempronius, sir,' I replied.

'Good. Then open the despatch, and read it. There is time before the house convenes?'

I looked at Laelius. He always had a fine sense of time, whereas I always had to look at the calibrated candles and work out the new hour.

He nodded. 'Yes, sir, there is time.'

'Then carry on.' The courier left, without a word. I broke the wax seal, as I had done many times before, expecting – what was I expecting? More of the same, I supposed. Scouting, engagement imminent . . . We had been hearing it for weeks.

'*Tiberius Gracchus Sempronius, Coss., Pr., Aed., Tr., Pl., Senatui Populoque Romano,*' I read. '*Ego exercitusque valemus—*'

'Yes, yes,' Fabius interrupted. 'The usual formalities. Skip all that, Publius. Get to the meat.'

'Yes, sir.' I cleared my throat. 'Yesterday, we captured a scouting party of the enemy's,' I read. Still 'the enemy', not 'Hannibal'. 'Thirty-eight Gauls. We made them talk. From them I learned the enemy's position and plans. They are encamped on the far side of the River Trebia, a tributary of the Po. We march at dawn to engage them.'

'Thank you, Publius,' Fabius yawned. 'Good news at last. I will inform the Senate that we can expect to hear of Sempronius' victory the day after next.'

'Excuse me, sir,' said Laelius from his corner, 'but how can you be so sure?'

'How? Come, come, Laelius. Have you not been writing down my history? Have you not learnt how the Roman army was forged in the furnace of war until it became the greatest fighting force the world has ever seen? Ask Publius. He has seen a Roman army in action. Invincible, wouldn't you say, Publius?'

'With respect, sir, we never joined battle.'

'No, but you've seen the discipline, the order. They're well provisioned and armed. How can any mercenary rabble match that, even if they did manage to cross the Alps? If they did, they must be exhausted. And Sempronius is an experienced commander. So is your uncle Gnaeus. This Hannibal is not. Why, he can hardly be much older than you two are. Isn't that right?'

'I can't really say, sir. I hardly saw him. But yes, he's certainly young.'

'There you are! Now, we have a little time, I hope, to continue my history before the sitting. Anything else from Sempronius, Publius?'

'Yes, there is a footnote, sir.'

'Oh? What's that?'

'He adds . . .' I swallowed hard, and looked again at the writing. 'He adds that they crucified the prisoners, sir.'

'Crucified them!' Fabius' voice was keen. He played with his beard, and the light and a breeze streamed in from the window behind him. I felt the morning air was cold. 'That's certainly a vigorous course of action, wouldn't you say?'

I felt sick at the thought. Yes, I had seen the Romans murdered by Hannibal at the Rhodanus and Ticinus. But that had seemed functional, war. The torture of Laelius' father was in a different league, I knew. Even so, the crucifixion of thirty-eight men seemed to me gratuitously cruel. I looked again at the number, xxxviii, and it seemed long. I saw the xs as ten is, the v as five is, and shuddered. As we were discussing the matter, they would be hanging there, dying in agony, alive. At least whoever cut out Priscus Laelius' tongue had then cut his throat.

Laelius answered Fabius, and saved me. 'They deserve worse than that for what they did to my father,' he said quietly. I was and am less sure. If cruelty piles on cruelty, who knows where it will end?

As Laelius and I were leaving the Senate that evening, one of the clerks called me back. 'The father of the house is asking for you,' he said. 'Please attend Fabius Pictor in his room.'

'What, just me?' I asked, looking at Laelius. 'Yes, sir. There is someone he wants you to meet – alone.'

My father had asked Laelius to have supper with us. 'All right,' I said. 'Laelius, just carry on. I'll see you at home. My father won't be there yet, but Cornelia will look after you.'

'I'll wait for you here, if you'd rather.'

'No, don't worry. I won't be long.'

'Ah, Publius,' said Fabius a few minutes later. 'Thank you for coming. 'There's someone I want you to meet who is also keen to meet you. Cato, step forward.'

He must have been behind the door when I came in. From my left, someone of around my age stepped forwards. That was the only similarity between us. He was small, and squat, thick set, with sallow skin. His arms were too short for the rest of him, and hung like a monkey's. His forehead was low, his nose fat and wide, his eyes deep in their sockets and too close together. To this day I maintain that he gave off a particularly rank smell. Sweat I was used to. This was something worse, acrid and sour.

'Publius, I want you to meet Marcus Porcius Cato. He is a client of Valerius Flaccus, whom of course you know.'

I nodded. 'I do, sir.' An arrogant and self-important senator, who gibed at Laelius whenever possible.

'Plaased t'meet you,' Cato said, or rather mumbled, looking at me from under dark brows.

'I beg your pardon?'

Fabius laughed. 'Ah, the accent! Cato is from Tusculum, Publius, though he has spent most of his life in the Sabine country.' Yes, I can believe that, I thought. Pig-farmers, no doubt. 'His people are farmers, who have won the contract to supply our expedition to Carthage. So I thought you two should meet, since you have interests in common.'

'I hear you saw 'im,' Cato said, scratching his nose. His toga was more of a gown than a toga, so ill-fitting that it flopped over his sandals. Still, Fabius can't see that, I thought, and he would want me to judge the substance, not the form. Both I have found wanting.

'I'm sorry. Saw whom?'

'That 'annibal.'

'Yes, I saw him,' I replied dryly.

'Come, come,' Fabius interjected, standing up behind his desk. 'Don't be so modest, Publius. As I'm sure you've heard, Cato, my pupil saved his father's life on the occasion he, ah, met Hannibal. He has been rightly and highly praised for his courage.'

'But you risked yir own, didn't you?' His diphthongs were like an owl screeching.

'Yes, I suppose I did. I—'

'You were lucky t' get out alive?'

'Yes, he was,' said Fabius proudly.

Cato turned to him. 'Seems to me, sir, there's a difference

'tween valuing courage high 'n' life cheap.' He snorted loudly, and wiped his nose on his sleeve.

'Ah, a *gnomon*,' Fabius remarked, nervously, I thought.

I was too astonished by Cato's rudeness to know what to say. 'I must be going, sir,' I managed, as calmly as I could.

'Quite, quite. Anyway, you'll be seeing more of Cato. Flaccus will be introducing him to the Senate tomorrow. Until the morning, good night, Publius.'

'Good night, sir.'

And they mocked Laelius as a *novus homo*, I thought angrily as I walked home. This Cato couldn't speak Latin, let alone Greek. And he probably had pig dung under his fingernails – if not his armpits. Still, I need not bother with him again. I would ignore him if our paths crossed in the Senate.

Events proved me wrong. I often wonder how I would have acted had I known just how wrong I could be.

At home, there was no sign of Laelius. 'Where is he?' I asked Festo.

'Gone home, master,' he said. 'In a hurry. Said he wasn't feeling well.'

'Oh. And Cornelia?'

'In her room. Said she'll see you and your father at supper.'

She did. She seemed flustered, and ill at ease. As soon as I sat down, I saw a bruise on her right cheek.

'Cornelia, what happened?'

'Oh, that,' she said, raising a hand to her bruise, and blushing. 'I . . . So stupid. I . . .'

'You what?' my father asked, looking up from his roast capon.

'I walked into a door. Just wasn't concentrating.'

'Well, please be more careful, Cornelia. We don't want any more wounded Scipios walking around for a while. And why have you got a scarf on?'

I had noticed that, but thought nothing of it. I looked

231

again. A fine piece of red silk. It had been my mother's, I was sure.

'I think I'm getting a chill,' Cornelia said, 'so I thought I would wrap up. That's all.'

We turned, or at least my father and I did, to talking about the Senate. Cornelia ate little, made her excuses and went to bed.

I must interrupt again. This is too important, although when I come to write up my fair copy I will make this a note in the margin.

Scipio just does not see. Even though he remembers the incident, he does not connect Laelius' abrupt departure with Cornelia's bruise, and covered neck. Scipio still loves Laelius as himself, and feels no danger from the evidence his friend soon will give. It is the fairest flowers that have the sharpest thorns. I feel a darkness, of the past and present. I pray I may be wrong.

The matters of equipment, money, munitions and men for the expedition to Carthage were settled. I learnt a great deal from following the discussions and plans in the Senate. Again and again my father had me go over how many spare bridles the army would need, how many nails and cooking-pots, hammers, swords, surveying equipment, dressings, spare colours, heads for *pila*, pitch for the ships and spare sails – quite apart from cooks and grooms, smiths and carpenters, engineers and couriers.

I worked so hard at the long lists that my head ached and my vision blurred. Laelius soaked up this information; I had to apply myself. But I thought of Quinta, now looking after Lucius, or trying to, and persevered. 'A hot meal and a dry tent.' I have always remembered.

Everything was ready, bar Sempronius, my uncle and their legions. When would they come? The whole Senate was restive, bored. Every day brought new reports of Carthaginian pirates attacking our merchant ships, now openly and at sea. There was also fresh trouble from the Illyrians, encouraged it was said by Carthaginian gold. It was time to strike, to 'cut off', as Fabius put it to the Senate, summing up the now-established plans, 'the snake's head'. I wondered if there weren't snakes more dangerous from the tail.

It was the middle of a sultry, airless morning when they came at last. The Senate was in session. Crispus Appius, the curule magistrate, was speaking. The double doors that led into the debating chamber swung open, and Crispus broke off. I was not alone in finding that a relief. The terror and exhilaration of seeing Hannibal's army had worn off. Sometimes I thought it had been a dream. My conscious misgivings and fears had gone, like the mist of early morning. Like everyone else, I expected news of victory, of the annihilation of the man who had led an army across the Alps in winter and wounded my father, consul of Rome.

One by one, the senators rose from their seats at what they saw. From our stools at Fabius' central seat, Laelius and I also saw. Three men, two of them officers from their clothing, stood crumpled, weary and dirty at the door. Unease rippled through the room like wind in corn. Some gasped and pointed, others shouted and gestured.

I felt Fabius' hand, squeezing my shoulder, felt his breath hot on my ear. 'What is it?' he hissed.

'Three messengers, sir. It looks bad. Call for silence. Let them speak.'

'Silence in the Curia,' Fabius roared, 'and we will all resume our seats. Are we barbarians? We will hear this news, favourable or ill, as the Romans that we are!'

Still muttering, staring round, frowning, the senators sat down. I saw my father to the right of Fabius, his face anxious and intent. The three men walked forward. They were tired, cowed and dusty. Two had blood on their cloaks, and the hair of all three was matted with sweat and dirt.

'Now, sir,' I whispered to Fabius.

'*Valetne exercitus senatus populique Romani?*' he began, the formulaic greeting, in a chamber now completely still.

'*Haud etiam valet,*' the man on the left interrupted. '*Haud!* – No, the army is certainly not well!' The anguished anger in his voice was clear, before his words were drowned by an incredulous, protesting roar. As I looked hard at him I saw that it was Scribonius under the dirt, which covered even his scar. His chin was hard set, his eyes sunken.

'Silence!' Fabius roared, stepping forward blindly into the open floor. 'Speak, man. Tell us.' The noise died down.

'*Patres et conscripti*, we have been defeated in battle,' Scribonius went on, 'at the River Trebia. A rout. We have lost one legion, perhaps more. The whereabouts of your colleague, the senator Sempronius, are unknown—'

'Is he alive?' someone shouted.

'I don't know,' Scribonius replied to a pregnant silence, sounding exhausted, dazed. 'We couldn't get to him. They cut us off, coming from our rear. It was impossible, fantastic. The shouts of "Bar-ca, Bar-ca, Bar-ca!" filled your inmost ear. It was a frenzy of killing, hacking, dying, and—' His voice broke, his head slumped.

'And?' said Fabius gently.

'And?' Scribonius paused, looked around, seemed to collect himself. Then, so quietly that I doubt to this day that the senators at the back could hear him, he said, his eyes locked on Fabius, 'And then I saw the River Trebia running red with Roman blood.'

The silence was deep and dismal. It can be much more frightening than noise.

My father broke it. 'Father of the house,' he said clearly and firmly, 'forgive me if, as consul, I intercede.'

His head hanging, Fabius nodded, and his long beard brushed his chest.

My father went on, more loudly. 'Praetor, go to the *rostra*. Tell the people. Guards, bring these three men chairs, and water. Fellow senators, consider now your questions. Then ask them, but in order, and in calm.'

So for the next few hours, we heard of the battle of the Trebia; of the first attack across the river at very first light, before our army had broken its fast; how Hannibal's soldiers, lightly armed, wading the river, then darting in threes and fours around and behind and between the maniples, had broken our *hastati*, then withdrawn; how, even then, Sempronius was giving orders to resume formation and have dry rations passed round, when the slingers' volleys began from above our army, high on the opposite bank; so many, said Scribonius, that the sky was dark and rained stones.

Our maniples took shelter under their shields. Few were killed, for at that range the stones had lost their strength, but the stratagem worked. Our army could not stay where it was. Sempronius had to advance or fall back. He was not a man to do the latter, so he gave the fatal command.

The hailing stones went on as our soldiers began to wade across the icy Trebia, their stomachs empty, their minds confused, but their orders at least clear − to advance up the opposite bank and engage the enemy. From behind them, with Sempronius and my uncle, Scribonius and the other tribunes could see few enemy soldiers on the opposite bank. It was dense with scrub. Then, as our first ranks of troops started to march up, rows of Hannibal's men 'popped up', Scribonius said, from the scrub, like 'puppets in a show'. Our *hastati* threw their *pila*, but uphill, and they had little effect. The rows of the enemy disappeared from view as suddenly as they had come, until two whole legions were committed, picking their way as best they could up the bank. Then, then it happened; and Scribonius told this part to a house so silent that we could hear the muffled clamour of the people gathered outside in the Forum, hoping to learn more when we had finished.

'The maniples couldn't keep order. Time after time, Sempronius told the trumpets to sound "File order, *file*", but across the water and at that distance the men couldn't hear. Anyway, it wouldn't have made any difference what order they were in. What happened next is something I have not seen in thirty years of war – and hope not to see again.'

Scribonius paused, and drank some water. He looked at the two men with him, almost willing them to take up the story. Both slowly shook their heads. The house was completely hushed, the senators leaning forward as if to draw the words to them.

'Horsemen,' he said, 'heavy horsemen. Not cavalry, like ours. They were in full armour, the horses too, and carried short, heavy lances. In three lines they came down the hill, steady, many, many hundreds of them, and wrought carnage in our muddled ranks. The order, the discipline, was incredible. If one was unhorsed, two more dismounted to join him and they formed a porcupine of bristling, stabbing spears against which our men, their *pila* thrown, were helpless. Our soldiers died like animals in an abattoir until the ranks coming after them slipped and fell in all the blood until they broke, and turned and moved back down the hill.

'The heavy horse came on against our men, bunched at the riverside, unable to regroup or get away. It was only when Sempronius saw the enemy infantry massing on the brow of the hill opposite—'

'How many?' my father asked.

'Thousands. More than that, I cannot say – only then did Sempronius give the command: "Withdraw!"'

No one spoke. Minds were racing, assimilating, until at last

Fabius said, 'So you withdrew in good order, with at least three legions still intact?'

Scribonius buried his face in his hands and rubbed his eyes; then looked up and around the chamber. His voice louder, clearer, firmer, as if he faced a rooted sorrow, he said clearly, 'No, sir, no – at least, not all of us. Gnaeus Scipio, who commanded the legion in reserve, must have done so. He was well in the rear. The rest of us were withdrawing when behind us, from over the brow of the hill, began a noise that would suit the Underworld, a high-pitched, wailing screech, rising and falling away.'

'The Carthaginian war-trumpet, the *corynx*,' someone said from the back.

'Whatever it was,' Scribonius went on, 'it was a signal and, as we were turning, from the trees around us cavalry burst out, light this time and nimble, and after them came screaming, naked Gauls. Sempronius screamed, "Lock shields!" but it was hopeless, confused. A group of Gauls drove between me, my colleagues here and Sempronius. I saw his colour-bearer cut down and killed. Sempronius felled the Gaul who killed him, seized the standard, and spurred his horse away towards the trees.

'We broke off, perhaps a dozen of us, and rode away. Two *turmae* of cavalry joined us. For the rest, I do not know. We came straight here. Of Scipio and his legion, in that broken country, we saw nothing. Nor were we pursued. We still hold the port of Pisae, through which we passed, and Placentia, I presume. We will hear more in time. What I know, you now know.' The traditional ending for messengers to the Senate. He was done. Scribonius stood up, threw back his cloak, and put his hand on the hilt of his sword.

'Reverend Fathers, I fled from an engagement. Father of the house, I offer my sword to your judgment.' The steel rang in the scabbard. Scribonius spun it round, and double-handed held the sword-point to his belly, just under his breastplate of dirtied bronze. Beside him, his two companions got to their feet, and did the same.

'I cannot see you,' Fabius said, 'but my ears tell me what you have done. In times of peace, I would pass the judgment, but Rome is at war. This is a matter for the consul present. Scipio, come forward and stand beside me.'

My heart was pounding as my father walked up to Fabius. My father's eyes locked on each of the three men, one by one. Then he turned to face the assembly. 'Should these three fall on their swords before us in shame?' he called out, and his voice echoed around. He scanned the faces around him. No one spoke. I saw Scribonius' hands begin to tremble, and sweat run down his face.

'Then I, Publius Cornelius Scipio, as consul, will judge. I say' – it was so still that Laelius breathing beside me sounded like a storm – 'I say enough Roman blood has been spent. These men were surrounded, trapped front and rear. I have felt the steel of Hannibal. None more than I wants him dead, or brought to us in chains. But I say to these soldiers, who are servants of Rome as are we all, sheathe your swords.' He turned back to Fabius, his sandals scuffing on the floor. 'Father of the house, I suggest you declare this session of the house ended, and that we senior magistrates continue to talk to these three men on our own.'

Order ended as autumn leaves before a north-east wind. Laelius and I walked out of the chamber together in a cacophony of noise. My mind was spinning. It wasn't that Scribonius had been spared. Hannibal had come. With five legions against him, he had won.

Over the next few days, I talked of nothing but the Trebia with my father, and with Laelius. With Laelius I drew up plans of what we understood to have happened at the battle. What Hannibal had done was brilliant, stupendous. He had used the land. But more than that, he had planned, right down to feeding his men before daylight. His timing seemed to have been perfect. I suggested to my father over supper that we send a deputation to Celtiberia to try to find out how Hannibal's army had been trained.

'A deputation? No, Publius.'

'But why not, Father?'

'Because we would never see them again. Remember Teuta, queen of the Illyrians?' I nodded. 'Well, I meant to tell you. We've learnt that Hannibal's brothers, Hasdrubal and Mago, now hold the whole of Celtiberia for Carthage. They each have large armies, and would make Teuta seem civilised. So no, we won't send a deputation. But we will send some spies. A good idea, Publius. Well done. I'll tell the Senate tomorrow.'

The Senate was in turmoil. Two schools of thought prevailed. The first was for invading Carthage immediately, the second for postponing that and sending a new army after Hannibal. The legions from the eastern seaboard had been sent for, and one of Rome's own two remaining legions was being prepared to march either north to Hannibal or south for Sicilia and Carthage.

Scribonius was in the chamber every day, to answer questions and advise. He had become morose, and withdrawn. I, a mere pupil, of course could not question him in the Senate. But two days after he had brought the news of the Trebia, I literally bumped into him as I was going into and he leaving the latrines.

'So, we meet again, sir,' he said with a wry smile. 'You know I had my misgivings about Hannibal. Then, no one would have listened had I expressed them. Now, they are too preoccupied to hear.'

'So which side are you on, Scribonius?'

He stiffened. 'As I have always been, sir, I am on the side of Rome.'

'Yes, but I mean are you for invading Carthage, or for going after Hannibal?'

'Invade Carthage, and leave Hannibal at your back?' He shook his head. There was, I saw, grey in his hair now. 'Madness.'

'So you'd go after him.'

'No.'

'I don't understand.'

'Hannibal would be my target, sir, certainly. But I wouldn't go after him. That would only mean that once again he'd pick his ground.'

'What, then?'

'I'd let him come to us, sir, that's what I'd do.'

'You mean you'd let him march on Rome?'

'Exactly. Send two of the eastern legions up to get behind him. Then wait for him here with the rest.'

'Why?'

'Because then we could fight him on our ground, sir, out on the plain. Not even his fancy horsemen could break our lines and maniples there, sir – and certainly not those naked Gauls. Anyway, good to see you again, sir. But excuse me, I must get back inside.'

I meant to discuss Scribonius' views with Fabius and my father. There was never time. That afternoon, a courier came with a despatch from my uncle Gnaeus, back behind the walls of Placentia. Laelius and I heard the hubbub generated by their arrival, even from Fabius' room where we were working. This time, my father and several of the senior senators joined us for the breaking of the seal – and, accompanying Valerius Flaccus, Cato was also there. This time, it was the senior Scipio who read out the despatch.

My uncle's news was good and bad. He and his legion had withdrawn in good order from the Trebia. Strangely, they had not been pursued. They had marched indirectly back towards

Placentia, camping properly each night, scouting not only for the enemy but also for survivors. The latter they had found; a hundred here, two hundred there. My uncle's strength was just over two legions.

As to the bad news, no one knew at first what had become of Sempronius. Then when, after five days, my uncle approached Placentia circumspectly from the north-east, he came to the place where Sempronius had crucified Hannibal's party of scouts. There, he wrote, they found Sempronius, nailed by hands and feet to a thirty-ninth stake in the middle of the desiccated Gauls, alive still amid the bloated vultures and crows. The birds had already picked out his eyes. He died within minutes of the stake being cut down. 'We have given his body,' my uncle wrote, 'a proper funeral. His ashes I hold here, ready to bring them or have them sent to Rome.'

The blood drained from my father's face as he read this. Fabius slumped in his chair. 'Savages! Filthy savages!' my father exploded. The other senators murmured in agreement. I thought of Euphantus, and something he had taught us about actions and reaction. But then, from what my father read, I realised the treatment of Sempronius was mild.

'I have also,' my uncle wrote, 'to record a serious breach of discipline in the field. Of our forces caught on the far side of the Trebia, five maniples managed to break away. They went north. Four stades from the enemy's position, in a sheltered bowl, they came upon Hannibal's camp, almost defenceless. Quite properly, they put it to the sword and fired all the wagons and gear, and swept round and east, recrossing the Trebia at its confluence with the Po and so coming to Placentia.

'But one of the centurions, Paulus the Bruttian, reported to me the rape of a woman in the camp. He and his men took no part in it, but the others did. First they tied several prisoners to stakes and made them watch. The woman was a Celtiberian. She was, the prisoners said, the wife of Hannibal the Carthaginian.

I have put those responsible under charges, and await . . .' My father's voice fell away.

In the silence, Cato farted. He was standing to my right. 'Bitch prob'ly begged for it,' he said casually.

Fabius turned his head towards Cato. When it came, his voice was icy, measured. 'Marcus Porcius Cato, what did you just say?'

'I said, sir,' he replied, 'that the bitch prob'ly begged for it. Prob'ly wanted more and—'

'You savage!' Fabius roared. 'Get out of my room, and out of this building! Valerius Flaccus, take your client away. Then I want to see you here, alone, in an hour. Is that clear?'

I discussed the rape with my father that evening. 'It is regrettable, of course,' he said, 'but that is war. Even so, Fabius' reaction to that insufferable Cato was correct, and my brother was right to arrest the miscreants—'

'Miscreants, Father? Is that all they were?'

'Calm, Publius, calm. You have been with soldiers. You know that most of them are only a penis and a brain, and of those the majority are more the former than the latter. What you haven't seen yet is what men do in true war. Anyway, women in general, let alone wives, shouldn't go on campaign. Now, I want to prepare for tomorrow. I'm going to vote for an attack on Carthage. Hannibal has been lucky. But he won't come near Rome.'

'No? What will he do, then, Father?'

'Oh, loot a bit, and then go home. I'll argue we should send two legions to reinforce my brother, though. I'll offer to lead them myself.'

Sleep would not come to me that night. If Hannibal had let his wife come with him, if she had marched with him, endured the Alps with him, they must have loved each other very much. What would the rape do to his mind, and to his purpose? Perhaps my father was right, and he was an adventurer, or had been before. But now? Laelius thought Hannibal would turn for Celtiberia. I was not so sure.

And I thought the plan to send legions behind him was wrong; better to leave his back open. It was summer. If he could cross the Alps in winter, in summer he could easily go back the way he had come. His grief and anger about his wife might drive him back. On the other hand, of course, it might drive him on. Which would it be?

My uncle's despatches from Placentia revealed nothing. His scouts could find no trace of Hannibal and his army, not on any point of the compass. Again he had disappeared. In Rome, the Senate was busy with the consular elections. My father's year – and Sempronius', had he lived – was almost at an end.

Meanwhile, the Senate decided, in case Hannibal was coming south, to station two armies to block his way. Two legions went to Ariminum, to block the road south along the Mare Adriaticum, and two garrisoned Lucca and Arretium, to do the same in Etruria. The pass from Forli through the Apennines into Etruria was the only way he could go, they argued. The alternative pass, from Bononia to Pistoia, led through the impassable marshes of the Arno river valley. If anyone besides me thought that the Alps, too, were allegedly impassable, he kept his counsel – as did I.

The two leading candidates for the consulship, Gaius Flaminius Nepos, and Gnaeus Servilius Geminus, were duly elected. Flaminius was the favoured candidate of the people. He had commanded our army with some success against the Insubres. I had only once heard him speak in the Senate, where he made some good points badly. As a soldier, my father thought, he was a hot-head; as a man, simply rude. Servilius was different, gentle and a scholar, and a cousin of ours through my mother's line.

As the autumn rains began, there was still no news of Hannibal. Because of that, Flaminius proposed to assume his consulship in the field. The augurs argued against this before

Fabius and then the whole Senate, saying it would be inauspicious. Consuls should first visit the temple of Jupiter, proclaim the Latin Festival on the Alban Mount, take the auspices before the seven augurs, call on the *pontifex maximus*, offer prayers on the Capitol . . . I remember the debate. It was long.

Flaminius ignored it, and went to Arretium. I saw him leave Rome, surrounded by a crowd of hangers-on eager for the spoils his imminent victory would bring. I am pleased to say that one of them was Cato. Valerius Flaccus had all but disowned him, but Flaminius had found him a worthy sycophant. Servilius had no choice but to follow suit, and went to take over our other army at Ariminum. What would have happened if it had been the other way around?

I must be brief now. These were events of moment, but not ones in which I played a part. The essence of the matter is that Hannibal did come south, and through the Arno valley. He emerged, to predictable astonishment, near the town of Faesolae, and proceeded to loot and burn, under the eyes of Flaminius' scouts.

All this we learned from Flaminius' daily despatches. Hannibal's horses had acute mange, he reported, and many of his men were sick from marsh fever. 'So he has no chance of victory. I ask the permission of the people and the Senate' – typical Flaminius, my father observed, to invert the usual order – 'to attack and eradicate this Carthaginian brigand at once.'

I know what the Senate's reply was. I wrote it down myself, dictated by Fabius after the debate. Flaminius was ordered to wait until Servilius and his army had joined him from Ariminum. He was on no account to act alone. 'Even Flaminius can wait for six or seven days,' Fabius said when he was done, and the couriers – one with orders for Flaminius, one for Servilius – had left. I remember looking at Laelius across the room. I could see in his face that he shared my doubts.

Hannibal, though, had other plans. Instead of waiting, or

marching straight for Flaminius at Arretium, he moved right across his front, south through the valley of the Chiana to Cortona – en route for Rome. So Flaminius informed us. Fabius ordered this information kept secret, to avoid panic in the city. Then, for three days, we heard nothing more.

I am conscious that my account is flagging, Bostar. I am about to introduce another messenger. This is becoming like some Greek plays in which, by means of an overt message, the dramatist saves himself from the difficulty of developing the plot covertly. Take the opening of Aeschylus' *Agamemnon*, for example. Well, at least I haven't yet produced a Euripidean *deus ex machina* to enliven my account. Even so, it seems flat and bald as I tell it. So please edit this for me, Bostar, when I am finished – if the verdict of my peers allows me that time.

Well, I can hardly use the στιχομυθία, *stichomythia*, the quick dialogue of the dramatists when they want to sharpen a play. What I can do, I will; and that is simply tell what I know, without my observations or feelings at the time, and then get on with the events in which I was actor, not audience.

I was at home, sitting in the atrium with Laelius and my father, talking. It was hot, and all the doors were open. The noise came gradually, building up as when you approach the sea. It came from beyond the Forum, from over by the Ravenna gate, the sound of many thousand voices.

'It's a huge crowd,' said my father. 'Something must have happened. Let's go and see.'

By the time we reached the Forum, they were on its far side. Coming towards us, surrounded by people, men and children, wailing women, was a loose line of about a hundred Roman soldiers, still in armour but unarmed. They walked slowly, some unsteadily, exhausted and confused. We pressed on into the swelling, groaning, screaming crowd and the Forum echoed to wails and ululations, waves of noise.

There was a little girl beside me, a dark-haired, large-eyed

urchin, sobbing softly as she tried to see. She climbed onto a
market stall beside us and looked. I watched the fear descend on
her like dark. Her eyes met mine, and I pushed closer to her.

'Now,' I heard her say to herself before my father pulled me
on, 'we're all going to die.'

With the soldiers was a small covered wagon, drawn by two
bloodstained mules. The men wove their way to the public *rostra*,
and one of them climbed up, past the prows of Carthaginian galleys
sunk in the first Punic war. Sensing he was about to speak, the
crowd fell still to hear.

'I am Quintus Ligarius,' the soldier called out, 'tribune to
Flaminius. He is dead. We have been defeated in a great battle'
– how those words, '*pugna magna victi sumus*', are burnt into me
– 'and the Carthaginian sent us to tell you so.' His voice broke
at that, and he leant forward on to the frame of the *rostra* for
support as hundreds of voices clamoured their questions. Ligarius
raised an arm for silence. Slowly, it came.

'There is more. Clear a space!' he called to the soldiers below
him, 'and bring them out.'

The crowd moved back in response to the soldiers' prompting.
Four of them went to the wagon, and each brought forward
a wicker basket glistening with gold. 'Tip them out!' Ligarius
ordered. The soldiers did as they were told. Not coins, but
thousands of gold rings tinkled and glistened and glittered on the
flagstones of the Forum. 'These,' Ligarius shouted, 'were taken
from our dead at Trasimenus. Hannibal told me to say that he
returns them, for Rome will now need all the gold it can get.'

Anything else he said was drowned in an explosion of grief and
anger as people jostled, scrambled forwards. I shall not dwell on
how, like rising heat, the panic spread throughout the city, on
how my father forced his way on to the *rostra*, and had the Senate
guards beat drums for silence, and how he stilled the crowd and
sent them home, and the soldiers to hospital. Suffice it to say that
I know well what happened at Lake Trasimenus, because over

those next long days we heard accounts of it from many men. They were weak from wounds and loss of blood and their long march, but their memories were all too clear.

This is what happened. Flaminius ignored the Senate's orders, and did not wait for Servilius. He left a garrison in Arretium under Cato's command, and set out with the rest of his force. Between Cortona and Perusia there is a lake called Trasimenus. Along it runs a pass, flanked by a U-shaped range of wooded hills. That is where Hannibal went, and that is where, in early-morning mist, Flaminius and his legions followed.

When our army were halfway along the pass, they saw enemy ranks massed at its head. Flaminius called for the attack, and that is when Hannibal sprang. From behind, his heavy infantry sealed the way back. From above, men who had been concealed in the trees came bursting, screaming the battle-cry 'Sim-il-ce! Sim-il-ce!' the name of Hannibal's wife, whom Romans had raped and wronged. So do our sins return to us. It is the justice of the gods.

It was not a battle: it was a slaughter. Still in marching order, our soldiers had no room to throw their *pila*, and some not even room to draw their swords. They died in their thousands, many of suffocation in the press, caught under dead or dying bodies, others drowning in the lake. Flaminius met his end at the hands of an Insubrian who recognised him, it was said, as the devastator of his country six years before. They chopped off Flaminius' head and left it impaled on the shaft of a *pilum*, while the killing went on under a sultry sun.

Our vanguard, of some four thousand men, managed to form battle order and, largely intact, forced and hacked their way out and up the hill. They marched north-east, making for the River Niccone, a tributary of the Tiber, which would have led them to Rome.

They were pursued by cavalry, surrounded, captured. The Carthaginian commander, whose name was Maharbal, let the allies and the auxiliaries go. Not the Romans, just over one thousand of them. They were disarmed and disembowelled, and left to die.

There was more to come. This was a time of dying, when all faces were gaunt and hope grew dark; when we functioned only because there was nothing else to do. Servilius had been on his way to Arretium as ordered. Sensibly, he had sent a force of some two thousand cavalry on ahead, under the command of one of his tribunes, Caius Centenius. They, too, were captured by the Carthaginians, and slaughtered to a man.

The day of that news, Fabius called a plenary meeting of the Senate. His eyes had failed completely now, and he had become morose and withdrawn. 'I do not grieve that the twilight of my life is being taken from me,' he said to me in his room. 'I grieve that I can be of such little help to Rome. Now, lead me to the Senate, Publius Cornelius Scipio. For this old man, you are appropriately named, and he will now do what he can.'

His speech was utterly compelling, spontaneous, measured, moving, delivered to a packed house which sat still throughout, transfixed. 'I am an old man now,' he began, 'and I have all but lost the power of my eyes.' He hung his head. I saw, incredibly, tears well up in his blind eyes. He wiped them away, his old hands mottled and grey, his fingers gnarled as an ancient olive tree, bent with years.

Then, suddenly, he snapped his head back and went on, his voice sonorous with power. 'I wish, on such a day as this, that the power of speech had also failed me, so that I would not be able to recount the sorrows that have fallen on us. But in this dark hour, reverend Fathers, let us now praise famous men, and our fathers who begat us. Remember how Aeneas endured the anger of the gods, the descent into Hades, the unrelenting hatred of Juno; how Romulus overcame all to found this city, and protect it; how, for her sake, many, many men have laid down their lives; remember Horatius Cocclus at the bridge, or aged Cincinnatus putting down the plough to take up his sword – for Rome.

'For Rome, we threw off the tyranny of the kings; for Rome, we developed our Republic, to this day unique in the world. Let that light die, and all the world will be dark, as even are my eyes. Let that light die, and all that will be left is the tyranny of Carthage, with its merchants greedy for money and power.' Fabius spoke for over an hour. When he was finished, there was in the Senate a new spirit. And it was only then that my father raised the matter of another part of the message Ligarius had been cursed to bring.

Hannibal had, it seemed, spared two thousand of our soldiers. But he wanted a ransom for them. He wanted one silver *denarius* from which the name of Rome had been excised. The Senate debated this for over an hour. Accepting the insult, some argued, was a small price to pay for the lives of two thousand men. But Fabius caught the mood of the Senate, though I was surprised by the harshness of what he declared. When all had had their say, he had Ligarius called in.

'Go back to Hannibal the Carthaginian, Quintus Ligarius,' Fabius ordered. 'Tell him that Rome has no need of such poor soldiers as he now has.'

Ligarius simply nodded. He left the debating chamber in silence, and was never seen again.

The consensus was that Hannibal would now march on Rome. There was, after all, nothing in his way. At Fabius' suggestion, my father was granted proconsular powers to see to Rome's mighty walls and supervise the destruction of all the bridges over the Tiber, bar one. Even that was to be torn down as soon as the legions of Servilius and those under my uncle's command were safe inside the walls.

Fabius sent five separate couriers with the same orders to both my uncle and Servilius. They were to come to Rome with all speed, leaving only small garrisons in Placentia and Ariminum. Servilius was to march north first, and make his way to Rome, avoiding battle at all costs. My uncle's legions, of course, would come by ship. He was empowered to requisition all the vessels he needed. Fabius also ordered Cato to remain in Arretium with his garrison, and defend it at all costs.

So we waited, and we worked, Laelius and I with my father, from dawn until supper after dusk, and then we went weary to welcome beds. In places, my father felt, the walls were weak; and the iron bars that prevented access along the city's aqueducts, an obvious weakness in our strength, he ordered reinforced. But it was to the training of the people that he devoted most time. 'Men defend walls, not walls men,' Fabius had said. So each day in the Forum my father organised exercises for the people in archery and slinging, in fire-fighting and first aid.

To Valerius Flaccus Fabius had been given the job of burning all the crops and farms within a narrow radius of Rome. With small detachments of the city guard, all on horseback, he went out to do that each day, crossing the Tiber by a hidden ford. I saw him returning in the evenings, blackened with smoke and sore from what must have been each time a very nervous ride.

Meanwhile, Fabius in person was attending to another aspect of Rome. He consulted the Sybilline books. From them he learnt that a vow had to be made to hold games in honour of Jupiter; a shrine had to be dedicated to Venus Erycina and to Mens. He held a series of *lectisterna*, ceremonial banquets offered to the images of the gods on their couches, one each for Jupiter and Juno, Neptune and Minerva, Mars and Venus, Apollo and Diana, Vulcan and Vesta, Mercury and Ceres. He made sure the people were involved, and so, in action, did Rome recover from the psychological blow of Trasimenus. As to the physical, the Roman people were, as Fabius had observed in his speech, 'as hardy as the vine, and would recover in time'. But, I remember wondering, had we the time?

Servilius and his legions arrived without incident, as then did my uncle. The barracks in the southern quarter were overflowing with men, and the whole city teemed with nervous life. Days turned to weeks. The brothels were always busy, and the baths, and the merchants' stalls. Each night, great bronze braziers, my father's doing, blazed along Rome's walls. Still Hannibal did not come. Busyness turned to boredom; we heard of fights, and petty wranglings. The city's mood began to fade and pall.

Laelius and I were sitting one morning on the parapet of the east wall, looking out along the Via Valeria.

'There's no point in looking that way,' came a familiar voice behind us, 'or any other way, for that matter.' We turned round.

'Scribonius!' I said. 'We haven't seen you for weeks. Where have you been?'

'Busy, like everyone. Your father's done a very good job. I hear you've worked as hard as he has – and you, Laelius.'

'The waiting's worse than the work,' Laelius replied. 'When do you think Hannibal will come, Scribonius?'

'I don't,' Scribonius said simply, moving to sit between us and the wall.

'You don't?'

'Why not?' I asked.

'Firstly, these walls. You two, more than anyone, should know how strong they are, and how well defended. What have we got here, for example?' he asked, looking along the walkway to one of my father's many stores. 'Pitch and tar and oil – and more arrows than there are Carthaginians, I should think.' He smiled at that, but then turned grave again.

'You mean he won't try because he hasn't got any siege equipment?' Laelius went on.

'Not just that, though it is a factor.'

'What do you mean, then?' I asked.

'Look west, sir – and you, Laelius.' We did so. 'What do you see?'

'Why, the Tiber of course,' I replied, 'running out to sea.'

'Exactly. Now, you two are well educated. Tell me what you know about the siege of Rhodes by Demetrius Poliorcetes.'

Laelius was always quicker. 'He abandoned it after two years.'

'Yes, but why?'

I understood. 'Because it, too, could be supplied by sea – as we could, by barges up the Tiber from Ostia.'

'Exactly, sir. Hannibal may not have siege equipment, but he certainly hasn't a fleet.'

'He could have sent for one from Carthage, and just be waiting for that,' Laelius said.

'Yes, he could – and he might have. But even if he has, I still don't think he'll attack Rome.'

'Because?' asked Laelius.

'Because that's the obvious thing to do, and he's never done the obvious. No, I think he'll burn and pillage until the winter, completely unopposed. Then he'll find a comfortable billet for the winter, and rest his men. I think he'll also try to get some of our allies to join him. Did you note that, after Trasimenus, the allies he captured were released unharmed?'

'Yes, that's a good point, Scribonius,' I said. 'He was trying to show that his fight is only with Rome.'

'And some cities, like Capua, might well break their treaties and allegiances with Rome,' offered Laelius.

'Well, we shall have to see. But for my money,' said Scribonius, 'the winter will be long.'

Hannibal did as Scribonius had predicted. We got reports of huge tracts of Roman farmland laid waste. Then he moved into Campania. Fabius' estate was one of the few he didn't burn, and that added to the pressure on my patron. Of course we knew that Fabius was beyond suspicion, but that didn't stop the whispers. I wondered where Hannibal got such information. From deserters, or prisoners, I imagined. But even before then, his topography was impeccable.

'He must have a mapmaker with him,' Laelius said.

I wondered. 'A mapmaker? No army that I've heard of has ever had such a thing.'

'No,' Laelius replied. 'But then, no army we'd heard of had ever crossed the Alps.'

I will not break my self-imposed silence. I will set this as a note in the margin of the fair copy, when I make it. Laelius was correct in his supposition, and that mapmaker was I. I had six assistants, and Hannibal's geographical knowledge of Italy was as good as any Roman's, even before he got there. For a civilised people, the Romans were, and still are, remarkably backward in cartography. The ancient Babylonians made cadastral maps. The Assyrians and Egyptians had topographical maps, some in relief, before Rome was born. The Persians made an art of making maps, and the Greeks made a science of that art. Alexander had his bematists, remarkably accurate surveyors and makers of maps. Two of them, Baeton and Diognetus, were even distinguished literary men. Yes, his empire seemed merely to realise eastwards – but he always knew where he was.

So, indeed, I made many maps for Hannibal the Carthaginian when I served him, and only to a Roman would that seem remarkable. But the greatest map of all is one we cannot make: that of a man's mind.

In the Senate, through the long, empty days, tempers rose and frayed. Fabius was criticised for doing nothing, especially by Caius Terentius Varro, a butcher's son and very obvious *novus homo* who had made a fortune in the slave trade and thereby had moved first into the equestrian ranks and, from there, to the Senate.

Varro was patron to two assistants of my age, like me doing their *triconium fori*, Caecilius Metellus and Mucius Scaevola. I had never exchanged more than a few words with either of them, though by instinct I liked the former as much as I disliked the latter. Metellus was squat and short and dark, his face covered in acne, Scaevola tall and lithe and blond. Yet Metellus was of impoverished patrician blood, and Scaevola the son of one of Varro's business associates who was also, allegedly, Varro's pimp. Laelius called them the 'short and long show'. They scurried about whenever Varro was speaking, passing him notes, checking papers, leaving the debating chamber as if on matters of the utmost importance and coming back in again with yet another note or chart. Their research was good, though, and Varro's information was always accurate and precise as he charted Hannibal's movements and explained how he would have countered them, had he been in command. At first most of the other senators smiled into their beards at his tirades, but as time went on they listened.

The winter came, and it seemed long. Capua had opened its gates, its merchants their wares, and its women, we heard, their legs to Hannibal and his army.

'Bloody Capuans!' my father exclaimed when we heard the news. 'Never could trust them. I argued years ago against accepting their alliance. And the worst thing is that Hannibal's men will have been paid.'

'Paid, Father?' I asked.

'Yes, paid, with Capuan gold. Richest city in Italy. That means Hannibal's mercenaries won't desert now.'

'You think they follow him for money?'

'Of course. Why else? Savages, that's all they are. Let's hope the good life in Capua softens them up for us, the animals. We'll deal with them, and then with Capua.'

I didn't say anything, of course, but I doubted Hannibal's men served him only for money. What I had seen at the Ticinus, and heard of at the Trebia and Trasimenus, was a thing of such unity and beauty as could come only from love. Great love for him – or, I suppose, great hate for us.

Then we heard that Hannibal had moved himself and most of his army out of Capua to a winter camp on nearby Mount Tifata, famous for its bitter winds. So, softened by Capua and its sybarites? I thought of Hannibal brooding, planning from his eyrie in the rain and winter winds.

Meanwhile, despite the accusations of inaction, Fabius was recruiting men, mostly in the north, away from Hannibal's scouts. Soon there was a fifth legion in Rome, training every day on the Campus Martius, and then the makings of a sixth. The Senate passed a special tax at Fabius' bidding, in order to buy horses in Liguria in the spring. It was clear that Fabius had a plan.

He would, I think, have led the army out himself, though blind and frail. But by the spring he was very ill. He had a fever, and was in bed at his home, close to ours. Laelius and I went back and forth to the Senate for him, with his orders and comments. One of us always stayed with him, though, and read aloud. Homer had replaced the historians in his affections.

One day, he had a terrible fit of coughing. His body-slave brought him an aromatic tea sweetened with honey, and helped him drink it with a spoon. That seemed to clear his chest. He asked me to bring my father to him. I did, but then he asked both Laelius and me to leave the room. We waited outside.

Coming out, my father closed the door very gently. He looked worried. 'This has been a terrible strain on him,' he said. 'You know, I don't suppose he'll ever finish his history now. Amazing to think he was a tribune in the last Punic war. Anyway, you two, there'll be action in the Senate tomorrow, and no time for carping about supplies.'

'What's going on, Father?' I asked.

'Fabius wants me to move that the consular elections be brought forward. He feels we're now ready, and can't afford to have the spring planting held back. So, with two new consuls, we'll march against Hannibal very soon.'

'We, Father? Will you be going? Will Laelius and I?'

'Yes and no – or, rather, no and yes. I am to stay, as prefect of the city. But yes, Publius, you and Laelius are to go on campaign. I want you there to see the destruction of the man who almost killed your father – and struck some deadly blows against Rome.'

I have been trying, Bostar, to be comprehensive and controlled. But I cannot resist it any longer. The memory of Cannae is calling me, and I must go there. So I shall, saying only that two new consuls were elected, Lucius Aemilius Paullus for the patricians, and Caius Terentius Varro for the people. Having sent reinforcements to all the garrisoned towns – like Arretium, where Cato still was, and Placentia – we left Rome within the week, to prayers and sacrifices for our safe return. Laelius and I had been assigned to Varro's staff, as had Metellus and Scaevola. I was, it seemed, to get to know both of them rather better, although I thought no more of it than that.

I did say to my father that I would have preferred Paullus' staff.

'Knowing that, I had Fabius assign you to Varro's,' he replied. 'No less than Laelius' late father, he and others like him are the face of the new Rome. The world is moving on, Publius, and I don't want you left behind with the old.'

'What is this "new" Rome, father?'

'You'll see – once we've dealt with Hannibal. The greatest trading empire the world has ever known. Upheld and fortified by the Republic, it will spread beyond the western sea. It needs the ambition of men like Varro and, in time, Metellus and Scaevola. Do you know that Scaevola's grandfather was my father's groom? Who would have dreamt of finding a Scaevola in the Senate? That can be good, if combined with the steadiness of families like ours. That combination, Publius, will be unstoppable. Roman laws and justice, Roman peace, right across the world.' His face darkened, then he smiled, and slapped me on the back. 'But first things first. And first of all is—'

'I know, Father. First of all is Hannibal.'

We were, then, six full legions and auxiliaries, with over four thousand cavalry – the horses had come safe from Liguria. So this was a vast army, well over sixty thousand men, the largest, my father assured me, Rome had ever put into the field at once. By the average of our scouts' reports, Hannibal had fewer than forty thousand. If we were careful, and fought him on ground that suited us, we could not lose. After all, we agreed, by cutting their way out at both the Trebia and Trasimenus our infantry had proved that they were more than a match for the Carthaginians, if they formed and kept their order, and fought as they knew.

We marched, along the Via Latina, south and east. After four days we came to burnt and blackened country not of our doing, to sacked villages and stores. We went on, along the Via Appia, towards Beneventum and then Venusia, where Hannibal had last been seen. Each time I looked back from my place near the consuls in the vanguard, the army stretched away behind us, further than the eye could see. Water was not a problem, nor supplies for the men; we had brought plenty on wagons from Rome. Forage for the horses and cattle was, though. Our foraging teams had to range far. Our progress was slow.

It was good to come to Beneventum, and see what Hannibal had done. He had not sacked it, he had erased it: only ruined walls stood to show where it had been. We had heard of this, but seeing it hardened the army's mood.

I grew more and more impressed by Paullus, on his alternate days of command. His commands were as clear and courteous as Varro's, unfortunately, were petulant and peevish. I wondered whether there was anything Laelius or I could do to make sure Paullus was in command on the crucial day. Metellus and Scaevola kept themselves to themselves, discussing things earnestly with each other in whispers or low voices as we rode. The first time I spoke to them, something began that to this day has never stopped.

I was seeing to my horse in the picket-line one evening.

'Where is he, then?' Scaevola's voice. I spun round. Metellus was behind him.

'Where's who?'

'Why, your fancy-boy, of course.'

I turned red as comprehension dawned. 'How dare you!' I managed, almost speechless.

'Oh! How dare I talk the truth to a great toff Scipio, staff of Rome? That what you mean?'

'Look, if you're implying—'

'Implying? I'm implying nothing. I'm stating a fact. You know it's illegal in a Roman army, don't you?'

'"It"? What do you mean?'

'Buggery, that's what I mean.'

If I'd been wearing a sword, I would have used it. Instead, I launched myself at Scaevola, and we wrestled, writhing on the ground as the horses stamped and whinnied in alarm. I got a punch in to his stomach; he managed a stinging blow to my right cheek. Then suddenly Metellus was beside us, shouting, 'Stop it! Stop it, you fools! We'll all be up on charges!' He managed to drag Scaevola off, and Scaevola and I glared at each other, panting, squatting on our haunches, across two strides of ground.

'Touched a raw nerve, did I?' Scaevola hissed.

'You're beneath contempt, you plebeian oaf.'

'Quick!' Metellus whispered. 'There's a sentry coming.'

They slipped away into the growing dark. They were not in the tent when I got back. Laelius was.

'What happened to your face?' he asked as I lay down on my bed.

'My face? Oh, I fell. It's nothing. Blow out the lamp, Laelius. It's time to sleep.'

'Oh, by the way, Scaevola was looking for you. Said he had a message.'

'Yes,' I replied, turning on my side. 'I got it, thanks.'

'He's really crude, don't you think, Publius? Keeps jeering at me about my fair skin – and other things.'

'I can imagine. But ignore him.' I fell into an uneasy sleep. I was ashamed; and not just of behaving like a soldier in a tavern brawl. Perhaps Scaevola had touched a nerve. Perhaps that nerve was raw.

The next morning, near Venusia, we left the Via Appia. Laelius and I rode behind Metellus and Scaevola, who turned once, and smirked at me. I ignored him. Laelius didn't notice. We headed east towards the sea. That, our scouts told us, was where we would find Hannibal. That night was the first time he showed his hand.

'Fire, fire!' I heard the shouts in the middle of the night, and with all the other staff officers was quickly up and out of the tent we shared. Against the far wall of the palisade, wagons were burning, and all round the camp rang calls of alarm. Fire-arrows again, I thought. Just like the Rhodanus.

Huffing and puffing, Varro appeared to find out what was wrong. Paullus was encamped across the valley; six legions together used up too much ground.

'Where were the sentries?' Varro demanded.

'The ones on picket duty are dead, sir,' the *primus pilus* replied. 'Throats cut.'

'And the cattle, mules and packhorses?'

'Driven off, sir.'

'By all the gods! Can none of my soldiers stay awake! And you, Scipio. You too, Laelius, and Metellus, Scaevola! What are you staring at! Go and find out what happened. I want a full report – in the morning. I'm going back to bed. Oh, and *primus pilus!*'

'Yes, sir?'

'I want the sentries inside the camp on charges. They should have sounded the alarm.' With that, Varro stomped off, knocking into a cooking tripod as he went. He swore loudly. I wanted to tell him that Hannibal's men would have made much less noise than that, and that our sentries could hardly be blamed for not warning of a danger they didn't hear or see. But I held my tongue, and with Laelius walked off towards the fires.

It was the same the next night, and the next it was Paullus' turn. The night after, there were no fires, but only an unearthly wailing noise that woke the whole camp. I wished Scribonius had been there to confirm what it was, but he had stayed in Rome as tribune to my father. Even so, I was sure that we had heard the Carthaginian *corynx* in full voice. Over subsequent nights, we grew acquainted with its howl, although that didn't mean we could sleep.

Yet by day, these raiders and disturbers of the night were nowhere to be found. Our progress slowed to four or five stades a day. Even Varro was cautious, feeling out the land ahead with thorough scouting. The nights were hot and airless. By day, Laelius and I rode between the two consuls as 'liaison officers', although, since they had little in common but their rank and almost nothing to say to each other, our duties were not hard. So much, I thought, for my father's 'new Rome'.

As we approached the town of Cannae, both our armies were nervous, restless, tired. No one among that more than sixty thousand can have had a full night's sleep for over a week. And there was some infection of the bowels in both camps. I had it, we all had it: diarrhoea that left the anus aching and the bowels sore. What I disliked most was having to dismount suddenly, handing my reins to anyone near, and squat down along the line of march. Even in an army, that is one thing that should be done in private.

Scaevola kept up his filthy digs. Once, when Laelius had to dash to the bushes, I overheard Scaevola say to Metellus, 'Easy for him. His arse is always open.' I bit my tongue. My time would come.

Such was the state of the Roman force that moved, credulous but cautious, towards Cannae. One morning – it was almost noon – we saw the dust come billowing towards us. Laelius and I, riding alongside Metellus and Scaevola, were two ranks behind Varro in the van. '*Poeni, Poeni!*' We heard the scouts' excited yells before they got to us. 'Carthaginians, Carthaginians!'

Hannibal, it seemed, was waiting for us. No feints, no hidden attacks. His camp and battle-lines were clear, the scouts informed us, serried in a crook of the River Aufidus just to the north of Cannae; before that, an empty, open plain; before that, a range of hills. It seemed perfect to Varro, too perfect to Paullus, at the council they called.

'So, he's not skulking any more,' said Varro. 'Open battle, then, and he'll taste Roman steel.'

'Indeed, indeed,' said Paullus, holding a perfumed sachet to his nose – advisedly, against the stench of so many men's defecation.

There was also the delicate matter of command. Battle the following day, and it would rest with Paullus. Delay a day, and with Varro.

'We should camp tomorrow, and let the men rest,' said Varro unsurprisingly. 'Delay,' Paullus replied, 'and he may be gone, or lay some trap for us.' So the discussion continued.

In the end, Hannibal decided the matter for us. Surrounded by one legion, which marched with locked shields, both consuls and their staffs went forward early that evening to inspect Hannibal's position. It was extraordinary.

We saw rows and rows of tents. We saw wagons, baggage

and animals. Fires were burning, but there was no one there. Not a single human being. On either side of the camp, and behind it, ran the reed-beds of the Aufidus; the town of Cannae took its name from *canna*, reed. From the slight rise where we had stopped, Varro ordered a party forward. Returning, they confirmed that what seemed, was.

'So,' said Varro reluctantly, his horse fretting under his great weight, 'we attack tomorrow.'

'Attack what?' Paullus asked derisively. 'An empty camp? The moment we enter it, he'll attack us from behind. It has to be a ruse. He's probably in those hills behind us, watching and waiting for us to do just what you suggest.'

'Pah!' spat Varro. 'This man's no fool. Would you take on six legions, on their ground? Look, this plain is perfect for us. He knows that, and has run away. I say we plunder and burn his camp tomorrow morning – under, esteemed colleague, your command – and then we hunt him down.'

'The day after,' Paullus said with thinly disguised irony. 'Under, of course, your command.' So the bickering went on.

Riding back to camp, Laelius and I were side by side. It was a beautiful afternoon, of pellucid light and azure sky, with a cool breeze from the sea. The world was alive in a spring of rising sap and singing skylarks overhead. The earth on which we rode was fecund, rich and red.

'Well, what do you think, Laelius?' I asked.

'We've got him now,' he said with a smile.

'But why should he let us catch him here? Why here, and anyway why isn't he in camp?'

'You always worry too much, Publius. You ought—'

Suddenly, from the bushes to our left, came the sound of a man singing in a deep voice, rising abruptly to ululating shrieks. Startled, ahead of us Varro and Paullus reined in, and the whole column stopped.

'Well, don't just sit there, you idiots!' shouted Varro. 'Do something! Scipio, Laelius, go and see what's going on!'

We dismounted and, with four legionaries, pushed into the juniper bushes from which the sound had come. In a little clearing, seated on a fallen holm-oak, we saw a man, his head a mass of wild and curly, unkempt hair, chin up, singing to the sky and waving his arms to the rhythm of his song. His clothes were rags, filthy and torn. His feet were bare and black with dirt.

'You!' I shouted. 'What are you doing?'

He broke off. 'Doing, master? Tentio dun't do, 'e sing!' He laughed, outrageously, uproariously, and, leaping to his feet, proceeded to dance round and round in a circle, swinging his tattered cloak like a pair of wings.

'Soldier!' I said to the man next to me. 'Go and tell the consuls all is well. It is a madman, nothing more. They should carry on to camp.' He nodded, and turned. 'Now you,' I shouted to the madman, 'come over here!'

Skipping nimbly, he did as he was told, and stood before us, panting, rolling his eyes, humming and muttering to himself something like 'battle, fighting, dead men here, battle fighting dead men here,' then, louder, his mouth drooling, 'Battle fighting dead—'.

'Shut up, you!' Laelius snapped. 'Tell us why you're here!'

Tentio looked shocked. He stood completely still, as if considering. 'Me 'ere?' he replied, looking at us with his head half-cocked. 'Me? Ha! No, no, no no. No me. 'Im!' he shrieked triumphantly, and his jaw lolled.

'Him?' I said. 'Who's "him"?'

'That 'Annibal, that 'oo. Know why 'e's 'ere? Do you, do you?' He began humming to himself again.

'Tell us,' Laelius shouted, reaching for his sword, 'or else—'

I put a hand on his arm. Stepping forward, 'Tell us,' I said gently.

In one quick move, mad Tentio was sitting on the ground

before us, leaning back on his hands. I squatted down beside him. His smell was rank, and almost overpowering. His eyes narrowed as he whispered to me: ''E's 'ere for the tomb!'

'The tomb?' I asked, puzzled. 'What tomb?'

'That tomb,' he said, jerking his head backwards, 'over there.'

'There's a tomb in those trees, is there?'

'Mm, mm, a tomb, tomb, big tomb, tomb of Cauno tomb!'

'Cauno?' I asked. 'Who was he?'

'Cauno Carthage, Carthage Cauno!'

'Cauno was a man from Carthage?'

He nodded, and suddenly looked scared. Looking nervously round at Laelius and the four soldiers, he beckoned to me to come close and whispered in my ear, 'Cauno came from Carthage here. With six daughters. Romans raped 'em. Girls killed 'emselves for shame. Cauno buried them 'ere, 'n' built a tomb. Then he killed 'self there, and cursed us Romans. That's why 'Annibal 'ere.' He reached out and pulled my face to his. I saw the blackheads all around his rolling eyes. 'Beware the vengeance of Cauno,' he hissed. With a scream, he bounded up, and ran away towards the trees.

'Shall I go after him, sir?' one of the soldiers asked.

'No,' I said, standing up. 'Let him go. He's no threat. But fan out. We'll search those trees.'

'What are we looking for?' asked Laelius.

'A tomb,' I answered.

'A tomb?' he gave back, incredulous.

I laughed. 'No, Laelius, I haven't gone mad too. But we're looking for a tomb.'

We found nothing.

On the short ride back to camp, I told Laelius what Tentio had told me. 'And do you believe him?' Laelius asked.

'Remember Euphantus, Laelius,' I replied. 'Anything is possible. Someone would have mentioned it if it had happened in living memory. But perhaps it did happen, long ago. Etymologically, it's possible too. "Cannae" could have come from "Cauno", as easily as from "*canna*".'

'Come on, Publius,' he laughed. 'You're getting carried away.'

'Am I? Then why do you think Hannibal's come here? Why here?'

He looked serious. 'I have to say, Publius, I don't know. The western coast I could understand, for ships to or from Carthage. But here? And the empty camp? It's all very strange, that's for sure.'

We finished the ride in silence, riding at the pace of the soldiers' walk beside us. I was thinking about the vengeance of Cauno.

The council in Paullus' tent was almost over when we returned. The plan, I soon gathered, was for ten maniples to stay behind and guard each camp, one legion to loot and burn Hannibal's camp, and the rest of the army to form battle order across the plain, facing away from the camp towards the hills – the only direction from which an attack could come. Paullus had agreed.

'Right, any questions?' Varro asked, belching and holding out his goblet to the slave-boy for more wine.

'Yes,' said the *primus pilus,* Flaevius. 'In what order do you want the maniples, sir?'

I sensed trouble. We had discussed this endlessly on the march. The tradition was that members of the same family stood side by side in the ranks. But Varro, unchallenged by Paullus, had suggested an innovation that seemed to me not only gratuitous, but wrong. I remember that when, in a rare break with his custom, Varro asked me my opinion, I had quoted Nestor's advice to the Greeks in Homer's *Iliad*: ʽκρῖνʼ ἄνδραζ κατὰ φῦλα, κατὰ φρήτραζ, Ἀγάμεμνονʼ, '*Arrange your men according to their clans, according to their tribes, Agamemnon*'.

'Trust you to come up with some poofter Greek nonsense, Scipio,' Scaevola had sneered. I suppose, with hindsight, it was pompous, especially to Varro, the son of a butcher and to Scaevola, the grandson of a groom.

'Shut up, Scaevola!' Varro shouted, to his credit. 'This is an army, not a nursery school! Anyway, we'll do it my way, when the time comes.' By that he meant that we would break up the families in the ranks. 'They'll be keener that way,' he said. 'This is the new Rome. I didn't get where I've got by relying on family or friends.'

Paullus had merely raised an eyebrow.

So I wasn't surprised when Flaevius' question simply got the answer, 'New way. Agreed, colleague?'

Paullus barely nodded. 'As you wish.'

I saw Flaevius stiffen. But he saluted, said, 'Yes, sir,' turned and left the tent.

That night, after supper, Laelius and the others in my tent went straight to sleep. I couldn't. Paullus had sent out three patrols to scout the woods behind us, to see if Hannibal's army was there. As far as I knew, they had not returned. I got up, put on an ordinary soldier's cloak from the pile at the tent entrance, and set off for the main gate of the camp.

All our campfires were burning. I heard the shifting of the horses in their pickets and, above the cicadas' ceaseless chirping, heard the voices round the fires. Maniple after ordered maniple I saw sitting, talking round their fires; they should have been asleep. As I passed, I heard them muttering and arguing in soft voices. 'At least it's Paullus. He's cautious.' 'So what?' from another. 'I don't like it. There's something strange.' Then, 'Shut up you lot, and get to sleep': a centurion, I assumed. 'Have you all checked your arms? We'll need sharp swords tomorrow.'

At the gate, in the light of flickering torches, I saw Flaevius, talking anxiously to the sentries. 'They should have been back at least an hour ago,' he said as I approached.

'I was thinking the same thing,' I said, stepping forward into the light.

'Who's that?' asked Flaevius sharply, turning round. I pulled back my cloak. 'Oh, it's you, sir. Sorry, I didn't recognise you.'

'No reason for you to have done so, Flaevius, with me in this cloak.'

But, Bostar, the memory is calling. It is strong, so let me run to it. Our men had found Hannibal's army, or part of it, hiding in the hills. Two of our patrols had been captured. The third returned, bringing two prisoners. We questioned them late into the night, and learned that it was a trap. Hannibal had more than half his army hiding in the reed-beds of the Aufidus. He had assumed we would sack his camp and face our main force the other way as we did so. Then he could take us in both front and rear.

I rode over on Varro's orders and explained this to a sleep-dazed Paullus as dawn was breaking. He decided to do nothing that day but stay in camp, and not be drawn by Hannibal's bait. So all day our army waited in its two camps, nervous, restless, hot, sharpening swords, re-fixing *pilum* heads, repairing boots and gear. I lay, like Laelius, in my tent and tried to doze. Actually, I remember trying to count the buzzing flies.

'Surprised you two don't have anything more, ah, interesting, to do.' Scaevola's crude vowels broke the silence.

'Why don't you just keep your filthy trap shut, Scaevola!' Laelius replied, half rising from his bed.

'Why don't you come and make me, pretty boy?'

I reached across, and put a hand on Laelius' knee. 'Ignore him, Laelius.'

He lay back. 'All right,' he said. 'But we'll settle this afterwards, Scaevola.'

'Ooh! I'm terrified!' Scaevola mocked.

'Knock it off, both of you,' came from Metellus. 'We'll need all the strength we've got.'

'For what?' Scaevola asked.

'To count the dead,' I answered.

In mid-afternoon, our scouts reported movement in Hannibal's camp: his men in the reed-beds were returning. From within the walls of our palisade, our little Rome, we saw the smoke of Hannibal's campfires renewed, billowing in the still summer air.

Later, we saw lines of cavalry and soldiers coming from the hills and moving towards the river, in a sweeping detour, on the far edge of the plain. They too were returning to their camp. Hannibal had given up his plan, we assumed. He was going to face us, sword on sword.

Shortly before the evening meal, Paullus and Varro came to our camp to address the men, as they had just done in the other camp; we had heard the cheers. We were to attack in the morning, under Varro's command. 'As Romans, on our soil and terms and in our manner,' said Varro, 'in the *triplex acies*, as we have always done,' and he stood there beaming like a basking lizard in the sun. Still, the men's cheering was genuine. At last a battle, on a plain – even without the customary ties of family. The camp's mood was one of confidence that we would win. I was still thinking of Cauno's vengeance, scratching at the feeling as a dog at fleas.

That night, those thoughts concatenated in my mind. My sleep was fitful. I went over my orders. They at least were clear – and very simple. Like Laelius, Metellus, Scaevola and the other staff officers, I was to accompany Varro, in command, and Paullus, observing, and be prepared to deliver messages in person to the different legions and maniples if, in the noise of battle, the trumpets were not enough. Varro's and Paullus' position was to be that same rise on which we had stopped and first seen Hannibal's empty camp. The legions' watchword was to be 'Telamon'. I thought of Frontinus, and what he found there. So, no feints or fripperies. As at Telamon, the legions of Rome would make a straight, frontal attack. Our scouts had reported, just before the failing of the light, that there were no signs of any Carthaginian tricks. Hannibal's army was in camp. There were, they were sure, no troops deployed at the flank or rear.

He is risking everything now, I thought. Why? Who is this man, who has dared to defy Rome? And why here at Cannae? He is heavily outnumbered, yet seems to have chosen the ground to suit us. Why? To the snores of Laelius, I slipped at last into troubled sleep, feeling utterly alone.

The trumpets woke us in the faintest half-light of the dawn. In the latrines, the men were joking, excited. Breakfast was early, too, on Varro's explicit orders the night before. Perhaps I've underestimated him, I thought, as I ate my bowl of porridge. He's learnt something from the Trebia after all. Then, of their own accord, the maniples began to form.

As the light strengthened, Laelius and I and the other officers rode out of the camp with Varro to the rise. I saw Paullus and his party coming to join us. There may have been only one consul in command, but two were going to watch. We found a group of camp-followers already at our position. They had a trestle-table up, and on to it from two hampers were unpacking fruit and flagons of water and wine. Flowing past us went the steady tramp of many men, saluting as they passed. Hannibal's men, we could see, were also beginning to form battle order.

'Good, good,' Varro said, munching an early pear, force-grown no doubt, in those great hot houses of the new *latifundia*, vast estates owned by *novi homines* like Varro and worked by armies of imported slaves. 'He's behaving like a soldier this time, not a bandit.'

'You really expect him just to fight us head on, Varro?' Paullus asked.

'What else can he do? He's nowhere to hide, or to run.'

'I agree, but that still doesn't explain why he came back to camp. It doesn't explain suicide.' This was quite a speech for Paullus.

'Always worrying, colleague,' Varro replied. 'It's simple. He's had his day, run out of ideas. They're like Gauls, Carthaginians. Impulsive. Then they just lie down and die. A cup of wine?'

'Isn't it a little early for that?' Paullus said sharply. 'And it's a bad example for the men.'

'Mind your own business, Paullus,' Varro retorted. 'Remember I'm in command.'

Whistling softly as we sat our horses and watched our lines forming on the plain, Laelius seemed as unconcerned as Varro. In accordance with their orders, the maniples were forming from the left flank, one line three deep slowly reaching across the knee-high grass. Some thousand strides from them, Hannibal's lines were also forming, but from the centre first. It was like children laying out draughts on a board. This was not a battle but a game.

On our right, Varro's ten trumpeters were sitting on the grass, joking, gossiping, making flower-chains. The whole occasion seemed dull, predetermined, like an exercise of my father's on Placentia's plains. The priests came in their white robes, cut open the entrails of a kid, and took the omens. They pronounced them good. Varro had the trumpeters sound the news, the soaring bi-tone that meant 'Propitious', and the soldiers raised a raucous, ragged cheer in response.

There was some warmth in the sun now. Hannibal's line, it seemed, was complete, his cavalry in four groups between the infantry and the camp. That, I thought, was strange. Our line was still extending. Our cavalry, which had been ordered to divide in half and take position at the edge of each flank, was still not in place, so long was our line.

'You see! Look at that,' Varro shouted when he noticed. 'We'll outflank him easily. He must be outnumbered two to one!'

'Why, why?' I asked myself, unaware that I was speaking out loud.

'Why what, Publius?' said Laelius.

'Why's he going to fight like this?'

'Because he has no choice, of course.'

Just then, from behind the Carthaginian line, the sky darkened suddenly with hundreds of flighting arrows that briefly shut out the sun. 'Trumpets!' shouted Varro. The command 'Raise shields' was already being obeyed, of the soldiers' own will. 'Pointless,' Varro said to no one in particular, 'at that range.' But I saw some men fall, like puppets on a stage. Then more arrows, then more, and our army's shields fluttered.

Varro mounted, moved to the edge of the rise, and peered intently ahead. 'All right, all right,' he said, coming back, and shouted suddenly, 'Trumpets, sound "advance at the run"!'

'No!' shouted Paullus. The trumpeters stopped, their instruments halfway to their lips, and looked from one consul to the other.

Varro, for once, didn't shout, but smiled. 'For the last time, Paullus, I am in command,' he said softly. 'Contradict my orders once more, and I'll have to ask you to leave the field.'

'But at the run? It's at least a thousand strides. They'll be exhausted! Can't you see that's exactly what he wants us to do, exactly why he's used the arrows?'

The two men eyed each other as we officers watched. Still staring at Paullus, Varro spoke in a firm, clear voice. 'Trumpets, as ordered.'

And that is how the killing of Cannae began.

The shouts of 'Tel-a-mon, Tel-a-mon!' came to us, a wall of sound, and as one man, the cavalry staying behind as ordered, our soldiers ran towards the waiting, stationary Carthaginian line. Just before the two lines would have met, and as our *hastati*, running, were throwing their *pila*, we saw something unprecedented in the history of war.

As easily and smoothly as a snake uncoils or a bird opens its wings, the centre of the Carthaginian line arched out. From straight, it became convex. The centre of our still-straight line broke on it, as a huge wave on a rock, and while the centre was engaged the rest of our line juddered to an uncertain stop, our men puzzled, milling, tripping in their ranks. A volley of javelins from both Carthaginian flanks caught them unawares, and we saw many fall as sixty thousand Roman soldiers collected themselves, resumed close order and blundered breathlessly on. Our straight line became a V.

'It's perfect,' offered Varro, farting. 'We'll encircle them soon.'

As the sun climbed and the fighting continued, it looked as if he was right. For a long time, until the sun was high, it was like two waves against each other, ebbing and flowing, but slowly ours was beginning to lap at the edges of Hannibal's. Our V's tips were enveloping his, and when ours met and surrounded him the battle would be all but over. Varro was right, I thought. I felt surprise that Hannibal's end should be so easy for us and so near.

'They're like ants, aren't they?' said Laelius, munching a pear.

'Yes, they are,' I replied, 'although I was thinking of them more like waves in the sea. It all seems strange from here. But why has he done it, I wonder?'

'Done what?'

'Why did he make his line convex?'

'Don't know.' He was unconcerned, chewing nonchalantly. 'Want a bite?'

'No, thanks,' I replied, screwing up my eyes and looking intently at what was going on below.

'I suppose he meant to break through our centre,' he went on. 'If he did, it hasn't worked.'

So the fighting went on, the mounds of dead and dying men

mounting in lines that merged at times but then retreated from each other like the tide. We sat on, silent and sweating in the summer sun, brushing away the languid flies, and watched. Sometimes a sudden roar or dying scream came to us, caught on the breeze, and sometimes a passing waft of the sickly smell of sweat and blood and faeces. You learn in war that most men defecate as they die. That is all some leave behind.

It was like a dance. But we were the dance, and Hannibal the dance-master. Just as our leading maniples were about to join, like two extended horns meeting at a point, Hannibal's centre began to fall back.

'Ha! You see,' shouted Varro beside me, interested now. 'They're breaking, running away! They don't want to feel how Roman pincers nip! Trumpets, sound "No quarter".'

'But colleague!' said Paullus.

'But nothing! Sound, you fools, sound!' They were doing so as Hannibal's centre went back and back and back and our men, no doubt weary, started in fours and fives to break rank and chase them. From convex, Hannibal's line became concave, just in time to drive the tips of our V back again. Then two things happened.

They were so straight and black and quick that I rubbed my eyes and looked again. One on each side of the battle, fast along the level plain, two columns of cavalry were coming on the gallop from the Carthaginian rear.

Varro was on his feet now, and pushed his way forward to the edge of the rise. 'By the— Trumpets!' he yelled, spittle spraying. 'Sound the cavalry advance!'

Too late. The two Carthaginian columns smashed into ours, which were still almost stationary. This was not cavalry as we knew it. The enemy horses and riders wore heavy armour, and ours were equipped as scouts. At least half of our two cavalry detachments fell where they stood, bowled over in a milling mess of broken legs and screams and wails of fear and pain that reached us above the roar of battle. We were transfixed.

'Look!' shouted Laelius, pointing, grabbing my arm. 'Look!'

I have been asked about it many times. Though at my trial they questioned my word, I say again that that is what took place. It was not the work of magic, as some whisper. It was the genius of a man. And, yes, though for this admission alone they might find me guilty, it was a thing of beauty that shines out in my memory like a ship's lantern in the night.

As we turned our eyes from the cavalry engagements, we saw the Carthaginian line . . . we saw it – this will seem absurd – we saw it double. To that, I swear. Like a folding ruler of four hinged pieces, its rear rank, two men deep, split in the middle and swung round, half turning each way. Before our eyes, the Carthaginians running, our men turning, confused, stopping, Hannibal's army began to surround ours.

Varro was sweating, swearing. 'By all the gods, what is happening? It's . . .'

'Reinforcements, sir?' I ventured.

'What?' he answered, staring at me with eyes that were wild and bloodshot from the best part of a day of wine. 'Reinforcements? Yes. Good idea. Not our guard here. Paullus, how many men did you leave to guard your precious camp?'

'Thirty maniples.'

'Well, I want them, now.'

'Why not the ones from your camp, colleague?'

'Why, you!' Varro roared, turning on him. It had all the makings of a brawl.

'If I may, sir,' I said clearly, putting a hand on Varro's arm but looking steadily at Paullus, 'I will ride to your colleague's camp and see your order carried out.'

'Thank you, Scipio,' Varro said, looking at me strangely. He turned away. 'Groom!' he shouted. 'My horse!'

'Let me come with you, Publius,' Laelius said as I reached forward for my reins.

'No. Stay here, Laelius. And keep these two from fighting! There's enough blood being spilt down there!' With a smile to him, I kicked my horse away, catching one last glimpse of our army, now surrounded by a tight and narrow band, and two cavalry engagements going on below. 'He'll never keep us penned in like that,' I thought. 'He's outnumbered almost three to one. Our maniples will break out.' I didn't want to miss that, so knew I'd better hurry. I passed Scaevola, returning from delivering some message. 'What, leaving already, Scipio?' he shouted to my back. I remember my shadow dancing beside me as I galloped in the fading sun. I reached the camp, gave my orders to a startled centurion, and turned my sweating horse.

How long had I been gone? How long does death take? It comes in many forms, and there were many, many deaths at Cannae. No place ever has known more. That place is burnt into my memory. Though I have never gone back there, it has never left my dreams.

There is, as I have said, a rise, from the top of which you see the plain below, the river and, beyond that, the sea, and the sea was glowing red from the sinking sun. I approached from the left of the rise, heading for the hillock from which I had come. But well before I reached it, I saw that there was no one there. The light, too, was dying, but I saw the bright blue of a consul's standard lying on the ground. I reined in sharply, panting, my heart pounding, blood pulsing in my head. Our army was still surrounded, but in a tighter band and I think I thought – or was that later? – of the steel bands round the oar-blades on the ship that had brought us back from the Rhodanus. The Roman army was dying in a band of steel.

Two large groups of our soldiers were running north, to the distant trees; they must have fought their way out. But the band of death had once more closed on the rest of Rome's great army.

Our men were packed too tight to fight, I realised, as I looked down, seeing the reds and browns of blood staining the trampled ground; and the shouting and screaming, the sounds of dying came to me like the noise of a distant sea where waves crash sibilant on a sea-beat shore.

'I must . . . Where is Laelius? And Varro? Cavalry? The other camp? This is impossible! He cannot have! Shall I . . . ? He has destroyed Rome!' My thoughts were tumbled, running together in my mind, but I remember that I shouted with all my being 'No, no, no!' and that the tears came, clouding my eyes, and I was angry with them, wiping them away with the back of my left hand, the other holding my horse's reins, when I saw coming towards me perhaps fifty horsemen, galloping towards me in a V. It was not fear – whatever was said at my trial. Make sure you record that, Bostar. It was not fear. I did not run away. There was nothing I could do.

I wrenched my horse's head round. Alone, I galloped from Cannae, weeping, screaming, sobbing, on and on away from there into a dank, warm, unforgiving lessening of the light.

Doing

Nomine ipso recreor.

By the very sound of his name I am refreshed.
CICERO, *Somnium Scipionis*

My mare's flight was sure. I dropped the reins, and hugged her neck, and rode, tears stinging my eyes. She laboured on the rise. Dread, not I, drove her on, and only when we came to the first trees did she slow. I sat up, looked back quickly into the last of the light. No cavalry. No pursuit. Why had they broken off? To let at least one officer live to tell the tale and raise the wail of Cannae? Then, to the north, I saw the feeding, flickering fires. Varro's camp, burning, and Paullus' too. So no, not to let me live. To let others die. Numb, tongue thick in my mouth, I did not want to live. No, that is too strong. Among and after so much death, the idea of life dies too.

Some ancient instinct made me kick my horse. She picked her way on, into the trees, their branches spreading like years, the sound of their leaves a threnody in the rising wind. And then the first drops came, thick and fat, dropping, plopping, rain to wash away the carnage that was Cannae. There must still be blood, now, many years later, being driven down further, deeper, seeping, feeding worms and the dark creatures of the earth.

Thunder growled and lightning streaked across the tree-screened sky as I rode on. Where? Dazed and dull, I didn't know. Wherever the mare wanted to go. I needed to urinate. I let it come. The warm flow was comforting, before its wetness joined that of the drenching rain. Branches caught my arms and face, brambles my legs. There was only my breathing and, for hours, relentless rain in that dark forest of the trees and of my mind. I dozed, I think. The mare's step faltered. I kicked her on. She faltered again, and slowed, and stopped, and I slipped off her and fell into a deep and dreamless sleep, lying on the dank and mossy, oozing ground.

A rustling, then a whispering, in the bushes to my right woke me. The rain had stopped. Above me through the trees I saw stars. My heartbeat quickened. In my groin and armpits, I felt sweat. I reached for the dagger on my thigh. Neither of the consuls nor, following their example, any of their officers had bothered to carry arms at Cannae. Quietly, quickly, I got to my feet. My horse had gone. I leant towards the noise, my dagger handle firm in my hand. I remembered Frontinus, and tugged the sleeve of my tunic down over my right hand. '*Quis istic est?*' I called out. 'Who's there?' Three quick drops of water landed on my forehead from the trees above. I heard more whispering.

'*Quis etiam es?*' replied a voice. 'Who are you?'

And they say I was a coward at Cannae, that I ran away. I drew myself up to my full height. '*Publius Cornelius Scipio sum,*' I answered clearly. '*Servo senatum populumque Romanum.* I am a servant of Rome.' I suppose I expected a spear, or a charge and a sword–thrust in the dark.

There was surprise, almost excitement in the reply from the same voice. '*Scipio! Immo vero, milites Romani sumus.* We're Roman soldiers!'

'Then come out,' I called. 'Show yourselves!'

First shadows in the dark, then in the starlight men, fourteen, sixteen, emerged from the bushes into the little clearing where I had slept.

'Which legion are you from?' I asked, slipping my dagger back into its sheath.

'The fourth, sir,' came a voice from the back.

'Are you a centurion?'

'I am, sir.'

'Then step forward, where I can see you.'

He had lost his helmet, and his shield. In fact, only two of those sixteen bedraggled Roman soldiers, for all I knew the only survivors of Cannae, still carried shields. The rest must have thrown theirs away in flight. I thought of the Spartan motto: ἢ τάν ἢ ἐπὶ τάν, 'With your shield or on it'. You left a battle either carrying your shield or, dead, being carried on it as a stretcher. But this was not the time for recrimination.

'What's your name, Centurion?'

'Sextus, sir.' His voice was deep, his accent from the south.

'Right, Sextus. Is this all of you?'

'I think so, sir. All I know of, anyway.'

'How did you get out?'

'We're from the same maniple, sir. We stuck together, and locked shields. Just cut our way out, before their horns closed.'

'Yes, I saw – I think.' My speech was slurred. I felt exhaustion in my bones and being. Command, command. I was a Scipio. 'I'll ask more later. Now, we need shelter, and food. They may be searching for us—'

'Or busy looting the camps, more likely, sir – or stripping the dead,' Sextus interjected.

'Yes, perhaps. But we mustn't stay here. We'll go . . .' I faltered. When I first learnt to swim, there were times when I almost drowned before I controlled myself and remembered the strokes that gave me mastery of the water. A part of me was asking, why should we bother to go anywhere: Rome was lost. Hannibal had won. We had never in all our history known a defeat like this . . .

'North,' I managed, shivering. 'We'll go north.' I took a deep breath, and gave my orders in a stronger voice. 'Single file. Swords drawn, those that have one. Follow me.'

'Begging your pardon, sir,' one of the soldiers said, 'but if it's food and shelter we're after, we'll find none that way.'

'No? Why not?'

'I'm from these parts, sir – or was, before I enlisted. We call this the Endless Wood. All we'll find going north is wolves and' – in the half-light I could not be sure, but I thought he made the sign against the evil eye – 'and ghouls and—'

'All right, soldier, all right,' I said wearily. 'And trolls, no doubt, and fairies. Where won't we, then?'

'West, sir, not north. In the village of Canusium. Only one for stades around.'

'Can you guide us there?'

'Yes, sir. And they won't find us there. It's a hidden place, on its own.'

'Then lead on, soldier. What's your name, by the way?'

'Pius, sir.'

'Pius? That's a rum name for a time like this. Still, I'm very glad to hear it. Pius, lead on. Sextus, bring up the rear.'

So, following Pius, we walked west in the dark, away from the black memory of Cannae, I thinking at first of no more than the need to move my feet and listen for pursuit. We walked and stumbled in single file through sparse woods of cork-oak and ilex, the ground thick with low bushes of bog myrtle and wort. Often I checked, as owls screeched or boars or other beasts moved in the bushes and the trees. Light rose behind us as we marched, and that comforted me. The sun will always rise over Italy, I thought, under Carthage or Rome. Carthage. Rome. That man in black at the Ticinus. Was he even now readying to march on Rome? Would her walls save her? Just before I left, my father had been organising the victory banquet, selecting the finest wines. He would not need them now. The wines of Falernia and Chios had become wormwood and gall. And Fabius? This news would surely kill him – if he was still alive. Who would take him the news? Us, or Hannibal himself?

Eventually, the sun up, the rain, which had started once more, easing, our brains and bodies numbed in wet weariness, Pius stopped. His eyes were red, his lips set tight. 'There, sir,' he whispered to me. 'See that ravine? Follow it up. Canusium is in the lee of the cliff, at the top.' I looked, and stiffened.

Smoke. Fires. Had the Carthaginians come? Pius saw the worry on my face, my narrowed eyes. 'I think it'll just be cooking fires, sir.'

I looked slowly at him, his oval, simple face crusted with dirt and blood, his cuirass filthy, his hair matted with sweat and gore, this peasant who fought and would have died for Rome. I smiled at him, and he smiled shyly back.

'Cooking, soldier?' I said. 'Let's hope the cooking's good.'

The path was narrow and treacherous. Below, a river ran through high, bouldered banks. Finches and wagtails, tits and wrens darted there, and a damp, dank smell of earthy rot rose up from the dark water below. Behind me as we moved on soldiers' swords rang on the hugging rocks. I passed the word. 'Silence! Sheathe swords!' A dip, a climb, a dip, and then I saw Canusium as the clouds cleared above us and the sun streamed through.

The dogs saw or smelt us first, and came on, yapping and snarling, as people emerged from the rows of round huts that fringed a levelled central meeting-place of beaten earth. Then a man, running towards us, relief, amazement, in his face, a Roman, and he was in my arms.

'Laelius!' I gasped into his shoulder. 'How did you get here? I thought that you were dead!'

He stepped back. We were both embarrassed at this show of feeling, with the soldiers behind us, the villagers before. 'I should be. But I thought the same of you. I—'

'We'll talk later. We need food, and rest. Let's—'

'One thing first, Publius. There are several hundred survivors here – asleep, I think.'

'Several hundred! How?'

'We met in the woods. Followed the river. When we came upon this village, we thought it a good place to hide.'

'As it is,' I said, looking around. I rubbed my eyes, cleared my throat. 'Column!' I shouted. 'Advance!' As Sextus passed me, I took his arm. 'You and one other, Sextus, picket duty. Back down the path. I'll have food sent to you, and relief.'

His face was haggard, but he nodded, and turned to go. With Laelius beside me on what was left of the widening path, I walked on.

'Publius,' he said, 'I should warn you. Scaevola is here, and several other officers.'

I stiffened. 'And Varro?'

Laelius' lips were stiff and set, his eyes blank yet wild. 'Dead.'

'Paullus?'

'I don't know.'

Villagers stood by their huts and watched as we walked in. They gave no greeting, but their silence was not sullen. They were dark-skinned and -eyed, mostly leather-clothed bar some who were dressed in animal skins above the hips and patched woollen leggings below. 'Who's the headman?' I asked Laelius.

'There isn't one. But there's a headwoman.'

'A woman? You're joking!'

'That's her straight ahead. Name's Bulla.'

Outside a larger hut that faced out on to the meeting place, I saw three women, their hair tied back, their leather skirts worn but clean, their arms crossed, their faces impassive. We walked up to them.

'Which of you is Bulla?' I asked.

'I am,' the middle of the three replied flatly, her face like a walnut shell of fine, wrinkled lines. She was in her late thirties, I guessed, the widow, no doubt, of the headman. I had often heard that the women took control.

'Then I ask you for shelter and food, for a while, for the Romans here.'

She screwed up her face, and spat, right at my feet. 'More than the others asked for.' She shot her words out. 'They just took.'

I looked across at Laelius. He spread his hands in apology. Scaevola, I assumed. 'In whose name do you ask, stranger?'

'In that of the Senate and people of Rome.'

'Rome? Pah! Here, stranger, Rome is just taxes – and war.'

'Then, Bulla, I ask as a man in need for men in need. If my, ah, friends have taken, I apologise. I ask you to forgive them. Men do strange things in time of war.'

'Very well, Roman. I accept your need – but not your war. Come, and eat.'

I gestured the men forward and followed Bulla into the hut, which was, I assumed, hers. There was little there: a low bed, a small chest, and a hearth whose smoke plumed upwards to a hole in the middle of the turf roof. Silently, heads hanging, the men with whom I had come followed me in and filled the hut and squatted down in two rows round the hearth, like mine their eyes smarting from the smoke.

'I haven't enough bowls,' Bulla said. 'But men who have almost shared death will surely now share food?'

'We will, Bulla, and gladly,' I replied. She grunted, and leant forward to fill the bowls she had from a blackened pot hanging over the fire. It was some kind of stew, of meat – rabbit I thought – and beans. It was good, though I took only a few spoonfuls before passing the bowl on. The food was dry in my mouth.

'You should eat more, Roman,' Bulla said to me.

'That's hard, when the heart is sick.'

'All the more reason to eat, before the body ails too.'

'I will, later. But my friend said there were more of us here. Where are they?'

She gestured with her arm. 'Asleep, in the huts around.'

'They posted no sentries?'

'No. Perhaps they didn't care.'

'That reminds me. Soldier,' I said to the one next to me, 'when you've finished, take some to Sextus and your other friend.'

'Neither is my friend, sir,' the man replied. 'Varro changed the order of the maniples. We fought alongside strangers, not our friends!'

'That's right!' another interjected. 'It broke our confidence, our routine—'

'Enough of that!' I snapped. 'You two, go and wake the other officers. I know that Mucius Scaevola is here. There may be more. Tell them I summon a council. Now, in here. The rest of you, clear out when you've finished. Go and get some rest.'

'You're in command?' Bulla asked me when all the others had gone.

'Command? Yes, I suppose so, at least until I see who else survived.'

'That is a heavy weight for young shoulders.'

'Is it? Not as heavy as the weight of loss that lies on Rome. I saw, I saw . . .' I began to shudder, and sob. She came over, sat down beside me and put her arms round me, and after Cannae I wept on the shoulder of a woman who did not even know my name.

That is what Laelius saw when he came in. 'Oh! I'm sorry,' I heard him say.

'Don't be sorry, Roman,' Bulla replied, her mouth above my head. 'Be glad that you see comfort given and received.'

'Come and sit with us, Laelius,' I said, breaking away from Bulla, 'and tell me what happened.'

'It was Paullus who . . .' he began. Then he faltered and buried his face in his hands.

'Paullus who what?' I asked, gently. He looked up at me. Our eyes met, and the bond was there.

'Paullus who ordered us to withdraw.'

'But Varro was in command.'

'I know, but he refused to move. Even when their cavalry came straight at us. "I'm a Roman, not a coward," he bellowed at Paullus. I think he was drunk.'

'That wouldn't surprise me. He'd been drinking all day.'

'Anyway, Paullus replied, "You may be a Roman, but you're a fool," and rode away. The other officers went with him.'

'You didn't?'

'Not straight away. I waited, waited, until they were within a *pilum*'s throw away – hundreds of them, Publius, heavy cavalry, bearing down on us.' There was anguish in his voice.

'I know. I saw. And then?'

'Then I grabbed Varro's reins, and tried to pull him away with me, but he swung at me with his staff and, and—'

'And?'

Laelius looked at me, and drew a deep breath. 'And a javelin caught him in the neck. I saw it. I saw him fall.'

'So what did you do?'

'Rode, of course. Rode for my life. I had no weapons. They didn't follow, at least not for a bit. Varro saved my life – not that he meant to. I looked back once, before the trees. You know, from the higher ground. They were stripping him naked. Then . . .'

'Then?'

'Then they held his body aloft on their spear-points. I heard them cheer.'

'And the consul's standard?'

'They stuffed it in his mouth.'

Beside me, Bulla spat into the fire. There was a sizzle, then no more. Like life, I thought. 'Animals!' she hissed.

'And you made it to the trees, as I did?'

'Yes. Then I met the others, first in ones and twos.'

'And Paullus?'

'As I said, I don't know. He wasn't with Scaevola and Metellus when I met them. You must ask them.'

'I can save you the trouble,' Scaevola said, pushing through the hut's flap and coming in. 'I don't know either. One moment he was there, then he wasn't. That's all I know.'

'What you mean, Scaevola, is that you deserted a Roman consul in the field!' I said to his flushing face, getting to my feet.

'I deserted? Look who's talking! Where were you at the time, fancy Scipio? Off in the bushes reading a little Greek poetry, were we?' My fists clenched.

Bulla stood up. 'I thought you'd called for a council, Roman, not a schoolroom brawl,' she snarled.

'Who's this old bag?' Scaevola snapped.

'This, Scaevola,' said Laelius flatly, 'is our host, and I urge you to remember that. She could send word to the Carthaginians that we're here.'

That calmed us, and just then Metellus and three more officers came in. I knew the other three, Claudius Postumus, Antonius Afer and Marcus Longinus. We all nodded at one another. They looked shocking, filthy, weary, even in that gloom. I suppose I did too.

'Is this all?' I asked.

'All the officers, anyway,' Afer replied.

'What, no centurions even, except Sextus?'

'Who's Sextus?' Laelius asked.

'He came in with me,' I replied. 'But he's on picket duty.'

'There's one *primus pilus*,' Postumus volunteered.

'Who?' I asked. 'What's his name?'

'Flaevius, I think,' said Postumus.

'Flaevius! I know him. Where is he?'

'Lying down. He's wounded.'

'Badly?'

'No. A sword–gash on the leg.'

'Can he walk?'

'Do you think we carried him here?' Scaevola retorted.

I ignored that. 'Go and get him, Postumus, will you?'

'Get him yourself. Who are you to order me around? You're not a consul yet.'

I took a deep breath, and caught Bulla's eye. She smiled.

'It's all right. I'll go,' said Laelius, and darted out.

'What do you want a *primus pilus* here for, anyway, Scipio?' Scaevola asked. 'I thought you wanted a council.'

'I do. But why exclude the most experienced soldier here?'

'Because he's not even commissioned, that's why.'

'Come on, Scaevola,' put in Metellus. 'Scipio has a point. We'll need all the help we can to get back to Rome.'

'Back to Rome!' Scaevola burst out. 'You're joking – or a fool. Hannibal will be on his way there today – if he hasn't already gone. I say, forget Rome. We should go—'

'I smell food,' Longinus said. 'Any left?'

'You and your bloody belly!' Scaevola jeered. 'Is that all you ever think about?'

I heard footsteps. 'Come in, Flaevius,' I said. 'Now you're here, let's start our council.' All eight of us sat in a circle on the ground. 'I suggest we each speak in turn, starting on my left with you, Longinus.'

'And I suggest, Scipio, that you stop suggesting,' Scaevola threw in.

'And I suggest, Scaevola,' retorted Afer, 'that if you two can't stop squabbling you both say nothing. We'll decide what to do by majority vote. Flaevius,' he went on, 'before we start, how many men do we have?' This seemed a good approach. I resolved to stay quiet, whatever Scaevola's taunts.

'Two hundred and seventy-nine, sir,' Flaevius replied.

'How many wounded?' Postumus asked.

'None as can't walk.'

'And weapons?' This from Laelius.

Flaevius frowned. 'Not good, sir. 'Fraid most threw their shields away. Under the circumstances, I haven't taken any action. But most have their swords, and some a *pilum* too.'

Scaevola laughed. 'So, we're going to fight our way back to Rome, are we?' He got up.

'Scaevola!' protested Afer.

'Don't worry. I shan't be long. I'll save us all a lot of discussion. Before we get to the marching order, I say it's very simple. The Republic's doomed. Rome's lost. I say we leave Italy, while and if we can.'

'And go where?' Longinus asked. The others were listening intently. Only Flaevius was looking at the ground.

'To Sicilia, to Catana. It's still a Roman city, and I have a cousin there. We're bound to find a ship along the coast.'

'And then?' Postumus asked.

'You fool!' Scaevola replied. 'What do you mean, "and then"? How should I know? But we'll be alive, at least!'

'Unless the Carthaginians have taken Sicilia, or do now,' Afer countered. 'Anyway, say we do find a ship. How do you propose to persuade its master to take us to Sicilia?'

'By telling him it's his only hope too – unless he wants to sail beyond the western sea to the Cassiterides. Rome's finished, I tell you! You all saw!'

So the discussion continued, growing more and more heated and wild, until it slowed and died like a fire that has no food. Silence settled. I thought of the madman: 'Beware the vengeance of Cauno!' I pushed the thought away. My back was stiff from sitting, my mind and body sore.

'Well,' I said, breaking the silence, 'Scaevola argued for one option. I have a second.'

'Oh yes!' scoffed Scaevola. 'We march back to Cannae and attack, I suppose – with you commanding from the rear, no doubt.'

I felt the blood flushing across my cheeks. I reached for the dagger on my thigh. Control, control. I stood up, and looked round. 'We go back to Rome.'

'You're mad, Scipio!' Scaevola sneered, getting to his feet.

'And you, Scaevola, are a traitor,' I said quietly.

It happened quickly. Scaevola threw himself at me, and we

were on the ground, rolling, scrabbling. I felt one of his thumbs pressing into my right eyeball, and I fumbled for the sheath on my thigh, twisted, rolled on to him and my dagger was at his throat and he froze.

'Just like a common thief,' he panted. 'I might have known.'

'Get up, Scaevola.'

He did so, after me, backing towards the wall. I moved with him, my dagger out.

'Right,' I called to the others behind me, regaining my breath and trying to slow my pounding heart. 'We have one for Rome, and one for Sicilia. What do you say?'

'Rome.' That from Laelius. Four others said the same, though without conviction.

'I say Sicilia,' said Postumus.

'And you, Flaevius?' I asked, keeping my eyes on Scaevola.

'I don't know what we'll find, sir, but I swore an oath. I am for Rome.'

'Good. Flaevius?'

'Yes, sir?'

'Bring two legionaries. Mucius Scaevola is under arrest. We will deliver him to Rome.'

'You really are mad, Scipio, and it can't be from too much sun!' scoffed Scaevola as Flaevius slipped out. 'What do you think you'll find, eh? And the rest of you?' He glared round the hut. Silence, but for the sound of a dog scratching itself at the door. 'I'll tell you. Hannibal, that's what. Or the city in flames. You'd be better to fall on your swords now.'

'Perhaps, Scaevola,' Laelius interjected, 'if we had any. Anyway, I'm not so sure. Hannibal's bound to strip the dead. That'll take him – what do you think, Publius?'

The handle of the dagger was sweaty in my hand. To strip the dead, so very many dead? A lifetime. He would need many wagons for the arms alone. 'I don't know. Days, anyway.' The truth was that I thought he might well leave them to the carrion–seekers and the worms. I thought we might find him at Rome.

The curtain across the door opened. I blinked at the sudden light. Flaevius came in, and after him two dishevelled, bleary soldiers.

'Right, lads,' Flaevius barked. 'Take him away,' he said, pointing to Scaevola. 'You'll find some rope somewhere. Tie his hands.'

Scaevola flicked the hair off his forehead and stepped forwards towards them. He paused in front of me and spat in my face. I stood facing where he had been until I heard them go, leaving his spit to trickle down my cheek.

'Laelius,' I said turning round, 'please summon a general assembly. Everyone except the pickets, on muster outside.'

After the hut's soft darkness, the sun shone like a threat. The light seemed a punishment. As we waited, ringed by the watching, waiting villagers, their faces set, their eyes cold, Postumus walked up to me. He was probably a year or so younger than I. His hair was blond, the colour of ripe wheat. His beard was wispy and matted with mud. His face was round and full like a melon. The colour of his eyes, which were too far apart, changed from green to topaz with the light. His upper lip was too big for the rest of his face. His voice was high and mellifluous.

'Scipio,' he began hesitantly.

'Yes?'

'I just wanted to say that I agree with you. I am for Rome.'

'Then why did you vote for Sicilia?'

'Not to run away. Because I thought that the best course. Survive. Regroup. It's suicide to go back to Rome. You saw what happened! Rome is finished.'

'Finished, Postumus?'

'Yes. That's what I mean. Our army is lost.'

I was so tired. I saw again in my mind's eye that carnage,

felt again amazement, incredulity, blank despair. I wanted to be sick at the memory, the pain. I rubbed my eyes, and looked at Postumus. 'Is Rome no more than an army?' He hesitated, opened his mouth, but said nothing, shifting his weight from foot to foot. 'Did an ancestor of yours not fight beside one of mine – and lose – against the Gauls at the battle of the Allia, Postumus, two hundred years ago?'

He nodded.

'And what did he do? Despair? Give up?'

'No, Scipio. He organised the defence of the Capitol.'

'Exactly. And, although the Gauls sacked Rome, she survived, thanks to the courage of your ancestors, and mine.' By now the soldiers had formed an uneven rectangle in front of us, shuffling, uncertain, scared and ragged, tired, shocked. Gnarled *triarii*, grey of beard; six or seven *hastati* younger than I, down still on their cheeks – I looked away from Postumus and at them, and what I said just came out. Laelius used to say it was the finest speech of my life. If it was, it was the one I was least prepared for. There is, perhaps, a moral there.

'Soldiers of Rome!' I shouted. 'Claudius Postumus and I have just been talking about the last time Rome was defeated in a great battle – that of the Allia, before the very walls of Rome. We lost, but those whose names and blood we carry did not despair. The senators refused the refuge of the Capitol, and died where they sat and waited in their chairs when the Gauls looted and pillaged and burned. Still, Rome did not despair.

'There were some potters outside Rome when the Gauls sacked it, men like you. Like me. Except they were outside Rome at the time because they had gone to collect clay. When they returned, they saw the city burning. What did they do? Return to Illyria or Magna Graeca or Dyrrhachium or wherever they or their people had come from? No. No. They were drawn, as now we are drawn, to Rome.'

'And they died for it!' shouted Scaevola, 'the foo—'. I saw

Flaevius chop him in the kidneys. I heard his grunt of pain and, as he doubled up, his hair tumble forward and spread like a shroud around his head.

'Yes, they died for their love of Rome. We may too. But they returned. So will we. And Rome, Rome will live!' I still remember the energy coursing through me. The greatest of our gifts comes to us through madness, provided it comes from the gods.

I stayed quiet, and looked at my audience. Few speakers remember that silence is at least as important as words, and sometimes more so. I sensed I had them. I also sensed, though, that uncertainty, not rhetoric, was the reason. They were weary, confused. I offered them at least the hope of the known, and Scaevola's Sicilia was unknown.

Doubtful, shifting, the men looked at each other, and at me. A group of silent vultures, dark and low and dense and menacing, crossed the sun overhead, their beaks and heads set for Cannae. I thought of the Roman bodies, piled and bloody, swelling and already, surely, stinking in the sun. Already the carrion-seekers would be glutted with gore. They take the eyes first, and all the soft parts, testicles and innards: these thoughts spun in my mind. I thought of Hannibal. Where was he? Exulting? Celebrating? Stripping the dead? Or marching, not yet sated, his purpose surging in him? Tides ebb and flow. Sometimes, through the strange motions of the moon or wind, perhaps, a vast breaker rises to smash unexpectedly on soft shore. Yes, I thought. Hannibal must even now be marching on Rome. I shook myself, cleared my throat – dry, I needed water – and went on as the sun shone and my brain burned.

'So we will go back to Rome. It is our duty and our destiny. We—'

'How?' someone shouted.

'How? We will walk back,' I replied, 'as we – well, as most of us – came.' That raised a nervous laugh. Officers on foot. I knew I had to build a sense that we were different, but the same. 'But,' I shouted, 'we'll need local knowledge. You, Pius. You led some of us here to Canusium. You know the ground.'

'I do, sir,' he called back, stepping forward.

'Well, could you lead us north?'

'I could, sir. Easy enough to follow the North Star. But why north?' he said uncertainly. 'Rome's—'

'I know where Rome is, soldier,' I shouted brusquely. 'And so does Hannibal. If he's bound for Rome, he'll take the direct route. So we won't. We'll go north-west before we turn south for Rome.'

The men shuffled their feet, and looked at each other uneasily. 'That'll take us through the Endless Wood, sir,' Pius called out. I heard murmurs of concern.

'So Roman soldiers fear fairies more than the Carthaginians? No, of course you don't. And anyway, no wood can be endless. Our way has an end, and that is Rome. We—'

'Look, Publius, look!' Laelius interrupted at my side. I followed his pointing arm, and all of us looked up to see. A flock of pigeons was flying overhead. From high above, a hawk plunged down, talons extended for the kill. It veered slightly, making for the last of the flock, but missed, and slowed and stalled and turned to regain height. Just then, when it was without its fatal gift of speed, in a group the pigeons turned on it, pecking at it in a flurry of wings, making a strange hooting that drowned the screech of the hawk. It broke off, and sped downwards, and away.

'It's an omen!' someone called out.

'Yes!' I shouted back. 'And the omen is good! The gods have spoken. So, soldiers, are we for Rome?'

A ragged chorus replied: 'Yes' or 'Aye' or 'Rome!'

'Then one more thing. We'll sleep by day and walk by night. Now, we all need rest and food. Flaevius, see to the wounded. Make sure they have their cuts dressed and salved. Tonight and tomorrow we rest. Tomorrow, at dusk, we leave. Officers, Pius, Sextus and Flaevius, back to the headwoman's hut. Flaevius, set pickets first. Assembly dismissed.'

Back in Bulla's hut, our eyes took time to adjust to the dark. 'I just wanted to discuss the practicalities of the march,' I said when we'd all sat down cross-legged on the earth.

'Practicalities?' Postumus asked. 'Like what?'

'Food, mostly. Pius, what will we find?'

He was drawing circles in the earth with his finger. He looked up. 'Little or nothing. We'll be ten, twelve days in the wood. Or more. It'll slow us a lot to walk only at night.'

'Yes, sir,' put in Sextus. 'I understand your thinking, but is that really necessary?'

'They're bound to be looking for survivors,' said Afer. 'I agree with Scipio. We should march only at night.'

'Right, that's settled. Back to food. Pius?'

'There are villages where the wood ends. I have an aunt in one. And I think Rufus in my maniple comes from thereabouts. Don't know what we'll find, though.'

'Little enough, if Hannibal came that way,' Laelius said.

'But in the wood?'

'Berries, sir, and rabbits. Pigeons. I have a sling.'

'No. No fires. No cooking, at least not until we're a long way north of here. Anyway, three hundred men would need a lot of rabbits – or pigeons. What about water, Pius?'

'No problem with that at least, sir. Plenty of streams and springs.'

'Still,' I went on, 'we'll need some water-skins just in case. Right, I think Laelius, Sextus, Postumus and I should stay here and plan these things. The rest of you, please go and start checking the men. Their boots especially: we can't have them giving out. Afer, please find the headwoman, Bulla, and ask her to come in.'

You see, after Cannae I did not just take command. I assumed it. It was as I was born to be. '*Ducunt volentem, nolentem trahunt,*' says my friend Ennius elegantly of good leaders in one of his poems. 'They lead the willing, and drag the unwilling.' That is all I then began. And why did I have us try to return to Rome? That is one thing that even my accusers grant was worthy of the Republic. The irony is they are wrong. It was not courage or loyalty. It was as rivers run to the sea, or sun follows the rain, or as man returns to the dust from which he came. Now I am as an old tree which has survived, but does not bloom. When will they cut me down?

The hut's curtain swung open. 'You sent for me, Roman,' Bulla said blandly.

'I am a Roman, but I have a name.'

'And what is that?'

'It is Scipio.'

'Then I will call you that. What do you want of me?'

I stood up, and walked over to her. 'Bulla, we have nothing to give you. But when we get back to Rome, I will send you gold.'

She laughed. 'Gold, Scipio? What would we do with that here?'

'Then what can we give you?'

'Peace. That is all we want. Peace to grow our crops and lead our lives.'

'But the war hasn't touched you here.'

'You know nothing. Not directly, no. This is, as you have found, a hidden place. But the Carthaginian has burnt many villages all around. The last market open to us was Cannae, and now he will burn it.'

I sucked in my cheeks. I knew it then. 'Bulla, I will bring you peace.'

She returned my gaze. There was a strange strength in her deep-brown eyes. 'So young, and so sure?' she said at last.

'Yes. So sure.'

'We shall see, Scipio. But you sent for me. What do you want?'

'Food, if you have any, for the march.'

She nodded. 'I see. Follow me. But you only.'

I followed her round the back of her hut, between two others to one in the last row. Instead of a curtain, it had a proper wooden door. She lifted a key which hung on a leather thong round her neck, and put it in the lock. The door creaked open. She stepped back. 'See for yourself. This is all we have – besides the clamps of corn. It is our winter store.'

From the rafters, hams hung. I tried to count them. Sixty, or seventy. I stepped back to the light. 'How many people live here, Bulla?'

'Forty families. Just under two hundred people.'

'So you have stored two hams for each family?'

'Not quite. We lost some pigs in the spring. The swineherd took them to the woods to root. They – and he – never returned.'

'Ah, yes. I have heard of the ghosts and ghouls of your woods.'

'Ghosts? Those who took our pigs were men – probably Carthaginians. Anyway, Scipio, you may take half our hams to feed you and your men.'

'Half? But will that leave you enough for the winter?'

'No, but we will survive. Take them.'

'Bulla?'

'Yes?'

'Why?'

'Why what?'

'Why this kindness?'

Again, those deep-brown eyes. 'Because you asked, and did not take.'

I found Flaevius mending his boots. I told him to arrange to take the hams and distribute them among the men. I went back to Bulla's hut, where Laelius, Afer and Metellus were already lying down on makeshift beds of skins. 'Where's Postumus?' I asked.

'He volunteered for picket duty,' Laelius replied, sitting up.

'Did he, now? Well, well.'

'And Sextus has arranged a roster for the night,' Afer continued.

'Good. So now, the best thing we can all do is sleep. Where did you get those skins, Laelius?'

'In the corner over there.'

But I couldn't sleep, or calm my buzzing brain. I heard the others' deep breathing, or snores. I got up, went out. It was getting dark – the second time the sun had set, I thought, on the carnage of Cannae. Was I mad? How would we ever get to Rome? If we did, would we find it burning? Hannibal had no siege equipment, they said. For him to sack Rome would be impossible. They had said the same of defeat at Cannae.

I walked past the food store, and up a little rise towards what looked like an orchard. I paused by an apple tree. Grey lichen covered its branches and crumbled at my touch. From the twisted twigs, little, wormed and wizened apples hung. It had not been an unusually dry summer. The trees beyond that one bore rich, if still unripe, fruit. I could not explain it, but for whatever reason, the tree I touched was dead.

I went to the trough at the meeting-place, found the cup and drank. The water tasted brackish, sour. I looked around in the dying light. All was quiet. I went back to Bulla's hut, took off my boots, lay down. I must have dozed.

I still wonder sometimes if I dreamt it. I felt her fingers following my body's lines, her warmth beside me and her smell. At her touch, my penis stiffened, and she slipped me into her. I reached my head up, and sank it between her breasts. I took Bulla's wet warmth as it was offered, in and out and revelling in the rhythm, driving the death of Cannae away with a power as ancient, but alive. When I woke in the morning, she was gone.

We left Canusium the next evening, the dirty, dishevelled, bedraggled remnants of a once-great Roman army, skulking in the dark.

'Remember, Scipio, to send us peace,' was the last thing Bulla told me.

I smiled. 'I will try. Bulla, thank you,' I began, but she had already turned away.

The next long weeks are blurred and muddled in my memory. They were a dark place in which I thought never to see light. The first week or so was easy enough. We had ham, and berries were plentiful. It did not rain, and concealing ourselves in thickets we slept or dozed like animals by day. Our smells grew rank, our bodies as black as our minds. We followed the stars as mariners do, though often turning east or west to avoid, Pius said, an impassable or difficult way. We learnt to know the many noises of the night. Two soldiers' wounds festered and turned gangrenous. The men died, delirious. We had no tools. We buried them under piles of leaves and stones.

The ham ran out. We began not only to feel hunger, but to fear it. We fed on acorns and roots. Our stomachs shrank and screamed. We grubbed for onions and garlic, like swine. But we saw no signs of Carthaginians as we moved north like thieves in the night.

Our progress slowed. Each morning in the early half-light I had an assembly to count the men and see how they were. First five or six, then eleven, twelve of them, then more, had to throw away their boots. The stitching had rotted. 'Never were any good,' one soldier said. Cheap leather, badly cured. Barefoot, these men fell further and further behind on each night's march. Sometimes they did not catch up with us until midday until, once, three did not catch up at all. I added boots to my list of things to do when I got back to Rome: find out who had the contract for supplying boots. I vowed that no man who fought for me would do so in second-rate boots.

So, the present insufferable and uncertain, I fixed my mind on the future. It was either that or the past, and I saw some of the men do that, withdraw within themselves, maudlin, to their memories. It is not the failure of the body, that march taught me, that matters. It is the response of the spirit. Those who died along the way did so from failure of spirit.

It began to happen in the third week, or was it the fourth? When I passed the word to march in the early evening, some men wouldn't move. We knew they had died, and we left them. What else could we do? That was one of the charges levied at my trial. That I deserted Roman soldiers in the field. It is one that I refused to answer. It is a memory that troubles me still. I am a hulk of memories.

The trees began to thin. The Endless Wood had ended, though Pius' estimate of how long its traverse would take had been very wrong. The only ghosts we had encountered were our own. Some two hundred of us hobbled and limped on. I meant to go on north for another two or three nights, and then turn west and south.

The land turned to low, rolling hills of grass and what had once been grain. Those fields were blackened now. Hannibal had been this way, it seemed, before Cannae. We passed sheepcotes of hurdles and dry-stone walls. Those that had not been long abandoned had been burnt and overturned. We saw flocks of goats, untended, already semi-wild. The billies stood their ground before us, though at a distance, and coughed and stamped and pawed the ground. It was a landscape of empty desolation. It was as if the whole of Italy had died.

We slept one day in an abandoned, ravaged village, sheltering like snakes in nooks of ruined buildings as hunger gnawed. I woke at noon, decided. I found the four fittest men. 'Slings, or snares. Go and catch us rabbits. As the light dies, we will build a fire. But be careful. Don't show yourselves on a skyline.' I found a store of barley in the floor of one hut, some desiccated carrots in a basket in the next. Pots were plentiful, as was wood. Already, my saliva was beginning to run.

The body. The mind. How strange that from those dreadful days I remember this. The four returned just before dusk with twelve rabbits. Twelve, between two hundred men. We huddled round, among the broken buildings, as the rabbits were skinned and the water boiled in twenty pots.

In the end, we each had little more than a spoonful, and the barley grains stuck in my throat. But it was the first hot food we had eaten in many weeks. It left me yearning for more, and almost wishing I had tasted none.

We moved on, following now the stars the Greeks call the Pleiades and we the Vergiliae, which sink in the west as day dawns. It seemed fitting that we should follow the path of the seven daughters of Atlas, turned into stars by Jupiter in pity at their suffering for their father. But only six sisters shine. The seventh, Merope, hid her light in shame at having had intercourse with a mortal, Sisyphus. I thought of her each night. Could we rekindle the light put out at Cannae?

Then, one morning, as the sun grew hot, I half woke just after I had fallen asleep in the lee of a broken wall under some chestnut trees, their leaves beginning to hint at yellow and brown. Colour is as fragile as life.

I heard a strange, steady, susurrating murmur from behind me. I looked up, and round. There was another roofless building, its walls half broken down. I listened. The noise came from there. I got up, and walked towards it. Then I caught the putrid, cloying, sweet and gagging smell. I held the crook of my left arm across my nose, the cloth of my torn shirt pungent with my own, familiar reek.

I looked over the wall, and I still see in my dreams what I then saw: a black, crawling mat of thousands and thousands of flies, feasting on the bodies of a man, a woman and a child. The man and woman lay on their backs, the many stabs and thrusts and slashes that had killed them festering and oozing, filled with feeding flies, and all around the bodies were columns of marching ants.

The man had been disembowelled, his guts stuffed into his mouth. The woman's dress was ricked up round her breasts. The brooding bruises on her thighs, the brown blood dried across her midriff, showed what had been done to her before she died. The child lay face down, its head a bloody pulp. Bloodstains on the earth beside it showed where it had been bashed.

I retched and turned away. There was nothing in my stomach to bring up, but my mouth was full of bitter bile.

The bodies fell apart when we moved them. An arm, a leg, a head. We buried those broken corpses, the men swearing, protesting, moaning, muttering that I had gone mad. I dug myself, swooning and shaking and sweating from the sun, and hunger, and the smell.

That evening, it was hard to move on. Doubt's room had no window, despair's dungeon no key. There was only the will to take one westward step, then another, through that night and all the others. I thought of Rufustinus, my *abecedarius*. *Potest quia posse videtur*: you can because you think you can. I chanted that. It became a rhythm that I walked to, drumming through my mind.

Men shuffled, stalled and stopped. I found light hemp rope in an abandoned house. I tied us all together in a line, and we lurched on. At least the land was not blackened now. There were no people, but we found villages intact, unsacked, and full of food. Then, one golden daybreak, from a meadowed rise of brimming autumn flowers of clovers, cranesbills, spurges, mallow, borages and thyme, across rolling hills, their coombes full of rolling morning ground mist, I saw beyond the fields the shining sea, the curving Tiber and, still there, substantial, the square, thick, embracing walls, and within them the seven hills of Rome.

The tears came, strong and fast and silent, running in my thick, matted beard and spilling onto cracked and blistered lips. I looked across at Laelius by my side. He was staring, wild, bemused.

'He hasn't,' he said. 'Publius, he hasn't sacked it!' The first words he had used for days.

Behind me, I heard the men mutter and gasp as they came up. 'You thought we'd find a smouldering shell?' My tongue was vast and heavy. Laelius nodded. 'Then why did you march?'

He turned to look at me. There were bits of straw and grass and mud in his hair and beard. His clothes were only rags and tatters. He was missing one boot, and torn cloth covered his left foot. He looked like a scarecrow after a season in the fields. So, I supposed, did I. 'I followed you, Publius, not Rome. But why were you so sure?'

'An instinct. No more. I feel I know his mind. But when we came closer, and saw he had not burnt or looted, I was sure.' I rubbed my eyes, turned round. 'Soldiers of Rome,' I called out. The words were clotted, clumsy, but they came. 'Today we walk on – to Rome.' There was a muffled, careworn cheer. 'Leave your swords, your packs. Leave everything. Flaevius, where is Scaevola?'

'Here, sir.' He pushed him forward. Scaevola did not look up. He hadn't spoken for many days. His hair covered his face. 'Cut him loose.'

'Sir?'

'Cut him loose.'

'But he'll escape.'

'I doubt it. But I will not have a Roman citizen enter his city bound. Scaevola, you know where the magistrates' offices are. Go there, and await your fate. Now, we move on.'

Beyond the next rise, the Via Praenestina ran straight and

true through well-tilled, hedged, deserted fields to the east gate which was, as I had expected, closed. So too, I could see as my eyes followed the great wall of blocks of mellow brown *tufa* stone, was the next gate, the Tiburtina. So the city knew of a defeat. Did they know how great, how shattering?

The sound of drums and trumpets came to us on the breeze: they had seen us. Some men tried to run towards the soaring walls. They were too weary, and they tripped and fell. The great gate swung open. The men held back. I walked in first, alone, and what I saw was black. What I heard was silence. My head was spinning. I saw a sea of faces, looks, women in the black clothes of mourning, girls with cropped and blackened hair, soldiers with soot-smeared heads and hands and legs. I saw a burly butcher in a blood-streaked smock. I heard the great bars of the gate behind us lodge fast in their sockets. We are home, I thought; and then my legs gave way.

I came to in – it seemed impossible, familiar – my room, my bed. I had been gone how long? Three months? Four? My eyes blurred. Everything was going round. I was naked under the cover. I had been washed. I felt that I had returned to the living. I saw several faces, and forced my eyes to focus on one.

'Father,' I whispered.

'Shh. Don't try to speak.' Someone held my head up. Another held a cup of sweet, scented, aromatic tea to my lips. I drank, and drifted away.

I lay like that for many days. A barber came and shaved me. I used a bedpan. There were slaves. I remember Festo feeding me warm porridge with a small wooden spoon. The next day it was a new slave I had not seen before, very old and missing his left arm.

'Where is Festo?' I asked him, weakly.

'Enlisted, master.'

'Enlisted?' I coughed. 'In what?'

'In a new legion, master.'

'A new legion?' I struggled to sit up. 'A new legion – of slaves?'

'This is the third, sir. Last proper legion left a month ago.'

'Left? Left for where?'

'For Sicilia, sir. Guess you don't know. You wasn't 'ere. Under your cousin Claudius Marcellus they've gone with the rest of the fleet to join those already there. To take Syracuse, they say.'

'But why Sicilia? What's been going on there?'

'Old King 'Ieron died, sir, while you was away. 'Is son sided with Carthage, that's wot. Gone to teach 'em a lesson, I 'ear.'

'And what about these new legions?'

'Anyone able-bodied from fourteen to sixty. Your father's training 'em on the Campus Martius right now. They're soon to sail, they say, to Celtiberia.'

'To Celtiberia! What's going on?' My head pounded. I had been having blinding headaches since we returned. My body ridding itself of accumulated strain, the doctor said.

'Can't say as I know rightly, master. 'Eard talk of an invasion, I 'ave. But you'd best ask your father. Now, let's get this soup into you.'

In the end, it wasn't from my father that I heard it. It was from Scribonius. He—

Yes, Aurio? What is it? We are working, can't you see?

Sorry, sir. But it's him again.

Who, Aurio, who?

Him. That Greek lad. Theo . . .

Ah! Theophilus! Then you were right to disturb me. Another letter, I suppose.

Yes, sir. From Theogenes.

Then hand it over. Thank you. You may go.

Well, Bostar. Well, well. Yes, I recognise Theogenes' hand
again. So, this should be it. The result of Cato's appeal. Read
it out to me, please. You can write its contents down later,
whatever it says. Here it is.

*With a tight, nervous smile, Scipio handed me the letter. I held his
eyes, he mine. I saw sadness in his, but also acceptance, relief. He
reached a hand out to my shoulder.*

'*Bostar of Chalcedon,*' *he said,* '*you are my very good friend. Now,
break the seal. No, just a moment. I want to hear this sitting in my
chair.*' *He turned, walked across the mosaic of Minerva, and sat down.*
'*Oh, Aurio!*' *he exclaimed.* '*The chair is too far back for me to see
my quincunx. I didn't notice earlier. Concentrating on my dictation,
I suppose. Isn't it strange that what we see depends on how we are
feeling when we see it?*'

*He got up, edged his chair forwards, sat down again and pulled the
folds of his toga over his knees. I heard the cowbells from the fields,
the wind wafting round the window's panes of selenite, and smelt the
salt tang of the sea.*

When Scipio was still, I began to read. '*My dear friend, I will come
straight to the point. Last night, your brother Lucius—*' *I gasped at
what I saw. I have since then copied it carefully, very carefully, into
this account.*

'*Read on, Bostar!*' *Scipio said firmly, calmly.* '*Do not fail me
now.*'

*I took a deep breath, and looked again at the words, so few for so
much, and resumed.* '*Last night your brother Lucius took his own life.
He—*' *I broke off again, for the shame, the bitter shame.*

'*Bostar, Bostar,*' *Scipio said gently.* '*Read on.*'

I raised my voice. '*He cut his wrists in his bath. His body-slave
found him this morning. I cannot tell you exactly what drove him to
do this, why he could not go on. I can tell you some of the pressure he
has been under from Cato, for whom hatred of the Scipios has become*

a habit, and from Cato's many friends. They have, it is said, been doctoring his wine with potions to unseat the mind. They had dead dogs thrown into his garden, and all manner of things. When he sent out for a harlot, they made sure she carried some disease. One they smeared with mutton fat to disgust him, and Theophilus himself once saw the carter urinating on the fruit he was delivering to your brother's villa.

'You know the treatment for suicides. This one is more refined. By the time you read this, your brother's body will not have been carried, but' – I felt tears well. I almost paused – 'will have been dragged by a mule past the tomb of the Scipios and out through the beggars' and the lepers' gate. You know the city dumps in the folds of the River Clitumnus. For disgracing the Roman Senate and people, the corpse of Lucius Cornelius Scipio, it has been decreed, will be dumped there. Anyone, of any rank, who seeks to tend the body or give it burial will face the loss of his right arm. Lictors have been sent to keep watch.'

I paused. From Scipio, nothing. I closed my eyes. This was, to my knowledge, without parallel or precedent. It was an unspeakable insult to Scipio, his family and blood. This was to try to extirpate his name.

But when it came, his voice was flat and level. 'Is that all, Bostar?'

I raised my head. 'No, Scipio.'

'Then read on.'

'As for Cato's appeal against the verdict, I can tell you that Laelius completed his evidence twelve days ago. Scribonius, summoned from western Celtiberia, arrived eight days ago and was dismissed only yesterday. People shun him in the Forum, so I assume that what he said displeased Cato and favoured you. I hear that Scribonius looks gaunt and old and haggard. There is talk that his governorship will not be renewed. Perhaps he will try to get word to you himself. I dare not make contact with him, or offer to help. I am sorry. I am already suffering for being known as your friend, but that is not important. As to the Carthaginian Senate, I have heard that their submission praised *you for your magnanimity, and that Cato has argued this proves you were not true to Rome.*

'When will the Senate give their ruling? As you know, the festival of the Lupercalia begins tomorrow. After that, the hearing will resume. So you have to wait, my friend, five or six days more at least, ten at the most. If the judgment goes against you, you will be arrested before I can get word to you. If it is for you, you will hear at once from me and many others who, still, count themselves your friend.'

Lucius had died, I thought, as he had lived. But so to insult the dead, and a family as old as Rome and, generation after generation, devoted to her service? For Cato, vengeance might be sweet. But its fruits would be bitter. What was being born was the death of the Republic of Rome. If Cato, a 'new man', was new knowledge, I would praise ignorance. For what man has not encountered, he has not destroyed.

Something had ended. One life. A second was now very finely balanced in the scales, and as I sat in silence with the man I loved, my master and my friend, I thought of the ancient things, the stars turning in the heavens, the timeless, teeming mating of the trees, the pollen entering invisible the domed roofs of the winds. That survives the ghosts of far forests killed for timber, or burnt, decayed. The earth invites it, and it will not be gone.

The minutes passed. The calibrated candles spluttered, and went out. The weak winter light began to lessen in the west. The room grew grey.

Scipio cleared his throat. 'So, my friend, the Lupercalia,' he said in an even voice. 'It is one of the many parts of my birthright denied me by war.'

He got up, and stretched. I heard his back crack. 'Anyway, Bostar, pretending to be a wolf and running through Rome naked — apart from a goatskin loincloth — is not, I think, something I would have much enjoyed, however honorific.' He paused, and rubbed his face. 'Lucius might have, but not I. Rather vulgar, don't you think? Now the festival of the wolves, remembering Rome's founders,

Romulus and Remus, suckled by a she-wolf, prolongs my life or assures my death.

'You must be tired, old friend. Let's have a break – until sunset, shall we say? I'm going – you'll know where. I'll come back when the light's gone, and have a bath, and then I propose we eat, and after that resume. Time, it seems, is something we do not have, Lupercalia or nay. So let's press on. Do you agree?'

I looked at his face, the sculpted brow and nose and chin, the deep lines on his cheeks, his eyes narrowed and dark. I nodded. He smiled, and cracked his fingers, then turned his signet ring round and round on his little finger. 'Please tell Aurio to prepare a bath, and Mulca our plans,' he said, and sighed, and left the room.

I knew where he was going. To the lake he loved, a stiff walk above the villa, looking down on to the sea. There is an island on it, where herons nest and call to each other and rear their young, and from which they find fish in the clear blue water that laps the oak-girt shore. There is a dead pine there, gaunt and solitary, lovely and forlorn. He loved that place. He used to praise the way of water, which patiently fills the place it comes to. I knew he would go there.

So, where was I? I must now be brief. I have ten days at the most; few days for many years.

Scribonius, Scipio. You had got to Scribonius.

Ah, yes. Thank you, Bostar. He came to visit me. I was by then able to get out of bed and greet him. He told me that the constitution had been suspended, and Fabius given supreme command as dictator. The Twelve Tables in the Forum had been taken down, and lodged in the temple of Vesta. We talked of Cannae.

'How did you find out?' I asked.

He frowned. 'When we heard nothing after Varro's last despatch, we began to fear the worst. Then we heard from Hannibal – the first time.'

I started, sucked in my breath. 'You what? I didn't know.'

'No. The doctors said you were to be told nothing until you were stronger.'

'I am now. So tell me, Scribonius. What did Hannibal do?'

'You'll remember the message he sent after Trasimenus?'

I nodded. 'How could I forget?'

'Well, this one was more, ah . . .' He shuddered, and chose his words with care. 'This one was more memorable.'

'What did he do?'

Scribonius cleared his throat, and grimaced. I noticed how the lines on both his cheeks had deepened, and grown. There were dark shadows of strain under his eyes. 'May I?' he asked, gesturing to the beechwood couch against the far wall of my room.

'Of course.'

He crossed the room with his precise, soldier's walk. I sat down on my bed, facing him. He looked at me keenly, and smiled. 'It's good to see you on the mend, sir.'

'It's good to be so, Scribonius. But tell me.'

He drew a deep breath. 'Hands.'

'Hands?'

'Yes. That was Hannibal's message. Twenty whole wagons, laden with, with . . .' He screwed his eyes shut and sucked in breath. 'With hands, thousands of Roman hands, cut from our soldiers of Cannae. I shall never forget the stench, the flies, the . . . That's what he sent. So, yes, we knew. And we never expected to see any of you alive again.'

I hung my head and exhaled deeply, slowly, wholly. Such sick savagery. 'Why, why?' I muttered. What demons were driving Hannibal? What hate? How could he contain so many dark and bitter things?

'So, no other survivors?' I asked.

Scribonius looked down at the floor. 'None that we know of.'

'And Paullus? If he had been in command . . .'

'We've heard nothing. But we know about Varro.'

'Varro! Who told you?'

'Laelius. He's been giving evidence to the Senate.'

'So he's all right?'

'Like you, weak. But you developed a fever. He's been on his feet for five, six days.'

I stood up. 'I must see him.'

'Indeed you must. In fact—'

I heard the voices, the footsteps, the sound of people coming down the corridor. There was a sharp knock at the door. Puzzled, I looked at Scribonius. He simply smiled. 'Come in!' I said, and the door swung open to two of the senatorial guard. They marched in, and snapped to attention, one on each side of the doorway. Slowly after them came – I remember the surge of joy – old Fabius, hobbling in very slowly on two sticks and, in his blindness, being led by a young boy, but alive. I moved towards him, to greet him, but sensed that would be wrong, and I stood still.

'Fabius!' I blurted out. He stopped. 'I, I . . .'

'You what?'

'I thought you would be dead.'

He fixed his unseeing eyes on me. They were watery. The cataracts had grown. He chuckled into his abundant, flowing beard, pure white, and shuffled forwards. 'Young man,' he said gravely. 'I do not have time to die. Now, let's get on.'

From behind him, around him, others came into the room. My father, my uncle Gnaeus, six senators I knew by name, then Laelius, Metellus, Postumus and Afer, then Flaevius, and even the soldier Pius, all sombre and intense.

Fabius spoke to a hushed, expectant room. His voice was flat and tired, but his blind eyes shone. 'Publius Cornelius Scipio, step forward.'

I did.

He raised his head, and his voice grew strong. 'Then, by the powers vested in me as father of the Senate, by those I hold from and for the people, we have come here in these dark days to honour you, Publius Cornelius Scipio, in the name of Rome. Bring it forward!'

An old clerk came forward, carrying with reverence before him something I had heard of, of course, but never seen. A *corona civica*, civic crown, a simple wreath of oak leaves. I looked round, amazed, mouth open, and caught my father's look, and felt his pride.

Fabius went on, 'We all know the significance of this: the reward for great bravery. None has been awarded for many years. When the light of the Republic was almost extinguished, this young man, we know from many accounts, ensured it did not die. Publius Cornelius Scipio, you have served the Republic and honoured your stock. Put on this crown with pride.'

I stepped forward, and took the wreath, and bowed my head, and put it on. As I did so, the room came alive with many voices saying the formulaic greeting: '*Salve, civis, haud indigne honore* . . .' I felt tears well up, but I choked them back. I had come home.

When the salutations had died down, Fabius' voice rang out: 'And this young man hereafter must share our deliberations through these dark days. And so I salute you, Publius Cornelius Scipio.' He paused, then added one word: 'Aedile.'

I gasped. An aedile, a magistrate of the city? I was at least five years too young. No one had told me of elections. Was this the will of the people? Was it unopposed? My head spun. Fabius went on, 'I must return to the Senate. There is much to be done. Those of you so appointed, hold your celebration. But remember, out of respect for our plight and for the dead of Cannae, no laughter, and no wine.' Fabius scratched his sticks across the floor. 'Boy,' he said, 'lead on.'

We all went down to the atrium. There were tables there, laid with bowls of fruit and cakes and pitchers of cordial. It was a sombre celebration, but I talked to my father and uncle and several of the senators and learned what was going on. There was still no sign of Hannibal. After Cannae, he had moved south, it seemed. Our daily scouts reported nothing, but our gates remained locked and our walls were manned by lookouts day and night. All those I talked to, once they had congratulated me, were full of Fabius' plans.

The old slave who had tended me was right. We had raised three new legions, of slaves and freedmen, young and old. They had been added to Cato's garrison at Arretium; it had been summoned back to Rome as soon as news of Cannae came. All clerks and scribes, all discharged veterans, all record-keepers and teachers, all priests but the *pontifex maximus*, all tax-collectors, all classes previously exempt from military service had been enlisted.

In the debate that followed the arrival of Hannibal's message of hands, Fabius had told the Senate that 'Rome will not die while even one Roman is left alive'. Some senators had suggested suing for peace, and sending emissaries direct to Carthage. Fabius had dismissed this out of hand. 'Peace!' he thundered. 'Peace? We will not utter that word while even one Carthaginian remains on Italian soil.' He had carried the house, with the exception of Valerius Flaccus, Cato's patron. From that agreement came his plan.

It was a simple one. Under my father and uncle, both given extraordinary, proconsular *imperium* and with Scribonius promoted to be their legate, our new legions and what was left of the legion still stationed at Placentia were to invade Celtiberia. They were to leave within the week, hence my father's desperate, intense training of his new troops. Fabius hoped that this would draw Hannibal to the defence of Celtiberia, either of his own volition, or because the Carthaginian Senate ordered him there, which they would do if our troops stopped, or at least disrupted, their supply of silver from their mines there.

They might even send him to Syracuse, Fabius reasoned, if Marcellus showed any signs of winning the siege. The news from there, so far, was good. There were in the city many Romans or friends of Rome, who did not support the new puppet king, Hieron's son, Hiero. Perhaps the gates would be opened, without a protracted siege. Marcellus' last despatch, certainly, had asked for more gold.

With Celtiberia and Sicilia settled, Fabius' intention was that both Metellus and my father should then invade Africa itself. Hannibal might not leave Italy for Celtiberia or Sicilia, but he would have to go if a Roman army was camped at Carthage's gates.

The spies we had sent to Celtiberia before I left for Cannae had returned. We knew of two Carthaginian armies, one stationed on the east coast at Carthagena under Hannibal's brother Hasdrubal, and the second on the west at Gades under his other brother, Mago. Our information was that their infantry were mostly Celtiberian, though their officers were either Carthaginian or mercenaries recruited from the Greeks, and their cavalry Numidians from northern Africa. 'If Carthage can hire, then we can too,' my father said.

'So you're taking money with you, Father?'

'Yes, lots. It's one thing we're not short of. Either to pay for a further legion we'll raise locally, or to try to bribe the Celtiberians to change sides.'

'May I not come with you, Father?'

'Certainly not, though I'd love that. But you must stay, with all those you led from Cannae. Fabius needs you, and so does Rome. You will be virtually alone.'

'I understand. Father, do we know how many men Hasdrubal and Mago have?'

'No, we don't. That's a worry, admittedly. But if they're

only Celtiberian tribesmen, we'll deal with them easily – out-numbered or not. But come, you look tired. Back upstairs to bed. Anyway, we all have work to do – and I for one don't enjoy a party without wine.'

Laelius came up to my room with me. If his repeated congratulations on my honour and new standing were insincere, I didn't notice. But I was thinking, and I said so as I lay back on my bed and he sat on the couch. 'If I'm an aedile, Laelius, I'll need a *quaestor*. You're good with numbers. Money is crucial, so why don't you become my financial secretary, my *quaestor aerarii*, and help me look after the public treasuries?'

So, I see. It may be true. One of the charges against Scipio is that he expropriated public money when his father was in Celtiberia. Certainly, much went unaccounted for. Scipio would have done no such thing. But Laelius? There is a Roman proverb about snakes lying silent in the grass. I hope I am wrong.

His face lit up. 'Do you mean it, Publius?'

'Of course I do. I'll ask Fabius as soon as I can.'

'But I'm too young to hold public office, for a start.'

'And too humbly born, you'll say next! None of that matters any more. No, it's a great plan! And it means we can work together every day.'

We talked about our march. I learnt that Scaevola had been found guilty of treason, and his whole family stripped of their rank. But he had volunteered for service in Celtiberia – as a legionary – and all charges against him had, quite rightly, been dropped. Perhaps I had misjudged him after all. As we were discussing him, I fell asleep where I lay.

When I woke, it was dark, and Laelius had gone. I shivered,

sat up and looked round. It was still so strange to be home. The house was silent. Where were my brother, Lucius, and my sister, Cornelia? It was time I saw them again. But there was something I had to do first. Pulling on a cloak, I left the room.

It was all unchanged, familiar, in and around the Forum. The only thing different was the quiet. The taverns, temples and brothels were deserted. To the west, though, from the smiths' quarter, came a steady din and clamour. Swords being made, and armour, and all the other accoutrements of war. I sat on a bench by the lake of Curtius, cloak wrapped around me, and dreamed. Was Roman soil still yielding men in plenty? I remembered the carnage of Cannae, and felt the pain. Where was Hannibal? What was he planning, and why? Above me, meteors streaked across a clear and starlit sky.

I went towards the temple of Vesta, where I intended to give thanks for my safe return and pray for Rome's delivery. I was crossing the street that ran past the public baths, empty and cold, and on to the Capena gate, when a voice startled me. 'Alms, sir, alms! Alms for a poor veteran, cold and hungry!' There was something in his voice I recognised; under the beggar's wheedling, a tone that I knew.

He was sitting in the shadows, his back against a closed street-stall. 'Come out,' I said, 'where I can see you.'

There was a grunt, and the sound of wheels or castors scratching on the flagged street. Into the starlight, on a low wooden trolley, propelled by his arms, came a legless man, poor indeed. 'Alms, sir, al—' As he looked up at me, recognition dawned. Despite the leather cap, the mass of matted beard, the filthy face, I knew Frontinus, and he me.

'Frontinus!' A sense of joy began in my belly and tingled down my legs. 'I thought you were dead!'

'By all rights should be, sir, should be. Left as good as, anyhow. But you, sir, you too. I heard no one survived Cannae.'

'A few of us, Frontinus, a few. But this is a marvel. By all the gods, you're alive! But . . . begging? I thought we looked after veterans.'

'We used to, sir. Then was then, but now is now.'

'Why didn't you contact my father?'

'I tried. No one would let me near him.'

'I want to hear it all, Frontinus. You saved my life, you know.'

'Aye, sir. I remember that night as if it were yesterday. You got away?'

'I did, Frontinus, I did – thanks to you. But we can't talk here. Are you hungry?'

'Always hungry, these days.'

'Then let's go to my home. There you shall eat, and we shall talk.'

'Begging your pardon, sir, but me go to the home of the Scipios? A beggar on the Palatine Hill? They'll call the Watch.'

'I won't let them. Anyway, I think you'll find the Watch is no more: enlisted. Come with me. Can I help?'

'I'm fine on this contraption, sir. You'll see, I'll race you there.'

One walking, one pushing, a youthful aedile and a faithful soldier went to the Scipios' home. This was a new Rome, indeed.

I woke up the cooks, and sat with Frontinus under the sputtering torches of the *tablinum*, as he wolfed down barley gruel and bread. Supplies in the city were low. As aedile, I would have much to do. I heard how, that night, the first of the two men on horseback had unseated him. 'The only disadvantage,' he said dryly, 'of a mule.' As he lay, stunned, on the ground they pinned him down. 'I thought they would cut my throat,' but for some reason they didn't. They checked me for the satchel, then cut my hamstrings and went after you.'

'What did you do?'

318

'That was good, sir,' he replied, wiping his mouth on his sleeve. 'Thank you. First hot food I've had for days. What did I do? I crawled. I was lucky. Found a village, and someone put me on a melon cart bound for Rome. Don't remember the journey. Delirious. By the time I got there, gangrene had set in. Surgeon just cut both legs off at the hip. I suppose there was nothing else he could do.'

I shook my head. War, war. All who survive it carry scars. 'How did you survive?'

'Begging. You saw me. A carpenter, brother of someone in my maniple at Telamon, made this trolley for me. Funny thing is, sir, that most of the time I still feel my legs are there.'

'Where do you sleep?'

'Where I can. Anyway, with Hannibal due I can't see it matters much.'

'You think he'll come?'

'Bound to. What's to stop him now?'

'We'll see, Frontinus, we'll see. But until then, you have somewhere to sleep.'

'Where's that, sir?'

'Here, in this house.'

'But—'

I raised my hand. 'No argument. I'll speak to my father in the morning. Now, let's see who's around to give you a bath. It'll have to be a woman slave, I'm afraid. As you'll have heard, all able-bodied men are now under arms.'

My father and his army left two days later; and yes, my father had agreed with enthusiasm to Frontinus' living with us. Rome's last remaining army marched through the Aurelian gate and across the flimsy pontoon bridge erected the day before to replace the Aelian bridge of the Tiber, torn down when news of Cannae came. My first task as aedile was to have the pontoons destroyed. I had already decided to do so by fire. From Ostia, Rome's port, the army would take ships, hastily constructed and little more than barges, stopping only if the winds allowed, at Sardinia or Corsica for water and at the Baliarides isles to recruit more mercenary slingers. That, at least, was the plan.

Gathered at the Campus Martius to see Rome's last hope go were all those left in the city. They were few enough, mostly women – and most of them were widows – or girls. There was no cheering, or weeping, no sadness, no joy. Fabius and my father and uncle were busy with the doddering *pontifex maximus*. My father would have marched, though, whatever the sacrifice revealed. I had heard his interview with the fussing priest, his instruction that, whatever the entrails showed, the priest was to pronounce the omens good.

'But this is sacrilege!' the *pontifex* spluttered.

'No,' my father replied. 'This is war.'

It was a winter's day. Grey, heavy clouds scudded low across the sky. Rain threatened. The north wind came in gusts, and made all of us clutch our cloaks. I felt my head begin to throb again. The only officer I spoke to was Scribonius, waiting by his fretting horse. All our trained horses had gone to Cannae, or to Syracuse. Those going to Celtiberia were young, and barely trained. I looked round at the massed ranks of shivering men.

'It's a large force, Scribonius,' I said, trying to be optimistic. They seemed to me bedraggled curs.

'Yes,' he replied. 'That's true. But not too large, I hope.'

'Too large? How could that be? Surely, the bigger the better.'

'Not in Celtiberia.'

'No? Why not?'

'I've fought there before, remember. Celtiberia is a country where large armies starve.'

'And small ones?'

'In Celtiberia, sir, small ones get beaten.' There was no hint of levity in his voice. 'Anyway, I'm more worried about the sea crossing. In winter, and in toy boats? We shouldn't have let Marcellus take the whole fleet to Sicilia. You know I thought it was madness. We'll make it across to Sardinia, but after that there's no shelter from the winter storms.'

'Yet you backed the decision at the council. I know. I was there.'

'Yes, I did. But only because I felt that the gain of surprise and the thin possibility of interception outweighed the risk.' He yawned. 'Sorry, sir. Didn't mean to depress you. Just tired. Been up all night – again. I'm sure everything will be fine.'

Late that night, as I fell asleep, I wondered. Scribonius' words went round and round in my mind. 'Celtiberia is a country where large armies starve, and small ones get beaten.' Everything in my father's plan depended on surprise. He needed to sack an unsuspecting Carthagena straight away, or starve. Doing the unexpected had worked for Hannibal. Would it for us? I felt a strange foreboding. I hoped I was wrong.

The next morning, in the dark of winter, after an early, cold breakfast, I walked through the wind and rain to the Senate to report to Fabius. It was as before, except that there were no guards, no life, few lights. Fabius' room was unchanged, except that it had a new item of furniture, a couch, and on it, wrapped in a cloak, lay Fabius, apparently asleep. I saw Laelius' cloak, over the back of a chair, and scrolls open on what had been his desk. So, he had got there before me. I moved on tiptoe towards my old desk.

'Good morning, Aedile.'

'Good morning, Reverend Father,' I spluttered, startled.

'You should not sound so surprised, Publius. I have lost the use of my eyes, not of my ears. Now,' he said, sitting up, 'what is your priority today?'

'First, the pontoon bridge.'

'Excellent. How do you intend to destroy it?'

'The easiest way. Fire, unless . . .'

'Unless what?'

'Unless you think the smoke would draw attention.'

'Ah.' He seemed very old and weary. 'You mean Hannibal.' He smiled and shook his head. 'I don't think, Publius, that one fire alone will bring him here. I think he knows where to find us.'

'And you think he'll come?'

'Who knows, who knows? As we have often discussed, it is hard enough to know one's own mind, let alone that of another. But we must assume he will come. We must be ready. We are.' Fabius struggled to his feet. 'Bring me my sticks. I must go to the latrine. Bowels not what they were.'

'Can I help you?'

'Publius, Publius,' he tutted. 'There are some things even an old, blind man must do on his own. I know the way, and the rest knows its own way. So, you'll see to the bridge?'

'Yes.'

'Any questions?'

'Two. First, where is Laelius?'

'Ah, Gaius Laelius. He has a good head for numbers, don't you think?'

'Yes, Reverend Father, I do.'

'So I sent him straight to the Treasury when he arrived. Indeed, I have an announcement to make this afternoon in the Senate.'

'What's that?'

'Laelius' appointment as your *quaestor aerarii* – no, don't thank me, Publius. It's no more than he deserves. But you'll need more help than that. There's much to be done. Have you anyone in mind?'

'Yes, sir. Postumus. Claudius Postumus.'

'But in Laelius' testimony—'

'I know, sir, but I trust him.'

'Very well. I'll see to his appointment to your staff. And the second thing?'

'Boots, sir.'

'Sorry? Boots?'

'Yes, boots.'

'What about them?'

'I want to find out who supplied them to our army at Cannae, sir. They were poor. They fell apart.'

'That's easy. I can tell you. Valerius Flaccus won the contract. His client Cato carried it out.'

'Cato! I meant to ask for him. Is he here?'

'Very much so. Indispensable, and so spared Celtiberia.' And Cannae, I almost added, and Cannae. 'Can't say as I'm much taken by him, but he's doing a good job. He's in charge of the corn supply. You'll find him in the granaries. Night and day, I'm told. Now, if you'll excuse me.'

Under Frontinus' and Postumus' joint command, I had as improbable a band of cripples, young boys and old men in their eighties as ever mustered go to burn the bridge. I saw that Flaevius was at his post. I had already made him prefect of the walls. He was doing a good job, reinforcing the lower ramparts, adding to stores of arrows, stones and oil. If – or when – Hannibal came, he would find us well prepared, and harder work than Cannae.

I walked on through that morning's drizzle, through the shuttered, silent, winter streets of mourning for Cannae towards the granaries in the lee of the south wall, through the potters' quarter, now still and empty, its yards deserted, its kilns cold. Dressed all in black, their faces pinched and grey, a group of women and girls passed me, bearing baskets of sand for the walls. '*Salvete, aedilis*' was all they muttered. We did not stop to talk of Cannae. What was there to say?

The ten granaries were tall and towering, stone-built and

limed. I went up to the first one. Locked. Through the ventilation shaft I saw only darkness. There was the heavy smell of grain. I found Cato in the third one, at a table poring by lamplight over ledgers and accounts. He was alone.

Scipio is ill again. He must have caught a chill last night, sitting by the lake. He is in bed with a fever. I can only hope it passes, and see that he is kept warm and drinks enough. But I wonder if this is an illness of the body, or the mind? He has given no response to his brother's suicide. Still, his will is adamantine. I sit by his bed, tablets on my knee. When he is awake, he dictates. Sick he may be, but his account goes on.

Cato looked up when I came in. 'Ah,' he said, 'the hero of Cannae. Greetings, Aedile, and 'gratulations on your 'ivic 'oun.' The dust from the piles of grain whirled and eddied in the light.

'My what?'

His piggy eyes were bright and eyed me keenly. 'Your 'ivic 'oun.'

'Ah, you mean my civic crown.'

'That's it. That's the one. Not wearing it, though, I see.'

'Marcus Porcius Cato, one doesn't wear the thing. It is a symbol of honour, that is all.'

He chewed the top of his stylus, pulled it out and belched. 'Damn beans. Just about all there is to eat now.'

'But what about all this grain?'

'Keeping it,' he said vehemently.

'For what?'

'Long siege. Could be. And corn keeps better than beans.'

'So you're using up the beans first?'

'You're quick.'

You see, I don't know where this animosity came from. It always was. 'Why don't you mix them?'

'Wot?'

'Start giving out some corn as well as beans?'

'Why?'

I sighed. 'Variety, Cato. To vary the people's diet.' He grimaced, screwed up his face, and scratched an ear. 'Oh, never mind. That's not what I came to see you for, anyway.'

'Oh, no? Wot then?' He pushed his chair back, and crossed his hands behind his head.

'Boots. Army boots.'

His eyes narrowed. 'What about them?' he said carefully.

'I understand from Fabius that your patron, Valerius Flaccus, was awarded the contract, and that you carried it out.'

'You understand right.'

'Well, I've checked the ledgers. The last order of boots before the one you placed was for the army that Sempronius was supposed to take to Sicilia.'

'Sounds right.'

'And that was for twenty thousand pairs, at twenty *denarii* each.'

'So?'

'So the order you met, for the armies of Paullus and Varro, was for forty thousand new pairs at thirty-five *denarii* a pair. That's quite a rise.'

'Nah, just inflation. Everything's shot up since that damn 'Annibal appeared. And leather's scarce. Tanneries are closed.'

'That's as may be, Cato. But quite apart from the fact that we should have had a discount for such volume, my real interest is in quality. You were paid a premium rate.'

'A fair rate, I'd say—'

'But for premium quality?'

'Of course. Nothing but the best.'

'You're lying.'

'I'm wot?'

'You heard me. Lying. Those boots were lousy. The leather was uncured, and the stitching was unwaxed. It rotted.'

Red spread across his face like a wine stain on a damask tablecloth. 'There may have been the odd bad pair,' he replied hesitantly. 'Inevitable, in such a large order.'

'The odd pair? I know about over two hundred pairs. On our march back from Cannae, they all failed.'

Cato got up, and leant over his table towards me. His arms, I noticed, never hung by his sides, but were held out and wide, as if casting around for something to do. 'If you're implying that—'

'I'm implying nothing. What I'm saying is that I'm going to be watching you. I'm going to check everything. And I see you supplied not only boots but horses' tack to my father. What I'm saying is that they had better be good. No, not just good. At those prices, they had better be the best. I won't have you and your patron growing rich while Romans die. Is that clear?'

Cato sneered, and sat down. 'So, a real busybody, are we, Aedile? Check anything you like. Some of us have work t' do.' He hunched over his ledgers. My point, I thought, was made. I turned, opened the door and walked away.

There was another personal matter I wanted to deal with. At Cannae, even if Varro had known what commands to give, our soldiers wouldn't have heard them. The trumpets' note was too low to cut through the vast noise of battle, and the command post was too far away. I could deal with the latter problem on my own, but with the first I needed help.

When I was a child, I had a long, thin, tin whistle. My father hated my playing it because its note was so piercing, high and clear. I had lost it long ago. I went to the tinsmiths' quarter, its little houses and workshops clustered along the street that rose and fell along the foot of the Viminalis Hill, its buildings all made of ancient, undressed stone. All was still, deserted, and the drizzle turned to sleet. I shivered, and pulled my fringed Asian cloak tight. There must be one tinsmith in Rome still plying his trade. Faintly, I heard the sound of hammer on anvil, and I followed the sound down a narrow alley past rooting pigs and chickens sheltering from the sleet.

The sound grew stronger. The smoke smell was safe. The alley opened out into a yard, and at the back of it was a lean-to forge, one man sitting by it, his back to me, his left arm rising and falling as he worked his hammer: his right arm, I saw, was shrivelled. Another man who could not serve in Rome's army. Still, he could contribute in another way.

'Greetings, smith,' I called out, drawing near. 'Your fire is welcome on a day like this, let alone your forge.'

He looked up, startled. 'And who—' His eyes opened wide as comprehension dawned. 'Aedile!' he spluttered. 'What are you doing here?'

'So, you recognise me,' I said, squatting down beside the forge.

'What Roman would not? Besides, one of the men you led back from Cannae was my brother's son. Our whole family thanks you. I— Let me get you a hot drink,' he said getting up. 'Some tea? Or food? We have beans, and a little pork. Or I could kill a chicken.'

'No, thank you, smith. But there is something you can do for me.'

The days that followed were full of work, anxieties and plans, although Postumus was proving an invaluable assistant, efficient and calm. We heard nothing from my father. We hadn't expected any news until the spring.

In my personal life, I learnt to love my sister, Cornelia, and loathe my brother, Lucius. She was extraordinary: tireless, efficient. She barely slept, seeing to our house, supervising, cooking, cleaning early in the mornings. Then she would go to the hospitals, sixteen of them prepared for casualties of the siege we all expected to come with the spring. She had a staff of hundreds of women and girls whom she was training, and she worked with them late into the night. She also ran the kitchens in the Senate, and we never wanted for wholesome food, if plain. For Fabius she made special dishes, because he could not digest most things. His favourites were custard, made from the milk of the goats penned on the edges of the Campus Martius, and millet porridge, sweetened with honey. 'In the early days of the Republic,' he used to say, 'there were two kinds of food. The first was a kind of porridge, and the second a kind of porridge. We have made progress, you see.' It was as close to levity as we ever got through those long, dark days.

By contrast, everything I gave Lucius to do he made a mess of. If helping Laelius with accounts, he got his numbers wrong. If helping Flavius with munitions, he dithered and dallied and annoyed the other men. I know he drank, despite Fabius' prohibition. And in a city of many women and few men, he never lacked diversion. To my regular question, 'Where have you been, Lucius?' he would reply, 'At play.'

I tried hard to understand and forgive him. He had never had a mother, or really a father, or a tutor. In his way he, too, was a victim of war. But then I learnt of something that turned me, and from that began a thick web of lies. It grew over the years, and now that I am of a mind to confront and to clear it, I cannot. Lucius is dead, and I must live – or die – with the consequences of my actions.

Four mornings in a row, when I walked from our villa to the Senate, I noticed a woman waiting at the crossroads where the road from our villa met the bottom of the hill. She was old and hunched, and always in the same black, cowled cloak. Each time I saw her, I greeted her, but she simply nodded and let me pass her by. I suppose I wondered what she was doing there, but there were many things on my mind. On the fifth morning, she stopped me.

'*Salvete, aedilis,*' she muttered.

'*Et vos, salvete,*' I replied. Her face was wrinkled, her mouth tight and pursed, but there was energy in her eyes. 'Have you something to say to me?' I asked gently.

She raised her chin, looked up at me, and cleared her throat. 'I respect you, *aedilis*, and your family. You are truly the staff of Rome. But . . .'

'But what?'

'Your brother,' she said flatly, looking away.

'What about him?'

'He—' She bit her lip, went on. 'He raped my daughter.'

'He what? When?'

'A week ago.'

I took the woman home. She told me it all, and I believed her. The girl was only twelve. I should have urged her to bring charges; I didn't. In my defence, the courts were closed: there were no jurors, and few magistrates. But the bag of gold I gave the woman was, I see now, ill-considered. I did not mean to buy her silence; I meant to compensate her for a wrong. She took the money. We had a tacit understanding. It was not the time to bring disgrace upon the Scipios. Both she and I did what we thought best for Rome.

I still do not know how Cato found out about it. The old woman is long dead, her daughter gone. He must have heard about it at the time. For years, Cato stored this secret up, and at my trial he made much of it. 'An early instance,' he declaimed, 'of this man subverting the course of justice. What other wrongs has he concealed? What other Romans had their rights denied them by Scipios' gold? What other mothers had their daughters ruined by that monster of depravity standing there?' Even now, it is a memory at which I shudder with pain. For the girl raped, and for her mother. For the shame at the trial, the shocked faces of the senators, my peers. But mostly for myself. In trying to do right, I did wrong.

I had a blazing argument with Lucius that evening. I said that if he ever did such a thing again, I would prosecute him myself.

'And you'd love that, wouldn't you?' he yelled. 'I'm telling you, she was a panting bitch. She begged for it, right there on the kitchen floor!' Almost the only words I ever had with Lucius were angry, and now he is no more.

I will pass quickly over the next months. They do not seem to matter in relation to what then came. My absolute priority, with Fabius, was to find and train more men. The few scouts we had reported nothing of Hannibal, wintering somewhere. So we sent out recruiting parties, far to the north, with a gold *solidarius* for each man who came. We sent messengers to every Roman colony, asking them to show their ties of *fides* to Rome. In tens and twenties, through the long winter, men came almost daily to Rome, some by light barge up the Tiber from Ostia, others by skiff across the sullen river, swollen by the winter rains. The city came to teem with many looks and tongues and accents, and soon Flaevius and I, much helped by Frontinus and Postumus, for whom I was finding a new respect, had our first legion to train.

Fabius' priority was ships, not men. 'Hannibal might win this war on land,' he had told the Senate. 'But he will lose it at sea.' His aim, by the spring, was to have a sufficient fleet to patrol and control the Internum Sea, right to the Pillars of Herakles – ah, the Hellenist in me again. All right, Cato. I will grant you one victory; one. Bostar, please Romanise that to 'Hercules'. Anyway, the fleet would deny Carthage her trade and Hannibal the siege equipment Fabius was sure he had sent for. So orders and money went out to shipyards in Massilia and Savona, Pisae and Populonia. To Greece went messages for mariners, and each day in the Senate the scribes' tables were full.

Laelius' overwhelming preoccupation was with paying for all this. As *quaestor aerarii*, he was supposed to report to me. But in practice I gave him a free hand. The Senate agreed that our reserves of gold and silver would have to suffice, at least until my father captured Carthaginian mines in Celtiberia. We could not risk men or ships for an expedition to the mines near Genua for more. Laelius observed that, at the rate we were spending, what the state had would not be enough. He proposed a special tax on private property. It was agreed, with Fabius, myself, in my father's name, and others paying double what was due.

From chests and cupboards in the houses of the Palatine, from under floorboards or from recesses in widows' chimneys, gold and silver came. Rome's mint had been closed. Staffing it with women, Laelius opened it again, reducing the silver content in the *denarius*, and the amount of bronze in the *as*. He introduced a new coin with a weight of two-thirds of the *denarius*, and named it optimistically the *victoriatus*. It had an image of Victory stamped on it, but a low – and erratic – silver content. You do not see it now. Anyway, it served well within the city to pay for goods in the market whose prices had risen, through shortage, by seven- or eightfold. So what an *as* had bought now cost a *victoriatus*.

Still we heard no news from Celtiberia. Let me be ordered, though, dispassionate. The days turned to weeks, the weeks to months. There were no festivals to mark the time. The Senate had decreed there should be none so long as Hannibal was on Italian soil.

We did have one despatch from Marcellus in Sicilia, brought through Ostia on a day of sudden sun by a Sardinian captain whose trade was in wine. The siege of Syracuse, Marcellus said, was going well. He had managed to cut off the city's water supply. With their cisterns, wells and rainfall, he estimated the inhabitants could last another two months, no more. He asked for more gold. The Senate decided that would have to wait until the fleet was ready and the seas secure. We could not risk our dwindling reserves.

It had been a normal, long day. First, hours of drill and training on the Campus Martius, then with Flaevius an inspection of the city's walls, and then administration in the Senate with Postumus and Laelius before the debate on Marcellus' despatch was called. It was long, and wearing. Valerius Flaccus proposed that I should march south with my new legion to go and join Metellus. 'And meet Hannibal on the way?' I replied. 'No, I am not a coward, if that is what some of you are thinking, but neither am I a fool.'

It was cold when at last I left the Senate. I had already decided to have a bath on my way home. Keeping the baths open was one luxury Fabius had sanctioned. 'Rome may be in grave trouble,' he said, 'but it will be clean.' Laelius came with me. There were three or four others already in the *tepidarium*. In the steam, it was hard to see. We undressed ourselves in the booths of Parian marble – the attendants were either among the dead of Cannae or with my father – and got in.

I remember the spreading, soothing warmth, the peace, the gurgling water flowing out and in. I lay back, and closed my eyes.

'Publius Cornelius Scipio, Aedile!' The shout seemed to come from a dream. 'Aedile Scipio!' Again and again, coming closer.

'I'm here!' I called out. Then I saw him by the edge of the bath beside me. He was one of the few Senate bailiffs not killed at Cannae or now with my father, Gaius Thurinus, an equestrian, a tiny hunchback who had always been excused military service on those grounds. But he was able, quick and keenly intelligent.

'Ah, there you are, Aedile.' Thurinus had a high, squeaky voice, more like a girl's than a man's. 'Fabius has sent for you! You're to come to the Senate at once.'

'But I'm having a bath, as you'll have noticed. Can't it wait?'

'You know Fabius, Aedile.' He disappeared again into the steam.

I did know Fabius. This must be very important. He was supposed to be resting on the couch in his room. He had taken to sleeping there most nights, rather than go home. Apart from the demands of work, there were usually not enough whole men to bear his litter home, and he found walking harder every day.

I got out, dried myself cursorily and dressed. Laelius came with me. Heads still dripping wet, we walked through the empty hall of the Senate, down echoing, deserted corridors to Fabius' room. It was dark in there; only one lamp had been lit. The brazier against the cold of early spring was low. At first I thought Fabius was alone. He was sitting behind his table, slumped in his chair, head in his hands. A man coughed in the corner. I turned towards him, but couldn't see his face.

'Publius? Laelius?' Fabius' voice was muffled. It came from behind his hands, as if he wanted to block out the world. 'I'm glad you've come. I thought you would. Laelius, please go to the kitchens and get us some warm wine.'

'Wine, sir?' Laelius was as astonished as I was.

'You heard me. A pitcher for four. We'll need it. Unwatered. Flavour it with nutmeg and cinnamon.'

'Yes, sir.' With an anxious glance at me – wine was of course forbidden – Laelius left the room.

'Now, Publius, sit down.' I did so, in the shadows opposite the still unknown man. There was dread in Fabius' voice, utter despair. He sucked in his breath sharply; I heard it rasp. He sat up, then hung his head down. 'Publius,' he muttered into his beard, 'after Trasimenus you heard me say in the Senate that I wished the power of speech had failed me, as well as my eyes.'

'Yes, sir. I remember.' What was going on?

'Well, now I wish I had no ears. For I must tell you . . . tell you what this man has told me.' His voice almost broke. He struggled to his feet, leaning on the edge of the table. 'I must tell you,' he went on, his voice stronger, strident, 'that your father and your uncle are dead, killed in Celtiberia, and at least half of their army – our army – is no more.'

I remember – what do I remember? My brain buzzes with the weariness of words. A mute, blind and utter incomprehension, disbelief, spreading down and right through my body, arms and belly, torso, hips and down my legs like a draught of strong wine when a man is hungry, tired and sore. It is the method of the mind. It prevents madness. That came with the outbreath, and with the inbreath came anger, hurt and fear. Half of me wanted to rage, to scream, to tear. The other burst with 'why?' and 'when?' and 'where?' I think I shook, but I got up and ran, ripping open the door, and ran and ran, hearing Fabius' vain call of 'Publius!' and it was raining as I ran on blindly, the rainwater mixing with the salt of my tears, on and on through Rome doomed, damned, forsaken, broken, shattered.

Home. I ran, eventually, breathless, winded, there and into my bed where I pulled up the covers, curled up and wept and shuddered as the rain poured down and lightning streaked across the sky.

I heard someone come in. I didn't care. I felt a body in the bed beside me, felt a hand first in my wet hair, then moving downwards, stroking, soothing, reaching for the part of me that was sore. His lips were soft on my neck, his hands firm, tracing circles on the cheeks of my bum. I felt my body warming. I wanted warmth.

'I love you, Publius, I love you.' Laelius nuzzled my ear, and his hands slipped up my legs, teasing up my hairs.

I felt my penis stiffen, and then I remembered and with all the life in me I turned violently and shoved, then set both my feet against his back and pushed. He fell on to the floor.

There was silence, except for the rain. Laelius got up in the dark, and went away.

*　　*　　*

DOING

*These places are black and deep. I am not sure that, in his illness,
Scipio should go there. Still, I cannot stop him. Life has a truth of
its own. But if he is not less feverish tomorrow, I will bleed him.
Physicians seek to treat the illness of the body. Yet it is the mind
that rules, and that is beyond physic; mine, at any rate.*

So came a blackness and a mourning built on mourning. The
man who had been in Fabius' room was Scribonius. I resented
the messenger as much as the message. He had lost his right
arm from the elbow down, trying to fend off, he said, the
sword-stroke that killed my father. He had been left for dead.
The Carthaginians and their Celtiberian mercenaries had not
stripped all the dead the day of the battle. Only my father and
uncle, whose corpses they had flayed. At nightfall, Scribonius
had crawled away while those who had defeated us drank and
burned and looted.

On Fabius' order, Scribonius dictated an account of my
father's last campaign. Cato produced it as evidence at my
trial. 'You see from this, Reverend Fathers,' he declaimed,
'the incompetence of the Scipios, and how, like the son, the
father, too, failed Rome – though in a different way.' The pain
swelled in me then, and the shame, and my head is loud with
the labour of words.

*I can imagine. He is feverish, and yet refuses to stop. He has so little
time. Or should we assume that the verdict, when it comes, will be
one of acquittal, and that therefore we shall have ample time to finish?
If so, perhaps I could persuade Scipio to rest, and leave this dictation for
a while. I will do that tomorrow – or try to – if the fever hasn't left him
by the morning. Apart from anything else, it is very hot in his bedroom.
To help him sweat the illness out, I have four braziers burning night
and day. I am bleeding him too, but it does not seem to help.*

335

Mulca, the cook, is also ill. Eight days ago, she cut her hand while she was slicing a joint of beef. That was bad enough, as she chided and chivvied the kitchen maids to do the cooking she couldn't. But now it's worse. The cut has become infected, and it is poisoning her blood. She is in bed, at times delirious. When she is clear-headed, she frets and worries.

'The bread,' she said when I visited her this morning. 'Who's making it?'

'Aurio is.'

'Yes, I taught him. Is it all right?'

'Yes, it's fine,' I said, and she slipped back into her troubled dreams.

I am doing what I can. I change her poultice twice a day, trying to draw off the poison. I give her my cordials. My usual ones have made no difference, so I'm trying one of juniper and ground weasel bones. It strengthens the blood. I learnt it from Artixes. I wonder how he is.

But the account. Scribonius' account. At first, my father and uncle were successful. They crossed the sea without incident, and landed at Emporiae. From there, they moved to a town called Cissa, which they captured. Hannibal had left his army's baggage there, and our booty was rich. In the town they captured a Celtiberian prince, Indibilis, chief of the Illergetes tribe, who controlled the north of Celtiberia from the Pireneos down to the Ebro. They took Indibilis as a hostage. His people, who had supported Carthage, now allied themselves with Rome and my father added two thousand Illergetian infantry and five hundred cavalry to his force.

As they marched south, the coastal town of Tarraco surrendered to them, and with it came twenty Carthaginian galleys stationed there. They crossed the Ebro, and built a proper camp near the city of Ibera. There, they joined battle with an almost equal force of Carthaginians, commanded by Hasdrubal,

Hannibal's brother, who had moved up from Carthagena in the south.

Hasdrubal's tactics were the same as Hannibal's at Cannae. As soon as we advanced, the Carthaginian centre gave ground until our army was being attacked on both sides by Hasdrubal's wings. But this time, the result was different. With my father fighting in person, our centre broke through and forced open the closing trap. Hasdrubal withdrew, with heavy losses. Scouts reported his brother Mago coming from Gades in the west.

Three weeks later, having hired four thousand more Celtiberian recruits, my father and uncle followed him south. Then the attacks began. Numidian cavalry, allies of Carthage in Africa, were something we had not seen before. They were horsemen of astonishing agility and speed. In groups of ten or twenty, they harassed and harried our line of march by day and our army's sleep at night. Some were armed with bows, and others with slings, and they could fire both with pinpoint accuracy on the gallop and be gone well before the range of a *pilum*'s throw. Casualties were few, but steady.

So it was a weary, nervous Roman army that entered the valley of the Baetis, not far from the village of Castulo. The armies were close now. The country became bleak and desolate, devoid of all vegetation but thick gorse, and we had therefore no wood to make a proper palisade. The ground was like flint and it proved impossible to use entrenching tools. Hasdrubal and Mago would seem to be forming their battle-line, but would then withdraw. When Hasdrubal turned and attacked, unexpectedly, we made a kind of rampart from pack-animals and baggage. It did not serve. The Numidians stung like bees disturbed. Somehow, in the confusion, Indibilis broke away from his guard and ran towards the Carthaginians. His tribesmen followed to a man.

Unprepared, outnumbered, encumbered by gear they could not leave in camp, for they had no camp, the Romans fell; my uncle to an arrow in the eye and then a spear in the side, my father to a sword. That both died early in the fighting was the only good that day: seeing them fallen, a great many maniples broke away in good order, and some six thousand of our troops, Scribonius believed, had survived. I wondered where.

I worked and worked. Anger began to mask the pain. A seed grew in me that was slow and strong and sure. Alone in my room, I filled tablet after tablet with diagrams and lists. I told no one. I worked late into the night, with sticks of charcoal drawing and re-drawing dispositions and troop movements on hides of goatskin stretched over frames. I went over and over in my mind what I had learnt on campaign with my father, the mistakes that he had made, that our system made him make. I analysed our strengths, our weaknesses. Again and again I relived Hannibal's manoeuvres; they became the stuff of my dreams.

I formed my plans, and ran through them again and again in that wasteland of those still, empty hours of the night before dawn when the spirit sinks and only owls hoot in the darkness before plunging, without pity, upon their prey. I pored over the few despatches we had received since Cannae from different corners of Italy, and I paid particular attention to Scribonius' account of my father's last, fatal campaign. When my plans were ready, I told Fabius the parts that concerned him, the means to my end and Rome's.

He was resting on the couch in his room. I noticed that his winter boots of carded wool had holes in their soles. I made a mental note to tell Cornelia, who would bring him new ones. He was very frail now, and losing weight. His cheeks were hollow, and the skin hung from his cheekbones like a lizard's flaps. Through his thinning beard, his jowls were grey.

For the next two hours, as the calibrated candles burned, I explained everything I had learnt, considered and planned. I had been silent before, I said, but now I was sure. Hannibal had innovated. Now, so would we. My first priority would be cavalry. Not only Hannibal, but now the Numidians had shown how crucial they were. Our tradition was disdainful of the skirmisher. I wanted that to change. I wanted our legionaries' armour to be less heavy too. And I proposed to abandon palisaded camps, and wagons. My army would travel light, without entrenching tools, for example, protecting itself with many more, faster scouts. Each man would carry his own rations, enough for three days. Our new fleet was ready. I would work in concert with it, and use it to provision my men. Next, I wanted to abandon our usual formation, the *triplex acies*. It was hard to break, but it could not bend; and, crucially for what I had in mind, though it could advance and retire, it could not wheel. The maniples work as a unit, I granted, but not as individuals. As the disasters that had befallen us had shown, it made no sense to separate *hastati*, *principes* and *triarii* on grounds of experience and age; those factors no longer applied.

Then there was the matter of command, which would be mine alone. To make flexibility possible, the whole army would take its orders in action directly from me, and to that end I proposed to make myself visible, highly visible, by wearing a scarlet cloak. I wanted my tribunes steeped in my plans, systems and thinking, so that one of them could take command if I was wounded or killed.

Finally, I explained to Fabius a new system of signalling I had invented. It was the matter to which I had given most thought. At Cannae – and before – I had noticed how cumbersome was our system of commands by trumpet: no fewer than thirty-eight different signals, and even those used to them found them hard to tell apart. The *triarii* used to say that you could tell your discharge for long service was coming up if at last you recognised them all.

It was hopeless. The commands were hard enough to make out without a helmet on, let alone with a helmet and in battle. I remembered the trumpets blaring in vain at Cannae. 'Face right!

Right face! Right about face!' as some of those death-girt soldiers made the turn to the left and others to the right when suddenly came, on Varro's inebriated orders, a higher note: 'Face about right!' Then suddenly an even higher note sounded: 'Face first about right, then left!' Then another: 'Close files!' and death flowed on and yes, yes, how well I remembered. Was it in such a shambles that my father died?

High-pitched tin whistles, not trumpets, were my solution, and there would be nine simple commands, no more. For 'Charge!' the trumpet would still do. But whistles would be used for the other eight, and each would have its own clear blast: 'Depth double', 'Depth half', 'Length double', 'Length half', 'Dress maniples by file leader', and then the vital three, 'Halt', 'Pursue' and 'Retire'. These would be heard, I was sure, even above the din of battle, when trumpets were drowned.

When I had finished, Fabius was silent for some time. Then he said, 'This is revolution, not evolution. You know, Publius, that there can now be few men anywhere around the Internum Sea whom we can enlist. We have scraped the cupboard bare. And what has it yielded us? About two legions?'

I nodded.

'And you are asking me to support your plan to take Rome's last hope, except Marcellus in Sicilia, to Celtiberia, leaving Rome ungarrisoned?'

'That's right, sir – although I propose to leave you with, say, fifteen maniples.'

'And those under strength?' Fabius shot back.

'Yes. But I hope to find the remnants of my father's army. And, as he did, I will hire troops—'

'If you can!'

'Yes, sir. If I can.'

'I see. I see.' Distracted, Fabius stroked his beard, closed tight his blind, rheumy eyes. The skin around them was thick and mottled, like the poorer vellum you see on market stalls. I looked away, staring at the fly spots on the ceiling. 'I understand your reasoning,' he said at last. 'If Hasdrubal and Mago now march on Italy and join their brother, we are lost. You could make that difficult or impossible, I agree. But you know what happened to your father. Why should you succeed where he failed? Why?' It was, I knew a rhetorical question. I said nothing.

He seemed to fall asleep. I was about to slip out of the room when, suddenly, he spoke again. 'But these are desperate times. Leave me to think about all this for two days. Now, I must rest.'

I got up to go. I was opening the door when Fabius stopped me.

'Publius?'

'Yes, sir?'

'You are a very remarkable young man.'

Laelius was waiting for me in the atrium when I got home. His face lit up when he saw me. He started to get up from his chair, saying 'Publius—'

'What are you doing here?' I interrupted. I was exhausted by the intensity and urgency with which I had told Fabius my plans. I wanted to be alone. But then I saw the rejection in his face, the bewilderment, the pain, as he slumped back into his seat.

'I . . . I just came to say . . .'

'To say what?'

'That I was sorry.'

'For what?'

'For—' He stopped, breathed out, and seemed to change his mind. He looked right at me across the room. 'Not for,' he went on. 'About. I just came to say I am sorry about your father, and your uncle. I . . .'

'That's good of you, Laelius,' I said. Silence hung between us like a pall. I needed to urinate. 'Sorry, but I must go to the latrine.'

'I'll leave, then.'

'No, don't. Please stay. Have you eaten?'

'No.'

'Then please eat with me. Call Cornelia, will you? I'm sure there will be enough for two.'

You see. I said I would be silent, but this is vital to what followed. Here is a man who has never been engaged emotionally. His friendships have been only with abstractions, not with people, with ideas, not with feelings. He barely knew parental love. His true life has been a casualty of war. He never played, it seems, or had a friendship but that with Laelius, and even that was hardly worthy of the name. He has never even faced the question of his own sexuality. He has never addressed what almost happened, what much of him wanted to happen, with Laelius the night he heard about his father's death. There need be no wrong in homosexuality. The Romans abhor it, but those like Cato who persecute it have never asked themselves why.

In the man lying ill in bed before me, I see a boy denied his youth, and as a result a man of enormous intellectual, but no emotional, intelligence. And I love him for his loss, for all the things that never came to him and those that never will. Having lost his youth, even the blessings of old age he must not look to have. He will never, for example, hold a grandchild hooded on his arm, and that is wounding to a Roman with their great sense of what they call 'memoria'. His life seems meteoric, and I see before me, I do believe, the greatest Roman ever to have lived, but he did so in spite of himself, in fury and in muddle, fled from himself, bound up in some dark shame. An adept of war, immured in an unadmitted pain, Scipio lost long ago the capacity for peace. Now he may have the time to seek it out, but no road leads back to the garden of our youth when it is gone.

We ate. We talked. Binding him to secrecy, I told Laelius my plans. We were reconciled. When he left, late in the night, when the whole household was asleep, we hugged. I yawned into his shoulder, and he was gone.

The next morning, before I went to the Campus Martius to see how the retraining of the troops and cavalry was going – whether Fabius agreed over Celtiberia or not, our practices had to change – I did something I had brooded on. When I had asked Fabius his opinion, he had said it was my concern. But he had agreed to spare me one of his new galleys for the purpose, and I knew that in doing so he was giving me tacit assent. He was very protective of our new fleet, and had it constantly at work, patrolling both the Internum and the Adriaticum seas, so to spare me a galley was generous indeed. But then, if he agreed to Celtiberia, he was about to spare me more.

Lucius was where I expected him to be: in his room, asleep. The place stank of sweat and sour wine. There were dirty clothes all over the floor. I tugged the curtains open, and the strengthening spring sunlight flooded in.

'Lucius!' I called. 'Get up!'

'What for?' he muttered under his bedclothes.

'Because I told you to.'

'Ah, big brother – now father, I suppose. Come to scold me?' He sat up, stretched and yawned. As the blanket fell down, I noticed that he was still in his tunic.

'Don't you even undress for bed any more, Lucius?'

'Publius, you're my brother, not my nanny. What do you want?'

'I thought you might enjoy a voyage. A little sea air will do you good.'

He leapt out of bed, excited. 'Where? I'd love to get out of here! Egypt, or Cyrene?'

'Nowhere as exotic, Brother. In case you hadn't noticed, there's a war going on.'

'So where am I going, then?'

'To Sicilia, to Marcellus and the siege of Syracuse. Barge to Ostia, and a galley will be waiting for you there. Get packed, and leave within the hour.' I turned to go.

'Publius, if you think I'm going to Sicilia, you're wrong.'

I stopped, but didn't turn round. 'Lucius, I will send an armed maniple here. You will make your way to Ostia with them as, ah, escort, if you won't go on your own. Out of respect for our father, I give you that choice. Only you can make it. Now, I must get on. Oh, and give my greetings to our cousin Claudius Marcellus. For you, I wish a fair wind. Goodbye.'

I . . . I still do not know whether . . . whether . . . Fabius actually . . .

He has fallen asleep. I will let him be. His fever is still strong. Aurio has just come in. He looks alarmed. He wants me to see to Mulca. I will go.

'Bring two braziers, Aurio. No, make it three,' I said, standing in Mulca's room.

'But Bostar, that—'

'Yes, that will make it hot in here. Very hot.' I put my hand on his shoulder, looked him in the eye. Aurio didn't flinch from my gaze. That wasn't like him, and suddenly I realised how much he cared. Did he love Mulca? I felt how mysterious and gentle are the links between people, like the roots of mushrooms underground. You cannot see them, but that doesn't mean they aren't there.

'Aurio, I have to try. Everything else has failed. We have to try and sweat the poison out of her.'

'Bostar.' Aurio's Adam's apple rose and fell, rose and fell as he fought for the words. 'Is she . . . Is Mulca dying?'

I looked over at her, lying on the bed asleep but tossing, fretting at the passing of her light. Her skin was grey, her hair streaked with sweat. She had lost a great deal of weight; the bones of her face stood out. 'Perhaps, Aurio,' I said as gently as I could. 'Perhaps.'

'So this heat could kill her?'
'Kill her, Aurio? Yes. Or cure.'

That soup was good, Bostar. Thank you. You fed me like a
baby with a spoon. But I feel strengthened. Now, where was
I? I must hurry. It has been four days already since Theogenes'
message. There may be little time left.

The last words you dictated were: 'I still do not know whether
Fabius actually'.

Oh yes, I remember. Thank you. I still do not know whether
Fabius actually agreed with me, or whether the news of Philip
of Macedon forced his hand. Three of our ships captured a
Macedonian galley halfway across the Mare Adriaticum. On
it were envoys from King Philip bound, they disclosed under
torture, for Italy and Hannibal. They were to offer him alliance
against Rome with Philip, who offered to invade the eastern
seaboard of the Adriaticum, and foment revolt in all Rome's
colonies. In time, he would even invade Italy. Together, they
would crush Rome.

'It is,' Fabius said in the Senate, 'as imperative as it is obvious
that this alliance must not take place. We cannot, for the time
being, challenge Hannibal in Italy. Equally, it seems, lacking
either the will or the siege equipment, he – for the time being
at least – cannot challenge us here. Rome stands safe within her
mighty walls, and so long as Rome stands, Italy does too. We
must broaden the theatre of war. And so, Fathers, I announce
my support for a daring plan put to me by Publius Cornelius
Scipio. It may seem reckless to you; but it is, I believe, our
only hope.'

Thus, without telling me first, did Fabius endorse my invasion
of Celtiberia. The Senate agreed, and there was much to be
done. My main priority was retraining the two legions I was to
take, and I began with a speech to them at an assembly on the

Campus Martius, now showing its first spring flowers. I couldn't be sure my voice would carry to so many men, stretching out in files in front of me, so I kept my speech very simple. But then, so was my plan.

'Soldiers of Rome,' I began, 'in this dark hour for Rome we are its light. And as our fathers' fathers would have done, we are going to respond to danger with daring. As my father did, we are going to invade Celtiberia.' I saw shock in the faces of the first ranks before me, heard mutterings of dismay. I raised my voice. 'I know what you will say: that we shall suffer the same fate, but to that I say no, doubly no! And that is because we are going to change.'

So I told them. I made three points. I said that we, Rome's last hope, would base our campaign on flexibility, mobility and clarity. These three. Nothing more. On the first, I said we would abandon the *triplex acies* – unless it seemed to suit the terrain or situation. We would also abandon the usual Roman practice of having infantry in our centre. Instead, we would keep the heavy infantry on our wings. Our centre, of light-armed troops, *velites*, would act as a sponge to draw the enemy in before our wings closed like, I said, a steel trap for rats. For mobility, we would take no wagons, wear lighter armour – that drew a ragged cheer – and each carry everything we might need. I said I proposed to treble the number of scouts and cavalry, who would be our eyes and ears. By clarity, I explained, I meant clarity of communication. I had brought my scarlet cape with me. I unfolded it, and let them see. I said there would be no more sessions trying to teach them the different trumpet-blasts. Finally, I asked them to share with me and with each other their thoughts and fears. 'We will fight and win,' I declaimed, 'because we will do so not as many Romans, but as one.' From my cloak pocket I took a plain tin whistle. My speech ended with a whistle blast, and the soldiers' tumultuous cheer.

The weeks that followed were obsessed and pure. They began

with Fabius, the two of us alone. 'So, another three weeks, you think, Publius? Apart from the retraining, what else are you waiting for?'

'The horses we've ordered from Liguria, of course. But I want your permission for something else.'

'What's that?'

'Boats, sir. Barges.'

'But I assumed you would be using our fleet. We have eighty galleys now, as you know.'

'I had thought so too, sir, but I've changed my mind. I think you will need them for your patrols. What's the use of my invading Celtiberia if, while I'm away, the Carthaginians send Hannibal siege equipment by sea, or Philip crosses over – or both? No, your patrols must not be interrupted. You were right to say that we might lose this war on land, but win it at sea. So keep your galleys, Reverend Father. The winter storms are over. Barges will do me.'

'But they'll take months to build!'

'Not necessarily. I've looked into that. The shipwrights explained that the time's taken up by fitting the copper joints and bands. That's slow and fiddly, plank by plank.'

'And the alternative, Publius?'

'Iron. Iron nails. If we just nailed the wood together, we'd have the barges I need in less than half the time.'

'But even I—'

'Forgive me, sir, but I know too. Iron nails will rust, and the barges will fall apart. I know that, but they'll still get us to Celtiberia.'

'And back?'

'We know the Carthaginians have a fleet – some galleys are stationed at Tarraco, others at Carthagena. I intend, sir, to come back in those galleys; or not at all.'

We went on to discuss which officers would come with me, and which stay. I said I wanted Laelius, Metellus, Afer and Pius.

I proposed that Frontinus, who would command the maniples I would leave in the city, and Postumus, who would take over from Laelius as *quaestor aerarii*, should stay, and that Flaevius should carry on as prefect of the walls.

Fabius readily agreed. 'And I'd like to keep Cato,' he said. 'He's become indispensable.'

'I've noticed.'

'Is that envy I detect in your voice, Publius?'

'No, sir. But I won't try to conceal my dislike for Cato – and my mistrust. And anyway, he doesn't know a *pilum* from a catapult. So by all means keep him.'

'What about Scribonius?'

'I don't want him.'

'Even though he's the most experienced soldier we have?'

'I grant that, sir, but in the old ways, not the new. I want officers with open minds. Anyway, you'll need him here if Hannibal appears.'

Then we discussed communications. Fabius agreed that we should send each other a despatch, if possible, at least twice a month. To that end, he suggested he put two fast galleys at our disposal as couriers. They would both accompany us to Celtiberia as protection for the barges, and then one would come straight back to Ostia, while the other waited off Celtiberia for my first despatch to Rome. I agreed.

'Where are you aiming for, Publius? Emporiae, like your father, and then march down the coast?'

'No, sir. My father went too far, too fast.'

'Where, then? Further north?'

'No, sir. I intend to go further, faster. We will sail to just north of Carthagena. To kill a snake, you must cut off its head.'

So, with Fabius' – and so also the Senate's – blessing, I gave my orders. None was disobeyed. Only once did anyone question me, and that was Frontinus when I told him to have our maniples arranged according to families and friends. I wanted those close ties, not the recruiting order, to determine who fought alongside whom.

'But the men in the maniples are getting used to each other now,' he protested.

'Frontinus,' I answered, 'I don't care how it was done before.'

I felt nothing on the morning of our departure. What could be done had been done, and it was time to go. My farewell to Cornelia was cold and distant. I felt she wanted to cry at seeing the last Scipio in Italy go off to war, and I had no time for tears. Only when I said goodbye to Frontinus did I feel a catch in my throat.

'Remember, Fabius will get despatches to me,' I told him. 'Be my eyes and ears, Frontinus, remember.'

'I will – if not your legs,' was his reply.

I left Fabius in his room in the Senate. He got up, and put his arms round me, and told me to take care – nothing more.

I must hurry, Bostar, I must hurry. There may be so little time. How many days has it been since Theogenes' last message? Five? Or is it four?

Four, Scipio, four.

Then I must hurry. I feel stronger. Aurio, please get us both some tea.

In single file, leading the horses, on full alert, early in the morning we slipped out of Rome, waded the Tiber and marched, protected by our scouts, to Ostia. The barges and two galleys were there. The crossing to Celtiberia was uneventful. A rope broke, and we lost six horses overboard, but nothing more. The seas were calm and kind, and dolphins darted and gleamed.

We saw no other ships. We reached Celtiberia, and followed the coast south. I moved from barge to barge, explaining my plans to each and every soldier, maniple by maniple. My plans were so simple, and so improbable, that I was sure they would work. Our men seemed to believe me. Laelius had doubts, but agreed to keep them to himself.

'Our real battle,' I told him, 'is with the minds of these men here. Remember Euphantus?' Laelius laughed. *'Potest quia posse videtur,'* he said.

At the core of my plans was a second new signalling system. If you divide an army, both halves must be able to communicate, even over a long distance, and it was this problem to which I had given most time, long before we had left Rome. If my solution worked, we would achieve our aim. So, day after day, we practised it. I had the barges on which the signalling stations were set move apart so far that they were almost out of sight of each other, and often truly so, thanks to the swell of the sea.

The Roman army now uses my system routinely. We used it in Syria, and in Macedonia. It will endure, when I am gone, and so I think it only right, despite the pressing of time, that I record it. If you find it arcane, Bostar, cut it out later.

There are twenty-one letters in the Roman alphabet – though that may have to grow as, whatever Cato's views, we absorb more Greek. I divided the letters into four groups of four, and one of five. I then had the letters listed on five tablets, numbered one to five. To each letter I also gave a number, and I made my signallers learn them by heart. Each signaller, a centurion, had two groups of transmitting signallers under his command – one on his left, the other on his right, each stationed behind a screen. Each group must have at least six burning torches ready, and the purpose of the screens was to conceal their light when they were not in use.

When the despatcher was ready to send a signal, he had two torches raised, and the recipient responded by also raising two torches. The torches were then withdrawn, and the message was passed. That involved spelling out the letters of each word. The number of torches exposed above the left-hand screen indicated the number of the tablet, and the number of torches above the right-hand screen indicated the letter on that tablet. I had never forgotten my father's observation that our Latin word for army, *exercitus*, comes from 'exercise'. We exercised and practised my new signalling system until everyone involved was adept at it. That proved crucial in what was to come.

The city of Carthagena, built I knew by Hannibal's father, Hamilcar, as the heart of Carthaginian power in Celtiberia, was formidably defended. Based on Scribonius' account and those of the spies we had sent to Celtiberia, I had drawn plans of it many times. Its walls rise above a sheltered bay, which leads out to the sea. To the west, its walls are higher, commanding a fertile, hill-girt plain and the roads to the mines of gold and silver inland and south. So it had to be, I reasoned, the seaward walls that were most vulnerable. To the north, a wide neck of hilly land juts out and protects the bay, making it a marvellous natural anchorage. But, of course, it also means that, by hugging the coast, we could approach unseen. And that is what we did. We disembarked at dusk, and camped among the hills and trees. I gave my orders. Well into the night, by torchlight the carpenters were busy, making ladders of escalade.

We woke before dawn and ate. I sent my signallers away first – two groups of them, one to the top of the hill in whose lee we had camped, the second well to the west, to the top of the first hill that looked down on the plain but also had a clear view of the western walls of Carthagena. That is where I went, with just ten men. Under Laelius' command, I had a thousand men, lightly armed, take ship: two hundred and fifty in each galley, the rest in barges. Under Metellus and Afer, the balance of our small force, just over nine thousand men, moved out, ready to attack the western walls.

It was simple. My main force attacked just after dawn. I saw them, scurrying, their fire-arrows blazing through the sky. I waited, waited, until I thought all the defenders would have been drawn to the western walls. Then I signalled, 'Laelius, attack!' and rode off to join Metellus and Afer. That was all.

By the time I had crossed the plain, the city's western gates were open, and our men were flooding in. We lost a few men in the eastern escalade when ladders broke. But, Laelius said, as I had hoped, they had found the eastern walls, and even the city streets, unmanned: everyone in Carthagena was high up on the western walls, and our soldiers had got to the western gates completely unopposed.

Our main force met only a small garrison of perhaps two thousand, all Celtiberian mercenaries except one Carthaginian, who was killed, Afer reported, resisting arrest. So, in exchange for five Romans dead and six wounded, Rome captured Carthagena. It is regarded as one of my greatest exploits. But I have told how simply it was done. Order, forethought, planning. Luck, yes. That too. But I have found that Fortuna smiles on those who prepare and plan. I sent a despatch at once to Fabius. That would give heart to Rome.

Our booty was prodigious. I found six thousand talents of gold in the treasury, and I added these to the war chests I had brought from Rome. There was a huge supply of munitions, metals, food. There were also numerous slaves, found cowering in the buildings and houses. Under Roman overseers, I had the skilled among them put to work immediately, making swords and shields.

The prisoners spoke no Latin. Several had a little Greek, and I asked them whether they and their fellows wanted to hang, or to join us. They asked what the terms were. I told them, and they agreed. One of them, Afitano, had heard of the remnants of my father's army. It had wintered, apparently, near Tarraco. I trusted Afitano implicitly. He had honest eyes. His long, soft brown eyelashes fluttered as he spoke. Once he had assured me that there were only two Carthaginian armies, one under Mago at Gades and the other under Hasdrubal inland near the River Tagus, subduing a tribe which had rebelled, I felt secure. I sent

Laelius off at once with the one remaining galley and all the barges, telling him to bring to us as many men as he could by ship. If there were more than ten thousand, he should have the rest start marching down the coast.

How quickly, I asked Afitano, could Mago get to Carthagena once he learnt we were here? He could have galleys in the harbour within two days, he replied. And his army of thirty thousand? By forced march, twelve days. It would be three or four weeks at least before I had all my reinforcements, and I did not know what state they would be in. So I did what Fabius would have done: I delayed.

From Afitano I learnt that Mago regularly sent out scouting galleys as far as Carthagena. When he gave me full details of the signals the city received and expected, I gave him a bag of gold. Four days later, a Carthaginian galley appeared. I made sure there were no Romans on the walls, and by flag Afitano signalled: 'All is well'. The ship responded, weighed anchor, and disappeared.

In the town the smiths were busy: we had warehouses full of gleaming new arms. The weeks passed. With two or three scouts, inconspicuous, I scouted every day. Leaving Afer in command, with only Metellus and two decurions I made a trip lasting six days. I found what I was looking for due west, inland, above the River Baetis, near where my father died. The site was perfect. A plan was growing in my mind.

When we got back, we found the town packed with Roman soldiers. They greeted me with joy. Laelius had packed eleven thousand into our already leaking barges, and gone back up the coast for three thousand more whom he had left marching towards us. So, with the Celtiberian mercenaries, I would soon have an army of twenty-five thousand. I decided it was time.

I sent for Afitano. 'Choose four men,' I told him, 'and four good horses. Take one man with you, and go to Gades. Tell Mago the Carthaginian that another Scipio has come to

Celtiberia, seeking revenge for the death of the last two Scipios who came here.'

Looking at me strangely, Afitano nodded. 'And the other two? I suppose they go to find . . . ?'

I smiled, I remember, standing there on the eastern walls of Carthagena, looking out to sea. 'Yes, to find Hasdrubal, and with the same message. Now go.'

The next morning, I resumed training. I would hide no more. The horses we had brought were much in need of exercise, and I had to teach my father's former troops and the Celtiberians our new way of war. Then Laelius arrived with the last of my father's army, and all day each day we all exercised on the plain before Carthagena, returning, dark with dust, at dusk. I often rode up the hill from which I had sent my signal to Laelius and watched my army training down below. My instinct that a battle is in the preparation, the planning, the perspective of the generals, grew and grew. Once the hand-to-hand fighting has started, there is little a commander can do. My plan for Mago had to be sure. He would know all the manoeuvres I had seen Hannibal execute. There would be others. How many, and what would they be?

Twelve days after I had sent my messengers, I gave new orders.

This is all dispassionate, factual, cerebral, clear — and lifeless. Again, nothing of his feelings. Perhaps it is the result of his fever. Perhaps it is because he is so conscious of time. Perhaps this is how it seemed to him at the time. I do not know. But though my fingers ache from so much writing, I will set it down.

We moved out of Carthagena. I had the walls which I might need again left intact, but all the buildings and houses pulled down or burnt. I had the wells — there were eight of them — poisoned by dropping dead goats down them. We made camp where we had done before, and I posted scouts and sentries and signalling-posts far afield.

I was sitting on a fallen tree, late at night, looking at the stars and thinking, when I saw the signal torches on the western hill. 'F-o-r-c-e a-p-p-r-o-a-c-h-i-n-g'. Mago! It could not be! I jumped up. 'F-r-o-m t-h-e n-o-r-t-h.' No, it could not be.

They arrived at dawn. By then, thanks to more signals, I knew who they were. Celtiberians, almost two thousand of them, all on short-legged, shaggy garrons, led by a tall, lithe man called Edeco. When Laelius led him up to me, in bad Latin and even worse Greek he called me king, said he was the prince of his tribe, the Edetani, and that he offered me

I see. 'Me'. Not Rome. Could Cato be right again?

his service and that of his people if I would rid them of the tyranny of Carthage. I replied that sounded fine to me.

So, I had more horsemen. But remembering what had happened to my father, I decided to keep them in reserve. I hardly ever played chess as a child. There was no time. Instead, I have played chess, with real pieces, as a man.

Under Afer, I left five hundred men and the remaining galley where we had landed. I wanted it ready to take Fabius the news I hoped — I knew? — I would be able to send. Then, as we were about to break camp, the second galley returned. I waded out myself to meet it, and reached eagerly for the single scroll the burly, wizened mate held out to me from the lower deck. I saw my name in Fabius' own careful handwriting. I wanted to open the scroll there and then, but knew that would be unseemly. I returned to the shore.

Fabius told me three things: that, cheered by our capture of Carthagena, he and Rome were well; that Hannibal at last had marched on Rome; and that Marcellus had captured Syracuse. All around me were men, expectant, hushed, with eyes only for me. I looked round them, and read again, this time aloud. Noise erupted – fear for Rome, joy for Syracuse, confusion, unease. I held up an arm for silence, and went on: 'But Hannibal had no siege equipment, and we were impregnable within our walls. Still, the people were fearful. So I led the way to the eastern wall below which Hannibal was camped. Cato and others saw the Carthaginian clearly, just out of catapult range, in black armour, on a huge, white, fretting horse.

'You will know the ground he and his army stood on,' I read, 'well-tilled and fertile in time of peace, watered by the Clitumnus stream, and owned by my family since the first days of Rome. Over the years, I have received many offers for it, but have never sold. I have now. There and then, I held a public auction for the land. Hannibal sent men forward to establish what was going on. We let them be. The land fetched its normal price. You will remember Aponius Celerius, who deals in wool – or used to, before this war. He bought the land. Hannibal went away.

'As for Syracuse—' The rest was lost in a huge, rolling, deafening cheer. Soldiers beat their sword-hilts against their shields, and tossed their helmets in the air. The tide, it seemed, was turning. It was time I made that clear here.

But Mago had beaten me to it. My scouts reported his army occupying the very ground I had chosen for myself. He could move further and faster than I had thought or Afitano had recognised. One should never underestimate one's enemy. He was encamped in the valley of the Baetis, in a strong position on hilly ground near the village of Baecula, not far from Castulo and its silver mines where my father died.

I knew the place. Mago had formed battle-order on a plateau, exactly where I had planned to, his rear protected by the river, the approaches on each flank difficult and rugged, while to his front the ground dropped in steep terraces from a ridge to the plain below.

When we got there and the men saw the enemy's position, they were disheartened. I said nothing, but withdrew into myself. We waited for three days, four. I went over and over the ground, every gully, every rise. There had to be a way. We were running out of water and supplies. I sent scouts to watch the entrances to the valley, in case Hasdrubal was even faster than his brother: my plan would not work if we were taken in the rear. That night, under the shining Vergiliae, I explained to my officers and all the centurions and decurions the full details of my plan, and I asked them to tell the men. 'We work as one man, and as one body,' I said.

I split my army into three. The signalling-stations, again, were crucial. Metellus led the attack, taking the light-armed soldiers and the Celtiberians, supported by five maniples of heavy infantry, straight up the slope towards Mago's centre. Our other two forces, one under me, one under Laelius, stayed at the foot of the rise, concealed by scrub and trees. I was banking on the fact that Mago would assume Metellus' force to be the standard, central Roman attack. Given the terrain, he would be unable to see how many men Metellus was leading.

The signal from a high hill to the west came just when I had hoped for it. Mago was leading his main force forward to defend the ridge. He was taking my bait. I heard the screams and shouts of Metellus' men engaging the enemy. I moved. Laelius went east, I west, and our forces climbed and scrambled up the two sides of the plateau. My men were breathless, glistening with sweat. I waited, resting them, just before the lip of the plateau. I saw Laelius' signal. He too was in position. I signalled back, 'Attack'. To Afer beside me, I said, 'Now!'

I did not fight at the battle of Baecula. I have been a general, not a soldier. With ten soldiers and my signalling-party, I stayed behind and watched Laelius' force and Afer's approaching Mago's from the rear. As I had ordered, my men marched steadily, in good order. I did not want them, as at Cannae, to reach the enemy exhausted from a run. In three columns each, exactly as ordered, they moved on. They must have been perhaps six hundred paces from Mago's army when his rear ranks noticed them and began to turn. 'Now!' I shouted to the signallers beside me. 'Signal "Now"!'

I heard the shrill tin whistles Laelius and Afer carried. Just as we had practised on the plain of Carthagena, my soldiers wheeled, the two forces joined and formed a crescent line right across the plateau, four men deep. They stopped. I heard the rhythmic beating of sword-hilt on shield. Another whistle, and they charged, some falling to enemy javelins or arrows. But I had the greatest advantage of a general. I had surprise on my side.

The sound of armoured, meeting men is like no other. A thunderous thud, a rolling ring, and then the screams begin. The Roman army used to keep its ranks in order, each a stride apart. The *principes*, our usual second line, held back while the *hastati* engaged, and the *triarii* waited for the *principes*. My orders were different. Our second, third and fourth ranks carried no *pila* and left their swords sheathed. They used their shields to shove, the second on the backs of the first, the third on the second, the fourth on the third. I called the manoeuvre my breaking-ram. So simply it was that we broke Mago's line at Baecula. It snapped, like a chicken's breastbone at a feast. Then my maniples broke up, as planned, and each fought units of a broken, milling, disjointed enemy army as the sun climbed, sweat poured, blood flowed. It was a hacking, stabbing, cutting, thrusting frenzy, and soon the grass was red with the blood of dead and dying men, and the air full of screams and grunts and groans. The death-screech of horses is a searing sound that cuts through the air.

The sun grew hot. I took off my helmet, and wiped the sweat away. I felt lice – we all had them – scurry on my scalp. I saw vultures gathering overhead. A group of twenty, thirty of the enemy broke off and began to run away. I did nothing. Let them go, I thought, and tell the tribes there is a new Scipio in Celtiberia.

In battle, you see thousands die but remember only one. I had moved closer to the fighting. One of our soldiers turned and stumbled across the plateau towards me in my scarlet cape, holding out his hands. I thought he wanted to give me something; I could not think what. As I reached out to him, I saw the sword-hilt in his stomach, just below his breastplate. The gleam of the iron handle shone out through the red. He didn't take my hand. Instead he gazed at me, open-mouthed, in wonder. A stream of blood sprang from his mouth, and he fell at my feet. I told the soldiers with me to move the corpse away, but that image has never left my mind.

The killing continued through the sultry, still, slow afternoon. Mago's army became a shrinking, then an encircled, band within a rampart of the bodies of their dead, over towards the west of the plateau. I felt for my whistle. I gave the orders. My men regrouped, attacked again, starting with a volley of *pila*. A standard hung limp in the middle of Mago's men. A puff of wind raised it and I saw, white on black, a scorpion, symbol of the house of Barca, of Hannibal. At last it fell, and all was done.

The dead and living, the wounded and the dying lay spent together on the bloody ground. The orderlies were busy with the wounded, and the bearers with carrying off our dead. I sent the living to the river to drink and wash, and moved among them, praising, encouraging. There was no elation, just exhaustion.

My men had paid good heed to my account of what had happened to Frontinus, and, rather than engage the enemy with sword, had ducked and cut hamstrings with their daggers. There were many Carthaginian wounded.

'What shall we do with them?' Laelius asked me. His face was grey with dust, his breastplate and forearms red and black with drying blood.

'What do you propose?'

'I ask my father's ghost that,' he replied. 'You saw what was done to him.'

One of the Carthaginians came crawling through the grass towards us, trailing blood. He was still only a boy, his forehead pimply, and his beard more down than hair. '*Hoodor*,' he panted feebly. 'Water!' So it was true what I had heard, that the polyglot Carthaginian army's common tongue was Greek.

I led Laelius away. 'Yes, I saw what was done to your father. And I remember what was done to our men after Trasimenus and Cannae, Laelius. But do you want to disembowel so many wounded, and leave them to die? Or cut off their feet, if not their hands, as Hannibal did?'

A sudden shout disturbed us. 'Sir, sir! Over here!'

He lay where he had fallen on his belly, blood still oozing from his mouth and nose and thighs. I waved off the settling flies. His armour was all black leather, his greaves studded with bronze, and beside him lay the standard of the Barcas, its white scorpion stained with blood. It could only be Mago, brother of Hannibal, and then I saw on his right hand, which still held a sword, the glint of a ring. I knelt down, forced the dead fingers open. From his little finger, I pulled off a gold ring. I wiped the blood off, and the scorpion on the face caught the last light of the sinking sun.

'Shall we flay him, sir?' asked a soldier beside me.

'Or crucify him, and leave him for the crows?' suggested a second.

'With his balls in his mouth first!' added another voice with a guffaw.

I stood up. I saw Pius. 'Bury him, Pius,' I ordered quietly, 'In his armour. With his sword.'

'But, sir—'

'No buts. Just do it.' I turned away. 'Oh, and Pius?'

'Yes, sir?'

'Mark the grave.'

Laelius was waiting. 'I heard your order, Publius. You—'

'Then you have your answer. Leave their wounded. Let those who can, crawl or limp away. Your father's ghost – nor mine, for that matter – will not be salved by more blood.'

A battle takes a day at most. Its consequence lasts long. We were a day burying our dead and seeing to our wounded, a second stripping the best of the arms from the Carthaginian dead. There were horses to round up and corral. There was Mago's camp to strip – I won much booty – and his tents and wagons to burn. By the fifth day, we were ready. That was a blessing. We had to get away from the smell of rotting flesh.

The march across country towards Gades almost broke us. I made a mistake; I have not made it again. A general should rest his men after a battle, and reconnoitre. I didn't. Sending two men with a despatch for Fabius, I pressed on. The land was hilly, barren, dry. Our rations of barley biscuit and salted fish were enough. Each man, myself included, carried his own. Water was different. We had filled our water-skins at Baecula. They began to run low. We learnt to leave our capes at night in hollows, suspended from scrubs just above the ground and in the morning there would be a little dew, enough to slack the rasping in the mouth. I rationed water: three mouthfuls per man, three times a day, and in the evening we dug water-holes where Edeco and his Edetani told us. The water was bitter, brackish, and the horses needed more.

'How far is the River Anas?' I asked Edeco through thickened, cracked and parched lips, as we sat our horses in the sun's glare.

'Three more days. No more.'

My orderly approached me with a water-skin. It was time for our midday drink, and as I had ordered I was brought the water last. I shook the skin. There was a dribble in it. I looked back at the long line of my men, sitting on the ground, resting. Those near were watching me. I held the skin up high, and turned it upside down. The water danced and sparkled to the ground. I saw the men pointing, approving, passing on word of what I had done.

'Column!' I shouted. 'March!' I wheeled my horse to follow the turning sun.

So we limped and sweated on. The flies were worse than the thirst. They clustered on the slightest wet or damp place on the body, the eyes, nostrils, ears and mouth. Each time I opened my mouth to speak, a black mass of flies darted in. Edeco and his Edetani found and killed a herd of onagers, the Celtiberian wild asses. They sucked on the raw livers in their thirst. Some of our men were disgusted; most, and I was one of them, were not, and did the same. We made bonfires, and feasted on the flesh. We came to the Anas. I posted many scouts. The rest of us drank and swam and splashed and sang, and, renewed, moved on.

My scouts reported an army coming from the south-west. The standards were white scorpions on black. Hasdrubal was coming to me, as I had planned. But my men were weak. I had to choose the perfect ground, but could not find it. I made appropriate plans. So came the battle remembered as that of Ilipa. I rolled my dice. A battle is a game.

It was a risky strategy. I knew that then; I know it now. Any commander knows you should force the enemy, if you can, to climb to you – as Mago had made us do at Baecula. I did the opposite. We camped at the bottom of a rise, a dried-up, rocky river-bed at our backs, and behind that a steep hill. There was, as Afer observed, nowhere to retreat to. I smiled.

I concealed my cavalry in ravines on either side, and posted four signalling-stations on the hilltops around. I told my army to rest, and sleep. That evening in the gloaming, I did not need to read the signals. I saw Hasdrubal's army massing at the top of the rise above. He must have thought that, like Flaminius at Trasimenus, this Roman army had walked into a trap. I called a council. It was heated, but I stuck to my plans, observing that, anyway, we now had no other choice. I gave my orders carefully, patiently, and went through them over and over again, drawing diagrams by firelight in the river's sand. I called an assembly of all the centurions and explained these plans again. We needed, I said, thirty thousand to fight as one man.

Hasdrubal attacked, as I had expected, at first light. But I had ordered my army to get up and eat and stand ready even before then. Hasdrubal was deceived by my screen. What he saw was a classic Roman formation, with the heavy *hastati* in our centre, the lighter troops on our wings. What he could not see was that our *hastati*, commanded by Metellus, were a screen, nothing more. Behind them I had the Celtiberians who had joined me at Carthagena. Commanded by Laelius and Afer, who knew they must wait for my signal and knew where to look for it, my experienced soldiers were not there, but on each wing, themselves screened by lightly armed *velites* and a sprinkling of Celtiberians. I was counting on Hasdrubal's main attack being by his heavy infantry against what he assumed was ours. Win that, and the battle is over.

Hasdrubal did as I had hoped. I was well up the hill above the river-bed, and I watched his infantry run down the rise and smash into the centre of our line. As I had planned and ordered, our centre gave way, soaking the enemy up like a sponge. They broke through, came to the river-bed, and turned.

'Now!' I ordered the signallers. 'Now!' The whistle-blasts shrilled out. Laelius' and Afer's wings wheeled. The net was closed.

Hasdrubal did as I had anticipated. Seeing his main force surrounded, he sent a second wave of cavalry and skirmishers charging down the hill at my men's undefended backs. As soon as I saw this, I ordered a second signal sent: 'Cavalry, now', for we were losing men, attacked front and rear. Edeco and his Edetani were a little late, but they appeared, screaming, whooping, slings throwing, arrows flowing, just in time to salve my rising fear, and behind them, slower on their larger Ligurian horses, came another wave of Roman horsemen, their mounts' hoofbeats loud and clear. I knew that we had won.

The signaller beside me pointed: 'Sir! Look over there!' Our western station was signalling. 'P-a-r-t-y b-r-e-a-k-i-n-g a-w-a-y. D-o r-e-s-e-r-v-e p-u-r-s-u-e.'

I felt a sudden alarm. I looked down below. Our armies seemed well matched in numbers. This had to be the vast majority of Hasdrubal's men. I couldn't see his standard. So, if he was breaking away, it could not be with many men. And my reserve was only of a hundred, and most of their horses were lame or suffering from mange. No, let Hasdrubal go, I thought, and tell what Scipio had done. Rumour, I have learnt, can be as potent as the sword. I had sent them signal 'N-o'.

We found Gades deserted, its gates open, its people gone. Everywhere were signs of hasty leaving. I hurried to the southern wall above the harbour, and felt a rush of joy at what I saw: the tide was out. Indeed, the tide had turned, and luck was labour's reward. Lying on their sides in the mud and sand of the harbour were more than forty galleys. I had a fleet. 'Mine!' I shouted to the soaring seagulls. 'Celtiberia is mine!'

It was. I travelled round it for almost two years, using the fleet and making sudden sorties inland. I made alliances with chiefs and princes. They paid tribute to me in silver, gold and precious stones of amethyst and ruby, beryl, emerald and topaz and glossopetri fallen from the moon. They fell on the ground in obeisance before me, and called me their king. I behaved like one, I own. They understood that, not the abstraction 'Rome'.

I recruited many Celtiberians to my army, and trained them well. I divided the country into two provinces, I left a core of Roman soldiers, and Metellus and Afer in command. With the rest of my army, with my treasure, on the crowded galleys, I set sail for Rome.

Mulca is dead. She slipped away in her sleep during the night. Aurio is grieving. In my way, so am I. I have not told Scipio. He has not asked, and though still in bed seems stronger and caught up in his story. I shall have to tell him before the burial. I hope he will be well enough to attend. I shall have to interview for a new cook – or should I wait until we know the result of Cato's appeal? Whatever that is, will we go back to Rome? Anyway, first let us try to finish this account. When Scipio is asleep, I work on it: not on editing, because I now feel that would be wrong. No, I am making two copies, which, when Scipio has finished, I shall send to Theogenes. He will see them safe against the vagaries of time.

When we landed at Ostia, I could see how things had changed. It was a port again, and hundreds of galleys and barges and skiffs and cutters and fishing boats jostled for space, and hawkers hustled wares on every quay. When I left, the market beyond the harbour wall had been an empty place, full of broken dreams. Now it was bustling and full. I knew from Fabius' despatches that Hannibal and his army were confined to the south, to Bruttium, shut in by Marcellus and his Sicilian legions. 'Hannibal has become a dog,' Fabius wrote, 'that barks but will not bite.' Even so, I had not thought to find normality so much resumed. But then, we are a trading nation, and thanks to Fabius we had control of the sea.

The crowds started at Ostia. They were there in their hundreds to greet me, showering me with flowers, pressing and touching me, some happy just to touch my cloak, and calling me the saviour of Rome. They lined the banks as my barge, decked with bunting, moved up the Tiber, the people cheering, rejoicing, hurrahing and calling out my name. In Rome, I found a party at the Tarpeian gate to greet me. Postumus and Frontinus and Flaevius were there. So was Lucius; he was drunk. Fabius had been carried there in a litter. It was good to see my friends again.

There was no rest, with troops to billet, reports to dictate, news to learn. The next day, Fabius told me, the Senate's hearings into those who had sided with Hannibal in Capua were due to commence. He wanted me to chair the hearings. Cato had already proposed summary execution of all involved. Fabius had opposed that. 'We have already known too much blood and division,' he said. 'Now, if all are willing, is the time for healing to begin. Besides, let us not forget that Hannibal is still on Italian soil. This cannot be the time for more Romans to die.'

So, in unaccustomed, uncomfortable white toga, bathed and oiled and with clean hair, I sat again in the much-depleted Senate, but this time in the father's chair. The first to appear before us was a magistrate and merchant, Titus Licinius Labienus. The charge against him was that he had actually invited Hannibal to stay with him, and he did not deny that the Carthaginian had stayed at his house.

Labienus was flustered and nervous. He kept repeating that he had had no choice; that he hoped to prevent the sack of Capua; that in his heart he had kept faith with Rome. I believed him. I could see that was not the view of some of my peers, especially Cato – elevated to the Senate while I was in Celtiberia, by the way, on Fabius' own nomination, for services to Rome. The questioning droned on.

Sitting behind Labienus was a man who interested me more, a servant or retainer. He was dark-skinned, but eastern, not Greek. From where? I could not be sure. He sat still, at peace in his own calm. He was dressed entirely in white cotton – blouse, tunic and trousers – and the same stuff was wrapped round his head. He had deep dark eyes, high cheekbones, a fine chiselled nose, a narrow mouth. When the midday recess came, I told the bailiff to have the man, but not his master, brought to my room.

It is strange to set this down. He is dictating it fast.

'You sent for me, Publius Cornelius Scipio,' he said in perfect Latin, standing in the doorway.

'I did. Close the door. Come in, and sit down.' I cleared the scrolls from my desk, and put them in a chest. When I looked up, he was sitting, watching me from his chair. 'So, tell me,' I began, 'is your master innocent?'

'Of what?' he asked.

'Of conniving with Hannibal, of course.'

'I do not know. I was not there.'

'No? Where were you then?'

'Am I on trial here, Scipio?'

I laughed, and leant back in my chair. I liked this man. 'Tell me, then, what is your name?'

'It is Bostar.'

'A strange name. From where?'

'From Chalcedon. But that was long ago.'

'Ah! The east. I thought so. And yet your Latin is perfect. Where did you learn it?'

★　　★　　★

*He was warm, curious like a boy. I told him what he wanted, and
more. We returned to the subject of Labienus. Strange things, I said,
were done in time of war, but I believed him to be a good man, and
I had found him to be a good magistrate, scrupulous and fair. He
had encouraged his sons to enlist, and as we spoke they were serving
with Marcellus' army. I said I thought the family were true servants
of Rome.*

*The hearing resumed. The evidence ended. Scipio moved for a
discharge. There was disagreement from Cato, but the majority was
with Scipio. That night he had Labienus and me join him for dinner.
He was eager to learn more of Hannibal – what he looked like, how
he talked, and what fuelled his hatred of Rome. Labienus' replies were
embarrassed and awkward, but frank. I said little, but my mind was
full. I felt a circle completing itself, as sure as the waxing and waning
of the moon.*

*'So, Labienus,' Scipio said when supper had been cleared away,
'you go back to Capua tomorrow?'*

*'I do, Scipio, I do,' Labienus replied with enthusiasm, 'thanks to
you.'*

*'Not just to me. But before you go I have a favour to ask of
you.'*

'Ask it. Anything,' said Labienus with relief.

'I ask you to release Bostar of Chalcedon to me.'

'But he is no slave. He is free!' Labienus stuttered.

Scipio's eyes turned on me. 'Bostar, will you now serve me?'

*My mind had been made up hours before. 'I will, Scipio, as
best I can.'*

*My parting from Labienus was warm. He agreed to send on my
few things, and that night in our lodgings I wrote a letter to Artixes
for Labienus to take to him. I asked Artixes to treat three of my
patients with a new potion I had been working on, and gave him
the recipe. I also asked him to look after the widow Apurnia and
her son, Hanno, and help them as he saw fit. 'They moved me,' I
wrote, 'in some strange way.' In the morning, Labienus offered me a*

bag of gold, due payment, he said, for what I had taught his sons.
I asked him to give the money to Artixes, who would know what
I wanted done with it. I said farewell to Labienus. He was glad,
understandably, to be leaving Rome. I was sorry to see him go, for
he had been good to me.

Time, time. I have never had it. Now I need it most, it flies away.
I must hurry Bostar. Please have me brought some tea, with lots
of honey. It will revive me. You know, when I was thirsty in
the deserts of Syria, it was not water I craved but tea. I have
two more things to say. Then, if I have time, much more.

Art, Bostar, old friend. Edit this for me, please, but let me
tell what I remember. So much had happened in the years I
had been gone. Epycides, an Athenian aristocrat and aesthete,
had been captured in Syracuse by Marcellus, who brought him
to Rome. He was one of many newcomers introduced to me
when I first got home. He had set himself up, under my cousin's
patronage, as a dealer in Greek art, beginning with the sculpture
and vases, mosaics and paintings, jewellery and terracottas that
Marcellus had taken in the sack of that great city, and shipped
carefully back to Rome. Epycides had sent for a cousin of his
from Athens, one Theogenes, whose skill was in restoration.
They made a team.

'What is the essence of this art you talk of, Epycides?' I asked
him at a banquet, the second time we met.

'If you have time, Scipio, I can show you,' he said. I didn't
have the time, but I made it. The next morning, Epycides and
Theogenes called for me. We walked to the warehouse quarter
in the north of the city, the people we passed greeting me, and
calling out my name. Theogenes opened the doors of a long,
broad, rectangular warehouse, and the light flooded in. I gasped
at what I saw. White marble, shimmering, glowing in the sun:
the shapes were ethereal, eternal, and danced before my eyes.

We walked in, and went in silence slowly down the avenue between statues of men and women, clothed and naked, in action and at rest. I stopped before one of a young man, standing in repose, his left foot forward, his right arm reaching outwards and beyond. Every muscle was sculpted clearly. There was to the body a noble simplicity, a calm grandeur – for this we need not words but eyes.

'You like it,' Theogenes softly said.

'Like it?' I replied in Greek. 'That is not the word. Tell me, Theogenes, Epycides, what were they trying to do?'

'Ah!' Epicydes sighed. 'That is the question! I think they were asking themselves what beauty is, and whether it lies in proportion.'

We stood and looked, and I left the world of statecraft and of war.

'It is a copy, but a good one,' Theogenes said at last. 'King Hiero had it made.'

'A copy of what?'

'Of the *Apoxyomenus* by the great sculptor Lysippus.'

'Lysippus? Tell me about him.'

So, most days, from those two Athenians did I start to learn – and buy. There are many Greek arts. None is without its masterpieces.

In the atrium of my house in Rome, Theogenes' long, fastidious fingers opened the lid of a sandalwood box. 'Now, Scipio, the pleasure that was mine is yours.' He stepped back from the table. 'Lift it out, and marvel.'

I did. Within the box was another of white marble, as wide as my face and as tall as my arm to the elbow. On each side the marble was inlaid with griffins of lapis-lazuli. The front and top were hinged. I opened the front by its tiny handle of silver, and gasped.

I already had one *clepsydra*, water clock, a poor Etruscan thing, and I now have many more. None that I had seen before or have seen since matched this.

The vessel from which the water flowed was of beaten gold, held up by threads of silk. The hole at its bottom through which the water flowed was a drilled diamond. The inverted bowl below was also of gold, and the hours were marked on a perfect Corinthian column to the side. A tiny figure of ivory, perfectly carved, a Muse I thought, perhaps Hora, held in one hand a rod which pointed, as she rose in the water, to the hours. I could think of no Latin adjective for this perfection. '*Poikilon*,' I said to Theogenes in Greek. 'It is exquisite!'

I knelt down. He joined me and we watched the water drip, the figure rise. 'But it is ivory,' I said. 'How can it float?'

'Because, Scipio,' and he smiled, showing his only flaw, those blackened, uneven teeth, 'it is hollow.'

'And the diamond? Why not just a hole in the gold?'

'Because dirt, like gossip, sticks in time, and the clock loses its accuracy. Dirt doesn't stick to a diamond.'

'Theogenes,' I said softly, standing up, 'it is the most beautiful object I have ever seen.'

'Beautiful, yes, but also accurate. Incredibly accurate. And it need be refilled only every other day because—'

'Because the hole in the top vessel is so small, am I right?' He nodded. 'Who made this wonder?'

'A man called Ctesibius, whom I have been sponsoring for some time. He's a Corinthian, and his father is a barber, of all things.'

I chuckled. 'Come, come, Theogenes. We all know about Corinthian barbers!'

He blushed slightly, and went on. 'Well, anyway, I was having my hair cut in his shop. I noticed he could raise and lower the mirrors almost by magic, so I asked him how. He showed me an intricate system of small pulleys in channels, operated from

a pull by the chair. I asked who'd made them. He said his son.
I asked to meet him. He said his son wasn't like that. I said, no,
I really wanted to meet him. I crossed the father's palm and was
shown to a little workshop out the back. I have never met such
talent, such dexterity. Strange, strange.' Theogenes stroked his
beard as he always did when he was thinking.

'Strange? Why?'

'Because the young man I met was deformed, a hunchback.
Little pig eyes, and the coarsest, podgy fingers. But Ctesibius
puts the beauty he lacks into the beauty he makes. One of its
fruits stands before you now.'

'It must have taken months to make!'

'No, years. Two and a half, to be exact. And that's reflected,
I'm afraid, in the price.'

'Ah, the price, Theogenes. Let's discuss that after lunch. You
must be hungry.' Closing the *clepsydra*'s door, I said: 'Let's go
into the *triclinium*. And after the price, you must tell me more
of Corinth. I should love to go there.'

As we walked together to the *triclinium*, I cocked my head
towards him so that I could the better smell.

'What is your perfume, by the way, Theogenes?'

He has made a science and an art of smell. 'In all other arts
I deal,' he likes to say. 'In this, I excel.'

'What do you think?'

'I would say the base is bergamot with star anise and' – I
sniffed again – 'camomile and, possibly, some lemon grass.'

He clapped his hands, delighted. 'My dear Scipio,' he said,
'you could not be more wrong! This perfume is something quite
new. Smell this.' He took from the pocket of his short cloak a
little phial, and held it out to me. 'This is its base. Smell,' he
said, stretching out the word as if all the beauty of all words
could lie in a scent.

'Well, Theogenes, perhaps I have smelt only army smells for
too long.' I took the phial, pulled out the cork and held it to

my nose. I gasped, and closed my eyes. This was a scent so fine, so delicate and deep, as to still the mind and quicken life.

'So, you approve.' He chuckled softly.

I opened my eyes, sniffed again: it was mysterious, ethereal. 'Approve? That's hardly the word, Theogenes. Is this a smell from earth, or from heaven? It's quite extraordinary. What is it?'

'This,' he said, taking back the phial, 'is ambergris.'

'Ambergris? I've never heard of it.'

'Nor had I, until two months ago. I bought it from a merchant who had, he said, paid a king's ransom for it.'

'Is it from the east? Parthia? Bithynia, perhaps?'

'No. Far from it. It comes from the north-west, or so the man said, from some islands hidden always in mist and rain, where there is nothing good but tin, and from the musk of a great fish like no other that swims in the cold waters there.'

'Theogenes, you're at it again.' I smiled, looked into those deep brown eyes of his, irises shining, so it always seemed, from a sea of ivory white. 'And this great fish talks as well, I suppose.'

'Of course, and dances!' He laughed his great belly-laugh. 'No, Scipio, I believe what they say. This fish is called a whale, a sperm-whale. I've seen drawings of it on Gaulish armbands and medallions, and I've talked to sailors who have seen them.'

'Well, well,' I said, turning from the Greek in which we had been conversing to Latin, *'nihil sub sole novum.* There is nothing new under the sun.' I heard the kitchen door bang. I smelled the smell of food. 'Come, Theogenes. Let's continue this conversation over lunch.'

But Theogenes never did tell me more about the whale, or about Corinth. We had just settled the price for the clock, and I had handed him the gold, when Cato burst in.

'So this is where you are! The Senate's messengers 'av been looking for you all over Rome! And I find you here with your Greek – ah – friend,' Cato sneered. Sweat shone on his forehead. He snorted to clear his nose. 'S'pose you've been talking about this art stuff. Don't you know there's a war on? Anyway, you're needed in the Senate. Now.'

And I was needed, that is true. The Senate was heated, fraught. Hannibal, it seemed, had not just barked but bitten. Slipping past Marcellus in the night, he had captured and sacked the city of Tarentum in the south. There were calls to send a second army against him, and at last wipe him out.

'It is dangerous,' old Fabius said, 'to attack a wolf cornered in its lair. There is a better way.'

So, within the month, did I again embark a Roman army for war. This time, though, I set sail not for Celtiberia but for Africa. I wanted to draw Hannibal there.

I besieged the city of Utica, satellite of Carthage. That was a ruse. It should have been Carthage, but I did not like the risks there – if attacked from the rear, I would have no place to turn but back to my ships and Rome. At Utica, though, I had plain on three sides of me. Anyway, I did not have to stay there long. Within two months, I heard that Hannibal had come. He and his army were inland. I followed cautiously, making much use of scouts. I knew I need not have worried when I saw the ground he had chosen for us.

I saw the sheen and shine and smoke of his army, camped on the side of a high hill that rose above a plain. But opposite that hill was another one. My scouts reported springs there, and said the water was good. Hannibal had chosen that place, it seemed, so that we would fight as equals on the plain. For stades around there was nothing, no topographical advantage either of us could use, only empty desert, flat, endless, studded with thin thorns. The plain's name, said the Numidian cavalry I had hired, was Zama. I went to my hill above it.

For days we sat and waited. My men were nervous and strained. There was no Roman there who had not lost a friend, a father, a brother, at Hannibal's hands. And in number, our armies were at best evenly matched. At night, if the wind was right, we could hear the babble of the enemy's voices, carried across the plain, and always the trumpeting of many elephants. They worried Laelius: as he observed, we had not faced them before. I went over and over the matter in my mind. I could not rehearse my solution, but again and again, for maniple after maniple, I drew diagrams in the sand.

Our supplies were running low. We had to fight, or go. The next morning, early, I put on my scarlet cape and went to do the thing that had been forming in my mind. As the sun filled the eastern sky, I mounted my horse and, ignoring protests from many, telling them to stay at their stations, I rode down the hill alone.

I was halfway across the plain when I saw a horseman coming down the other hill towards me. I knew it was he. I had last seen him, fleetingly, at the Ticinus, sixteen years before. My heart was pounding. My mind was clear.

He sat easy on his horse, not even holding the reins. Both our mounts slowed of their own accord, as we came near each other. I sat and looked at him, and he at me. It was true what we had heard: Hannibal's left eye-socket was empty.

'How did you lose your eye?' I asked him in Greek, after a long silence.

'That does not matter now, Roman,' he answered in Latin. His voice was low and deep, his torso short and stocky, his breastplate black and stained. I saw his hair was going grey. 'It is the least of what I have suffered.' His tone changed. 'Anyway, what do you want? Why did you come?'

'Why did you?'

He laughed. His teeth were brown and broken, the skin of his neck blotchy and lined. 'Curiosity. I wanted to see the great general of Rome before I beat him. I have heard of your battles in Celtiberia. Brilliant tactics, I admit.'

'Brilliant, Hannibal? Hardly. I was only doing what you taught me.'

So, before the battle of Zama, two generals talked together as men.

I offered Hannibal peace.

He snorted. 'You Romans make a desert, and you call it a peace,' he said.

I asked him why we had to fight. He said because of an oath he had sworn as a child, because of what we had done to his wife, Similce, to his father's grave. 'And because . . . because . . . because I know nothing else.'

'But you can learn the ways of peace!' I replied. My horse fretted at the flies.

He smiled, and shifted in his saddle. 'No, Scipio, and certainly not under the rule of Rome. Now, I know that you can skip, but can you dance as well? If you can, we shall see who can dance the longer!' With that, he wheeled his horse, and rode away.

'Hannibal!' I shouted. He turned his head. 'I have something for you.' Reaching into the pocket of my tunic, I kicked my horse forward and held out my open palm to him. On it was Mago's signet ring. He took it, looked at me intently, and rode away.

The next morning, I had my army woken very early to be fed. My scouts reported Hannibal's army doing the same. I chuckled, and cancelled my orders. 'Let the men sleep until dawn,' I said. In the full light, two armies moved down two hills to the plain. I stayed back, with my customary signallers and ten men. I saw a group of horsemen on the hill opposite. Hannibal, I assumed.

My army waited in the classic *triplex acies* as I had ordered, commanded by Afer, with our cavalry on the wings. It looked like a draughts board, perfectly formed in squares. It was not to attack until what I hoped for had happened. Hannibal's army was one long line, four deep, with perhaps a hundred elephants behind.

Then Hannibal surprised me. I saw among the horsemen the flashing of bronze mirrors. So, yes, that was him. From his army's wings, two large forces of cavalry broke into a canter, then a gallop, heading towards my greater forces. 'Engage', I signalled with my whistle. Between the two armies, in the middle of the plain, the cavalry clashed. Another set of flashes, and the Carthaginians broke off and veered away, westwards. My men followed. What was Hannibal's plan?

Banging swords on shields, his line then advanced on mine at the run. Could I have been wrong? But three or four hundred strides before Hannibal's line would have broken on my *hastati*, something as beautiful as I have ever seen in war took place. With perfect precision, his line became two columns, opening up an avenue between. And then came what I had expected.

Gleaming with armour, daubed with garish paints, Hannibal's trumpeting elephants bore down in rows of three on my lines, thundering up the gap between his columns, halted now. I shut my eyes, breathed out. There was no point in trying to signal over that noise. I had to rely on my plans.

Just in time, my men performed the manoeuvre I had asked for. The *triplex acies* became ten columns, with wide avenues in between, bristling on both sides with *pila*. Most of the elephants, as I had hoped, charged harmlessly down the avenues. Three broke into one of my columns, and flattened it like corn in heavy rain. But then, as ordered, reforming a line as best they could, my remaining soldiers advanced at the run and as I watched that sweet-sour sweat came, beginning in my groin.

It was bitter, Zama, bloody, hand to practised hand and man to seasoned man. There were no manoeuvres, no other tactics that I could have planned. Hannibal's first line and mine simply killed each other. The second lines fought on the corpses of the first. His third line foundered on the planted *pila* of my *triarii*, but he almost broke them with his fourth.

The fighting was even, desperate. I do not know how it

would have ended if my cavalry had not returned, or most of them, and attacked Hannibal's army from the rear. Slowly, his line was breaking, just as a wall of sand is broken by the tide. Time after time, my cavalry broke off, regrouped, and charged again as the hot sun climbed. Whatever the historians record, the battle of Zama was won not on the plain but in a cavalry encounter far out in the sands. I had invested heavily in my cavalry. I had learnt to do so from him.

I saw the group of horsemen opposite me leaving, climbing up the hill. Holding back, Afer and a *turma* of my cavalry saw them too. Half of them started to wheel round to pursue. But Afer waited. His helmet caught the sun and I knew that he was looking up at me. I ordered the signal. 'No. No. Do not pursue.'

I had won. But that was not my victory. You see, I let him go. I let him live. I wanted him to be free, free . . .

The long day waned. The slow moon climbed. He was conscious only sometimes through the still, light night. He asked for water once. Supporting his head on my arm, I gave him some, and dozed in the chair by his bed.

He woke at dawn, and called my name. I leant forward, and he tried to sit up, raising his head from the pillow. His right hand seized my arm and clutched me. His eyes were burning, wild. 'Omnia fui, Bostar,' he croaked, 'et nihil expedit. Ni-hil. Nil. I have been everything, and it amounts to no-thing. Nothing.'

He coughed, fell back, exhaled. His grip loosened on my arm. He seemed to fall asleep. The spring sun strengthened, and filled the room with brimming light. The dust mites tumbled in the air. I heard the cowbells from the far fields toll. Time passed. All was still. I stirred, uncomfortable in my chair. Scipio's eyes opened. He looked younger, clearer, as if his fever had left him, and gone elsewhere. It does that. It is as fickle as the flight of a butterfly.

He looked at me, and smiled. 'Bostar, old friend,' he whispered, 'please get Aurio, and carry me to my chair.'

Aurio was still asleep, lying wrapped in a cloak, outside in the hall, right beside the door. I woke him gently. We carried the man we served to his study, and sat him in his beloved chair. Aurio stepped back. I stayed there as Scipio leant forward, pulling on the arms of his chair, staring through the window as if seeing for the first time what was there.

'I see the sun,' he said in wonder. 'I see my quinces are in bud. My quincunx. Bostar, spring. Spring is here.' With that, he slumped back, and his eyes closed. I heard the rattle in his throat, and Publius Cornelius Scipio Africanus died.

We shall bury him today, as he told me years ago he wanted, in a white woollen toga, with his signet ring still on his hand, on the island in the lake.

The dead pine there is bleached white by the sun, and its limbs reach out across the sky like the fingers of a hand, outstretched, seeking absolution. The herons that nest there will salve his soul as, each evening at the fading of the light, they return from fishing, floating downward to darkness on extended wings. Water laps against the stones of the island, endless, formless, free.

As he had pre-ordained when we first came here from Rome, I read Scipio's will this morning while Aurio was washing and laying out the body. As is customary, Scipio lodged a will with the Vestal Virgins in Rome, but he feared that Cato would not shrink from the profanity of opening it, before it could be made public, and distorting its terms. If Cato does intercept that will, he will find that it is blank. Thus, from the grave, will Scipio frustrate him still.

The one I have is the real will, properly notarised and witnessed. Cato will not be able to challenge its terms, and there will be no money from Scipio for Cato's Rome. Still, I am amazed. Scipio amassed a vast fortune. There is gold deposited with bankers in Rome and Capua, Massilia and Carthagena, Antioch and even Carthage. Perhaps Cato was right all along. It does not matter now.

I shall make the arrangements Scipio set out. All his slaves on the estate here are to be freed, each with an annuity for life. He has left a considerable fortune to his sister, Cornelia. There are handsome bequests to Aurio and Macro, the estate bailiff, and to Mulca: I will see that given to her next of kin; Scipio died assuming her alive. Frontinus inherits the estate, and the house in Rome. Scipio's library here is to go to the public library that he has left money for building in Rome. Will Cato let that be done? I do not know. Some, certainly, will support the plan. They know, if Cato does not, that a society without books is barren. And if those books are only Greek at first, Rome can learn from them and make a literature of her own. In time, I think, captive Greece will take her captor captive — though by culture, not arms. It is a process Scipio began, and will be a product of the peace that Scipio won.

All the rest of his financial legacy, vast riches, is mine. So I must go, and do what must be done. In Capua, I believe, I shall find that what men think ended is beginning, and that what they think separate is one. In Capua, the cycle turns. That is the song inside me, like water flowing under ice.

I leave much unresolved, and Scipio much untold. After his African campaign, he returned to Rome and was awarded a triumph and the honorific Africanus, although Cato and his party opposed both things. In the consular elections, he defeated Cato in a carping campaign. He devoted himself to Greek art, and to beautifying the city. He became patron of the poet Ennius, and encouraged him to emulate the Greeks, especially the Iliad and Odyssey of Homer. He proposed the building of a public library and theatre, both bitterly opposed by Cato. He married his sister, Cornelia, to Postumus, now adopted son of Fabius Pictor, and known for his looks as Fabius Pulcher. With Lucius as reluctant legate — and me as his mapmaker — he led an army into Macedonia and defeated Philip at the battle of Cynoscephalae. The supposedly invincible Greek phalanx crumbled before Scipio and his veterans and their new way of war. He returned to Rome, having made a treaty with Philip that many said he should not have done, to find that Cato's party had taken over all the important offices of state. But still he had the people's support and using that he held lavish funeral games for Fabius Pictor, who had died while we were away. There were questions in the Senate about cost. Scipio refused to answer them, or to say where the money had come from. 'How dare you question the cost of the funeral of a man to whom you owe your lives?' he said. He bought this estate here at Liternum, and began to spend much of his time here. But soon he found Rome facing a new threat, this time from the waxing power of Antiochus, the great Seleucid king. Again, Scipio led out a Roman army, and I was by his side. Again, he won, again he showed clemency, and with Antiochus signed a peace which Cato argued vehemently was inimical to Rome.

That proved the catalyst for Cato's impeachment of Scipio and his brother, and the trial. I suppose I should record the formal charges against Scipio. There were ten.

(i) *That, in Celtiberia, he took for himself gold and silver which should have been lodged with the treasury in Rome.*

(ii) *That, in Celtiberia, he made alliances with many Celtiberians, enemies of Rome.*

(iii) *That, after the battle of Zama, his clemency towards Carthage was contrary to Rome's interests.*

(iv) *That he accepted bribes from Carthage in return for favourable terms of peace.*

(v) *That, after defeating Philip of Macedon, he and his brother, Lucius, accepted bribes from him to withdraw Rome's legions.*

(vi) *That, after defeating Antiochus of Syria, he and his brother, Lucius, accepted bribes from him to withdraw Rome's legions.*

(vii) *That, after each of his four campaigns, he dallied in Rome and devoted himself to Greek art and other interests, rather than safeguarding the interests of Rome.*

(viii) *That, by his Hellenism, he subverted the virtues of Rome.*

(ix) *That, in one Bostar of Chalcedon, he had an unnatural*

> companion, not even a citizen, to whom he disclosed the
> business of the state.
> (x) That, throughout his life, he set himself above the will of
> the Senate and people of Rome.

How much of this is true? At the trial Laelius confirmed the first, for example. I have no doubt that much of what Scipio did was wrong, but that is a philosophical view, not a legal one. Much of what Scipio did was at a time when the constitution was suspended. He was his own law and he has died as he lived, an enigma. And the ninth charge? It was never as they thought it. 'Unnatural'. What does that mean? It is a charge of which I am proud.

For myself, I have not told of my time with Hannibal. I have hinted at aspects of my own past, but more than that I leave unsaid. Like the flash of a fish in a pond, I leave unfinished my account of Labienus, his sons, Artixes, Apurnia and my studies.

What else have I left unsaid, undone? I have not finished the two copies I was making to send to Theogenes. I shall not do so now. The account itself is incomplete: let its copies be more so, like the memories of dreams. More importantly, there is much that remains unaddressed in Cato's doings, and his implacable enmity to anything that is not of Rome. And there is much that I could add – like my belief that Laelius tried to rape Cornelia all those years ago in Rome, when Cornelia wore a scarf around her neck at supper. In that rejection and violence began the canker of Laelius. Its fruit was his treachery at the trial. All things connect, if we can see.

But I prefer to leave these matters as men after me may find them, and this account like Scipio – magnificent, perhaps, but marred. Now let him enter the serene gravity of the rain, the hill's passage to the sea. Scipio is dead, and I hold deep in my body the dark seed of his sleep. It is finished. I leave off words now. Let them settle, and this account take on such meaning as will celebrate the absence of what does not belong. That which has been has ended. A new time has begun.

EPILOGUE

It is cold here on the edges of Rome's empire. Bostar said it was best to be away, where no one knows us and we are free. He came for me in Capua. He talked to my mother, Apurnia, and took me from the place where I was born. We travelled. He bought this house for us, here in Macedonia, high in the hills that reach up from the shore. As I look out, I see the shining sea, and each day I seek the sight of the ship's sails that I am waiting for, and the man that they will bring.

Otherwise, I want for nothing. I walk in the deer-filled mountains, and hear the querulous cries of darting quails. I have a tutor, servants, and ample gold to pay the carters and pedlars for the goods they bring. I read and read again this account that Bostar gave me of the life of Scipio, whom he served, and to which he suggested that I add an epilogue.

I see that Bostar leaves many things unanswered. That is his choice. But it seems to me important to record the result of Scipio's trial – or, more accurately, of Cato's appeal against the judgment of that trial. I heard the decision in Capua the day before Bostar came. Everyone in Italy heard the news in days. Scipio must have died two days before it came. The result was acquittal.

If Scipio died of a heart broken and a mind too strained, it need not so have been. He could have returned to Rome and, once more, assumed the station that was, even I knew, utterly his own. Who has not heard of Scipio Africanus, the brilliant general, the Philhellene, the saviour of Rome? In Capua, people used to say he was a god. From this account, I see that he was very much a man, and one I wish I had known. Bostar says no one could know him, because he did not know himself. But

Bostar also says that people loved him in spite and because of that lack, that longing, in him. I am not sure I understand.

Or would Cato have made Scipio's return impossible? I do not know, and see no use in dwelling on these things. So I wait, as Bostar told me. He has gone to Bithynia, where there is a man hiding from the vengeance of Rome.

I am Hanno, the son of Hannibal whom he has never known. Bostar told me that in Capua, and my mother, sobbing, confirmed that it was so. I had never seen her cry before. My father was, she said, like a meteor that is not consumed but burns beyond the furthest stars. She said I was the child of the greatest hunger for love that could be known. Whose? I asked her. Yours, or his? She would not say. We left her crying, alone. But her tears seemed to me of joy, not pain, and now I am to meet the man who moved my mother so – and who gave me much of what I am, and might yet be.

I am young. The events that Scipio has described formed the world, and begat me. Bostar will find my father, and bring him here. Then we three will learn the ways of love and life, not death and war. The sky is bright and blue. The light is clear and pure.

CHRONOLOGY

The Rise of Rome

209 BC	Scipio invades Celtiberia (Spain); captures Carthagena
208	Battle of Baecula
206	Battle of Ilipa
	Celtiberia divided into two provinces
204	Scipio returns to Rome; elected consul; invades Africa
203	Hannibal recalled to Africa from Italy
202	Battle of Zama
	Fabius Pictor publishes first history of Rome
200	Rome declares war against Macedon
197	Battle of Cynoscephalae: Philip defeated
195	Cato elected consul
194	Scipio elected consul a second time
192–189	Syrian war between Rome and Antiochus
189	Battle of Magnesia: Antiochus defeated
188	Trial of the Scipios begins
184	Cato elected censor
182	Deaths of Scipio and Hannibal
167	Direct taxation of Roman citizens abolished
149	Death of Cato
149–146	Third Punic war; Carthage destroyed; Africa becomes a Roman province
148–146	Fourth Macedonian war; Macedonia becomes a Roman province
146	Corinth destroyed
	Roman Republic at its zenith

ALSO AVAILABLE FROM CANONGATE

CARTHAGE

ROSS LECKIE

After 300 years of acrimony and two bitter wars, the great
Mediterranean powers of Rome and Carthage clash for the
final, fateful time. *Carthage* concludes the internationally
acclaimed trilogy that began with *Hannibal* and continued
with *Scipio*.

As with all the best writing in this genre, Leckie makes
Carthage relevant to a contemporary audience through
his exploration of human drives, political intrigue and the
process of history-making itself. A self-contained story of
politics and power, love and hope, pain and loss, *Carthage* is a
tragic tale, with important parallels for our own times. It is a
remarkable finale to an extraordinary trilogy.

'The final volume of Ross Leckie's Punic trilogy is the most
interesting . . . imaginative but convincing detail makes the
reader a tourist to a lost world.' *Herald*

'A considerable achievement in which learning has been
enlightened by the imagination. Perhaps most remarkable
has been the manner in which he has contrived to bring
Carthage itself and the Carthage culture to life . . . a fast and
gripping narrative.' *Scotsman*

Turn the page for a short extract from the book.

£7.99

ISBN 978 1 84767 101 1

From Hanno's memoir, found among his papers in the citadel of Carthage

We are surrounded now. They have broken through the walls, and possess the city, bar this citadel where I am; I, Hanno, son of a legend and a slave; Bostar, bent with years, who has been my guardian, mentor and friend, father I never had; Fetopa, my wife, whom I have learned to love in as many ways as rain comes.

Here with me also are our four children Fetopa holds as a hen does her chicks against the deepening of the dark; Artixes, a doctor and man learned in many things; Halax, rich in the lore of plants and animals, a hunchback but my friend; Tancinus, once a Roman, now no man; some hundred of my people who have come with me to the farthest reach of hope and of endurance. And I have the sacred books, the soul of Carthage.

High on the sacred mountain Jebel-bou-Kournine, still our beacon burns. I will see its light tonight, and our strength will be renewed. We will mock the Romans. The walls girding us are thick and strong, built, our legends tell us, not by any man but by Tanit-pene-Baal, great goddess of the moon and of forgetfulness. We have time, water, food. None of the Romans, not even Scipio, whoever helps him, can know of all our secret stores and cisterns, deep hewn from rock when Rome was only huddled huts, squatting by the Tiber. So let them seek the ruins' shelter from this summer sun that beats and pounds and sears the brain.

I can see the sea from here, hear the water's sounding, ceaseless sibilance. And from the sea, help may come before I do that which otherwise will be done. The wood is seasoned, dry. The pyre stands by. Meanwhile, let me write – and others too – of how it came to be that, once again, Rome confronted Carthage.

I begin that which now is almost ended. I go back, back. To Macedonia, and to a boy waiting, waiting for his father, Hannibal. Yes, let that be where I begin. I shut my eyes against my people's noise. Blind, I see. Eyes open again, sweat plopping off my forehead from the heat, the stench of many people and no wind, eyes only on the vellum here before me and the goose-quill's point, I write.

HANNIBAL

ROSS LECKIE

This fictional autobiographical narrative of breathtaking
range and power is the first book in the bestselling *Books
of Hannibal* trilogy. Ross Leckie not only presents a vivid
re-creation of the great struggle of the Punic wars and the
profoundly bloody battle for Rome, but succeeds in bringing
the almost-mythical figure of Hannibal, the man born and
bred to lead the Carthaginian army, to life.

'In Leckie's descriptions it's possible to smell the stench of
sweat and fear, hear the roars of warhorses and elephants,
see the blood-stained armour. Informative and utterly
compelling.' *The Times*

'Enthralling . . . The politics of Hannibal's makeshift alliances,
the corrosion of his humanity and the ghastly mechanics of
war are brilliantly described.' *Independent*

'Visually rich and satisfyingly credible in detail . . . Its
triumph is to bring the world of Carthage to life again.'
Spectator

£7.99

ISBN 978 1 84767 099 1